THE PRODIGAL DAUGHTER

ELIZABETH BASDEN

Blue Muse Books

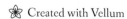

For Nathan

PROLOGUE

The day I met Rick and Mary Parrish was a typical east Texas summer day: so hot and humid that the road looked wet, and the crickets and grasshoppers crunched under your tires on the black-top. I was only six months out from the whistleblower trials, still driving my fancy little BMW convertible, still struggling to make the monthly lease payments, still trying to understand the situation in which I'd found myself. I knew I was going to have to give up the convertible soon, so I drove it with the top down every chance I had.

Not that day, though. If I did, I'd arrive at the Parrishes' double-wide with stringy, windblown hair and that didn't figure into my plan. I was just going to go there, face these people down, and hope they'd move out on their own. Looking back, I'm amazed at how smug I was about people I presumed were deadbeats facing eviction or foreclosure or bankruptcy. Even back in 2014 there were a lot of people still hurting from the recession, and my law practice—such as it was—dealt with many of them.

I'd worn my big-city attorney clothes to meet the Parrishes—a black pantsuit with white pinstripes and black kitten-heel pumps—hoping to impress the residents of Sundown Acres with my professionalism. Unlike the lawyers on television, figuring out what to wear always seemed to be a challenge for me, but that day I thought I'd gotten summer professional chic just right.

The woefully-thin file from Danford Investments, Ltd. was on the passenger seat, and a map I'd found on the internet got me as far as Kaufman County Road 1622. There were no streets for Sundown Acres on the map, and I wasn't really sure what I'd find. Google Earth just showed heavy trees inside a rectangular block with a few rooftops peeking out from under the leaves. Although the site map in the Danford file had 20 smaller blocks inside a long rectangle, many of the blocks looked empty in a satellite photo.

Two of the small lots on Danford's site map had 'Parrish' on them, and, since this matched the name on the letter I'd received after sending Danford's demand letters to the residents of Sundown Acres, I planned to start there. This was, of course, just after the mortgage meltdown, and like so many other companies, Danford had bought a cheap package of defaulted loans, hoping to foreclose and sell the properties to make big money. At the time, it was the biggest piece of legal work on my plate, and I was hoping to impress Danford and get more work from them. God and the IRS knew I needed the money.

Sundown Acres squatted about eight miles southeast of Kaufman and not quite as far east and south as Gunbarrel City (I kid you not) in the sandy oakland of east Texas. The billboard for the development loomed up from a weedy corner where two unnumbered roads joined, the paper peeling but the development name still readable in faded red, touting large half-acre lots for sale. Lower down, someone had spray painted 'SCREWED UP ACRES' in green across the bottom, and no one had bothered to disagree.

A hundred feet behind the sign, a freshly-painted, horizontal white board fence marked the Parrishes' two lots. They'd bought the corner lot on the main road itself but had turned their double-wide trailer to face the inside of the property, grading a sandy driveway up to the trailer and a detached metal shop/garage.

The Parrishes had built a brick base around the double-wide and a deck surrounded by mature flower beds spilling over with clumps of white and yellow daisies, black-eyed susans—two of the few flowers I know. Some faded purple flowers struggled to survive the heat in the shadier areas, with the thick green blades left from the spring flowers hiding the base of the trailer. The driveway tracked the line between their two lots and continued past the house to the big shop with aluminum siding. The flower pots next to the steps had been cleverly moved into the shade so the leggy white, pink, and red blooms would live a little while longer in the hot Texas sun. Overall, the whole property was well-tended and pretty and, in my head, I imagined taking some pictures on my phone to send to Danford to show them how well this property would resell post-foreclosure. Tidy house, tidy foreclosure, tidy fee. I could do this.

I pulled into the drive and parked behind a light blue Chevy pickup truck, took a deep breath and gathered my bag and the Danford file. My heels immediately sank deep in warm sand, and, as I struggled to pull them out of the sand, I realized I'd worn the wrong shoes for this visit.

Usually, a residential foreclosure in Texas is a simple matter. You send out demand letters, have a notice posted on a previously-designated bulletin board somewhere in the county courthouse, then you stand up on the first Tuesday of the month on those courthouse steps and read a script about the loan and the lender's intent to foreclose to an audience (if there is one), take bids (if there are any), and bid for the lender if no one else buys the property. Then you march into the courthouse, file a new deed, and you're done. The whole process is set up by statute and pays me a flat $500 per loan.

When you figure in filing and mailing different notices and letters, the five minutes spent on the courthouse steps is really the easiest part. The biggest problem I've had is my greediness, taking loans for several properties in different counties. They all must be read on the first Tuesday of the month, so I cover a lot of Texas ground in a few hours. The worst day was six foreclosures in four separate counties between 10 am and 4 pm on a cold and blustery

Tuesday in March my first year doing foreclosures, but—since I made $3,000 in that one day—my complaints were blown away with the north wind as I ended my second foreclosure on the steps of the courthouse in Corsicana.

Back then, I didn't really think much about the people who'd lived in the houses I was foreclosing. It was all about the legal work, and I was pretty much determined to get as much work as I could until I could figure things out and get a job. I'd convinced myself that the reason most of the demand letters I sent were returned by the post office was because the homeowners had already moved on to different (and hopefully better) circumstances.

The Sundown Acres demand letters elicited a quick response from a Mrs. Mary Parrish, informing me that the loan referenced was a fraud. Mrs. Parrish's letter and the details she included made me wary, and Doug Garner, the director at Danford working with me, was persuaded that a visit to Sundown Acres would be a good idea, an extra charge not covered by the flat fee. The letter not only had a lot of detail, it was grammatically perfect, centered on the page, and Mrs. Parrish sounded like she spoke for all the residents of Sundown Acres. I called her to make an appointment, and her soft voice seemed pretty confident.

I knew the woman who opened the door was the Mary Parrish who'd responded to the demand letter. She was as tidy as the yard around the trailer, with short gray hair cut in the Dorothy Hamill bob my grandmother wore for forty years. Her small frame carried about ten pounds more around the middle than she probably should (not that I'm one to judge, since I carry more myself than I should). While she didn't wear a lot of makeup, her hair was combed and curled, and the turquoise velour sweat suit she wore was neat and clean. Her face was lined, but it was mostly laugh lines around her mouth and sky-blue eyes.

She smiled and showed me into the living room, where she'd muted the sound on the big-screen television attached to the wall, still running a daytime game show where contestants dressed up like chickens and clowns. The matching brown leatherette sofa and pair of recliners were large for the room, but everything was pushed back to the walls, leaving a wide path from the front door to the kitchen and a dinette set in dark brown.

She offered iced tea, which I accepted, knowing that sharing a glass of iced tea on a hot summer day in Texas is usually the best way to break down barriers in awkward conversations. While she worked the automatic ice dispenser, I walked over to what could only be called a wall of honor. One large photo of a Dallas police officer in full dress uniform looked slightly faded and blue, but the other of an Army sergeant was topped by a flag, folded in a triangle and preserved in a wood and glass shadow box.

"I'm so sorry for your loss," I said as I turned and accepted the glass of tea. Mrs. Parrish joined me at the wall, and we stood for a moment, looking at the young sergeant, forever trapped in the 1990s.

"Our son Thomas," she said, straightening the sergeant's frame. "He was killed in Afghanistan during Operation Enduring Freedom." She nodded with her head at the photo of the police officer. "That's my husband Rick. He's out in his shop, but I know he heard your car, so he'll be up soon."

It was clear we were going to wait for Mr. Parrish before our conversation about the foreclosure, so I moved to another grouping of pictures, more recent this time. One showed a tall young man in a cap and gown with his arms around Mrs. Parrish and an older version of the cop. "Is this your grandson?"

She smiled. "That's Todd. He's 24."

I leaned closer to peer at the smiling boy, who had Mary Parrish's sky blue eyes. "Nice looking young man. You must be proud of him." Her smile seemed to fade a bit, but she nodded. An awkward silence descended, so I prodded on. "Is he in college?"

She hesitated, looking at the picture of the young man. "He's working for a landscape company. He's very talented with plants—he does all the planting in our yard." She paused, rocking a bit on her toes. "He hasn't had it easy. His father died when he was nine, and then his mother remarried a few years later. He lived with us after she moved to Canada with her new husband." She turned and gestured to the well-tended yard in front of the trailer. "We moved out here in part to give him a place to always come home to."

I turned too, and gazed out at the carefully placed flowers and bushes. "Ah. It's beautiful out there." I never know what to say about plants. They live and die without human intervention, and it seems particularly arrogant of humans to claim pride in what they do. The fact they typically choose to die in my care seems to support my ambivalence.

The front door creaked open, and a tall, beefy man with a gray buzzcut stepped inside. I turned with some relief as Mary Parrish introduced us. "My husband, Rick. Honey, this is that attorney who wrote and called, Lacey Benedict." She turned to me. "You're the first one brave enough to come visit," she said with a cheeky grin, and I had a suspicion she wasn't that worried about my presence in their home.

Rick Parrish was tall—really tall—and I like to think I'd recognize him as a cop any day. Even though his hair was gray, it was still thick and bushy, flat on the top and showing pink scalp on the sides. He was probably in his late sixties, but his arms were well-muscled and tanned in the short-sleeved red t-shirt he wore. I'd stepped forward with my professional smile in place and extended my hand for the obligatory handshake before I realized that Rick Parrish's brown eyes were clouded by more than shadow. The hand he extended was a good six inches to the left of mine, so I moved over and took his hand, shaking it firmly. Mary Parrish had moved to the kitchen to pour him some tea, talking all the while.

"Let's sit at the table, and I'll get you the documents I was talking about in my letter," she said from around the corner. I stepped back, unsure if Rick Parrish needed assistance, but he walked past me as if he could see where he was going, heading right to the chair on the near end of the table. This was a man who wouldn't let a thing like blindness slow him down. I took a seat to his left and put my slim Danford file a few safe inches from my sweating tea glass. After setting a plastic glass of tea carefully at Rick's left hand, Mary Parrish disappeared into one of the bedrooms beyond the door.

I could tell Rick was someone who could sit still and quiet, but I was raised by my grandmother to be polite, and it's probably one of my better qualities. Sitting in silence with Rick Parrish was something I just couldn't do, so I spoke first. "I see you were a Dallas police officer."

"Thirty-eight years," he rumbled in a deep, quiet voice. "Till my eyes gave out on me." He took a sip of his tea, his eyes focusing somewhere near my head. "Eyes were bad after Vietnam, but they seemed to get worse at the end. For the last ten years, I've not been able to see much of anything."

Ten years. My stomach began to churn as I realized he'd been blind when they bought the house, when they'd signed loan documents. Before I could think of anything to say, Mary returned with a blue and white file box. "I think the chemicals they sprayed on the jungle over there hurt his eyes," she said with the ease of a long-held belief.

Rick had clearly heard this before. "Even if it did, none of the doctors at the VA would say, Mary."

Mary rolled her eyes at me, two girls sharing secrets. "Of course they'd say that. But it's just not right." She saw I'd drunk half my tea already and started to rise. "More tea?"

I turned her down, fearing more iced tea would mean I'd have to ask to borrow the bathroom, something I could never get used to when visiting someone else's home. I also saw my plans for a quick visit going down that same toilet; her file box was neatly organized, but it was completely full. Alarm bells were going off in my head, and I knew I needed to get this meeting back on track.

I pulled the Danford file a tad closer to draw attention to it and tried my grown-up, lawyerly voice as I looked Mary Parrish in the eye. "Mrs. Parrish, you said the documents referenced for the loan on the property were in error. Which document do you believe was an error?"

She eyed me over the rim of her tea glass before taking a sip, and now I was sure she was enjoying this. "Call me Mary, dear, and yes, very much so. Your letter talks about loans for the acre of land we supposedly bought from Sundown back in 2007." I didn't like the word *supposedly*, but I didn't interrupt. "Well, it turns out that Sundown didn't deed us the land we thought we'd bought. Instead, Sundown kept our down payment money—kept everyone's money— and didn't file any deed transfers." She looked over at her husband and took another sip of her iced tea. Rick Parrish was sitting quietly, his hands cupped around the plastic cup of iced tea. "So, we never got the land we were told we bought. It's not in our names."

My mind spun over the implications of her story before I spoke. "Is it the same for everyone on the ten acres?"

Mary Parrish watched me processing, and I think she felt a bit sorry for me. "From what I can research, Miss Benedict, they did that on every property they developed, all fourteen developments across Texas."

She put on a pair of reading glasses and began to pull folders marked with name variations of 'Sundown' out of her file box, stacking them between us. I opened the one for Sundown Acres. "When Clay and Marty King over on the back of the development wanted to deed over their second lot to their son and daughter-in-law in 2012, the title company said that the Kings didn't really own an acre at all. In fact, none of us owned any part of the land." She slid a photocopied plat map over toward me and spun it around so I could see the writing. "The land had never been divided up into lots officially—they're all still owned by Sundown." The map from her folder looked like mine from Danford's loan file, but where mine had shown the rectangle subdivided into twenty smaller rectangles, hers was one big block with 'Sundown Properties, Ltd.' across the middle. "A lot of people have just left. They can't sell their homesite to anyone, can't leave it to their families, can't even use it to get a loan." She wasn't enjoying the conversation as much now.

She took off her glasses and looked over at her husband with tears in her eyes. "We lived with Rick's mother over in Garland for almost 20 years—she'd been suffering from dementia that long." One tear slid down beside her nose before she wiped it away with her hand. "When she passed in 2007, we used the money from the sale of her house to buy the trailer and make the $2500 down payment on the land. We'd never bought a house before, and we didn't know." Rick's face was as set as stone as she talked, but I could see a little tic under one of those sightless eyes. Mary reached out to take his hand, and his thick, calloused fingers closed over hers. "They knew when they saw us coming that we didn't know anything about loans or titles or mortgages. Rick was blind, and I was dumb."

I tried to explain to Doug at Danford later, without going into too much detail, how confident Mary Parrish had been in her facts and how many documents she'd gathered. Turns out Sundown Properties, Ltd., the company that had developed Sundown Acres, had been a scam like others organized in the prime mortgage heyday. It all depended on the gullibility of people who wanted a bit more land than your usual quarter-acre lot and were first-time buyers who didn't understand the process. A surveyor who'd faked the surveys (and later committed suicide) and a sham title company were in on the scheme as well.

As I explained to Doug, Sundown Properties had 'sold' these Kaufman county lots to twelve different couples or individuals, but they'd never divided the ten acres or deeded them to anyone at all. Mary and Rick had paid $25,000 for their two lots, paying the ten percent down payment in cash and the balance in a loan from Sundown. The residents had canceled checks and other documentation that showed they'd paid their monthly payments to Sundown faithfully until 2012, when Mary had organized their neighbors, and they all stopped making payments. Since it appeared Sundown had ceased operations in 2010, who had received those two years of payments was anybody's guess.

Nothing happened until 2014, when a new company had written to all the residents, demanding past-due payments on loans it had purchased from the now-defunct Sundown. When they threatened foreclosure, Mary's response was similar to the one she had sent me and Danford. After that, several companies who bought the notes down the line had sent similar demands, and Mary's response each time became more succinct: *We were the victims of fraud,* she would write in response to their demand letters, *but so are you.*

I left my card with the Parrishes that day and took some of the copies Mary'd given me from her neatly labeled files to send to Danford. By the time I spoke with Doug, I'd worked out a bit more of the fraud against Danford. Our predecessors in interest in the loan purchase had clearly known about the fraud, but then so had their predecessors, right up the line to Sundown. Doug went off to discuss what to do with his partners.

Land changes hands frequently in Texas. Even if someone had bought the property from whoever thought they owned it now, no new deed had ever been filed with the Kaufman County Clerk. It would cost a fortune to unwind it all, even if Danford won. In the end, Danford wrote off the loss of the $500 per loan and considered my work on the file to have saved them the money for a complicated lawsuit. I don't know if Danford sold the notes down the line to some other unsuspecting buyer, but I'd like to think they didn't.

I went out to the Parrishes' property after that to explain the situation, but aside from receiving Christmas cards each year signed by Mary Parrish for herself and Rick, I didn't hear from the Parrishes again until they called me four years later about their grandson Todd and the murder of Carrie Ames.

CHAPTER ONE

M ary Parrish first left a voice mail, then called several more times while I was in court on Friday. Todd, the blue-eyed grandson in the living room pictures, had been arrested for what appeared to be a homicide, and they needed my help. Although I told them I didn't practice criminal law, I still felt sorry about what had happened to them, so I went back out to Sundown Acres the next afternoon to hear the story, carrying a half-dozen snickerdoodle cookies with me. Mary served us coffee instead of iced tea this time, but we sat in the same places at the table. It was Groundhog Day, and I felt like I was trapped in a time loop.

The double-wide trailer was still just as clean and neat, but Rick and Mary had aged far more that they should have in four years. Todd's girlfriend, Carrie Ames, had been found dead last Sunday night in her apartment in Dallas, and the Collin county sheriff's deputies had come to arrest him on Thursday at a house where Todd was digging a French drain. Bail had been set at half a million dollars. Todd and his grandparents didn't have the money to get him out, and

—as I knew all too well—they couldn't use their home to raise a bond. They'd been unable to reach Todd's mother Lori, but they doubted she could gather the $50,000 for the bond. Right now, Todd was being held in the Collin county lockup instead of the Dallas county jail, so it could have been worse.

"Todd wouldn't do this. Isn't that right, honey?" Mary said again, and we both looked over at Rick. His eyes were cloudier now than they'd been when we first met, but they still looked directly at your face when he greeted you. Right now, his eyes were fixed on the coffee cup he cradled with both hands.

"We looked you up," he said quietly without raising his head, and I felt my heart race, just like it had done for five years now, anytime anyone discovered who I was. He raised his sightless eyes to mine, and I swear to god, it felt like he could see me, perhaps see beyond what I hoped was a professional façade. "You risked your career to right a wrong that was being done to all those investors. There's a wrong being done here. Can't you help us?"

He lifted the brown pottery mug halfway to his lips but lowered it again without taking a sip of his coffee. "He'd never do something that could end him up inside a room for the rest of his life. He can't breathe inside—I can't imagine what this is doing to him. He has claustrophobia. He's had it since his father died, and nothing can make him stay indoors." He smiled with a memory. "Lord knows we tried over the years." The smiled faded. "Mary's right. Todd wouldn't —couldn't—do this. He's had some trouble over the years, but nothing serious. After thirty-eight years as a cop, I'd know if my grandson was capable of doing this."

I was suddenly glad he couldn't see me, because I knew better than most that people could surprise you, disappoint you, even betray you. I kept my eyes on him, even though I knew Mary was looking at me, silently pleading for me to help them.

"I wish I could help you, I truly do." I took a fortifying sip of my own coffee, diluted with as much sweetened non-dairy creamer as I could manage, and tried not to choke. "But I don't practice criminal law."

"You say you deal with traffic tickets on your website," Mary put in reproachfully. "That's criminal law."

I finally looked at her, and then wished I hadn't. Her red-rimmed eyes were the same blue as those of the grandson in his pictures on the memorial wall, and I recognized that look. It was the same pleading expression I'd seen for four years on the faces of home-owners dealing with a foreclosure, the same desperation I faced as a creditor's attorney when I attended a bankruptcy hearing. *Believe me, listen to me, help me.*

I tried to defend my website. "I have an attorney who takes care of those traffic tickets for my clients, and that's why it's there." I knew where this was headed, and I didn't like it one bit. "Look, I know a criminal defense attorney. He's very, very good, but he will be expensive, and I don't even know if he takes these kinds of cases. But I'll talk to him."

Mary closed her eyes, and she reached to take Rick's hand. I watched his fingers close over hers and wondered if I could force myself to be in the same room with Rob Gerard one more time.

CHAPTER TWO

What I'd told the Parrishes wasn't really a lie. I knew a criminal defense attorney, and I knew he was very, very good. I would even speak to him, if I could get in to see him. What I didn't know was whether he would speak to me.

I was under cross-examination the last time Rob Gerard had spoken to me. His client, Bill Stephenson—my former managing partner—had been on trial for fraud, and I was the government's main witness in securities trials against him and his clients. Gerard hadn't pulled any punches. He'd portrayed me not only as a disgruntled former employee but had also hinted to the jury that I'd had a secret crush on Bill. He'd led them to think that because Bill hadn't returned my 'fumbling' attempts to attract him, I'd filed a whistle-blower complaint with various securities agencies to get my revenge.

Some of his questions were achingly personal: *How many times had Bill and I worked late in his high-rise apartment, preparing opinions or meeting with clients? How often had I rushed to take care of Bill's dry-cleaning or buy a gift for his teenage daughter—tasks that no other self-respecting associate would have done?* The answers to the questions were always that yes, I'd stayed late or worked too much or spent too many evenings there or just wanted to do Bill a favor. And if I had done so in a misplaced sense of hero-worship, well, that was just as unfortunate as my choice of employment.

Regardless of my reasons for reporting, the jury could clearly see that Bill had knowingly assisted the firm's clients in preparing documents for their investors that exaggerated or flat out lied about risky business propositions. Gerard couldn't pinpoint any knowledge of Bill's activities on my part, but he made me as unlikable as possible to the jury. His disdain for me during the cross was palpable, and his disgust when he shook his head as he completed his closing argument to the jury caused several of them to glance at me for a reaction. I'd found a place to rest my eyes (a dark brown spot on the wall a few inches above the judge's right shoulder) and I kept my face as expressionless as I could.

I kept them there through the closing arguments, through three hours of excruciating jury instructions read by the judge, and through Gerard's disclosure to the Court while the jury was still out— announcing a settlement between Bill and the government. All the criminal charges against Bill were dropped when he agreed to work with the government against his former clients. Now, while several of Bill's clients serve prison sentences and their assets have been seized, Bill's settlement was fully paid, and he's well on his way to making it big on the speaker's circuit. I heard he brings in thousands for dinner and luncheon speeches. Five years later, I was still struggling to recover from my three short years at Stephenson and Associates.

In my nightmares since, Gerard has become my career's cross-examiner, the ever-present voice in my head: *Why did I take that client? Didn't I know she'd ultimately stiff me on the bill? Did I need an office or assistant? How would I get clients? Who did I think I was, taking on a legal matter I didn't really understand? What kind of lawyer struggles to make ends meet?* He prosecutes me without pity or prejudice, ruthlessly re-opening the wounds I feel every day. I see his icy blue eyes under those black brows looking at me with derision or mockery—as my answer merits—and even the careful civility in his questions feels like an indictment of my life choices.

And here I was, at the receptionist's desk in his office. Although I'd pegged Gerard as another high-rise type like my old boss, his office in a converted bungalow in the State-Thomas section of Dallas was entirely the opposite of my expectation. The street was mostly law or accounting offices, and signs for three or four small firms sharing a remodeled Victorian house would be posted next to the brightly painted front doors. I'd sat in my parked car for half an hour before I came in, pretending I was checking my makeup (which had already faded off in this heat) and my voice mail (still no new work), but nothing had come along to stop me from committing this folly.

The Gerard Firm occupied a house by itself, a two-story, Crafts-man-style house painted a light tan with dark green paint on the shutters and trim on the porch posts. On the wide front porch, there were pots waiting for plants in the spring, and two hooks for a porch swing. I would have loved an office like this, with the parlor on the right of the central staircase fitted as a waiting area, the dining room to the left converted into cheerful, light-filled areas of desks with plants and pictures of children and families. I could hear people chatting and laughing around the corner and a high-speed printer chugging out documents. The bell above the door jingled when I pushed it open, and one of the women I'd heard laughing came out to greet me with a smile. I returned it and spoke with as much confidence as possible over the pounding in my head.

"Hi." I smiled with as many teeth as I could. "I need to see Rob Gerard. Is he available?"

She cocked her head and apologized with, it seemed, real regret. "I'm sorry, he's not available right now. Would you like to leave a note?"

Before I could answer, the man himself came down the hallway from the back of the house with a mug in his hand. He looked as piratical as ever, tall and prematurely silver-haired, with those black eyebrows raised in amazement.

"Lacey Benedict Arnold, as I live and breathe." His smile was as mocking as the nickname he'd given me in the Dallas press, but to my surprise, he didn't seem angry, even though I had to have been the main reason his client had settled and been disbarred. "What brings you to my door?"

I took a deep breath. "I need a criminal defense attorney. Will you help me?"

———

THE FURNITURE IN GERARD'S UPSTAIRS OFFICE WAS DARK WOOD and leather, and the chair I sat in was so big I felt like a little kid in the principal's office. Or maybe that was me. Either way, I'm sure Gerard meant the furniture to dwarf anyone sitting there, while he took a seat behind a desk that was big enough to be a bed.

I was appalled. Why did my brain go there? *That's enough of that*, I told myself. Gerard was a handsome man, but I preferred my men kind and supportive, not cruel and cynical. I didn't want the coffee I'd accepted from the friendly receptionist, but I'd needed something to do with my hands, so I just cradled the cup and enjoyed the warmth. He took a sip of his own coffee before setting the cup on a coaster on his desk. *Of course, this jerk has coasters*, I thought.

"So. You're in trouble?"

I was instantly angry, and to my dismay and embarrassment, I could feel hot tears at the corners of my eyes. "You'd like that, wouldn't you?" As soon as the words left my mouth, I wished I could call them back. Gerard only smiled slightly. He looked at the coffee cup and moved it slightly, centering it on its coaster.

My face flushing, I resettled myself in his office chair. It was slightly lower than his, and I assumed that was intentional. "Actually, I have a client referral for you." There—that put us on a more equal footing, I told myself. I was simply another attorney referring a case to a colleague.

"You have a white-collar criminal referral? I'd heard you were doing mostly real estate law these days."

"Been checking up on me, have you?" This time, I was the one taking a calm sip of my coffee and looking at him over the rim of the cup. Luckily, the coffee wasn't hot, so it didn't scald me, but it was a shock. I'd not wanted to take cream or sugar, since Gerard had taken his black, and I'd wanted to look just as tough. I regretted it now, since the coffee was espresso strength and bitter enough to make my mouth pucker. He watched me struggle it down only a slight lift of those black eyebrows, and I remembered how blank his face could look when he was waiting for a witness to answer. He'd mastered the art of staying still after posing a question, letting the uncomfortable silence stretch out further and further, until a witness found herself filling it with answers she'd wished she hadn't divulged. It had worked like a charm when I was a nervous witness, but this time, I knew the trick and waited him out.

He finally smiled and picked up his coffee cup, saluting me mockingly. "You've gotten better at that," he said before calmly taking a sip with no mouth puckering. "I hear things—Dallas isn't that big a town where the legal community is concerned. I heard you were doing some commercial real estate litigation." He leaned back in his chair. "Quite a departure from M&A work, isn't it?"

Mergers and acquisitions were a long time ago, I thought. Years, decades, centuries. Gerard would be fully aware that no transactional firm in Dallas—or even a transactional section of a larger firm—would give me a job after the Stephenson debacle ended. "Not that far," I said, with a shake of my head. I put my cup on the coaster on my side of his desk and leaned back myself. I crossed my right leg casually over my left, noticing with concern that my pencil skirt slid pretty high on my thigh as I did so. This suit was over five years old, one of the few suits I still owned, bought back when I was working for Bill Stephenson and making six figures a year. I was also a few pounds lighter then, and the suit was a bit tighter now. The rest of my high-priced attorney wardrobe was sold in consignment stores, one outfit at a time, along with most of the expensive leather shoes and purses that were bought to match. I tugged the skirt down, hoping Gerard hadn't noticed.

"But let's talk about this referral, shall we?" He set the cup back down and flexed his arms over his head in a stretch. "What've you got?"

"It's not white-collar," I confessed, "but you're the only criminal lawyer I know."

I told him what I already knew, stumbling a bit over the facts in my nervousness. Mary Parrish had upgraded her research skills since the Sundown Acres matter, and the file folder she handed me about Carrie Ames' murder contained printouts from news stories online. The picture at the head of one article showed that Carrie Ames had been a petite blond with intelligent blue eyes and an elfin cast to her features. She'd grown up in Breeland, a medium-sized town northeast of Dallas, and was survived by her parents and two older sisters, who were married with children of their own. She had been living in Dallas and had been employed at an urgent care facility located in east Dallas. Other than those bare facts, the articles revealed little about Carrie, but more about her death.

She'd been discovered about 10 pm on Sunday night by her roommate, a young woman named Naomi Jackson, who'd returned late from spending the day with her sister at the University of North Texas in Denton. Although the police hadn't released many details about Carrie's death, Naomi had been interviewed by the *Dallas Morning News* and was pretty chatty about what she'd seen. Besides the tearful disbelief, Naomi knew that Carrie had been last seen alive by a group of friends who'd met in Carrie and Naomi's living room late Sunday afternoon. Naomi found Carrie with a head wound and blood pooling around her. As a medical assistant, Naomi knew to check for a pulse, but when she touched Carrie's cold skin, she called 911 and hadn't started CPR.

After that, information in the reporting was mostly secondhand. Witnesses had told police that Carrie's boyfriend, Todd Parrish, had argued with her after the rest of the group had left, but had been unable to say why. On Thursday morning, the police in Princeton had arrested him on site at his landscaping job. Bail had been set at half a million, but Todd's grandparents weren't sure they could afford both a bond for bail and an attorney to represent him.

I hadn't even finished the story before Gerard started shaking his head at me. "What?" I asked, irritated.

He held up his thumb. "Number one. I don't practice that kind of criminal law." He raised his pointer finger and aimed it at me like a gun. "Number two. Grandparents couldn't afford me—even if I did practice that kind of criminal law. Number three—"

"Before you raise that middle finger at me," I broke in hotly, "you've practiced that kind of law before. I know you were an assistant DA out of law school."

"Been checking up on me, have you?" he countered.

"I checked you out before you deposed me five years ago," I confessed. The reminder of how we met chilled the air, but he didn't look away.

"Number three," he said as he added that middle finger to the other two, "I don't do *pro bono* work."

"They need help," I said, leaning forward. "They don't believe their grandson could have done this—"

He interrupted me. "No one believes their grandchild could be a killer, but every day, killers prove that supposition incorrect." He threaded those blasted fingers together behind his head, his eyes daring me to challenge him. "No one knows what someone else is capable of," he said, echoing my thoughts from a few days before. "Maybe that argument people heard got out of hand, and grandson struck out in anger. Who knows?"

I slumped a little in the expensive leather chair. This wasn't my field and I couldn't argue psychology with him, but I did believe what the Parrishes said. "Todd Parrish has never had a violent episode in his life. He and Carrie were planning to be married this year, and his grandparents say they were really in love."

"And maybe girlfriend was breaking it off with him." Gerard looked at the ceiling as he argued the hypothetical. "She tells him it's over, and he gets angry." He looked back at me, black eyebrows lifted. "You said she had a head wound. Did boyfriend push her? Hit her? What do you know about cause of death? If it was a push, the DA will probably plead him down to voluntary manslaughter."

I shook my head. "God, you're cynical. Why would he plead guilty if he didn't do it?"

Gerard laughed and sat forward. "People plead guilty and settle things all the time to avoid a trial." He looked me in the eye. "You should know that."

I shoved up from the chair, my voice loud in the quiet room. "This isn't about me and Bill Stephenson. The Parrishes asked me who the best criminal defense attorney was, and I told them it was you." He raised his eyebrows sardonically. "Yes, you. Just because you eviscerated me on the stand doesn't mean I don't recognize you're brilliant at what you do." I reached down for my bag as Gerard rose.

"Ms. Benedict." I looked up at him quickly, and I knew he could tell what I was thinking. On cross-examination, he'd called me 'Lacey' and called Bill 'Mr. Stephenson,' highlighting the age difference between us, making me sound like a young assistant with a crush on her boss. To hear him call me by my last name now was simply infuriating. We stared at each other for a full ten seconds.

He sighed and held up a hand. "Lacey. Sit. Let me at least help you find the right counsel for grandson. I doubt you know the best criminal law attorneys in Dallas." He was right. While I knew the attorney that took my traffic ticket cases, my legal network in Dallas was defined more by who still spoke to me rather than quality. I sat, a little huffily, and put my bag back down on the floor.

While I watched, he drank the rest of his coffee and turned his chair to look out the back window, the one looking out over a backyard filled with trees. I took the opportunity to look around the office.

If the converted house was a surprise, the office was even more so. Bill Stephenson's office had exemplified the man he believed he was: sharp, smooth, and polished, with an expensive modern standing desk —kept completely clean except for whatever file Bill was working on at the time—and a credenza with metal sculptures spaced perfectly under a "me wall" filled with diplomas, certificates, and pictures of Bill with politicians and celebrities (many of whom have since conveniently forgotten the previous connection).

Rob Gerard's office was two upstairs bedrooms of the old house joined to form one large room, with windows on the three outer walls, which had been painted a few shades darker than the exterior. The floor was hardwood—probably original—and the furniture was heavy dark wood, slightly scuffed and worn on the corners. His desk was covered with stacks of papers and files, labeled in a dark, thick writing that reminded me of his eyebrows. The credenza along the wall had more stacks and files that towered precariously, hiding in part some small pictures in wooden frames. Some had children in them— strange, since I'd never imagined Gerard as a father. I guess we see what we want to see about people.

I heard his chair creak, and I looked back at him to find him looking at me, that faint smile on his face that made me think he could read my mind. I flushed but didn't break the silence. Once learned, that lesson sticks. For the space of a few heartbeats, we just looked at each other.

"I'll help the grandson right now." He said, and I exhaled the breath I didn't realize I was holding, but before I could speak, he continued. "I'm right—they can't afford me." He held up a hand to stop me from interrupting. "But they can afford you."

My words fell all over themselves. "But I'm not a—I don't—"

He raised his voice over my denials. "I know you're not. But what's needed right now isn't trial work or negotiation. It's the grunt work, the details, the due diligence of information and investigation. You're definitely capable of that. Bill Stephenson said you were the best associate he'd ever had." He stood. "If you're all wrong, and grandson did do this, we can talk about getting them different counsel for the trial."

As that statement robbed the breath from my lungs, he went to the office door, shouting down the stairs. "Carmen! Bring a pad and come up here."

For the next few minutes, the woman I met at the reception desk —Carmen—and I discussed details: the Parrishes' names, address, phone number, and Todd's information in order to prepare an engagement agreement. I scrolled through the contact information on my phone and gave her numbers, but I could barely concentrate on the details for the pounding in my head. Considering all the different areas of the law I'd had to learn in the past five years to pay my bills, criminal law shouldn't be a stretch. But I'd sworn after the whistle-blower trials to never be involved in any criminal law matters again. Now it looked like I'd be doing it after all.

Finally, Carmen left to call the Parrishes and arrange for signature of the engagement agreement, and I was left alone with Rob Gerard. We fell back into waiting for the other to speak, but this time, I broke the silence.

"I don't understand what you're getting out of this." The statement came out rather more harshly than I intended, so I tried again. "While I appreciate you doing this..."

Gerard grinned at me, a genuine and rather disarming grin that I'd never seen before, and one I'd prefer not to see now. "I think the words you're looking for are 'thank you.'"

I frowned at him, more to give myself time than out of displeasure. With that relaxed, easy grin, he was less the cynical and disdainful attorney I remembered and more someone I could like. And I didn't like that.

"Yes, thank you. But why are you doing this?"

He shrugged and looked away. "I remember doing things out of a sense of justice." He straightened the closest stack of files on his desk, lining the straight edges of the bottommost manila folder with the corner of the desk. Then he looked directly at me. "Isn't that how they got you to take them on? Doing the right thing again?" A sardonic smile edged at his lips. "It's a character flaw of yours, isn't it? Truth, justice, and apple pie?"

Stung, I reached again for my bag and tucked my phone away, trying too quickly to zip it and catching a bit of the torn lining in the zipper's teeth for my trouble. Now that he was doing the nice thing and giving in to my request, I was determined not to snipe back at him. As I struggled to unthread the lining from the zipper, Gerard waited. When I gave up, hoping I'd be able to open it outside and get my keys out, he spoke quietly.

"Forgive me, Benedict. I know you're trying to do a nice thing for them." I looked back at him, startled, to see him smiling at me again. "It's been a long time since I've felt like jousting at a windmill. Maybe it's time." He glanced at his calendar. "I've got an appointment in a few minutes, but why don't we meet tomorrow morning for coffee and discuss the next steps?"

I rose, looping my bag over my shoulder. "I am grateful to you," I said, and was a bit dismayed to hear my own grudging tone. How would this ever work if I couldn't even be polite? I held my hand out, and Gerard looked at it for a moment before taking it in his.

"I do have a condition, though," he said as he held my hand in his. I didn't want to pull it away, but I was afraid mine would start to sweat the longer he held it, so I tugged a bit.

"What condition?"

He released my hand and stuck both of his in the back pockets of his jeans. "I want to know why you didn't take the whistleblower award from the SEC."

For the second time, he robbed me of my breath, but this time, he didn't speak while I recovered. We stood in silence for a moment, and then I made up my mind. "I'll tell you why, if you tell me why Bill Stephenson decided to settle the trial before the jury returned a verdict."

We looked at each other for a few seconds, and then we both nodded. Deal.

———

I GOT OUT TO MY CAR AND RESTED MY HEAD ON THE STEERING wheel, willing myself not to be sick. It had been years since I'd thought this much about the Bill Stephenson part of my life.

The six months surrounding the whistleblower trials had been pretty confusing, with depositions, attorney meetings, federal and state agent interviews, and I surfed along. The press, including the legal press, had picked up the story, and I ended up changing my cell phone number to avoid calls from reporters hoping for more details— details I was not going to provide even if I had them. I convinced myself for a few weeks that the change in phone number was the reason I didn't get any follow-up calls from law firms I'd applied to. After three months, that excuse lost all believability, but it took a call with a recruiter I'd registered with to really bring home the message that I was now radioactive. She was kind and polite, but she explained the situation with excruciating clarity. While I might be able to move to another city and practice transactional securities law, Dallas firms wouldn't hire someone they couldn't trust—and they couldn't trust me. Was I interested in looking in other major cities like Atlanta or Chicago?

I considered it for a few days while I continued to spend into my savings, but it was mostly for form's sake. Dallas was home, and I didn't think I could really be that far away from my father. Even though my brother took the main responsibility for Dad, I tried to be there for them both. I remember staying in bed for several days, trying to avoid life and family until Sara, my sister-in-law and one of my closest friends, came to drag me out for tacos and a tough discussion about the rest of my life. I felt nervous and excited and frightened and overwhelmed—much like I did leaving Gerard's office that afternoon.

After leaving Gerard, I joined the thousands heading to the suburbs in rush hour, my windows cracked for a breath of the surprisingly warm and muggy air. Dad lived with Ryan and Sara in Plano, just north of Dallas, in a remodeled eighties brick ranch that looked like all the other remodeled houses on their street. Ryan and Sara were both teachers, and it was only because of Dad's disability and pension that they could afford a house in this neighborhood. I didn't begrudge them the financial assistance: on his best days, Dad needed a lot of help, and now that the Alzheimer's had progressed, he couldn't live alone. For several years, we'd thought he was just a bit forgetful, that his memory was failing a little. By the time his ability to do his work as an engineer was endangered by his failure to follow up or to remember to report findings, I'd done enough research to see that Dad had already passed into the early stages of the disease. Tests only confirmed what we already knew.

Dad's decline had already started when I filed my whistleblower complaint with the government. I'd even discussed what I was seeing at Stephenson's office with Dad, and it was he who encouraged me to do the right thing. By the time the trials began to roll around more than a year later, Dad's short-term memory was pretty much gone, and I really didn't want to start from scratch explaining the situation every time we met, so we didn't discuss it in front of him. Ryan and Sara had moved him into their house at that point, fixing up the family room over their garage as a bedroom and sitting room for Dad, a move which caused a short-term war in their household, since my fourteen-year-old nephew claimed he had been planning to take that space (even though Sara rolled her eyes and talked about him having to climb over her cold dead body to get there).

Five years down the road, Dad was no longer able to have that much autonomy, and the stairs had become a challenge. With their son Michael off to college at Texas A&M, Sara had decided to take a leave of absence this school year as we made some hard choices. Her parents were both still alive and living together up in Sherman, and we told her she won the award for best Benedict. We had to decide what to do for him, and tonight Ryan had called a family dinner meeting. I'd spent the morning preparing for the next day's foreclosures and dreading the interaction with Rob Gerard, so I hadn't even really been thinking about what I was headed to this afternoon.

While I was looking forward to Sara's lasagna, the meeting with Gerard had left me a bit queasy, and the thought of discussing long-term care for Dad only deepened the nausea.

Once I was off the highway, I cracked my window to get some fresh air. After almost an hour in crowded Dallas traffic, Ryan and Sara's suburban neighborhood seemed deserted, with most driveways empty even at 6 pm. February is usually the coldest month in Dallas, but the air this evening matched my mood: ominous and heavy. The weather people were forecasting a cold front tomorrow, but it didn't feel like winter tonight.

Some of the houses in the neighborhood were stubbornly still lit with Christmas lights, and I even saw a tree in one window. When we were young, Dad would have the Christmas tree down and lights packed up by New Year's night. I was always slightly envious of those who left theirs up through the Feast of Epiphany on January 6. People with lights up in the first week of February were either defiant or crazy or both. Last year, Dad loved the artificial tree with its blinking lights so much that they moved it to his sitting room and left it up until well past Memorial Day. This year, Dad seemed to barely notice us, much less the decorations. A social worker we'd worked with told me that Alzheimer's robs its victims of their joy as well as their memories, and I get that now.

I knocked lightly on the front door but let myself in with my key, and, as I'd hoped, the queasiness eased as soon as I smelled Sara's marinara sauce. I went in to find Dad dozing in his over-stuffed recliner in the living room, Alex Trebec silently responding to contestants on the muted television. The last year had aged Dad so much; his hair—never very thick—had receded to a short circle of gray around the back of his head, and his face had gained a softness with age that I'd not wanted to notice. His doctor had warned us that, in this stage of the disease, Dad might be agitated or even combative, but that hadn't occurred yet. He simply seemed to move in a fog, barely noticing us or anything around him. He spoke little, and when he did, his conversation was disjointed and out of context, as if we were strangers on a train who didn't know each other at all.

I didn't want to disturb him, so I sat on the ottoman next to the chair and waited, letting the silence in the house seep into me and ease the stress away. I knew when he opened his eyes they'd be the same light gray as mine, but his would be unfocused and dazed. His blond hair had resisted gray for a long time, but over the last few years, the graying—like everything else—had seemed to accelerate. Ryan and I both had our mother's very straight and light brown hair; when she committed suicide when we were teenagers, Ryan had dyed his hair a yellow blond that clashed with his skin tone and quickly grew brown roots, and then he added highlights of various other colors as the mood struck. Dad let him go through the phases, showing no shock or surprise when Ryan showed up with a mohawk or a piercing. Ryan said now that he was acting out because he was trying to show his creativity in a family of boring go-alongers, but I think he was doing everything within his control to distance himself from the woman who had chosen to leave us long before she'd ended her life. Now we seemed to be losing our father, the one person who'd been steady as a rock—boring even, to a teenager—and again, there was nothing we could do.

My dad opened his eyes and looked into mine. I threaded my fingers through his hot and dry ones. We'd discovered that sometimes touch helped with the confusion he seemed to feel. For a moment, I thought he might have recognized me, but then he moved his head slightly to look past me at the television. I watched him as we sat there together. *Family ties for 200, Alex,* I thought wearily.

———

DINNER WENT PRETTY MUCH AS I'D EXPECTED, SARA'S delicious lasagna brightening the dull, too-warm air in the house. She makes it just like I like it, extra saucy, with cheese oozing from every square. But even her cooking couldn't make the conversation easier.

Sara and Ryan met their senior year in high school, and they've been a couple ever since, steadily weathering Ryan's college career and teaching, their infertility and subsequent adoption, and now their care of Dad. Sara is the sort of person whose comforting presence feels like a soft warm blanket when it's cold. I could not imagine what she saw in my goofy brother, whose hair the year they met had looked like the mane of one of those rainbow ponies little girls collect. He already had several ear piercings by that time, and for a while had a stud lodged in his eyebrow. During that year, I couldn't look at him without getting distracted by the bright silver dot winking at me through the eyebrow hairs. Sara had clearly seen something in his weird, impulsive nature that appealed to her. She says he makes her laugh.

"The facility is just about a mile away," Ryan told me before I'd finished my first helping of lasagna. He nudged a brochure across the table. On the front, a silver-haired woman happily showed a partially-constructed afghan to a young girl. They were both laughing, and I wondered what was so funny about knitting. I didn't pick it up.

I wanted to ask if we were sure Dad needed full-time care, but it felt wrong to ask that in front of Sara, who'd put her career on hold to stay with Dad this year, so I just swiped my garlic bread in the left-over sauce puddled on my plate. The question was moot at this point. I'd seen Dad wander into the kitchen earlier, and watched as Sara gently walked him back to the living room. He'd recently taken to refusing food, so Ryan had sat with him at a TV tray and, with the ease of habit, determinedly encouraged him to eat the healthy meal Sara'd prepped.

"This facility doesn't have space right now, but if we get him on the waiting list, they'll evaluate him and see how much care he needs and where he could be placed," Ryan doggedly continued while I finished my slice of garlic bread and considered how many calories another square of lasagna would have. Italian food—whether it was Sara's lasagna or pizza or minestrone—is my idea of comfort food, and I needed comfort tonight. I didn't want to think about the openings on the waiting list, which I was pretty sure only happened when someone died.

"Lace." Sara sounded sad and a bit regretful, her face sympathetic. "Ryan and I have considered every option we can. We thought about moving Ian to our room downstairs, but sometimes he wanders during the night, and I'm afraid he'd go outside."

I wiped my hands on my napkin and then sat still to think, as if I could find some answers they'd not considered. "I know you have. And I appreciate you both doing everything you could." I took a breath. "I'm hoping by mid-year I can help out too." I pushed my plate forward a bit, surreptitiously nudging the brochure a little further away.

"The long-term care insurance will cover about 50-75% of the cost, depending on the facility and the care he needs, and Dad's disability payment should just about cover the rest until he's able to draw social security next year," Ryan said. "We need to talk about selling the rest of the farm at some point, but Sara is going to do some substitute teaching for the rest of the year, and we'll be fine." He looked over at Sara, who smiled gently at him and nodded. He looked back at me and nudged the brochure a little closer to me.

I looked up at him. He looked so like my mother it made my head hurt. "He's already gone, isn't he?" For a moment, Ryan just stared back at me. Then he exhaled a deep, deep breath and nodded.

CHAPTER THREE

The cold front we'd been warned about blew through in the early hours on Tuesday, and the north wind was bracing, to say the least. I parked in the cheap pay-by-the-hour lot a block from the courthouse, waving to Sameer, the attendant, who was still directing attorneys and litigants frantically trying to park in order to make the 8:30 am docket call. He was bundled up to his eyebrows, but he waggled his flag at me. I'd settle up with him when I finished my foreclosures.

The Courthouse Café is a one-room lunch counter that serves breakfast and lunch, and it opens at 5 am and closes at 2 pm. It's not the place to come to if you're worried about having floors clean enough for eating off of, but since I never eat off the floors, it suits me just fine. The windows were dirty and fogged, but the smell of bacon and coffee that blew outside on the warm air as I opened the door just made me happy. I saluted Curtis, who was making coffee behind the counter. The 'Two' Breakfast (two eggs, two thin strips of bacon, and two halves of buttered white toast) was $4.99, an amazing price for anything in downtown Dallas, and I usually ate in the Café when I had to be in the county courthouse early. As cheap breakfasts go, it's filling and quick, and the over-easy eggs are always perfectly cooked, the greasy edges just starting to curl and brown. If you want to get a parking space in the closest lots, you have to come early. Snagging a parking space on the cheap and breakfast for less than five bucks is the perfect way to start a day spent in front of a judge who probably got up on the wrong side of the bench that morning.

You might think a place like this wouldn't attract the high-priced attorneys that worked both the state and federal courthouses around the plaza, but you'd be wrong. There's a mix of people that eat here: some you suspect might be homeless, while others are clearly attorneys in thousand-dollar suits. It was one of the few places that had been here in the courthouse plaza before downtown Dallas had gone through a rejuvenation a few years ago, Curtis had told me, and he had owned the building for more than 20 years. The unheated top floor he leased out to a yoga company that had converted the long, narrow space into a studio. During the summer, the rising heat and lack of air conditioning upstairs was perfect for hot yoga, and in the winter, the classes kept their sweats and scarves on.

The Café occupied its own long and narrow building next to a hotel built in the 30s, a blocky edifice without much charm or detail that had stubbornly resisted gentrification and renewal, and still rented rooms out by the day or the week or, I have long suspected, the hour. The Café seemed to huddle there, between the pay-by-the-hour parking lot and the hotel, and business was steady Monday through Friday, the only days the Café was open. Curtis fed veterans down on their luck for free, the attorneys rubbed shoulders with the hotel residents, and everyone seemed to get along just fine. Curtis had been enforcing a "no-phone" rule in the Café for years, and any time someone new didn't see one of the signs on the walls and started talking on their cell phone, the transgressor would be politely asked to go outside. There was no television or radio or speakers playing music, so it was the perfect place to review your notes before heading to a hearing or trial, the only background noise the gentle turning of the ceiling fans and Leslie's tuneless humming as he made pancakes.

The Café was only half-full this close to 8:30 am, since most of the early docket crowd had left to go check in before hearings began. I spotted Gerard immediately, sitting at one of the little four-tops that hugged the wall across from the counter. He was in a light blue dress shirt that matched his eyes (damn him), and his red- and navy-striped tie was tucked in between the third and fourth buttons of his shirt so he wouldn't drag it in his plate. He was reading a legal document and finishing scrambled eggs that he'd doctored with hot sauce. Never having seen the need to mask the taste of eggs with vinegary Louisiana hot sauce myself, I felt a bit superior. I'd also dressed up a bit today since I had to cry foreclosures at the courthouse. I'd learned that—if my client actually wanted to get someone to bid on a property —it helped if I looked the part of client representative.

I slung my long wool dress coat over the back of one of the chairs and put my briefcase on the chair seat. Both were of really good quality from my Stephenson days. We seldom had the chance to wear heavy coats in Texas, so this one had gotten little wear in the seven years I'd had it. The briefcase had been soft and supple Italian leather when I'd bought it, and it had just gotten softer and more mellow over the years. When I'd sold most of my suits and dresses after my unemployment days, Sara had gone through my closet with me. She'd been responsible for me buying the right things before, and then was responsible for the good quality things I'd kept. As it turns out, she was right in assuming I would still need some dressy clothes to meet with clients or other attorneys. I was opening my own office and would be the 'partner' responsible for bringing in clients, and I would need to look the part. I wasn't so sure, since the idea of having my own firm was barely comprehensible then. She was right though, and the fact that I had the black pantsuit to wear with my black heeled boots today was wholly thanks to her.

By the time I finished unwrapping my scarf and taking off my gloves (we really get out the cold-weather gear when we can), Gerard was finished with his eggs and was drinking coffee. Curtis came out from behind the counter to bring my breakfast, and he grinned at me. "Looking good today, Lacey," he said as he set down the melamine plate. "Coffee?"

"No coffee this morning, and thank you, right backatcha, handsome," I said, winking at him. Curtis is sixty, about a hundred pounds overweight, and is married to Leslie, the tall black man working the pancake batter at the back. His coffee is made in a pot that I think is original to the building, and tastes like 1970. I avoid it at all costs, which Curtis knows.

"I heard you, Lacey Benedict," Leslie shouted from the back. "Stay away from my man." Curtis grinned and headed back behind the counter.

Gerard watched all the goings on from his seat as he pulled his tie out of his shirt and rebuttoned. "Guess we know where you eat breakfast before docket call."

I shrugged, silently pleased that we'd met in a place where people seemed to *like me.* His office, maybe even the federal courthouse—those were his types of places, but I'd made a place for myself where I could, and not even Rob Gerard or Bill Stephenson could take that away from me.

I started to pull out the legal pad from my briefcase, but Gerard waved me toward my eggs. "We've got time—eat." I was irritated at his tone, but I was hungry, so I let it go to attend to my breakfast. His attention was diverted by an attorney who came by the table and spoke to him. I didn't expect him to introduce me, so I was startled when he did. The attorney, a pretty famous Dallas real estate specialist, was clearly trying to place me, and started to ask me what firm I was with. Gerard smoothly interrupted him, and they talked for a moment while I salted and peppered my eggs, my cheeks hot with embarrassment. *I'll never get used to this,* I thought, *never.*

I watched them talk for a minute, Gerard looking like a younger, gray-haired Sean Connery. *Thank god he didn't have a Scottish accent too,* I thought with a smirk, *or women would faint when he walked by.* When his phone beeped discreetly, Gerard excused himself to go outside to make a call, and the other attorney moved on. Curtis refilled Gerard's coffee and my water, and he murmured, "You okay?" I nodded, using my toast to swipe through the egg yolk on my plate.

"Rob Gerard's not a bad guy," Curtis continued.

I swallowed the last bite of toast, not touching that statement. My jury was still out on that one. "I've never seen him here."

"Oh, he doesn't come here much anymore," Curtis said. "He spends more time at Cabell these days," he said, referring to the federal courthouse a few blocks away. This was true; most of Gerard's civil cases would be heard in federal court at the big federal building. The big white Dallas county court building where most of my evictions or collections cases were heard didn't have any criminal cases. Those were heard at the imposing criminal courthouse over by the county jail on the other side of the highway.

"He used to be here more often when he was working with Higginson," he added. "What was that—about five years ago?" I nodded.

Higginson and Botwell was a large firm that had split up a few years before—something that seemed to happen to many large local firms. They formed, swelled for a few years with the hiring of new attorneys or laterals and carve outs of sections from other firms, and then they died or were carved up when those same partners left for new, better firms. I'd known Gerard was with Higginson, but now I wondered if he'd left before the implosion, or as a result of it. Gerard takes on both civil and criminal cases for his high-dollar clients, and occupies a fairly unique place in the Dallas legal market.

Curtis seemed suddenly to remember what else was just about five years ago. He patted my shoulder, then picked up my empty plate and abruptly turned back toward the counter, and I felt the rush of cold air as Gerard came back in from outside. His ears and nose were tipped with red, and he sat, cupping his hands around the thick coffee mug with some relief. "Dead of winter and height of summer, I curse Curtis's no-phone policy."

I pulled my legal pad out and started digging for a pen. Gerard watched me for a moment, and then handed me his. "Thanks," I said, uncapping it. It was a beautiful Mont Blanc, and I scribbled at the top of the page with it, enjoying the heavy feel. I wondered for a moment if he'd notice if I kept it.

"Where do we start?" I asked. I hated feeling completely clueless about this investigation, but I really had no idea what Gerard expected me to do. I thought I was going to be a kind of associate for him, something I was used to after Bill Stephenson. Given his reference to tilting at windmills, it made sense. Last night, I'd re-read a bit of the Cervantes story of crazy Don Quixote who thought windmills were giants, and whose sidekick, Sancho Panza, rode a mule while he attempted to keep Quixote on the straight and narrow. The thought of Gerard as a demented knight made me smile inside.

Over the next hour, Gerard took me through the facts we knew and mapped out an interview schedule. He'd done some research on Carrie Ames, her parents, her roommate Naomi Jackson, Todd Parrish, and he'd even called someone he knew at the police department and had the names of several of Carrie's friends who had seen her at the meeting on Sunday. He handed me a sheaf of printouts, and we theorized on who had the most information and who would be available during the week. Because he had the contacts with the police department and the DA's office, he'd make some calls to see what he could find out. I was absurdly pleased at the thought of this new research.

For a few minutes, I felt the pleasure of working with a partner. I'd missed that. Working alone on cases isn't easy: there's no one to argue ideas with, no one to tell you when your ideas are inspired or just simple crap. Despite Gerard's clear disdain for me and my skills as an attorney back when we sat on opposite sides of the courtroom, we seemed to work well enough together now. However, when I told him I had several foreclosures and two prove-ups for default judgments to get done this week, his eyebrows lifted and settled, and I felt defensive all over again. "I have to make a living," I said, recapping his expensive pen and jamming my notes in my bag.

"I get that," he said mildly, and I felt foolish for being defensive.

"I remember CrimLaw from law school," I said, hoping to sound smart, "and our goal is to raise enough reasonable doubt about Todd Parrish's guilt, right?"

Gerard leaned back in his chair and looked at me. "Right now, Benedict, I just want to know more about this girl and what was happening in her life before she was killed." He stretched for a moment, and then began to pack away his notes. "Try not to piss anybody off, okay? We just need a sense of who these people are right now. By the way, I have to visit grandson, but I can't get there till tomorrow. Do you want to meet me there?"

I couldn't help but be excited. This might be out of my specialty now—I'd been doing bits and pieces of transactional work like contracts for construction or real estate agreements and taking on some minor real estate litigation—but it had been so long since I'd really learned something new. "Absolutely. What time?"

"Easy now," he said with that grin, and, even though he was only ten or so years older than I was, I felt like my excitement was childish. Then he leaned in close enough for me to smell his expensive cologne. "I get a bit excited with every new case too. It's like watching reality TV and seeing someone else's world." I hid a smile.

Curtis came by and delivered our checks, and Gerard reached for mine. When I opened my mouth to object, he shook his head. "Benedict, don't be silly. Your five-dollar breakfast won't break me." As he stood up to take Curtis a credit card, I remembered a time or two in the last few years when that five dollars would have broken me.

———

You 'cry' a foreclosure when you sell, as a trustee, property that a lender has a lien on. In the past, someone actually held the paper deed 'of trust' and then announced (or like a town crier, 'cried') the sale in the middle of town. Now, the county clerk has the electronic record of the lien, and paper deeds are a formality.

One of the documents I have to file before announcing the foreclosure of a lien is a notice telling the world that I've been appointed by the lender to sell the property and recover their loan funds. Because this document becomes a matter of public record, the public can then contact me and try—unsuccessfully—to get me to give them special consideration before the sale takes place. It happens a few times a year. I politely decline to sell the property before my client actually owns it.

The myth of getting a bargain at the foreclosure sale persists. On the first Tuesday of each month, the larger Texas county courthouses are mobbed with people trying to snap up a bargain. I've heard about people who buy property cheap when the sheriff forecloses for unpaid taxes, or for pennies when a lender wants to recover the money on a home equity loan, and then they fix that property up and sell it for tens of thousands of dollars of profit.

I've never seen it work that way, but hope springs eternal every month at the county courthouse.

In reality, at most foreclosure sales, I mostly just wait for a minute or so after reading the notice, and then bid for my lender-client. There's not even really any organization to it. 'Foreclosure services' try to organize lender representatives to cry their foreclosures in front of audiences and roving 'specialists' with important-looking clipboards. Ice cream vendors sometimes hawk their wares across the street in the summer months. The whole thing takes on a circus feel, but I usually just go and read my script and hope that the wind doesn't blow me over on an exposed forecourt in Waxahachie or that I won't fall down the granite courthouse steps in Decatur again.

Today, as I stood in the February wind on the north side of the Dallas courthouse and the sky started spitting sleet, my hope was that Gerard would stop finding my discomfort amusing. He stood at the back of a crowd as I began my spiel for my first property, grinning that crooked smile, black eyebrows winging up as the foreclosure specialists ran over to squawk about my positioning. The stinging sleet pellets blew into my face as I ignored him and read my notices. For a minute, I thought he might bid on one just to annoy me, but when I looked up again, he was gone.

CHAPTER FOUR

After finishing the last foreclosure, I decided to go ahead and leave the courthouse and get started. The foreclosure crowd had quickly thinned out when the temperature warmed and the sleet turned to an icy rain. Gerard had given me addresses and phone numbers for all the witnesses I needed to interview for him. I was amazed that he'd had been able to get the information he had—middle names, home address, property owned, places of employment. Most of the research I do is using clerk's records for property information and documents, and those are available either free or through pay services at all the Texas counties. Gerard used an investigative database that did background searches on individuals for a fee. As a result, he took for granted information I could never have obtained that gave me oodles of data to pore over.

I paid Sameer and sat in my car checking my email while the rain tapped against the windows and the defroster worked on the glaze on the windshield. Danford and another note buyer had contacted me for new foreclosure files, I saw with some satisfaction. I'd worked to make my foreclosure documents as clean and reusable as possible so that I could earn the maximum on each file, and each new file for a lender tended to boost that profit margin.

I also had an email from Gerard, letting me know that Todd was still in Collin county's jail in Princeton, since the Dallas county facility was so full they couldn't accept a transfer. We'd have to drive up to Princeton tomorrow, an hour-long slog through traffic each way. As I pulled into my driveway, I tried to envision my calendar for the next day so that I could move things around if possible. I left my car running and changed clothes quickly, putting on jeans and thick-heeled boots with a puffy jacket and scarf, pulling my hair up in a clip. It's days like this I'm glad I keep it long.

Prior to the Great Depression, Ross Avenue was lined with mansions. Over the years, the huge houses were first cut up into apartments, then bulldozed completely to become commercial strip centers. After that, the cheap dry cleaners, resale shops, and convenience stores took over. Recently, the area had been cleaned up and repainted, experiencing what real estate agents call a 'renaissance' (and social scientists call 'gentrification'). Papa's Deli had strenuously resisted either. As it had since 1972, it served sandwiches, soup, salads, and coffee so strong it probably didn't need a cup. Papa's runs out of an end unit, sharing space with a takeout pizza joint, a dry cleaner, and a derelict massage parlor that had long ago given up on happy endings. It was about half a mile from my place, so I was familiar with their take-out counter, but I rarely ate in. There were only a few cracked vinyl booths, and these were usually occupied by the medical students and workers from Baylor Hospital a mile away.

Ross Avenue Urgent Care, where Naomi Jackson and Carrie Ames had worked together, was right across the street. Naomi was a redhead so petite that I topped her by a good three inches, and I've never been known for my height. She'd agreed to take a late lunch at Papa's to meet me, and she was already plowing her way through an

enormous cobb salad when I got there. My stomach growled as I realized how long it had been since breakfast with Gerard. She was
tucked back into one of the few booths with her phone in one hand
and a fork in the other. Her brown eyes were a bit bloodshot, and her
red hair and maroon scrubs clashed with her purple jacket. I
wondered if she noticed.

She pushed her horn-rimmed glasses further up on her nose
before reaching out to shake my hand. "I'm sorry I have to keep
eating, but I only get half an hour for lunch." She forked up some
lettuce and chicken. "This cold weather means everyone's called in
sick, so we're slammed."

One of the hardest things for me when I'm interviewing is what
they call 'establishing a rapport' with your subject. You're supposed to
talk about things that put your subject at ease, and, in return, they're
supposed to open up more. I tend to jump right in to whatever I
wanted to talk about, so I'd been reading some books about how to
make people more comfortable. In one, they suggested talking about
someone's name and inquiring where it had come from.

I dug for a pen in my bag and found Gerard's expensive Mont
Blanc pen—score. "Naomi...that's such an interesting name." I looked
at her dark red hair and leapt. "Were you named for Naomi Judd, the
singer?"

Naomi's brow wrinkled, and she peered at me through her black-
rimmed glasses. It was clear she had never heard of the country
singer. She tucked the ruffage she'd just started chewing into a cheek
to answer me. "No, my mother wanted us all to have names from the
Bible, so she named me for Ruth's mother-in-law." She crunched
through another bite while I tried to remember who Ruth was. "My
younger sister was unlucky and got Ruth." I nodded as if I knew who
these people were and tried to think of a follow-up that would
quickly get us closer to Carrie, but Naomi did it for me.

"That's why Carrie and I got along so well," she said, looking
down into her salad. She took a deep breath and stabbed a chicken
strip, delicately dipping it into a container of purplish dressing before

biting off the end. "My family was rabidly Pentecostal, so I got the whole over-religious background thing." She looked at me. "Ours was everything but the snakes. Healing, speaking in tongues, you name it. Pretty hard and colorless. Carrie's family was just JW."

I wrote JW on my pad with Gerard's pen and started to ask, but she continued. "You know, Jehovah's Witness."

"I don't know much about them, really," I confessed. Her chomping on that salad was starting to make me hungry, but I didn't want to interrupt her flow by going to the counter to order something.

"Carrie's family is really into it," Naomi said before taking another bite. "Her dad is like an area elder or something, and her whole family is really involved with the church. I think that's why the shunning hurt her so much."

I was lost. "Wait. What shunning?"

Naomi looked at her watch, then set the remnants of her salad to one side. "So. Carrie met Todd a couple of years ago. When they started dating, the church got all up into it, and told her they had to stop because he was worldly." She made air quotes around 'worldly,' so I added them to my notes. She drew on the straw in her soft drink, shuffling it around to get the last drops with her final slurp. "Instead, she moved to Dallas and stopped going to church and stuff. And her mother and sisters and everyone else she knows haven't spoken to her since. I mean, I don't go to church anymore, and trust me, my mother hasn't let me forget it, but she still speaks to me. They shut Carrie out completely." She tipped her cup up to get a piece of ice and began to crunch it.

I scribbled 'shunning?' on my notepad. I could tell Naomi was poised to leave, and I tried to think what information I needed from her before she bolted. "You know I represent Todd, right?"

She finished crunching the ice cube and nodded. "Yeah, I get that, but there is no way that guy could have..." She paused, tears welling in her brown eyes. "There's no way he could have done *that*." She pinched the bridge of her nose in a gesture I hadn't seen since my grandmother died ten years ago, but it seemed to work and the unshed tears didn't fall. "I don't want to talk about that. Do I have to?" I shook my head. We had her statement to the police. "She and Todd were just crazy about each other. That's why I couldn't believe she was going back." She put the lid on her cup.

I felt like I was running to catch up. "Going back where?"

Naomi started gathering her purse and gloves. "To the church." She slid out of the booth and zipped up her purple jacket. This time she didn't bother to stop the tears, and they slid down behind her glasses. "She was going back to that cult."

———

NAOMI HAD TOLD ME I COULD TEXT HER TO ARRANGE A FOLLOW-up, so I must not have done too badly. I stood at the counter to read the menu posted on the wall as the freezing rain tapped on the windows. I shivered and finally decided on a bowl of butternut squash soup. While I waited for it to arrive, I looked up 'Jehovah's Witness' on my phone. Wikipedia to the rescue, I thought, scrolling through.

Jehovah's Witnesses is a millenarian restorationist Christian denomination with nontrinitarian beliefs distinct from mainstream Christianity.

Well, that was clear as mud.

The group reports a worldwide membership of 8.45 million adherents involved in evangelism and an annual Memorial attendance of around 20 million. Jehovah's Witnesses are directed by the Governing Body of Jehovah's Witnesses, a group of elders in Warwick, New York, which establishes all doctrines based on its interpretations of the Bible. They believe that the destruction of the present world system at Armageddon is imminent, and that the

establishment of God's kingdom over the earth is the only solution
for all problems faced by humanity.

I spooned up the thick soup while I tapped on links. The Wikipedia entry must have been written by some church followers, I thought, since it was pretty positive. I had a vague memory of someone knocking on our door before we moved to my grandmother's farm, and I wondered if they were Jehovah's Witnesses.

At the end of a long paragraph, I found it.

Congregational disciplinary actions include disfellowshipping, their term for formal expulsion and shunning. Baptized individuals who formally leave are considered disassociated and are also shunned. Disfellowshipped and disassociated individuals may eventually be reinstated if deemed repentant.

A click on a link took me to another section on disfellowshipping and shunning, with their procedures and Biblical justification. As I read further, I tried to imagine what Carrie Ames could have done that would merit this type of discipline. The entry said that Jehovah's Witnesses who continue to speak to or associate with a disfellowshipped person are said to be sharing in their 'wicked works' and, while the shunned individual can continue to attend 'Kingdom Hall' services, no one speaks to them. Understandably, most of the shunned people move away.

I pressed the button to close the phone window, suddenly chilled.

———

I MUST HAVE SAT THERE, THINKING ABOUT CARRIE AMES AND—I have to admit—myself for half an hour before the manager came over to tell me they were closing early because of the weather. A look outside confirmed that the temperature had taken a nosedive, and the rain was freezing as soon as it hit the ground. They'd already wrapped up the stuff in the deli case while I was sitting there woolgathering.

I bundled up and tried to walk to my car without falling on the freezing asphalt. I had only half a mile to get home, but I realized I had practically no food in the house. I stopped at a small neighborhood grocery a block from Papa's, where the rest of my side of town had already shopped in response to the dire predictions of the weathercasters on the local news. I snagged the last, slightly smashed loaf of bread and a box of packaged hot chocolate mix and headed for home. The half mile took me almost half an hour, as cars ahead and behind me inched along, sliding on the glazed streets. The rain continued to fall and freeze, and I kept the defroster on high as I moved slowly along.

I pulled into my carport on the side of the house on Gaston Avenue where I'd lived for the last five years. My landladies occupied the front of the rambling brick house, and my one-bedroom apartment was the last of two that had been carved into the house in the 60s, but were slowly being renovated back into the main house. Because of the positioning of the house and my carport, I was able to park right beside my door, and the overhang kept my sidewalk from getting iced over at all. During the summer, the cement was shaded from the sun, and I had a little enclosed patio beside the door. I kept promising myself each spring I'd buy some lawn furniture and plants, but the intense heat of our summers didn't inspire you to sit outside, so I'd put it off, and by winter I'd be glad I didn't spend the money.

The heater inside was running almost non-stop to keep up with the dip in temperature. Although I usually turn it down during the day, I'd edged it up when I came home to change clothes before meeting Naomi. I don't think the cat had moved all day. She was still in her little bed by the couch (and a convenient floor vent), her long fluffy tail just covering her nose with its gray smudge. I shook a little dry food into her bowl, hoping to tempt her out, but she just looked at me.

Rummaging in the pantry revealed some chocolate chip cookies that were only partly stale; I heated hot water on the stove and made a cup of instant hot chocolate, then curled up with my laptop by the cat and the heater vent. I knew I needed to do more research on the Jehovah's Witnesses, but I honestly could not face the information about shunning right then. I turned on the TV and flipped through the channels until I found a black and white *I Love Lucy* episode, which I watched while I listened to voice mail. Both of my client meetings for the next day had canceled because of the weather, leaving my schedule wide open for a visit to the Collin county jail. I looked up the directions and, while they printed out, I texted Gerard and told him I was good to go, asking what time he wanted to meet.

Almost immediately the phone rang, showing his name on the screen. My thumb hesitated over the Answer icon, and then I hit Decline. I pulled up messaging instead. *What is it?* I texted. The phone started ringing again. Gerard.

Irritated, I answered. "What?" I said grumpily.

"And hello to you too, Benedict." Without his black eyebrows beetling at me, his voice reminded me of the Gerard in my night-mares, too close and too real.

"Don't you text?" I asked him, and then immediately realized how nasty I sounded. So much for attempting to be civil.

He just laughed softly—a sound much too intimate for this conversation. "Not too much. Fat fingers." Ha. *There's nothing fat on that body*, I thought, then instantly felt my cheeks heat. Thankfully, this time he couldn't see me. "Did you get home okay?"

I pulled my phone away from my ear and checked the display. Who was this? "Gerard, don't start getting all nice on me. You're freaking me out." I took a breath, hearing my grandmother lecturing me in my head. "Yes, I got home okay. Even stopped at the grocery store just in case I get snowed in." We both chuckled. In Texas, let it get overcast during the winter, and everyone stocks up on bread, milk, and anything else left on the shelves, lest they get snowed in and starve.

"Assuming the roads are clear, I'll pick you up at 9. I'll bring the four-wheel drive."

This gesture was totally unexpected and completely unwelcome.

Two hours of Gerard to Princeton and back? Even my grandmother couldn't expect me to be polite for that long. "I can drive and meet you there. I just printed out the directions."

"Benedict, the forecast is for freezing all night—this stuff's not going anywhere. I'd put this off, but it's much easier to get in and talk to grandson while he's up in Princeton."

"His name is Todd, and..." I couldn't say what I was really thinking, but Gerard did it for me.

"You don't want to spend that much time alone with me." God, when he said it, it sounded petty and mean. "I get it, Benedict."

"No, I can do it. And I appreciate it." I swallowed hard. "My car doesn't have four-wheel drive, so that'll work."

Gerard's voice was a little rough and abrupt. "Fine. See you at 9."

He hung up before I could give him my address, but then, I guess at some point, I'd been the subject of one of his investigations. I'm sure he knew more about me than I did.

———

Four hours later, the lights and television flickered off, and the heater went silent, the vents ticking. Because of the old electrical wiring in this 'transitioning' neighborhood, this tended to happen when the wind blew, or when it rained, or when someone shot at a transformer. I closed my laptop, picked up the cat, and headed to the bedroom to add another blanket to the bed.

I'd learned some important things about the Jehovah's Witnesses from various sites on the internet. First, people who were 'ex-JW' seemed to be pretty angry. There were sites dedicated to 'exposing the truth' and meetups for groups of former Jehovah's Witnesses all across the globe. YouTube videos featured earnest speakers who talked about their experiences and the church, and hours of posts replayed hearings about child abuse allegations or medical issues. I found an image of the Jehovah's Witnesses governance committee, or 'governing body': a group of men, mostly white and all very old. *Just*

the kind of people who'd understand young people and their problems,
I thought cynically as I peered at the image.

Second, Naomi seemed to be right. One website said that the
Watch Tower Bible and Tract Society—the official name for the
church—was a cult that became a church. Watch Tower... the name
gave me a shiver. After hours of reading and listening to horror stories
about being disfellowshipped and shunned, I realized Carrie's experience wasn't unique.

One young man was interviewed for a web documentary that had
segments for church dogma, service, education, and disfellowshipping, among others. He was a vividly handsome young man with
liquid brown eyes, but his language was simple and direct. He
seemed to have been disfellowshipped for some vague sexual activity
that I'm pretty sure I engaged in during high school. The camera was
placed over the interviewer's shoulder, so the subject looked right into
the camera as he talked about his experiences.

"You grow up completely surrounded by Friends. You go to
Kingdom Hall with them, you work with them, you live with them,
you travel with them, you go out in service with them—your every
waking moment is spent with these people. And then you screw up
in some way, and the punishment isn't just that you can't go to
Kingdom Hall anymore. It's that you lose your whole world." His
eyes bored into the interviewer. "I can't tell you how it feels to have
your mother never speak to you again. And I can't talk to her. She
believes—she is convinced by the Friends—that if she speaks to me
she risks her relationship with God. She'd for sure be risking disfellowshipping herself." His eyes narrowed, but he didn't cry; in fact, he
seemed oddly disconnected from his words. "How could I do that to
her?"

In response to the interviewer's question, he looked down at his
hands as he explained his feelings of doubt. "Do I ever consider going
back? Yeah, all the time. To see my family, to be accepted again? I
think about it every day. Will I do it?" He looked back into the
camera. "I don't know." His mouth twisted. "The people that I know

who've gone back? They're so isolated and miserable outside that going back is the only alternative to ending it all."

I bookmarked his interview before my battery went dead, and then I shut the laptop down, curling into the cat for more than warmth. Sometime during the night, I woke when the heat and electricity came back on, then went back to dreams and sleep.

CHAPTER FIVE

I wish I could say I felt the Force flicker in the neighborhood when Gerard drove his black Range Rover up to my curb at 9 am, but the truth was, I was a bit distracted and didn't even notice. The rain had stopped overnight, but when the cloud cover moved on, the temperature dropped another ten degrees. The resulting ice on the wires and trees meant the power had gone off again. I was lucky enough to have a gas hot water heater, but no power for lights in my windowless bathroom and no heat in the apartment. I'd stood under the hot shower till the water ran cold, and then dashed into my closet to pile on warm clothes.

The sky was vividly blue and clear. Power lines across east Dallas would be downed by frozen tree limbs, so it might be a while before we had electricity. My landladies, a pair of sisters whose family had owned the large prairie style mansion where I had a small apartment, took the cat back for the day—as they should, since the cat wasn't really mine. A few months ago, they'd decided I needed a pet, and gifted me with the white and gray cat. She's the laziest animal I've ever known. When I leave for work, she's in her bed. When I return, she's still in her bed. She either stays there all day, or she's learned the sound of my car and rushes back to the bed just to torment me. Since I loved Hattie and Sallie Shelton like the weird, wild aunts I never had, I let the cat stay in my apartment, but I planned to install a cat door in the one interior door we shared so that it could go back to their side of the house and perhaps be happier and more active there.

If there is a typical senior citizen these days, the Shelton sisters don't qualify. They were conceived almost the moment their father returned injured from the war in Europe in 1944, and they came of age in the sixties, where they apparently engaged in every protest, concert, and love-in they found. Even if half the stories they tell aren't true, they've lived remarkable lives. I also believe that they own massive amounts of Dallas real estate. This house was their ancestral home, which they bought and renovated when they moved back here a decade ago, but they also seem to be at least partial owners of other residential buildings all over east Dallas. At one frighteningly pecunious point in the last five years, they tried to hire me to perform some evictions for their management company. I declined, thinking it might not be a good mix of personal and business, but since then, I've seen that management company's signs popping up in multiple locations in the neighborhood.

Tomas, the handyman who lives in the apartment above the garage, had lightly sanded the sidewalk out front yesterday, so I was able to walk to Gerard's Range Rover with some dignity, but there was no way to climb into the high passenger seat without scrambling and scrabbling for hand holds. Gerard, damn him, just watched from the driver's seat. For a moment, I wished for a good old-fashioned chivalrous gentleman to give a delicate lady a boost. I glared at him, daring him to comment, when a whiff of coffee from the cupholder hit me. *A warming cupholder, of course*, I thought sourly. It did hold two cups, which gave me hope.

He smiled that crooked smile and handed me a warm paper cup. As we pulled away, he wished me a good morning, but I held up a hand to stop any further pleasantries until I'd had a few sips. I assumed it would be black, but it was a fragrant cinnamon latte, and I may have purred as I drank.

A few blocks later, Gerard's smile was gone, replaced by cursing that would have made that delicate lady's ears burn, and I was smiling into my coffee cup. While the streets in Gerard's upper-class neighborhood were already well on their way to being cleared, the streets in my neighborhood were still partially blocked by tree limbs or cars that had been pulled over when their drivers could no longer steer on the ice. I knew that his streets would have been serviced by Highland Park, a small inner-city municipality where the truly rich lived, while my streets were firmly under Dallas maintenance and services, and might take days to clear. He drove expertly, but he also snarled—really snarled—when the other drivers didn't. I ruined his intensity by laughing from my passenger side of the car. We finally made it onto the Central Expressway, where cars inched along until they reached the sanded bridges, speeding up just to slow down where the sanding ended.

Gerard relaxed once we'd begun to slowly head north, but I had started to tense up again, realizing that the condition of the roads would lengthen the journey up to Princeton and back exponentially. He smelled just as expensive as the Range Rover was, and I wondered how much he charged his clients. He'd only asked the Parrishes for a $5,000 deposit, but I knew Bill Stephenson had paid him at least my previous annual salary to get to trial.

With a satellite talk radio station playing softly in the background, we talked a bit about the weather and speculated about whether the courts would cancel hearings or trials, since judges, clerks, and bailiffs would be just as unable to travel as the general public. As we reached the northern suburbs, it became clear that the weather up here had been much worse: cars left outside had a thick coat of ice, and Plano and Allen were ghost towns. School had been canceled all over the Metroplex, and children seemed to be the only ones out and about, shaking tree limbs to make icicles fall and skating on iced-over driveways.

We exited on County Road 89 and headed northeast. The roads here were less well-sanded, and I kept quiet so Gerard could concentrate. I was startled when he pulled off into the parking lot of an obviously-closed restaurant. He put the Range Rover in park and turned in his seat to face me. Suddenly, we seemed far too close to each other, and I felt a rush of blood to my face. I turned toward him, pressing my back into the door's armrest.

"Let's talk about how we interview grandson," Gerard began, and I was immediately indignant. I'd like to think it was just about Gerard's use of 'grandson' again, but I knew some of it was because of my pounding heart. He seemed really big and close in here.

"He's our client. Don't you think you could call him by his name?"

Gerard didn't immediately react or answer, but simply looked at me, then half-smiled. "What?" I asked crossly.

"Who would have ever thought we'd share a client, Benedict?"

"Not me," I admitted grudgingly as I looked out the windshield at the darkened plate glass windows of the restaurant. "This whole situation feels about as surreal as it gets."

Gerard reeled off the facts he'd learned since we spoke. "Our client was arraigned on murder charges on Friday afternoon. He was assigned a public defender for the arraignment, where he plead not guilty. I called the PD, Jill Whitehead, and she's happy to reassign him to us. He's refused to give a statement or confession or even give any real information to her. She says he's seemed to be almost catatonic the couple of times they've met, and he's not been helpful at all."

"His grandad said that Todd's got claustrophobia pretty bad," I said, as I slipped out of my thick puffy jacket. Now that we were sitting still, the windows were beginning to fog with the heat inside. I dug in my bag for my notes. Gerard waited, arm on the steering wheel, watching me. When my hand closed over the Mont Blanc in the bottom of my bag, I thought for a moment, then held it out to him. He grinned and took it, tucking it away in an inner pocket of his jacket.

I flipped through my notes. "Here it is. Todd's got a diagnosed anxiety disorder and depression. It's aggravated by being in closed spaces, and he takes medication for it." I looked up at Gerard. "Will he be able to take that while he's in custody?"

He nodded. "Yes, but only with a doctor's note and a new prescription given to the facility medical staff. They'll administer it to him." He looked at the café's storefront, where there were the beginnings of signs of life. "Have you had breakfast?"

I looked at the lights coming on behind fogged windows, and opened my door. Fresh air, space, and food. "I could eat."

––––––––

WE WERE THE ONLY CUSTOMERS IN THE CAFÉ FOR THE FIRST fifteen minutes. The couple who owned the place were calling employees to see if they could come in, and the husband was manning the cooktop till they could get the kitchen staffed. I figured the easiest thing on the menu was an omelet, so I ordered a ham and cheese omelet and sourdough toast. Gerard echoed my order to the wife, who took a break from calls to pour some water for us. She seemed to be new to the front of house setup, so we both decided to avoid the coffee she was making.

I had a text from Naomi Jackson, letting me know that Carrie's family wasn't going to have a funeral, so the ex-JW Sunday afternoon group was going to meet in a sort of memorial in East Dallas on the coming Sunday. I let Gerard know, then took a risk to make a suggestion. "I was thinking we could stop and talk to Carrie's mother and father while we're up here in Princeton." Gerard frowned a little. "What?"

"You'll see," he warned ominously. "Victim family interviews aren't easy, even if you don't represent the accused killer." He smiled his thanks at the wife, who slid our plates in front of us.

I didn't expect much, but the omelets were huge and fluffy, stuffed with large chunks of ham and stringy with cheddar cheese. Since dinner last night had been only the stale cookies and instant hot chocolate, I was starving. Gerard finished his first, but I wasn't far behind. Husband came out to talk for a minute, and he and Gerard exchanged some manly discussion of the weather while I basked in post-protein bliss. All too soon, Gerard asked for the bill. I started to dig into my bag for my wallet, but Gerard waved me off. "Case expense," he said, and I chose to believe him. I could get used to free breakfasts.

Back in the Range Rover and on the road, we talked a bit more about the interview with Todd. I'd never been in a county jail facility, and I asked Gerard if it was much like what I'd seen on television.

"Dallas county's facility will be more like what you'd see on a crime show," he explained. "Collin county's north facility in Princeton is still a bit small-town." We drove past the Princeton city limit sign, and I understood what he meant.

While the Dallas-Fort Worth metroplex (as it's called) continues to grow north, most of Collin county on the northeast of the quadrant has stayed pretty rural. The town of Princeton has taken zoning to the extreme, so growth here has been gradual. There are some high dollar residential developments, but they've been built back into the trees on the edges of town. There's a large organic grocery store and a national chain coffeeshop downtown, but there's no mall or strip commercial centers, and the large club stores can't get approval to move in.

The Collin county jail was on the northern edge of town, a square cement block building that didn't look very big, surrounded by almost-empty parking lots. Gerard gave me a some tips as he parked a few spaces from the door. "Don't bring your bag. You'll need your driver's license and bar card, and you can bring a pen and your pad. Other than that, you'd have to leave it all at the guard gate anyway, so make sure you have nothing else in your pockets." I tucked my phone into my bag and zipped it, leaving it on the passenger floorboard.

He locked the Range Rover with a beep and stuffed the keys in his jacket pocket. It had started to cloud over again which, oddly enough, made it a little warmer, but we still needed our scarves and jackets.

At the counter inside, uniformed guards sat watching closed circuit views of the grounds and main walkways. We were the only visitors, but the guards were still extremely professional as they greeted us. Since I'd never been to this facility, I had to show my bar card and ID, and then go through a palmprint registration to get into the interview rooms.

We took an elevator down a floor, and I realized that most of the facility was underground. There was a long, windowless hallway from the elevator to the holding area, and the least claustrophobic person would still feel anxious as they walked along the long white box. Cameras were placed to cover every inch of the space, and the thought of all those eyes on me was creepy. Even Gerard seemed grim, and we didn't speak as we moved along.

Gerard had notified them that we were there to see Todd Parrish, and by the time we made it through the security checkpoints, Todd was waiting for us in an interview room with an armed guard just outside the door. I was surprised there weren't any phones or glass panels like there were on *Law and Order* or other television shows, but I wanted to be cool, so I said nothing to Gerard.

Todd slumped in his chair, his eyes lowered to his hands in his lap. His short brown hair was spiky and damp, and he smelled of fear and sweat. I could immediately see that this was no longer the naïve young man from the memorial wall. The bright orange of his jumpsuit washed out a complexion that looked pasty and sick under a landscape-worker's tan. He glanced up at me quickly when I started to speak, and I was shocked at how haggard he looked. His pupils were dilated so fully that there was only a thin rim of blue, and his face didn't change expression when I introduced us and explained that his grandparents had hired us to help him. His breathing was shallow and quick, he rocked slightly in the chair, and a pulse pounded at his throat and temple.

He kept his eyes on me as I spoke. Gerard sat back and nodded at me to continue. I didn't know what I was doing—surely Gerard saw that—but Todd was so out of it that I'm not sure it mattered. I decided to get right to it.

"Todd, can you tell us what happened when you and Carrie argued on Sunday?" He looked at me, but I couldn't tell if he was comprehending what I was saying, so I started again. "Todd, do you remember talking to Carrie last Sunday?"

He looked at me for a long moment, and then he looked down and nodded tightly.

"Good." I looked at Gerard, who nodded at me to go on. "Did you and she have an argument?"

Todd nodded again without looking up, one distinct head bob. "Can you tell us what it was about?" This time, he shook his head, once, then twice, and then he continued to shake his head in agitation.

"That's okay, Todd." I sat back in my chair and looked at Gerard.

He sat forward and spoke sharply. "Todd." Todd finally looked at him. "We're going to get your medication to the facility, and then we need to talk again. You're going to have to tell us what happened."

Todd looked at his lap, then nodded again and continued to rock slightly in his chair.

I looked over at Gerard. "Don't we want to ask—" He cut me off with a headshake. Okay, so no asking about the murder.

Gerard stood and the guard entered the room again. Rewind the entry, and you've got our exit, but with much deep breathing when we finally got outside. Both of us.

Gerard and I sat in the Range Rover, checking our voicemail and emails. "Well, that didn't go like I planned," he said as he scrolled.

"Re-thinking strategy?"

He looked over at me. "Until we get him some medication, I don't think he's going to be much help." He ran a hand over his hair in a gesture I'd seen at the defense table in the courtroom, and I'd decided then that he was thinking when he did that. Apparently, I was right.

"Let's swing by the girl's parents' house. I can get Carmen on to the grandparents and see if we can get his medication. If that doesn't work, we'll see about getting the transfer expedited. Dallas county has better medical facilities."

I looked through the windshield at the sterile facility with its small exercise yard, ice shining on the wire fencing in the bright cold sunlight. I didn't know if he was guilty or innocent, but I wanted to get Todd back outdoors where he belonged.

CHAPTER SIX

Much of Princeton had been built in the early 1990s as a bedroom community to Dallas, springing up from farmland purchased by hopeful developers. Those early developers built three or more streets with a connecting cul-de-sac at the end, named the streets after their sons or daughters or wives, then promptly went out of business when Princeton didn't immediately prosper.

Samuel and Leah Ames owned a small, three-bedroom brick house on Janice Lane, in a neighborhood of other small, three-bedroom brick houses on streets named Jeremy, Jennifer, and Justin—not coincidentally, three of the most popular children's names of the 1990s. The Ames' one-story house, like those of its neighbors, was built of sandy brown brick with neutral trim, garages tucked around on the alley in the back. Although the neighborhood had some mature trees, an unremarkable central sidewalk and front door were flanked by double-hung windows with screens, and narrow flowerbeds wrapped around the house with low-cut shrubs hiding the concrete foundation. Despite the trees and shrubs, the whole thing felt lifeless to me.

There were three cars pulled in tight at the front curb of the Ames' house, all a few years old, all compacts, and two with child seats in the back. The front sidewalk was sanded, so I didn't slip and slide as I walked up to the door. Gerard had been little or no help to me; he was parked across the street talking on his phone, and he'd mouthed 'good luck' to me as I got out. I might have growled in response—my head was pounding at the thought of this interview. I shivered and pulled my coat tighter around me to give me a bit of comfort. The wind had picked up during the day, and pieces of ice fell from the branches with a jingle of discordant crystal. A squirrel chattered at me from the bole of a tree, clearly offended that I was disturbing the peace of the neighborhood.

Yeah, I don't want me here either, I told him silently, knocking lightly on the dark green door. I was prepared to turn away if no one answered, but it was opened almost immediately by a woman I knew was Carrie's mother. Like Carrie, she had light blond hair, but where Carrie's had been cut short, Leah Ames' hair was drawn back in a long braid down her back. She had slightly worn Scandinavian features, with dark blue eyes and high cheekbones, and was a bit taller than I. Her face had that large-eyed, elvish look that so impressed me from the pictures in the paper, but this woman looked time-worn. She was dressed simply in a plain light blue button-down oxford shirt and loose navy slacks. Her hands seemed to have a story of their own, with reddened and swollen knuckles that screamed arthritis to me.

I jumped right in with the short intro Gerard and I had worked out on the drive over. "Mrs. Ames, my name is Lacey Benedict, and I'm an attorney working on the circumstances of your daughter's death. May I come in?"

She murmured something I took to be acquiescence, and I stepped forward; she stepped back almost automatically, and I continued inside, feeling like I was leading in a compulsory dance. Her eyes had a slightly glazed expression, and I felt vaguely guilty.

The door led right into the living room, a small space with too much furniture. There were two full-size couches and two large recliners and two other, smaller chairs, with a coffee table and bookshelf wedged in as well. It was also unbearably hot after the cold fresh air outside. A couple of floral bouquets were wilting in the heat, and the smell of lilies and chrysanthemums—something I found depressing and cloying even in the best of times—was overwhelming. I unbuttoned my coat, but didn't want to take it off without being invited. While I'd had meetings and even confrontations with people who were unfriendly (such as widows and orphans whose home I was foreclosing), I'd never been in this situation, and I didn't know how this would go. I sensed that rapport-building was a waste of time—especially since I might be asked to leave once she figured out that I represented the man accused of killing her daughter.

Leah Ames stood in the middle of the living room, not speaking, not even really looking at me, and I realized she wasn't going to lead this little meeting. "Shall we sit?" I asked, and moved toward one of the sofas. She followed me, her knotted hands working together, and perched on the edge of the sofa adjacent to mine.

I looked at a long, low floral arrangement on the coffee table. The chrysanthemums, carnations, and lilies were white, and the edges of the flowers were starting to brown. "That's beautiful," I said, leaning toward it to stroke a glossy ivy leaf.

"My office sent it," Leah said, staring down at the arrangement. "I told them it was unnecessary, but it seemed to make them happy." She sounded bewildered at the notion. She had a bit of a midwestern accent, the vowels sounding flat and slightly singsong to my Texan ear.

"I'm so sorry for your loss," I began—my standard condolence line—but Leah broke into my flow.

She looked at me, directly at me, for the first time since greeting me at the door. "My daughter died two years ago." She must have seen my frown because her eyes left mine then. "If she hadn't met that boy—that Todd. It's his fault."

My heart stuttered. Was she saying she knew Todd had killed her?

"Ma'am? What do you mean? How was Todd Parrish at fault?"

Her eyes filled with tears as she looked at me, exhaustion etching her face with lines I was pretty sure hadn't been there before. "He led her astray. She met him, and she left the Truth." Her reddened hands fluttered in the air then came back together nervously, twisting and tangling. With their swollen knuckles, the nervous wringing looked painful. "She stopped listening to her father and me. He was worldly and led her astray, and she—" She broke off, her breath shallow and fast.

"Mama? What's going on?" A young woman, round with advanced pregnancy, came into the room. Like Carrie, she shared her mother's fair hair, but where Carrie and Leah had smaller, more delicate features, this woman's eyes were green and large, and her face was fuller and rounder. She went directly to her mother and looked over at me. "Who are you?"

I stood, but didn't approach. "I'm Lacey Benedict, an attorney working on the circumstances around Carrie's death." I hated how tentative I sounded.

The young woman put her arm protectively around Leah Ames. "It's too soon for this, you understand?" She didn't seem angry, just resigned. "I'm Jenny, Carrie's sister. If you have questions, you can contact me."

I nodded and put my business card on the coffee table. "If you'd just drop me an email with your contact information, I'll call you next time. I'm so sorry for your loss." Leah just stood in her daughter's embrace, hands doing that nervous dance with each other as I left. I didn't hold out much hope for an email.

Outside, I took a deep, bracing breath of the cold air and headed across the street. In the Range Rover, Gerard was talking on a headset, jotting notes on a small pad with his fancy pen.

"I know, but we're going to have to produce that file next week. The judge denied our protective order on Friday. Let's get the privilege log out the same day, and see what we can withhold, all right?" He waited, listening to the caller. "I think we can keep that back, but not the emails." He looked at me, black eyebrows winging up interrogatively. "Okay, let me know what the client says. I'll be working from home this afternoon." He disconnected, writing a final note and capping his pen.

"Bad?" He asked when I'd climbed in and buckled my seat belt.

"Let's just say I'm glad I don't have to do that every day." I adjusted the heater vent, shutting off the warm flow. I was still hot from inside the house.

Gerard put the truck in drive and moved away from the curb. "The PD up here still has paper files, so I want to swing by her office and pick up a copy. She said they'd have it ready." He turned back onto the main road through town.

In a few short sentences, I told him about my experience with Carrie Ames' mother and sister. Just recounting it made me feel teary. He pulled up to a stop sign, and, with a glance in the rear-view mirror at the empty road behind us, put the truck in park. He turned in the seat to face me.

"Let it go."

I looked over at him, too irritated by his tone to mind his nearness. "Excuse me?"

"I said, let it go. You have to move past the emotion."

I was stunned. Who did he think he was? "What? Let go of the fact that the woman is devastated by her daughter's death and probably feels so guilty about cutting her out of their lives that she'll never get over it?" I crossed my arms over my chest and pounding heart, and looked out the windshield at the frost-covered landscape. "Sure, I'll just let it go and sing a song from my castle of ice."

Gerard ignored my sarcasm and beetled those eyebrows at me. "If you can't learn to let it go, you won't be an effective interviewer. You have to push aside your empathy or sympathy or whatever and just ask questions."

I didn't reply. I hated that he was right. I hated that I hadn't been able to face Leah Ames' grief and guilt and go ahead and do the job. But more, I hated that he was right. I might just hate him. I was sure I wasn't going to reply to his rightness. Instead, I looked away and seethed.

He put the truck in drive and pulled through the intersection. We drove in silence for a few minutes, and I swore to myself that I wouldn't break it. I'd learned that lesson better than he ever knew. We pulled up to a storefront on the main town square with Law Office painted on the window. Gerard put the truck in park and muttered, "Be right back" before getting out of the truck.

I let myself feel a little superior as he slammed the door: he'd spoken first this time. He immediately opened the door and poked his head back in. "That didn't count."

Jerk.

CHAPTER SEVEN

L aw school teaches you nothing.
      Okay, that's a bit overdramatic, and not exactly true. Let me try again.

Law school teaches you how to be rich. You see wealthy, successful lawyers on TV, you see them in the courthouse or the airport, talking on their expensive phones about hearings or settings or motions to quash. You go to law school and the talk is about grades, and interviews, and six-figure salaries: which firms are hiring 1-Ls for summer clerkships, which are not; which firms will be on campus for interviews and what they pay first-year associates; what grades you have to get to get interviews or law review or judicial clerkships.

What you're learning is that law school is only a tool to get you to the most prestigious or high-paying jobs. And so your three years in law school are geared towards that, before you ever realize that only the top 20% of law students will get clerkships with law firms after their second year, and an even smaller number get clerkships for their first summer break. You don't understand that it usually takes massive student loans to get through law school, loans you might not be able to pay back once you're out. There's a saying that you hear in law school that's partially true: 'A-Students become judges; B-Students become professors, and C-Students become rich.' I managed to get solid As and Bs and still avoid all three results.

Bill Stephenson was introduced to me by my Secured Transactions professor in my second year. I wasn't one of the stellar students who'd worked their first summer, so I'd taken a graduate class in finance over the break, playing with the idea of getting my MBA at the same time. It wasn't that I was a business nerd—I just loved the information. I'd always been that way, sharing my love of data with my dad. Where his enthusiasm dovetailed into the engineering work he did, mine stayed with the information. I love digging through data to find the shining nugget inside. It's like a treasure hunt, and I win by getting the best nuggets of information.

Bill saw the data geek in me and knew what I could do for his team. We would research investor transactions and then provide reports to his clients about the target companies, who would then provide our reports to investors. Bill realized I could spot issues or gaps in the information we'd been provided, and he would craft an opinion or report using the details. What I didn't know at the time was that Bill wasn't always putting the information we'd found into the reports, depending on the client and what they wanted to see or give to their investors. I'd been so entranced by the data treasure trove I'd discovered that I rarely reviewed the reports Bill was supplying the clients, and I wasn't important enough to be named as attorney of record until the very end. In fact, it was me being named on a report that spurred me to file the whistleblower complaint.

This felt like one of those treasure hunts. Once I'd started researching the Jehovah's Witnesses and their connection to Carrie Ames' life, I couldn't stop. After meeting Carrie's mother, I was even more curious about the church that had shunned Carrie. While Gerard went into the public defender's office to get a copy of their file, I texted Naomi and asked her if she knew any of Carrie's ex-JW friends. I thought I could start there, with their own experiences. She responded almost immediately, sending me the name '*Adam Garrison--Shepherd*' and a number.

This guy seems to know everybody. Carrie used him as her reference on our rental application.

In for a penny, I thought, and texted him.

Hi. My name is Lacey Benedict, and I'm an attorney working on the Carrie Ames matter. Would you be willing to talk with me? I'm trying to understand her life a bit.

Before Gerard returned, I had a response.

I'll be at Hipster Haven in Deep Ellum tomorrow night after the studio--about midnight. I can meet you there for an hour.

Studio? Midnight? Sounded like a musician to me. It had been a long time since I'd hung out with musicians after midnight; at this stage of my life, I'd need a nap tomorrow afternoon. I searched unsuccessfully in my bag for a pen to jot the note in my calendar and then borrowed Gerard's Mont Blanc from the cupholder.

The drive back to Dallas went much quicker than the drive out to Princeton. Although the temperatures hovered around freezing, the bright winter sun had melted the ice patches that weren't in shadow. There were still few cars on the road at noon, and Gerard was an expert driver. I noticed he didn't take any of the calls that came in while he was driving; I didn't know if that was because he didn't want to take them while I was in the car with him, or if he didn't multitask. He also didn't say much. I couldn't tell at that point if we were still trying to compete for silences or not, but I wasn't in the mood to talk either. Leah Ames' tear-ravaged face was still very clear in my mind. I closed my eyes and tried to think happy thoughts—you know, puppies and sunflowers and meadows with babbling brooks.

I didn't realize I'd fallen asleep until I woke up with a start as

Gerard turned off to exit the expressway. A boyfriend once told me, to my intense mortification, that I had snored when I fell asleep on a flight to Cabo San Lucas, and I've tried to be careful to stay awake when I'm upright ever since. There's no good way to ask if you did snore, I've found, so instead you just try to act like you were just meditating or resting your eyes while considering deep, philosophical thoughts. Out of my peripheral vision, I tried to see if Gerard had noticed. He was staring out the windshield with a moody, unsmiling expression. I thought I'd go for nonchalance.

"I'll go meet with this Garrison-Shepherd guy tomorrow night, but I've got two default judgments in the morning. I don't know what I'll be able to do tomorrow." I rubbed my eyes as covertly as I could. "How do you want me to report what I'm doing?"

"Just drop me an email at the end of the week with daily time entries." He seemed gruff and unhappy. If he'd been a friend, I'd have asked him what was going on; he wasn't, so I didn't. But my curiosity was aroused, and that's never a good thing.

"So I noticed some pictures of kids in your office. Are those yours? Are you divorced?"

Gerard pulled up at a light and looked over at me with a mocking smile. "Benedict, is that an attempt at small talk?"

I felt the blood rush to my cheeks. "I was just trying to be friendly, Gerard." I desperately wished that I could have slammed my way out of the car, but it was freezing outside, and we were still half a mile from my place. "I don't know why you have to be such an ass." I looked out my window, watching as the blocks slid by, cozy Tudor-style homes, then big industrial modern condominium complexes, both bookended by rundown shopping centers with neighborhood pizza stores, taco joints, and postal centers. Finally, we turned on my block, and I gathered my bag, scarf, and coat.

"I'll drop my time to you on Friday and let you know what I find out," I ground out as I heaved myself out of the car.

"Be safe, Benedict," I heard him say as I slammed the truck door.

I was in and turning up the heat in the freezing apartment before I realized he hadn't answered my question at all.

———

I HAD A NOTE AND LASAGNA FROM SARA WAITING FOR ME, AND IT changed the course of my day.

My brother brought Sara home for the first time when they were seniors in high school. They'd been paired for a biology project, and Ryan was desperately trying to impress her. We were still living on our grandmother's farm, and Ryan was driving a pickup that was almost as old as he was. He was not a vintage car guy; he just didn't care. His sarcastic attitude and constantly changing hair color (along with some piercings that violated all the dress codes) did not endear him to teachers, but the non-athlete, non-preppy, non-brainiac kids— all those who were left out of any of the popular cliques—thought he was the epitome of anti-authoritarian cool.

In reality, Ryan was pretty sweet and charming, even with the safety pin in his ear. His antiestablishment leanings only went so far as to rebel against the norms for hair and piercings. He was polite to teachers, administrators, and parents, and he worked hard to avoid taking sides in any disagreement. He's a Libra, and he says that means he can see both sides to any argument. He'd have made a good lawyer, and our father pushed him hard in that direction.

It wasn't to be. Ryan and Sara shared a love for science and math, and that first biology project set a pattern for them: Ryan became a high school science teacher, while Sara usually runs a math tutoring franchise. Since she was off for the year, she turned her science leanings into recipe experimentation. On a good weekend, we can expect to test sauces, entrees, or casseroles, and some of those have made their way into my freezer. After an experiment gone wrong, Ryan, their son Michael, and I have been subjected to multiple versions of Very Bad Things; when I could, I'd freeze those as well, so I wouldn't hurt Sara's feelings. At some point, you forget which are good or bad, and my freezer is like a box of Harry Potter's jelly beans—you just don't know what you'll get.

I was hoping the power had come back on and the casseroles in my freezer had survived. I'd deliberately not opened the fridge or freezer this morning so that things would stay cold or frozen, but I was really desperate for a good, hot ziti casserole from September or even a mediocre baked veggie au gratin from November's Thanksgiving experiments.

Instead, I found the cat back in her bed, a small loaf of garlic bread, and note from Sara, with an uncooked lasagna from the other night's batch tucked inside a small cooler filled with ice. The power was still off, but I had a small gas stove in my tiny kitchen, so I turned the oven on and popped the lasagna in to cook while I read her note.

> Lace,
>
> Thought I'd stop by and see how you survived the ice storm. Miss Hattie was out checking on her early daffodils and let me in, so I left you lasagna for your dinner.
>
> Ryan has put your dad on the waiting list at that home we talked about—more later.
>
> Much love!
> Sara

I chewed the inside of my cheek for a few seconds. Was the lasagna to comfort me for bad news? Or celebrate good news? I couldn't tell. I decided to delay any consideration until I'd eaten and wasn't so cranky. I opened my laptop and started looking for treasure.

———

A FEW HOURS LATER, STUFFED WITH LASAGNA AND GARLIC bread, I sat in front of the oven on a kitchen chair and balanced my laptop on my knees. The battery-operated thermostat showed it was 56 in the house, but it felt like below freezing to me. I was bundled in sweats over thermals with an afghan around my shoulders, and I was seriously considering a visit to the Shelton sisters, who had the only wood-burning fireplace left in the structure. I'd moved the cat's bed (with her in it) to the kitchen, and had the door open on the warming oven. It wasn't the most efficient use of gas I'd ever seen, but I was starting to get feeling back in my toes.

I'd been able to connect to the internet through the hotspot on my phone, and learned quite a bit about Adam Garrison, who had web pages and a YouTube channel with a regular video podcast called 'The Shepherd.' He had over 75,000 followers. Apparently, the Watch Tower organization had labeled Garrison an 'apostate,' a word they used to describe someone they believed was attacking their religion. I could see their point. I watched several episodes of the podcast and finally had to stop. Like Naomi, he described the religion as a cult, and even though nothing I'd seen so far differed from that opinion, I didn't like to think of someone like Carrie's mom and sisters as part of that. Garrison didn't just discuss the Jehovah's Witnesses and their beliefs: he exposed them, ravaged them, and was brutal in his every indictment of their hypocrisy. He was a treasure trove of factual information about the church, though, once you got past his obvious bitterness.

I didn't know how much Gerard knew about the religion/cult, so I noted some important facts for my report:

- The 'Watch Tower Bible and Tract Society' was started as a publishing endeavor in the late 19th century by Charles Taze Russell, a Pennsylvanian minister. He was later accused of adultery, fraud, and unethical business practices, among other things. According to the Watch Tower organization, there was no truth to the allegations, but differences of opinion as to that remain. He created a Bible study group, and its members promoted publications and other products created by Russell and his allies.

- The religion that formed around Russell's teachings gained ground in the early years of the 20th century when Russell and others predicted that the second coming of Christ would come soon and could be pinpointed to an exact date. It wouldn't become known as the 'Jehovah's Witnesses' until the early 1930s.

- Russell himself had an interesting and peculiar take on the date for the end of the world that he published in a book called *Millennial Dawn*: after visiting the Great Pyramid in Giza, he believed that the huge pyramid was the only true 'witness' to the power of the Judeo-Christian god called Jehovah.

- Russell used measurements found in the Great Pyramid to predict that the 'end times' would culminate in Armageddon in October 1914. When October 1914 passed with no cataclysmic catastrophe (except for the beginnings of World War I), Russell and his successors changed the meanings of the dates and predicted Armageddon in 1918, 1920, and then every few years, including 1951 and 1975. After a while, the group stopped predicting dates and claimed the end was 'coming soon.' According to some, the next date is about 20 years away.

- The Jehovah's Witnesses don't vote or serve in the military, they don't smoke or accept homosexuality, and they don't allow some medical procedures, including blood transfusions. Their 'services' are held at 'Kingdom Halls,' and they believe they have a duty to convert others by knocking on the doors of strangers to preach to them.

I was startled to find that there were about 20 Kingdom Halls within an hour's drive of my apartment. They must just fade into the background because I couldn't remember seeing them at all.

I found a website that presented numerous pages of 'facts' about the Jehovah's Witnesses and arguments against them, and I scrolled through, checking what they had to say about shunning. I had a feeling that this action against Carrie Ames by the Jehovah's Witnesses was the key to her murder. Could someone from the church be responsible? Had something Carrie had done so angered someone that shunning her hadn't been enough of a punishment? Several websites talked about shunning, and one mentioned that the reason 'ex-JWs' most often gave for disfellowshipping had to do with sexual transgressions. I wondered what that meant.

My laptop battery was at about 10% when the power flickered back on. I made sure the heater clicked on, plugged the computer into the charger, and moved the cat's bed to the heater vent in the living room. I had to prepare for the two default judgment hearings for Thursday morning, and now that the printer would work again, I saved my notes and spent an hour or so prepping outlines and printing the orders I was hoping the judge would sign.

A defendant in a Texas lawsuit has only a certain number of days to file an answer after they've been served. If no answer is filed, the plaintiff can go and ask the judge to sign an order granting them all the relief they ask for. It should be a no-brainer for the judge: there's no argument from the other side for the judge to listen to, so—by law —he or she should just assume the allegations in the plaintiff's complaint are true and sign a judgment.

I wish.

My first default judgment hearing back four years ago was a bloodbath, and—because I was the only one in front of the judge that day—it was me that was bleeding. I heard later that judges sometimes target novice attorneys doing default judgments and 'teach' them about litigation by eviscerating them in their first few hearings. I didn't know any of that then; all I knew was that I was unprepared and ill-equipped to deal with examination on subjects I didn't understand well.

Since then, I've gone ahead and prepared for every default hearing as if the judge was my worst enemy, that he or she would be out to get me, and that my client's entire business would go down in flames if I lost. It's the only way I know to prepare thoroughly. I don't know how other attorneys practice in court—since leaving Stephenson's firm, my only legal contacts are friends from law school who practice out of state, and none of them are litigators.

I also had a couple of evictions, but those are pretty much slam-dunks, so I just prepped the exhibits for those. Once I had all that done, I nibbled at some leftover garlic bread and got back on my almost fully-charged laptop. I pulled up Adam Garrison's podcast to listen to while I scrolled through ex-JW websites.

Garrison was a church official—an elder—before leaving the organization six years ago at 28. His YouTube videos were made in a studio with motivational graffiti on the walls, him behind a radio-style microphone with headphones on, showing a still-young man with shaved head, intense brown eyes, and muscular arms and shoulders encased in a tight-fitting t-shirt. Each podcast covered a particular aspect of the religion or its followers, and Garrison would speak fervently about the hypocrisy of the church or its governing body, the group of older men who ran the entire global organization. Sometimes he'd interview another ex-JW about their experiences, and I noticed he seemed to have a lot of knowledge about the inner workings of the church, even this many years after leaving.

There was a new video from him about the Jehovah's Witnesses' refusal to accept blood transfusions. He was an arm-waver, and, as I watched him discussing the procedure for refusing transfusions and other medical treatments, I realized he's someone who can't be still, whose body constantly expresses what he's feeling.

"It's insane, I tell you," he raged as he made a fist and pounded it once on the table. "They even show pictures of these kids at conventions, kids who had such *unwavering faith* that they refused a blood transfusion themselves, making their parents so proud." His voice dripped with sarcasm, and he leaned forward, his eyes boring into the camera. He enunciated each word. "So. Proud. These parents were so proud, as their children died from the results of this horrific policy.

The church and the liaison committees who stop the doctors from these procedures point to obscure verses in the Bible to justify the practice, as if God is to blame." He leaned back, his arms crossing over his chest and his upper lip curling. I felt a chill at the coldness in his face. "Those parents should be jailed and convicted of murder, along with the governing body members who push their agenda on those helpless children."

I stopped the stream, looking into that face, frozen in anger and bitterness. If he felt so strongly about this, would he have allowed Carrie Ames to return to the church?

CHAPTER EIGHT

Thursday dawned bright and blue. A west wind on the back side of the cold front brought in a little west Texas dust and warmth, and I itched to go to White Rock Lake for a long walk. Instead I was due in justice court for the default judgment hearings and two eviction proceedings on the early 8:30 am docket.

Courtroom work is still a challenge for me, five years into doing litigation. When I started trying to build a practice after the securities trials and my subsequent blackballing, I assumed I'd be doing the same type of work I'd done for Bill: research, analysis, reporting. But when you're alone in a practice, there's no partner to assign you research, no clients brought in to analyze, no one to read the reports. I had no idea how or where to find clients, or how to develop a law practice.

I started by taking all the legal continuing education I could find, in every discipline or practice area. I quickly realized that family law wasn't something I was prepared for. I couldn't tell if never having been married or having children would make it easier or harder for me to represent a spouse or parent in the dissolution of a marriage and the subsequent parceling out of property, children, and pets.

During the trials of Bill and his partners—both federal and state—I spent days waiting to be called in as a witness. Several times, I'd be told to be at the courthouse, only to nervously wait outside the courtroom all day and never be pulled in. In my second and third years of law school, I'd been so sure of my eventual practice focus that I hadn't participated in mock trial or the legal clinics, so I'd never been inside a courtroom until the year of the trials. My curiosity was aroused by my own experiences, and I'd spend wait times in the courtrooms up and down the halls, watching bench and jury trials, hearings, and court-ordered depositions. Because I had a bar card, I was able to sit in on jury selections and custody disputes, and I often thought—from the gallery side of the gate— *I could do that.*

It's not as easy as it looks.

Today, I had two quick evictions and two default judgments. I was in front of Justice Hubert Laughlin, a Republican justice of the peace on the edge of mandatory retirement age. He keeps getting elected because he says and does nothing controversial outside of his courtroom, where he is king. Democrats have given up posting a candidate opposite him because the showing for candidates running against him is so demoralizing to the other Democratic candidates up and down the ticket. He's tall and gaunt and white-haired, and the scuttlebutt around the courthouse credits the pinkness of his beak-like nose to heavy drinking. He has these deep-set blue eyes that look sleepy until you step outside of his courtroom rules, and then they blaze at you across the bench.

His bailiff, court reporter, and court clerk are all his contemporaries, and if you get on the wrong side of one, you're on the wrong side of them all. Judge Laughlin starts his 8:30 am docket at precisely 8:25, and I only know this because I am almost always early to court. After my first few terrifying appearances, I realized that I could gauge a judge's mood (and therefore his or her tendency to make idiosyncratic rulings) if I watched a few hearings before mine.

This morning, I had two hearings set at the same time where the defendant hadn't filed an answer to the lawsuit. I checked in with the bailiff, Sergeant Carew, by 8:15 and was nodding off in one of the pews with all the other attorneys when a woman burst into the courtroom. She was tall and broad with hair in dreadlocks down her back, but the most startling thing about her was the fake (I assumed, from this distance) coonskin hat she wore. Her skin was tanned nut brown, and she could have been anywhere from 50 to 80. She looked around wildly as she came in, and I'm pretty sure the other attorneys felt the same ripple of fear that I did. All the cases set for 8:30 were default hearings, so an obvious non-lawyer in the courtroom could only mean one of us was about to be surprised by a *pro se* defendant—in non-Latin, a defendant acting on their own behalf.

The coonskin cap woman marched up to the uniformed bailiff, and they spoke in low voices. She shook her head so hard the raccoon tail bobbed back and forth, and all of us held our breath as the bailiff looked out into the gallery. My heart sank when he caught my eye and crooked a finger at me. I joined them at the bailiff's desk.

He tipped his head toward the woman and spoke quietly. "Ms. Benedict, this lady says she's Sophia Barnstead, and she didn't receive proper notice of the hearing."

"That's right, that's right. I didn't get nothing about this," the woman declared. "I just came 'cause one of my neighbors said she saw something posted on my door a couple of weeks ago." She drew herself up in indignation. "I never saw it myself."

I looked at Sergeant Carew, and he looked back at me. He'd been doing this work for god only knew how many years, and he'd probably seen it all, but I'd never had this happen to me in an eviction case. With evictions, you send a notice to vacate by mail, but it's also a good idea to post them on the door as well, so that tenants who don't check their mail will still see that they're being evicted. Then you file a suit for eviction and have it served by a constable, set a hearing, and you're good to go. Most people move out before you ever get to the hearing.

Sergeant Carew looked at the clock, which was edging toward 8:25 am, and I knew what he was thinking. Justice Laughlin liked eviction cases to go quickly, with no fuss and no muss, and definitely no defendants showing up to complain about service. I was pretty sure I had the constable's return of service in my file, and all the eviction notices were posted weeks ago—I thought I even took a picture of the envelope taped to her door. I couldn't check my phone right now because the judge required all cellphones to be turned off in his courtroom, and if he came in while I was thumbing through photos, he'd have the coordinator reschedule all my hearings. I had absolutely no idea what to do.

Sergeant Carew abruptly turned away, went to the chamber door behind the bench, swept it open, and a moment later Justice Laughlin came through looking like a bald eagle in black robes. I backed up behind the gate before he got to the bench, but Ms. Barnstead wasn't as quick. Justice Laughlin turned in her direction, and I saw the raccoon tail quiver as she looked back at him.

"Madam, are you lost?" Justice Laughlin's tone was icy, and he looked like a hawk about to sweep in for the kill.

Sergeant Carew stepped forward and whispered to the judge, whose eyes immediately swept the gallery to find me. "Miss Benedict, Sergeant Carew tells me you're responsible for this situation."

"Permission to approach, your honor?" He nodded, and I stepped forward to the raised wooden desk. "This lady says she wasn't noticed for the hearing, but I posted the eviction notice on her door three weeks ago, the suit was served by a constable to an adult in the household, and I mailed and posted this hearing notice on her door more than five days ago." I tried to keep my voice as steady as I could, but even I could hear a little quiver at the end. Sophia Barnstead stepped up beside me, and I noticed a slight gamey smell about her.

"You have documentation, I presume." It wasn't a question.

"Yes, sir, I do. Both of the mailed notice, the return of service, and a photo of all the posted notices." I hoped. "With your permission, your honor, I can step outside and pull up the photo."

Next to me, Sophia Barnstead began to rustle alarmingly. "I never got no notice! I never got nothing!" she began. Justice Laughlin interrupted her.

"I've not given you permission to speak, madam."

Ms. Barnstead shut her mouth abruptly and glared at the judge, who looked back at me.

"You have two minutes, Miss Benedict. You're second on the docket, and I expect you to be ready. You're excused."

"Yes, your honor." I practically ran to the back of the courtroom, pulling my phone out of my pocket and turning it on. Two minutes later, the Barnstead folder in my hand and the thankfully-clear picture of the eviction notice posting pulled up, I was back. Sophia Barnstead was seated at the defense table tapping her fingers on the table while another attorney stood in front of Justice Laughlin, giving the facts of his case in a low tone. The bailiff went out to call the defendant's name in the hall and the judge and attorney waited. After three calls, the judge succinctly found for the landlord, signing his name on the proffered order with a flourish.

I was up.

The bailiff called the case—*Handlebar Properties vs. Barnstead*—and I stepped forward towards the bench. Sophia Barnstead rose. Justice Laughlin motioned me to stop. "Miss Benedict, since you have a live defendant, you can use the counsel tables. Miss Barnstead, you may sit while she presents her case." Sophia Barnstead sat down with a *hmph*.

I stood at the plaintiff's table, my folder open and spread, and waited for him to give permission, my stomach turning. "Counsel, it's your application: begin."

I recited the facts over rumbling and rustling from the defense table: my client had a lease, Ms. Barnstead was the tenant, she failed to pay her monthly rent three months in a row, we sent out 'pay or else' notices and posted them on her door three weeks ago, and when she failed to catch up her rent, I filed an eviction case, had it served by a constable to an adult in the household, and noticed Ms. Barnstead of the eviction hearing—posting it on her door and by mail. When the judge gave permission, I entered copies of the service return and notices and the certified mail receipts into evidence, and even showed him the picture of the posting of the notice of hearing on her door.

I stepped back to the table, still standing. As far as I could see, I'd followed every procedural rule. My client should be granted possession of Ms. Barnstead's apartment.

Sophia Barnstead rose. "I didn't get no notice of nothing, Judge." She turned in my direction and pointed a finger at me. "She's lying. That's all there is to it." She folded her arms. "Why, if my neighbor Dorothy hadn't told me about seeing some letter on my door, I wouldn't know this was even happening. There weren't no letter when I got home from Houston."

Justice Laughlin raised a hand and stopped the flow of words. "Miss Barnstead, am I to understand you are challenging service of the eviction complaint and the notice of this hearing?"

"That's what I said, innit?" Sophia wasn't about to be intimidated by Hubert Laughlin. "She cain't prove I signed nothing."

Justice Laughlin looked at his computer for a minute or so, and then turned and looked at me. "Miss Benedict, the clerk's system doesn't yet show the constable's return of service, and your green cards showing delivery of the notice of this hearing haven't been returned yet, is that true?"

I admitted that they had not. Eviction proceedings go pretty quickly, and sometimes the post office is slow returning certified mail cards showing delivery.

Justice Laughlin drummed his fingers on the bench. "I don't like slowing down my docket for an eviction, Miss Benedict." I felt vaguely guilty at his words, as if I could have predicted Sophia Barnstead and her display when I set the eviction for hearing. "You and Miss Barnstead need to see the court's coordinator and reset this hearing for next week. You will bring me evidence of notice and service. Miss Barnstead will thus have notice of the hearing set next

week, and will need to address the facts of the eviction at that point."
He looked down his nose at Sophia Barnstead. "Do you understand,
madam?"

"I do, your honor." She looked triumphantly at me. "I'll be here,
and we'll see who knows how to do court better."

I shuffled my papers into the file marked Barnstead and followed
her out of the courtroom.

———

THREE HOURS LATER, I WAS FINALLY DONE FOR THE DAY. I'D
hoped Justice Laughlin would go easy on me in the two default hearings and the other eviction, but instead he grilled me on every fact
and allegation, checking over service and notice documentation like
he'd never seen it before. As if he blamed me for Sophia Barnstead, I
had to wait to present my default prove-ups until the coordinator
could squeeze me in between other cases. The other attorneys gave
me commiserating glances as they left after their hearings.

After paying Sameer, I sat in my car. I had a meeting with the
Shepherd tonight, but it was a long time till midnight. I had a voice
mail from Gerard telling me that they'd been able to get a prescription to Collin county jail for Todd, so he'd probably be able to get his
medication soon. I thought of Todd and how panicked he'd seemed;
as I sat there in my car, I understood all too well how it felt to be
trapped.

I started the car and drove east to White Rock Lake.

White Rock Lake is a small, manmade lake on the east side of
Dallas circled by large palatial homes and quirky art deco cottages.
Once a playground for the post-war wealthy of Dallas, the lake is now
a tiny jewel surrounded by parks and paths, and it's my favorite place
to do what little exercise I can force myself to do.

On an sunny winter weekday, men and women with large
strollers and walkers in fleeces dragged about by their dogs were the
only people on the paths. By late afternoon, even in this cold weather,

cyclists would be speeding by, crushing that extra ten miles before ending their day, and rowers would be sculling across the glass-like surface of the water.

I am not, nor have I ever been, an athlete. I was too uncoordinated to play sports in school, and solitary athletic activities bore me. I've tried it all: jogging, running, yoga, Pilates, cross-fit, weightlifting, even rowing and kayaking. I never found the endorphin high that everyone promised, and I've been known to get distracted and forget to move to other equipment at the gym or to trip over other people while trying to jog. I fell asleep in child's pose once and had to be helped up by three yoga instructors when my legs wouldn't wake up. So now I just start out and walk, and I keep walking until I'm done. The biggest benefit is that it requires no expensive equipment, clothing, or shoes, so it was something I didn't have to give up when my finances dried up. The main drawback is I sometimes find myself a couple of miles from where I started, and I have to walk back, tired and ready to move on, and I sometimes get lost. While I walk, I can let pressures and worries slide off me like water off a duck's back.

Walking at White Rock is a pleasure: big, mature trees shade winding paths that end in scenic overlooks or small piers, and I never get lost or tired of looking at the view. Even though today there was a bit of wind, the sunshine was bright and the air was clean. I left my phone in the car and walked for an hour, sometimes dodging a jogger or stroller-pushing parent, just enjoying the sun on my face and the air filling my lungs. The slight sound of my steps on the concrete path was rhythmic but not regular, and I concentrated on that for a long time, just letting things slide away. I let Justice Laughlin go, I let Sophia Barnstead go, I let my worries about my dad or money or work go—hell, I even let Gerard and Todd Parrish go. Time enough for that later in the day.

CHAPTER NINE

I've never worked at night. I have friends who do, and who are able to sleep virtually on command, preparing themselves to stay awake, eating and living on a different schedule than the rest of us. I thought I'd be able to nap for a few hours in the evening and be fresh and ready by midnight to meet with Adam Garrison. It didn't quite work out that way.

After a very early dinner, I was wired and unable to fall asleep. I tried everything, and finally nodded off about 9. When I woke at 11:15, the alarm on my phone had been beeping for about 30 minutes. I was groggy and had a slight headache that my quick shower couldn't wash away.

Instead of getting to Hipster Haven half an hour early like I planned, I rushed in the door a few minutes before midnight. A quick look around didn't show any single males eating alone, so I assumed I'd still beat him to the place. The hostess put me in a booth at the front that looked out onto the busy street, and I faced the door so I could see him when he came in. I dug for a pen and was rewarded with Gerard's Mont Blanc, which I'd apparently kept the day before. I flipped over to a clean page in my pad and felt ready, if not exactly steady.

Hipster Haven is a quirky semi-vegetarian café in Deep Ellum, the part of Dallas where goth and leather clubs went to die—or get trendy, depending on the whim of the public. Since HH is open 24/7, it's busy at all hours with slightly and not-so-slightly inebriated partygoers trying to sober up or stop the munchies before going home. The dishes on the menu are mostly meat-free, but they warn people that doesn't mean vegetarian. They have a few items that are "certified vegan" or "gluten-free" or "nut-free" but I think you take your chances if you have a real allergy. The waitstaff and kitchen crew are all young and slightly edgy, with a lot of tattoos, vividly-dyed hairstyles, and piercings they wear with pride.

Not having any dietary restrictions myself, I breathed in the slightly greasy air and looked over the large menu, my stomach growling. Food here is cheap and the portions large. I was leaning toward the chilaquiles when the door swept open with a rush of cold air to let in a couple and a man alone. It was definitely Garrison. He was shorter than I'd assumed from his video podcast—maybe a few inches under six feet—but the intensity that shone through on the internet was apparent the moment he walked in. He was bundled up in a khaki green parka, and his shoulders looked massive.

He came right to my table. "Lacey Benedict?"

I stood up and shook his hand. As the waitress came by, he caught her arm and wrapped her in a side hug. "Hey, Shelley. How's Henry's leg?"

"Hi, Adam." She turned her face into his shoulder, her voice muffled. "The vet said no walks for a couple of weeks, but it looks like he'll be okay." She disentangled and pushed back her jet black hair. "Chilaquiles tonight?"

"Sounds good, darlin'. Thanks." He slid into the booth opposite me. While he took off his coat and scarf, Shelley remembered I existed and took my order for chilaquiles. I felt slightly miffed when she gave me a look that told me she thought I was copying Garrison. I chalked it up to feeling cranky and tired.

Under his coat, Garrison was wearing a long-sleeved shirt that was just as snug as the short-sleeved one he'd worn on the video, and the muscles in his chest and shoulders stretched the fabric. It felt like vanity to me, and I wondered how much of a contrast he was now to how he must have been when he was a Jehovah's Witness.

Garrison had no problems jumping right into conversations. "So, you're representing Todd?"

I nodded. "I'm really just helping out the attorney that took the case, Rob Gerard."

Garrison leaned forward and pounced. "That's right—you're like a securities lawyer, aren't you?"

So the internet had done its work. "I used to be. I'm just a general business lawyer now. I know Todd's grandparents." I looked back steadily. *There. Let him make more of that if he wanted.*

He drummed his fingers on the table and then looked around, seeming to lose interest. "So what do you want to know?" Shelley dropped off two water glasses, and he smiled at her as she left again. "If you're going to ask me for an alibi, I don't have one." He looked at me, that smile twisting a bit. "I was home alone that Sunday night."

I watched as he slipped a straw out of its paper covering. "I'm trying to find out more about Carrie. Todd's not really able to help us much right now." I didn't think this guy needed to know about Todd's mental state at the moment.

Garrison stretched his arms over the top of the banquette cushion and looked over the patrons in the restaurant while talking to me, something I found odd and vaguely insulting. "I met Carrie and her family about eight years ago. The Organization had asked me to move to the new Kingdom Hall in Princeton because they were splitting up another Kingdom Hall that had gotten too large." He looked back at me. "You know how that works?" I shook my head, Gerard's pen flying over the page, and he leaned forward, back in video podcast mode. "Watch Tower doesn't like Kingdom Halls to get too big. They only want about 80 to 120 or so Friends in any Kingdom Hall. So when one gets too large, they split it up into separate congregations meeting at different times in one building, or they build a new Kingdom Hall some distance away and have some Friends move to that one."

He took a sip of his water through the straw, and I took that pause to stop him.

"Why?"

"Why what?"

"Why do they not want Kingdom Halls to get bigger than 120 people?" I held the pen over my pad, waiting for what I was sure would be a logical answer, and was surprised when Garrison hesitated. He was pretty much completely still, and for a man who seemed to never stop moving, the stillness was noticeable.

After a moment, he ran his hand over his smoothly shaven head, a gesture that was oddly reminiscent of Gerard's movement when he was thinking. "It's one of those things that are policy, and if there was a reason for it, it's not one that's stated." His eyes met mine. "There are a lot of policies like that in the Organization. They don't tell the rank and file members the reasons for what they do."

"Who is 'they'?"

He looked at me as if I'd grown horns. "*The Organization.*" He leaned forward. "The governing body, the administration, the corporations, the committees, the overseers, the whole bloody mess."

"Ah." I didn't really understand, but I noted it down. "I'm sorry—you were saying you met her and her family about eight years ago?"

"Right. Her father was an elder at the Kingdom Hall in Princeton. Nice man—they're both nice people, he and Leah."

"I met her yesterday. She seems really upset at Carrie's death."

Garrison tilted his head and looked at me, considering. Then he shook his head. "I doubt if it's completely because of Carrie's death. You have to understand—in her mind, Carrie died when she left the truth."

It was odd to hear him echo Leah's words. "Her mom said that.

She really made no effort to reach out to Carrie?" I took a sip of water. "I cannot imagine just cutting my immediate family out of my life because they have different beliefs."

He shook his head again, then looked out over the restaurant at the patrons eating and talking. "The JW aren't raised to think like you do," he said, watching a couple taking a selfie in front of a graffiti'd wall. "They're told that interaction with people like you—the 'worldly' people—is wrong. And it's unhealthy for them to get too close to you." He looked back at me and crooked a bit of a grin. "Eventually, after Armageddon, they'll end up in an earthly paradise and you'll be vulture food, so it's not wise to get too close." His smile faded. "When a JW leaves or is disfellowshipped, they're doomed to the same fate."

He sat back as Shelley placed plates in front of us. We spent a minute or so testing the chilaquiles, adding salsa or hot sauce, passing the salt and pepper back and forth. The portion was huge, but I was starving, well into the eighteenth hour of my day. The vivid orange yolks of the fried eggs were runny and the green chile sauce was plentiful, dripping down over the edges of tortilla chips. I added a little sour cream to mine and dug in.

Garrison drizzled hot sauce over his chilaquiles and forked a huge, dripping bite. He chewed for a moment, remembering. "Carrie was such a sweet girl. She was 16 when I met her, super bright...a good student." He dipped a tortilla chip into the green chile sauce and crunched into it, then picked up his fork again. "She got that from her dad. Sam's a really intelligent guy—he's an up and coming man in the Organization in this region. He's been an elder, and now circuit overseer, and he may even end up in administration at Warwick." He stopped, his fork poised above his plate, looking out the window into the night. "He and I used to have these great talks. They weren't really arguments or debates, just discussions." He looked down at his plate and then cut another bite. "He was part of the reason I left, really."

I watched while he chewed. "Why *did* you leave?"

"I couldn't take the intellectual hypocrisy." He pointed his fork at me, sliding easily into teacher mode. "Consider it. A whole religion based on the measurements of a pyramid taken by one guy almost a hundred and fifty years ago. None of the dates they've ever predicted have come true. And yet men like Sam Ames put that aside and willfully allow themselves to be deluded." He shook his head and forked up another bite. "I started collecting books in my 20s, and I actually read them. Stuff just didn't make sense. But when I'd raise those issues with Sam, he'd just shake his head and smile and tell me I had to listen to the men who were appointed by God to be our shepherds, and have faith that God had inspired them." His voice rose as he spoke, and he looked into my eyes. "That's not faith. That's blind, sheep-like obedience. And after a while, that becomes intolerable."

His intensity was a little unnerving, just like it had been in his YouTube video. "I read on your website bio that you'd been an elder too. Weren't you a little young?" I got a particularly spicy green chile in my next bite, so I nibbled some tortilla with sour cream to even out the heat.

He shook his head. "The word 'elder' in the Jehovah's Witnesses doesn't mean someone who's old. It's more of a title in the Organization. You're supposed to lead the congregation—you know about ministerial servants?" I shook my head, jotting down the term.

He leaned forward, elbows on the table, confident and teaching now. "Ministerial servants are assistants to the elders—they're the guys who help do the administrative work in the congregation and take turns giving parts in the meetings." He waited for me to catch up with my notes while also eating. "So elders are the men who lead the flock and take care of them, keeping them safe from the harmful wolves outside. The elders' handbook is called 'Shepherd The Flock of God.'" He grimaced. "At least that's how they view it. They're really there to help the sheep be indoctrinated by the Organization." He cut off another bite of chilaquiles and sopped it in the green chile sauce.

"I notice you call yourself 'The Shepherd.' Do you still consider yourself an elder?" I made a note and looked up. Garrison was chewing and looking at me.

"Do you know the parable of the 99 sheep?" I shook my head. He took a sip of water and put his fork down, folding his hands together and entering teaching mode so smoothly it seemed effortless.

"Jesus told a parable of a shepherd who has a hundred sheep, and one gets lost on the mountainside. The shepherd leaves the 99 sheep who are safe, and goes out to find the one that's lost." He stared out the window for a moment, then sighed and looked back at me, his face tightening. "The JWs like to compare themselves to the shepherd that's out there looking for the one sheep. It's a lie. Instead, they ignore the one lost sheep, telling themselves it's Jehovah's justice for that sheep's sins." His voice rose and his words oddly became more formal. "They're more concerned with making sure that the 99 sheep stay in the pen, docile and too frightened to think, than helping the poor lambs who've lost their way." He picked up his fork and stabbed it into a bite of chilaquile.

"And so *you* shepherd the lost lambs?" I tried to ask the question lightly, but some of my cynicism must have come through.

"Who else is going to?" he shot back at me, his voice rising. "People need to know that these kids are not only unprepared for the world, they've been actively damaged by the Organization."

Shelley came by to refill my water and looked at us both a bit anxiously. Garrison smiled at her, and I felt him relax a little.

"It's just a YouTube channel name," he said to me, with a smile that didn't quite reach his eyes. "It works for the advertisers."

"And the thousands of followers." He acknowledged the comment with a little head nod. I decided I didn't want to make an enemy here, so I moved on. "You and Carrie must have had a good relationship for her to call you when she left."

"I liked her. We had a lot in common. Carrie finished high school—I was proud of her for that. Both of her sisters quit high school early to go out into full-time ministry—you know, back when the JWs knocked on doors. They both were married and having babies by the time they were 20." He cut into the last bit of his chilaquiles. "That's not unusual, by the way. The JW don't think much of education." He chewed for a minute. "Carrie had my cell phone number, and she stayed in touch with me after I left—which could have gotten her in trouble." He looked out the window as some young people went by, their laughter audible through the glass. "She didn't say much, just let me know what was going on with her and her dad. She was struggling by then, pretty unhappy about the non-answers she'd gotten to questions." He looked back at me. "If you ask too many questions, or show that you're not completely on board, you'll have to be counseled by the elders or ministerial servants. If you don't go out into field service enough, you'll get a visit." He dropped his fork in his empty plate with a clatter.

"Was Carrie that unhappy with what was going on?"

He nodded. "A lot of young people just go along—it's what they've been taught to do, and with no outside influences, there's no one to tell them otherwise." He sighed. "I did, for years. It took Sam and other elders telling me to seek answers in the writings of the Organization to wake me up."

"Why was that?"

"Because the writings don't make sense." He leaned forward, his hands making fists on either side of his plate. "Go back far enough, find books that are old enough, and you realize the writers—no, let's be clear, the Watch Tower Organization is a flawed and confused earthly corporation that was started to make money, and is now predicated on a need for power. Well, power and money." At my look, he added, "Check on the Organization's finances, if you don't believe me. They've moved into real estate speculation and lending. They've come full circle on the backs of JW volunteers and loans." His voice rose and he brought his fists down on the table, and the water in my glass sloshed over the edge. "Sorry." He laughed and used his paper napkin to absorb the small puddle.

I'd reached my limit with the chilaquiles, so I pushed my plate aside and scribbled a note down about the Organization's books. "How long had you been out before Carrie left the church?"

He pushed his plate aside and sat back in the booth. "I left six years ago this coming spring. I think Carrie left what—more than two years ago? You do the math." He looked up with a smile at Shelley as she appeared to take our plates. "Coffee, darlin', ok?"

She nodded and patted his shoulder.

"I know Carrie put you down as a reference for her job and her apartment."

He nodded. "A lot of the kids in Dallas who leave know me. You have no idea how hard it is for them. These are kids who've never done anything for themselves. They either live with their parents until they get married, or they room with another JW family. They work in a company owned by a JW if possible, and all their friends are JW. If they leave, they leave everything behind." He shook his head, his face flushing with his anger. "The JW praise anti-intellectualism so much that parents who allow their children to go to college may be shunned. Did you hear about the family in Michigan a few years ago that allowed their children to go to college and were then shunned—the wife killed her husband and children and then herself in desperation?" I shook my head, appalled. "It's not always that bad, but it's bad. Some never finish high school, and few go to college. We grow up learning nothing but the most basic of job skills, and we have no idea how to work or interact in the world."

"Did Carrie have those kinds of problems?"

"Maybe." He smiled at Shelley when she set the coffee in front of him and refilled my water glass. "Sam and Leah were good parents, and the family was close. I think Carrie missed them more than anything else." He poured cream in his coffee. "In the last two years, she's helped some of the other JWs who came out and were just—" he paused, searching for the word—"broken." He shook his head. "Groups form as they look for connection and try to understand the world."

"What are they trying to understand?"

"Everything." He shook his head again. "We were never taught to do anything for ourselves. They don't teach us how to think or reason or analyze anything. We get out, and everything is just crazy." He stirred his coffee and watched as the white cream swirled into the coffee. "You're suddenly free, free to do anything you want—drinking, smoking, sex, drugs. And so many kids have no idea how to judge things for themselves or what to believe. Our whole lives, we've been told to just obey. Some do—or they don't, and get kicked out. Some decide to leave, knowing they'll lose it all when they do."

I wondered if he realized that he moved freely back and forth between 'us' and 'them.' "Did you lose it all when you left?"

He shook his head. "I was a little different. I worked at a national electronics store chain, so I didn't lose my job. I had my own apartment already. But all my friends, and all my family. None of them could or would speak to me." He looked back toward the window, the neon lights from the still-open bar across the street lighting his face with red. "They still don't."

I couldn't imagine it. "How do you deal with that?"

He shrugged and looked back at me. "Me? It made me tough. I joined a gym and would go work out every time I thought about going back." He laughed ruefully and a dimple flashed. I could see the charisma that Shelley—and I presume others—saw. "I got in great shape."

"Was Carrie tough?"

He looked down at his coffee again. "Tough? No." He laughed. "She was smart though—she packed her car and came to Dallas. Before she did, she got in touch with me. By the time she got here, I had an ex-JW lined up to give her sleeping space on her couch. Ann Thornton. Really nice lady." He looked around the restaurant again, then back at me. "Carrie was able to find a job and get her life going." He sipped his coffee and shook his head. "Some don't make it. They have no idea how to set boundaries for themselves. They drink, do drugs, have addiction problems. They just go crazy, and they don't know how to survive. The support group helps them learn how to survive."

"But Carrie didn't survive, did she?"

He paused, set his coffee mug carefully on the table, and pushed it away from himself a little before looking at me. "No, she didn't."

I looked down at my notes. Every time he turned on the intense eye contact, I felt nervous and didn't ask questions—I just let him talk. I was starting to think it was intentional. "Had she told you she was planning to return to the church?"

He leaned forward, suddenly intense again. "You keep referring to it as a 'church.' It's not a church—it's an *organization*." He stressed the word with heavy emphasis, and I sensed we were about to get back into podcast mode. He leaned back and exhaled as he rubbed his hand over his smoothly shaven head. "She wasn't going back to a religion and a God. She was going back to a company." I could feel his eyes boring into my head, willing me to look back up. "Did you know that Watch Tower was started as a publishing company?"

I made a note and met his eyes. I did know that, but I could tell he was about to lecture, so I shook my head. "When Russell started the Organization, its purpose was to publish the Great Pyramid series, and then other books, and sell them. But he used his Bible Students Association to do it, calling them 'porters.' Friends who go out knocking on doors are called 'publishers.' They say it's because they're 'publishing the word of God,' but that's not what it really means." He took another sip of his coffee, just getting going. "For years, Bethel—the big complex in New York—was all about literal book publishing and printing."

My memory was triggered. "Your bio said you were a Bethelite—does that mean you worked there?"

He nodded, eyes on me. "Yep. For two years. It's why I started collecting the books. By the time I was there, electronic publishing was taking over, and I thought the printed books would be a thing of the past pretty soon. So I started picking up the print books when I could."

He leaned back. "But you didn't come here to talk about me." He played with his coffee cup but kept his eyes on me. "You think Todd killed her?"

I didn't answer that. "Do you?"

He shrugged, looking at the remains of his coffee, then ran a hand over his head again, as if he missed the hair there. "I don't know. It doesn't seem likely. They seemed really in love." He looked back at me. "Maybe it was a crime of passion."

"That's what I'm thinking. But what passion?" I leaned forward and put Gerard's pen down. "You didn't say—what did you think when Carrie told you she was going back?"

He leaned in, eyes fixed on mine. "I thought she was being influenced. But kids go back, all the time. If they're lucky, their parents or family stay in touch, and the pressure to go back is really heavy."

"And if they're not lucky?"

He looked out the window, the neon lights flashing across his handsome, bleak face, and I could feel him withdrawing from the conversation. "If they're not lucky, as far as their family is concerned, they might as well be dead."

————

After Garrison and I halved the bill a bit later, I walked back down the street to the space where I parked my car, turning the conversation over in my mind. It was well after 2 am, and my steps dragged over the two short blocks. A laughing foursome dressed in black split into couples to go around me, and a homeless man gave me a look before going on to other, better-dressed potential donors. Even though it was still cold, the extreme chill of the past few days was gone. A south wind had brought moisture in, and they were calling for rain for the next few days.

I got in my car and sat behind the wheel for a few minutes. Something about Garrison and his story nagged at me, but I was too tired to follow it through. I usually make notes after an interview or meeting,

but there was no way I'd be able to do that tonight. I suddenly wished
Gerard and I were on better terms. The thought of being able to
explore the facts and discuss them with someone else was starting to
seem really attractive.

I gave in to impulse and texted Gerard.

*I met with Garrison. Some interesting insight about Carrie and her
family and the church. I'll write up a report this weekend.*

My phone immediately rang.

"You could have just texted me, Gerard."

"You know better than that, Benedict." His voice was low and
husky, and for a bad moment, I imagined him in bed. Not good, not
good.

"Well, I hope I didn't disturb you."

"No, just me and Bella trying to stay warm." I really didn't need
to envision him with some Highland Park trophy woman in bed, but I
couldn't help myself. I gave into it for a moment before he spoke
again. "So the Garrison thing went well?"

"Yeah, he's something." Just talking made me see the interview
clearer. "I think he's being evasive, but I'm not sure about what." I
closed my eyes and pictured Garrison: his intense brown eyes, his
shaved head, his broad shoulders. "I don't think he's lying—just not
telling me some things."

"How about coffee tomorrow? You sound beat."

"Yeah, I've still got to drive home."

"Jesus, Benedict, go home. We can talk tomorrow." He put the
phone on speaker, and I could imagine him looking at his calendar.
"How about 3 pm at that coffee shop near your place? Café au Lait?"

"That'll work. I've got a lunch, but I should be done by then."

He came back on the phone. "Be safe, Benedict."

I pressed disconnect, then started the car. It was going to take
everything I had to stay awake as I drove home.

CHAPTER TEN

It started to rain during the night, a slow, steady, cold rain that lightened to mist and deepened to heavy driving rain at various times. Without a reason to get up till almost noon, I snuggled in and slept to the sound of it falling. When I finally got up at 11, I felt almost normal again. I didn't remember feeding the cat when I came in from meeting with Garrison, but I must have. She was curled up in her bed when I emerged from the shower and just watched me without moving.

I was meeting a client and friend, Dr. Amie Pascal, for lunch. She was a practicing child psychologist, and I'd represented her last year when two divorcing parents each subpoenaed her to appear in their custody dispute—each claiming she represented their interest. They'd wanted hours of deposition and document production from her files, and both had named her as a witness to appear in their court proceedings, since each claimed that the other was a damaging influence on their eight-year-old child. According to Amie, they were both right.

Although she was only ten or so years older than I, Amie was far more sophisticated than I'd ever be. She chose to work with children rather than adults, but I'd found her to be insightful and accurate in assessing my own issues. She was also incredibly kind, and loved the Mexican restaurants that sprang up on every corner of Dallas, full of tacos, margaritas, and street corn. Me too.

Dr. Amie whipped into the restaurant, rain streaming from her umbrella. As usual, I felt slightly grungy next to her. She's what she calls (with some sarcasm) 'aristocratic Creole,' and she reminds me of the Frenchwomen I met when I was in Paris the summer after I finished law school. Her pink and gold umbrella matched her chic rain boots, and the paisley-patterned scarf tied around her neck complimented the gray winter wool pantsuit she wore. In contrast, I'd prepped for a day in the cold rain with a cream fisherman's turtle-neck, jeans, and leather boots. I did put some makeup on, though, since this wasn't my first lunch with Dr. Amie and her discerning eye.

Sure enough, the first thing she did after a quick hug was peer into my face, her hands cupping my cheeks. "Cherie, you look tired," she pronounced in her Louisiana accent. It's not French, but not quite southern either. "But I see traces of eyeshadow and mascara, so I'm proud of you." She kissed both of my cheeks before letting me go.

"And as always, you look amazing." The restaurant's owner swept up to drop off guacamole and chips, and she spoke to him for a minute, remembering his name from our last visit and asking about his holiday travel to see his family in Mexico. I watched with my usual smile. It's hard to be around Dr. Amie and not be charmed by her.

"So, my dear." She focused back on me with a flourish, snatching a chip from the basket. She nibbled on an edge before salting her half of the basket a bit, the gold signet ring on her right hand flashing. "That text you sent me was wholly unhelpful. Can I look up the psychology of cults?? Of course I can, but why would I want to?" She laughed at my frown. "Never fear, I did, my dear, I did. But the price of the research is the story!"

I told her what I could while we decimated the guacamole, the chunky avocado mixture disappearing long before the description of my interview with The Shepherd. She seemed particularly interested in Adam Garrison and his persuasive nature, given his history with the Jehovah's Witnesses.

Once we'd ordered our lunch (chile relleno for Dr. Amie and cheese enchiladas for me), I got down to business. "It's amazing to me that a woman in this day and age would allow herself to be part of such a repressive patriarchal religion. I mean, they have internet there —surely they can see that there's a better life out here."

Dr. Amie tilted her head to the side. "My dear, they believe it's a better life *in there*." When I frowned and started to reply, she continued. "Do you think that it is the friends of a battered woman who convince her to leave? Of course not. It's the abuser themselves."

My jaw dropped. "You're comparing someone in the Jehovah's Witnesses to someone in a domestic violence situation?"

She shrugged. "It's a paradigm that is often used, cherie. The abuse may be different, but the psychological torment is very similar." She smiled at the owner, who'd dropped off her mango margarita. Since she doesn't keep her office open after noon on Fridays, she considers a margarita at Friday lunch her reward for a week well done. "A victim of domestic violence will stay and defend her abuser against all doubters—the good times are so good, he's just angry and frustrated, or, even worse, it's her own fault too—until the abuser crosses some invisible line. And then she leaves." She sipped her margarita and made a delicate, pleased 'mm.' "They coined the term 'brainwashing' for a reason, cherie. The victim begins to see everything from the point of view of the abuser—or in our case, the cult— and makes excuses that can explain away even the worst abuses."

I considered this while waiting for my water glass to be refilled. "You know, one of the things I saw in a video was that the Jehovah's Witnesses redefine words like 'truth' and 'friends.' It's a way of distorting reality, isn't it?"

Dr. Amie nodded, then broke a chip into smaller pieces to dip into salsa. "Imagine being born into the religion. You'd know nothing else." She nibbled a chip thoughtfully. "Abusers redefine reality to convince the victim that life outside the relationship would be far, far worse than whatever the victim suffers inside it."

"Best life ever," I murmured.

"Pardon?"

"I saw this on a blog—some of them use the hashtag '#bestlifeever' in social media. They've been convinced that the life they lead is the best life ever, and that the rest of us are miserable and unhappy in our worldliness."

"There's another one," Dr. Amie said. "The word 'worldly' means sophisticated and aware to us."

"True. Carrie's roommate mentioned that it's considered a derogatory term to them." I swirled a chip in my little salsa bowl. "But she'd been out for almost three years. Why go back into it?"

Dr. Amie sipped the mango margarita again. "Why would an abused woman go back to her abuser? Because it's familiar, my dear." She delicately dabbed salt from the corner of her mouth with her napkin. "When someone who has been abused leaves the abuser, they're usually leaving *home*." She shook her head as she emphasized the word. "You've said poor Carrie was cut off from family, friends— all she knew. Perhaps she yearned for the familiar—for her home."

I dipped another chip in my salsa bowl. "Even if the familiar is psychologically abusive? You should hear some of these stories, Amie." The tomato salsa was spicy and burned the tip of my tongue with a pleasant tingle. "These kids are sheltered—I get that—but they don't go to college, many are taken out of school and home schooled"—I made sure to do the air quotes around 'home schooled' to emphasize my opinion of taking a child out of school so they could do hours of service to the religion—"and you should hear the stories they tell of learning *not* to make friends with outsiders who'll burn in the fires of Armageddon."

Amie made a face and shook her head. "I've heard some of them firsthand. I've had a few children as patients when their parents flee fundamentalist religions." She leaned forward and tapped the table with a pink-polished nail to make sure I was listening. "But Lacey, sometimes the unknown is more frightening than the worst psychological or physical abuse."

I leaned back as a waiter placed our entrees in front of us. When he left to get the water pitcher to refill our glasses, I shook my head. "It's just not normal."

She tested the sauce on her chile and dabbed a bit of salsa on top. "You understand that 'normal' is different for each person." She used her knife and fork to cut off a small bite from her chile, but paused to look at me. "Remember how to cook a lobster?"

I dipped a bite of cheese enchilada into the crema at the edge of my plate before answering. "Start in cold water and slowly heat it up, so the lobster doesn't know it's boiling." The cheese enchilada was perfect, the corn tortilla thin and tightly rolled, the cheese inside hot and creamy.

Dr. Amie nodded approvingly. "Just like with an abuse victim, 'normal' changes all the time. The victim believes she is the one who causes the negative changes, and the abuser is responsible for all the positive ones."

"We're not talking about gently boiling water," I argued. "The things these people go through—it's awful."

She looked out the window at the rain beading the glass. "It is, indeed. Religious groups add a layer of fear that makes the abuse particularly damaging. It's not just the earthly disapproval that affects the victim. You can add a powerful, vengeful, and unforgiving deity to the mix." She looked back at me. "And you can't really argue with God."

"One girl I saw interviewed in a documentary said that she'd been sexually abused by a JW foster parent." I heard my voice rise, and lowered it. "And they didn't even believe her because there wasn't another witness." I shook my head and took another sip of water. "This Shepherd guy told me that the young people who leave have no idea how to act or think for themselves. He compared them to lost sheep." I considered how full I was, and then cut off another bite of cheese enchilada. "But I think he really likes that analogy because he calls himself 'The Shepherd.'" I smirked. "It works for him, even though he doesn't seem very loving and shepherd-like."

"And was your victim a lost lamb? She seems to have had a lot of support here in Dallas."

I thought about it. "She was in a support group, but Garrison did say she had helped some other people who had come out."

"Mmm." Dr. Amie took another sip of her margarita as she considered. "I suppose one way to help yourself is to help others."

She set her glass down with a thump. "But ultimately, my dear, I don't buy it." She lifted a forkful of rice to her mouth and then shook her head as she chewed the bite. "Carrie didn't seem like your typical lost soul. You described some of the young people who have left this church and gone a little Rumspringa." At my look, she explained, "That's what the Amish call it when their young people go a little crazy when they leave home. Most go back and resume their Amish lifestyle, but some stay outside." She took a sip of iced water. "Your Carrie doesn't sound like that. She sounds like she had a good support system of friends, employer, and boyfriend outside the Jehovah's Witnesses. Her going back inside doesn't seem to fit that." She picked up her fork and pointed it at me before cutting off another bite. "You're missing something, cherie."

I stopped eating and stared at her. In a few sentences, she seemed to clarify my own feelings about Carrie: that she was a strong, capable young woman who had established a stable life outside and wouldn't —without a strong motive—go back into that closed-off world.

———

I'D EXPECTED GERARD TO LOOK OUT OF PLACE WHEN HE strolled into Café au Lait a bit before 3 that afternoon, but he'd shed his suit coat and tie and wore a long black trench open over his light blue shirt and navy dress pants. He looked just like the other businessmen who frequented the place for meetings.

A few years ago, Felix and Marie Haught bought one of the unlovely and almost-derelict warehouses in this part of town and performed massive renovations to turn it into a commercial bakery. They kept the enclosed front offices, and Marie—who is straight-from-Paris French—turned one of the large, brightly-lit spaces into Café au Lait. She got rid of the false dropped ceilings and kept the wooden beams, and she exposed the red brick walls that were behind some ugly wood paneling straight out of the 1970s. She found old glass and wood bakery cases and created a long concrete counter where you order while admiring two enormous espresso machines, complete with copper fittings. The three tables are 12-foot long wooden ones that I thought were vintage refectory tables, but Marie confessed that she'd had a carpenter make them with some reclaimed wood. Seating is on pew-like benches, and at lunch, you sit elbow to elbow with all the other patrons—and like it.

Even though I'd stuffed myself with cheese enchiladas at lunch, it's really hard to come in this place and just have coffee. Felix and his staff run the bakery in three 8-hour shifts, so there's always the smell of fresh baked bread to make you crazy. The cases hold quiche, croissants, baguettes, and specialty breads I could never pronounce or recreate. Marie fills baskets at the end of the counter with day-old bread at a discount, and I learned from her that stale brioche makes the best French toast.

I was almost finished transcribing my notes on the Garrison interview at the end of one table when Gerard came in, his eyes widening as he took in the room. I love to see people impressed by what the Haughts have done here—it feels like a bit of France, a bit of Texas, and a bit of something indefinable and lovely, all at the same time.

"Wow, this place is—what is *that*?" he asked, his eyes lighting up at the remains of my cinnamon knot, which is Marie's novel use of leftover croissant dough, dotted with cinnamon and butter and tied in a knot about half the size of the typical cinnamon roll. They're small and sold by the dozen...or a single one or two, if you're nice to the counter staff.

I pulled my plate a little closer to me. "Get your own, Gerard."

He just laughed and went to the counter, where he proceeded to flirt and sweet talk his way into four (four!) cinnamon knots and a very large cup of coffee. He sat across from me and spread a napkin over his lap.

"So I met with Garrison last night...." I trailed off when Gerard lifted a hand to me, much like I had two days before when I had my first sip of coffee. I closed my laptop and watched him devour all four cinnamon knots and drink half of a large coffee, and I felt my crankiness slip away just as quickly as the pastry disappeared.

He finally wiped his mouth with his napkin and sat back with a sigh. "That. Was. Amazing."

I grinned at him. I knew that feeling. "You act like you haven't eaten all day."

"I hadn't. Got a call from a court coordinator who likes me this morning about 8:15. One of my civil cases is blowing up, and opposing counsel was in the judge's chambers trying to get a TRO. I threw on a suit and got to the courthouse before the judge granted it *ex parte*." He took another sip of coffee. "Barely had time to let Bella out in the backyard before I left, and we've been off and running since then."

I tried not to let the little click in my head about 'Bella' be audible. So he slept with a dog and not a trophy girlfriend. *Didn't mean anything.*

He put an arm across the back of the bench and raised one of those black eyebrows. "So how was the chat with Garrison?"

I opened my laptop to pull up my notes, but he shook his head. "Wait, Benedict. Don't give me data yet—just your impressions of him."

I closed the laptop one more time and stared at the logo on the top, re-running bits of the interview in my mind. Finally I found the word I wanted.

"He's charismatic. I didn't realize from the YouTube videos just how powerful that would be." I shook my head. "They should call him 'The Preacher' instead of 'The Shepherd'—he reminds me of one of those televangelists." I took a sip of my latte and tried to think about Garrison's personality quirks. "I'm not sure I like him."

"Hmmm...I'm getting the feeling you think he's a possible suspect." Gerard took a sip of his coffee and waited.

"I...I don't know." This wasn't something I'd really thought about, and I didn't know how to respond. Gerard did need to be warned about my interviewing limitations, though. After all, he was depending on my gathering of facts for this case.

I took a deep breath. "You need to understand, Gerard, I'm more comfortable with facts and data than people." He quirked an eyebrow at me but waited for me to continue. I looked away. "I'm trying to learn those things, like creating a rapport or listening to body language, but it's just not my forte. I can't tell when people are lying or telling the truth." My cheeks flaming, I looked back to see him tilting his head to the side and watching me. My cheeks burned hotter.

"Benedict, I think you probably pick up on more than you believe you do." He didn't sound like he was mocking me, and I relaxed a little. "You just have to think of it as collecting data. Sit back and relax for a minute."

I tried, I really tried.

"Tell me why you felt like he was a televangelist."

I thought about Garrison's manner when he started talking about the Jehovah's Witnesses. "He's very intense when he slips into this preacher mode. He leans forward, and makes direct eye contact, holding it until it's a bit uncomfortable, to tell you the truth. He uses his hands, and he always seems to be moving." I remembered his speech about blood transfusions in the video. "He seems to know exactly which words to emphasize or when to pause for effect. Maybe he's had some training as a speaker, I don't know." I caught the word I wanted. "He's *slick*."

"See, Benedict, all that is data." He reached for my legal pad, and turned to a blank page. "Try this sometime." He picked up his Mont Blanc pen and stared at it for a second before looking at me with an eyebrow raised. I shrugged and tried to look innocent. He drew a line down the page vertically, pointing with the pen to the left side of the line. "Record your notes about what was said on this side. Then over here," he said, pointing to the right side of the line, "record people's expressions or actions right across from their words." He put his pen in his pocket and sat back. "Put his words to his actions, and the overall impression is that of someone who is a persuader."

"That's exactly it! He seems like he's constantly trying to persuade." I thought for a few seconds. "And that's exactly what Jehovah's Witnesses do—they try to persuade." I opened my laptop for the Garrison data sheet. "He was an elder, and had been very active in the church for a long time before he left." I grimaced and rolled my eyes. "The *organization*. Garrison made that clear. He says it's more like a corporation than a church." I looked up at Gerard. "I'm not sure any of that is helpful."

"You said last night he seemed evasive." Gerard rubbed his hand over his hair, and I smiled a little, remembering Garrison's similar habit.

"What?" Gerard said a little defensively.

My cheeks burned a little. "Oh, Garrison does something like that—rubbing your hand over your head—but he's shaved bald, and it looks more like he's scrubbing his scalp." I stopped—something about that nudged at my memory. "Wait, wait, wait."

I scanned my notes, trying to remember when Garrison rubbed his head and what he was talking about. "You do that when you're thinking, right?" Gerard nodded, but said nothing.

"Garrison's the kind of guy who likes to know everything—and I mean everything. I think he was rubbing his head when he didn't know the answer to the question I asked him." I found the note I was thinking of. "I asked him why the church"—I frowned—"the *Organization* liked to keep Kingdom Halls smaller than about 120 people. He didn't know, and when he was trying to come up with the right answer, he rubbed his head."

I looked up at Gerard. "It's not an important thing, but I noticed him doing that several times while we were talking."

Gerard nodded. "It's a tell."

"A what?"

"It's a poker term. You know what a 'pokerface' is, right?" I nodded. "Well, a 'tell' is a particular motion or facial expression or tic or micro-expression a player makes when they're bluffing—essentially lying—about their hand." He lifted and lowered his eyebrows once. "Almost everyone has them. Noticing them—and connecting them to what's being said—will make you a good interviewer."

I caught my breath. "Everyone has them?" I asked, the words thin and thready.

Gerard nodded, his eyes on mine. "Pretty much everyone, Benedict."

We looked at each other, and I felt my heart pounding out the seconds in my throat until he spoke again.

"Even you."

———

TELEVISION AND MOVIES HAVE GIVEN THE PUBLIC A BADLY skewed vision of how litigation works. From *Perry Mason* to *A Few Good Men* and *Law and Order*, it looks like the first time an attorney talks to a witness is in trial, in front of a judge and jury. The reality is that discovery involves hours of document review and deposition testimony. The attorneys ask a witness or defendant—if he or she hasn't raised a Fifth Amendment privilege against self-incrimination —hours of questions first. It's exhaustive and exhausting for all parties involved.

In the civil trial brought by the government against Bill Stephenson, I was deposed for over 18 hours—first by the government, and then by Gerard for Stephenson, and then by the attorneys for Stephenson's clients, who were also being sued by the government, and being prosecuted in criminal proceedings as well. The depositions were spread out over several weeks, and many of the questions were repetitive. How was I instructed to do research? Were these the emails from Bill to me with my instructions? What verbal instructions did I receive? Did I look at the finished reports? Did I ever meet with the clients? With the clients' investors? Most of the questions were accompanied by documents to review and authenticate, which takes a long series of questions, and to which all the defense counsel objected.

Gerard had raised one question multiple times, in multiple ways. When did I know Bill Stephenson wasn't providing the full research to the clients or their investors? The clients' defense counsel would seize on this as proof that Stephenson, of his own initiative, didn't notify his clients that there were problems with the investments—and thus the clients were blameless. Stephenson had his own documentation showing the clients' decisions about what to include in reports, however, and that argument went nowhere.

But Gerard had persisted, asking me again in trial as if he didn't believe the answer I'd given in deposition: I realized Bill was knowingly editing my reports, and once I confirmed he knew what he was doing and had conspired with his clients to leave out negative information before investors saw it, I blew the whistle and told the federal and state agencies.

It wasn't a lie. Exactly.

All along, Gerard had insinuated that I was in love with Bill Stephenson. I wasn't. Oh, don't get me wrong: Bill was—and is—a vibrant and attractive older man. He's always impeccably dressed and his manners are courtly and just this side of flirtatious. But just because the snake is pretty doesn't mean it's not also poisonous. I didn't realize it at first. I was mesmerized and flattered and in way over my head, and I realized it and got out, reporting Bill along the way.

If I didn't report him the moment I suspected, if I didn't rush out to accuse a man of career-ending illegal conduct, if I waited until I was sure, that's something I have to live with. I never lied.

And now I looked right back in Gerard's eyes, my heart pounding.

"What's *your* tell, Gerard?"

He looked at me, that right eyebrow slightly raised, and then slowly smiled. "Anyone else would ask me what their own tell was, Benedict." He swirled the last bit of coffee in his mug and picked up his crumb-strewn plate. "I need more coffee. Need anything?"

I shook my head and then watched him sweet talk the young woman at the counter into another cup and four more cinnamon knots.

While he devoured his second round of pastries, I finished telling him about the Shepherd's interview. He sat back and stretched, the surest sign of a man with a full stomach.

"So what's your theory, Benedict? This Shepherd was so angry that our victim was going back to the cult he lost control and killed her?" He shook his head. "You've taken the prevailing theory about grandson and just substituted The Shepherd for him. That doesn't create reasonable doubt; it's just another, less plausible theory." He took a long sip of his coffee.

"But the Shepherd doesn't have an alibi, and his personality is much more emotional than Todd's."

Gerard looked skeptical. "He sounds like a salesman, but is he that invested in what the people in this support group do?" He considered for a moment, then shook his head again. "Sorry, Benedict. It just doesn't seem to work for me, but maybe there's something else we don't know."

I felt frustrated. There wasn't enough data gathered yet, and I wasn't really comfortable trying to come up with possible answers. "I still want to talk to a few more people."

Gerard crossed his arms over his chest. "Okay. We've been able to get grandson his meds, and we should try to get a better statement. Saturdays are busy days at the county jails because of all the visiting relatives, but the attorney interview rooms are usually free." He stood, and—to my surprise—took our plates and mugs to the busser station, then came back and picked up his coat, wrapping his dark gray scarf around his neck. "Got any weekend plans, Benedict?"

CHAPTER ELEVEN

I agreed to meet Gerard at the Collin county jail facility in Princeton on Saturday morning. There was no way I was doing the drive with him this time. He'd told me I'd be doing the interview, and I wanted to think about the questions while I drove. I'd spent the evening before making some notes for questions using his divided sheet method, and I'd record Todd's answers along with notes about his physical actions or characteristics while answering the questions. I still wasn't sure about how well this would work, but maybe it would help me know where to go in the follow-up questions.

It was still raining, but the drive to Princeton only took about 45 minutes this time. Gerard's Range Rover was parked in the lot with the engine running when I got there. Unlike last time, the lot was full, and it took me a few minutes to stalk a family leaving in a 1990s Buick to get a space. I'd forgotten my umbrella, so I pulled up the hood on my black jacket and ran for the entrance. Gerard met me just inside the doors. The sign-in process took a lot less time since my palmprint was already in the system, and we were down in the attorney interview room before Todd arrived.

Gerard was pacing the tiny room when the guard brought Todd in and cuffed his leg to the chair. I stood to one side, but Gerard seemed to recognize a need for us to be calm and seated, so he pulled a chair up to the table and sat down. I sat across from Todd.

He was still pale and a bit shaky, but he seemed more present today. I reintroduced us, and he first shook my hand, then Gerard's. We had some paperwork to sign, so we got that out of the way first, and then Todd spoke up.

"I'm sorry about last time. I remember you being here, but I don't really remember what we talked about." His voice shook a little, and I wondered if this was his normal state. If so, he'd make a terrible witness on the stand. Overall, he was an average-looking young guy with light brown hair and those pale blue Parrish eyes, his skin tanned dark from working outside. He seemed cleaner and more put together today, but there was still an aura of fear that surrounded him.

"It's fine, Todd." I tried to make my voice calm and low, advice from one of my books on interviewing. "We just asked you a few questions, but I can ask them again." I pulled my notes closer and started with an easy question I hoped would ease him into the others. "How did you and Carrie meet?"

He breathed in sharply through his nose and looked down at his hands. The nails were clean and cut short, but years of landscape work had left the round nails circled with stains from soil and chemicals. "I went to work for a landscape company up here in Princeton about four years ago. Carrie was their office manager." He smiled wanly. "She really ran the place. She's so smart." His voice faltered on the last word. "She *was* so smart." He paused, his light blue eyes blinking rapidly.

I didn't want him to lose focus in grief. "Did you and she get along right away?"

He laughed shortly, his face brightening a bit at the memory.

"Not at all. The first time she talked to me was when she was yelling at me for getting paperwork in late. I was a crew chief, and I was supposed to put in a daily report with the names of the workers that showed up and their hours, and then tie those to the projects we worked on that day." He grimaced. "I love plants and trees, but I suck at paperwork—I always have."

He sat back in his chair, looking at the dingy acoustic tiles on the ceiling. "She took a breath to yell some more, and I slid in a dinner invite." He smiled at the memory. "I think it shocked her so much she didn't know what to say, but she stopped yelling." He laughed a little. "And said no."

I heard Gerard laugh, and I smiled, enjoying the joy on Todd's face. "She didn't like you?"

Todd shook his head and looked down at his hands again. "She told me later she thought I was cute that day. I don't know how—I was probably covered in dirt and who knows what else." He picked at the stained skin at the edge of his thumbnail. "Landscape work isn't the cleanest job out there." He looked up at me. "See, I was 'world-ly'—that's the word they use—'worldly'—and she couldn't go out with me."

"Who is 'they'?"

"The JW—Jehovah's Witnesses. Carrie's family is deep into it, and she was still living at home with her parents when we met." He looked at me and then Gerard. "Do her parents know?"

I nodded. "I talked to her mother a few days ago. She's pretty upset."

Todd's eyes narrowed, and he barked a harsh laugh. "You know she didn't speak to Carrie after Carrie moved to Dallas? Not once." He shook his head again, his eyes filling with tears. "It hurt her more than she let on."

"Did her family object to you so much?"

He nodded. "Her father is an elder, and that seemed to make it worse. It didn't help that she wanted to leave anyway."

This was new. I made a note to come back to that. "I presume she eventually said yes. So what happened then?"

"She didn't say yes until after she'd moved out of their house." He cleared his throat. "Could I have some water?"

Gerard got up and spoke to the guard outside the door.

"Was this when she moved to Dallas?"

He shook his head. "First, she moved in with a friend of hers. She was really just sleeping in a bed in someone else's room while she figured out what to do." Gerard put the water bottle in front of him, and he twisted it open and took a quick sip before continuing. "We went out a few times, but we met over in McKinney or Plano. I hated sneaking around, but I could tell she was the one—you know, *the one* —and I knew she was worth it."

He yawned. "I'm sorry. I have to take my meds on their schedule here, and I had some this morning. I'm getting a little sleepy." He took another sip of water and rubbed his eyes.

I scanned my notes, skipping over some more background questions, trying to decide what was important and how to ease him into what happened the night she was killed. I asked him what happened when Carrie left the Jehovah's Witnesses.

"She'd been living with her friend for a few months when she told her parents. She'd been questioning things for a long time, and the whole argument about seeing me just pushed it all over the edge." He crossed his arms over his chest in an unconscious self-hug. "I loved her. I knew it, and I'd told her. She didn't say it back, but she felt it." He stopped talking for a moment.

"What happened then?" I asked quietly.

He lifted his eyebrows and laughed sharply. "We both got fired." I looked up from my notes in surprise, and he caught my look and laughed again, this time more in amusement, and relaxed his arms. "Yeah, I know. When she left, she got fired, and so did I. The owner of the company we worked for is an elder in the JW. When everything happened, he told us we couldn't work for him anymore." He leaned forward and put his elbows on the table. "They were so sure we were sleeping together. We weren't, not then. But they blamed me for Carrie's leaving." He looked off to the door where the guard watched through a glass panel. "I wish it had been because of us—but it wasn't. She'd come to believe that the JW wasn't what they said it was. She didn't believe it was the Truth anymore."

"So she left the church?"

Todd frowned, an odd reflection of the Shepherd. "It's not a church. Carrie always says it's an organization, like a business." He sighed, and then stifled a yawn again, apologizing under his breath. "She wanted them to know she was leaving. Some people just stop going to Kingdom Hall—they 'fade away.'" He made air quotes around the phrase, and I made a note. "Carrie thought it was important that they understand why she was leaving, but her father had just been made a circuit overseer, and she didn't want to get him in trouble." I wrote 'circuit overseer' in my notes, trying to remember where I'd heard the phrase before. "So she did that instead—she just stopped going to Kingdom Hall or out in service or anything. She just faded away, she said."

"When was this?"

"A little over two years ago. Right before she moved to Dallas. She got in touch with Adam about that time, and he helped her find a place to stay and a job." He yawned hugely, unable to stifle it. "I'm sorry. This is so rude, but I think I'm about done."

I felt Gerard move behind me, and I decided to get to the important stuff. "Just a few more questions, Todd. Do you remember the night Carrie died?"

He nodded, looking down. "Yeah. I'll never forget it." He took another deep breath, and I recognized the breathing as a tool to decrease anxiety. He stared at the table. "The last time we talked, we argued."

"What did you argue about?"

Todd looked up at me, and I could see the misery in his eyes. "She was going back to the JW. I was trying to talk her out of it."

"Were you angry with her?" I noted down his answers as fast as I could, trying to note his expressions on the other side of the page.

He gripped the table edge. "Of course I was!" He started to rise and the shackles on his ankles rattled. The guard opened the door and looked warningly at him. Todd nodded at him, and then sat back down and spoke a bit more quietly after the guard shut the door. "Of course I was. The last two years have been the happiest of my life. For her to go back to that cult—to leave me—I couldn't stand it." He choked out the words, tears starting to spill over.

"Would you have joined with her?"

My question seemed to startle him out of his grief. "Joined? The JW?" He shook his head. "After hearing about it for three years, living that pain with her?" The air seemed to go out of him. "No, I couldn't join with her."

I leaned forward, willing him to make eye contact. "Todd, what happened when you were fighting?"

He looked up at me. "What do you think happened? We argued, we yelled at each other, we cried." He clenched his hands together on the table, staring at me. "I know what you're getting at. I didn't kill her. I didn't want her to go back, but I didn't kill her."

"So she was alive when you left her?"

His hands twisted until the knuckles whitened. Todd looked at them and pressed his lips together for a moment as tears streamed down his face. "Of course she was."

———

THE RAIN HAD STOPPED WHEN WE CAME OUT OF THE JAIL facility, and we stood in the weak sunlight for a minute.

"He's lying, isn't he?" I asked Gerard.

He lifted and moved his hand in a 'maybe/maybe not' motion. "Toward the end, he was being evasive. Did you note his actions?"

I raised my legal pad. "Yeah, for all the good it will be."

"You never know, Benedict. It might be helpful."

He kicked my rear passenger tire, hands in his jacket pocket. "Who do you interview next?"

I thought for a moment. "Garrison invited me to the memorial the support group is having tomorrow night. They'd wanted it to be outside, but the forecast is for more rain." We both looked skyward. "I'm hoping they'll all be willing to talk with me."

"Good, good. Keep looking for another suspect." He still seemed agitated, even though we weren't inside anymore. He rocked on the balls of his feet as he looked at the barren branches of a tree next to the parking lot. He was casually dressed today in jeans and a cream colored turtleneck under a navy peacoat, and I thought he looked a little like a sailor in from a long sea voyage. *Ahoy, matey.*

Enough of this. "Well, I'd better get back. I'm going to stop in Plano to see my dad before going back to Dallas." I had an urge to hum Barry Manilow's *Mandy* now, and when I hum or sing, I should always be alone.

"Got a hot Saturday night date, Benedict?"

I frowned. "Maybe. What's it to you, Gerard?"

He smiled, his eyebrows lifting slightly in that way he had, making me feel foolish for my defensiveness. "Be safe, Benedict."

———

I HUMMED THAT STUPID SONG THE REST OF THE DAY. AT ONE point, my dad heard it and picked up the humming. If there's anyone in the world who is worse at carrying a tune than me, it's my dad. We had a few great minutes of trying to remember the words to the song. At this point, going further back in his memory is actually better, and he remembered more than I did. Sitting with him and laughing over our attempts to imitate Barry Manilow made me wonder if we were overreacting to his current situation. I left still humming and made it home before evening fell.

All in all, it wasn't a bad day.

My 'date' for the evening was a twosome: my landladies, the

Shelton sisters. About once a month, they took pity on my single state and invited me over for dinner. Occasionally, they also invited some poor man they'd discovered in their social world, and he'd show up, like a dapper and fragrant lamb to the slaughter, only to find he had a blind date who came in through the connecting door in the laundry room, a ready-made but uninformed escort for the evening. They promised no date tonight, so I didn't bother to change clothes before letting myself in with a quick knock and loud greeting. I'd once barged in on Sallie entertaining a gentlemen friend in the kitchen in a state of partial undress, and have announced myself loudly ever since.

Hattie is the best cook I've ever met. Sallie says she should have become a chef when she was younger, pointedly mentioning Julia Child and all the female chefs that came up through the ranks in the 1960s and 1970s, but Hattie was wife to a professor who became a college dean, and she used her skills to entertain for him. I wonder sometimes if she regrets her choices, but if she does, she never says.

I checked the kitchen first, and Hattie was at the stove, using tongs to lift a steamer basket filled with tiny round potatoes. "What's for dinner?" I asked, giving her a side hug when she'd set down her burden. She's a tall, spare woman, tanned and lithe. She reminds me of actresses in the 1930s who wore men's clothes as they smoked cigarettes and drank bourbon, and played golf and tennis with handsome men.

"Evening, dearie." She patted my shoulder with a mittened hand. "*Coq au vin.*"

I squinted and translated. "Chicken in wine?"

"*French* chicken in wine," Sallie trilled as she swept into the kitchen to give me an exuberant hug. She's at least six inches shorter than Hattie, a 1970s-something 'It Girl' with swinging silver hair and the style of a model without the svelte figure.

I hazarded a guess. "Julia Child?"

Sallie patted my arm. "You're such a smart girl. I think Hattie has all of dear Julia's recipes memorized."

Hattie simply lifted an eyebrow and transferred chicken thighs to a platter.

"Wait." I goggled. "When you say 'dear Julia'...did you know her?"

Sallie laughed. "Of course we did, my dear. I had a house in Montecito when Julia moved there in...when was it, Hattie?"

Hattie paused to think. "I came to stay with you after George died in 2001. She was there then."

Sallie was bored with the subject by then, and she flapped a hand as she leaned in to sniff the platter Hattie was loading. "So sometime before that. Hat, that smells wonderful."

I leaned in too and inhaled deeply. There were so many benefits to living in the Shelton house, but truly, this was my favorite.

Hattie smiled a little. "You two should have been here when I flamed the pan a couple of hours ago." She smoothed a finger over one of her perfectly-arched eyebrows. "I may have lost some eyelashes."

We each carried a platter in to the dining room, where Hattie had laid a table for (I was relieved to confirm) three with beautiful china, silver, and crystal. When the Shelton sisters combined households, they told me, they decided which of their several sets they'd keep, and kept only the ones that 'gave them pleasure to see on the table.' Even their everyday dishes are lovely—they have one set they use that is more delicate and thin, with scalloped edges painted with flowers, and another that is thick, vibrantly colored pottery. Once, when washing up after dinner, I mentioned that I assumed the floral dishes were much more valuable than the thick pottery, and almost dropped a plate when Sallie pointed out that the pottery set was hand-fired in Italy, and one piece was far more valuable than the entire beautiful but mass-produced china set.

Tonight, Hattie served dinner in elegant shallow Delftware bowls, and lovely etched crystal glasses held a red wine she told me was the same Beaujolais used in the *coq au vin*. We had a crisp green salad after the main course (in what Sallie told me was the French fashion), and a tiny smidgen of a cheese course. By the time Hattie brought out small dishes of pastry and coffee, I'd warned her I could eat no more.

I was wrong. The pastry was a simple deconstructed pear tart, a tiny piece of crust on bottom, several thin slices of pear poached in wine, and a drizzle of caramel gracing the top. It was light and flavorful and soothing, the perfect final touch to a perfect meal, and Sallie and I both applauded as we finished.

During the meal, the discussion was light and amusing—the ladies had worked long and hard to instill in me the art of small talk and casual conversation. When we had pushed the remains of our meal to one side to enjoy coffee, Sallie pounced.

"Tell me about the man in the Range Rover." Her tone was deceptively light.

I looked at Hattie. "I'm surprised she waited this long."

Hattie took a sip of coffee. "I made her promise she'd wait until dessert was done." She looked pointedly at the bite of pastry still in my dish. "You could torment her if you wanted."

Sallie laughed. "I can wait."

I pushed the dish a bit further away. "You don't have to. He's just an attorney I'm working with on a case." The sisters looked at each other. "What?"

Sallie leaned over and patted my hand. "You just don't mention other lawyers much, dear."

I took a deep breath. "I don't work with many. This guy is a criminal law specialist, and I'm really just doing some legwork for him." I briefly told them about the Parrishes, and Carrie Ames. When I mentioned the Jehovah's Witnesses, Hattie frowned and turned to her sister.

"Sal, do you remember Ed and Sally Navarro?"

Sallie tilted her head and focused on her sister. "Boston?"

Hattie nodded and turned to me. "What do you know about 1975 and that group?"

I started to shake my head and then remembered. "The end of the world?"

Hattie nodded. "George and I were living in Boston at the time while he finished his dissertation. We'd only been married a couple of years. Sallie and her second husband, Ken, were in New York—Upper East side, right, Sal?" Sallie nodded.

"There was this couple living in the apartment next to us. They'd joined the Jehovah's Witnesses a few years before, and had been convinced—their whole group there in Boston was convinced—that the world was ending in the fall of 1975." Hattie shook her head and took another sip of her coffee. "They'd sold their house, quit their jobs —and he had a pretty good job at the College—and they moved in with some other people in the church to preach to the rest of us and wait for the end."

"I'd come to stay with Hattie for a while," Sallie broke in. She looked down, and Hattie reached over to hold her hand. "It was just after Haley died."

"Ah." I didn't know what to say—Sallie and her husband's baby daughter had died suddenly, but I didn't know anything about the circumstances.

"I remember Sally well because we had the same name," Sallie clarified, "just different spelling." She gave Hattie's hand a last squeeze and then poured herself and Hattie more coffee. "Such a shame."

I stayed quiet and waited for Hattie to continue after helping herself to cream. "They'd sold their home at a steep discount—remember, this was the depths of the 1970s and a very bad time here in the States." She took a sip and added a bit more cream. "Ed worked as a supervisor in the cafeteria at the College, and he quit his job to preach to the rest of us and wait to be taken up in some kind of rapture or something. He lost his pension and benefits, and they worked knocking on doors instead. They moved into the apartment next to us that winter after it all fell apart. Sally cried constantly." She looked at her sister. "The other Sally, not you." She shook her head. "Ed still hadn't found a job in May when George graduated and we moved away."

"I read something about them setting dates for Armageddon, but not specifics." My coffee was cold, but I sipped a little, hoping they'd continue talking.

Sallie said quietly, "I cried constantly too. We bonded over our losses." She lifted her cup to her lips and then lowered it. "I remember her talking about giving up her family by going in, and giving up all their friends by coming out." She shook her head, remembering. "So sad. I was lucky to have Hat then."

I watched them smile at each other, feeling a little envious. Ryan and I were close, but not like this.

Sallie smiled at me, her mood shifting and her warm brown eyes dancing. "This is all very *Columbo*! What's next in the investigation?"

I sent her a mock frown and picked up the last bite of pear tart, licking the caramel off my fingers. "I am no Columbo, lady. Wasn't he the rumpled guy who could make anyone talk?" I shook my head. "If only I could do that." I stacked my cup and saucer on my now-empty dessert plate. "I'm meeting Carrie's support group tomorrow afternoon, so maybe I can practice working on people mired in grief."

Hattie chucked quietly. "Are you still reading that book on establishing rapport in sales?"

"Yes." I adjusted the handle of the coffee cup to line up with the flowers on the saucer, and sighed. "It's not working too well. Gerard suggested that I take notes on people's expressions as they tell me things to better see when they're nervous or uneasy. That doesn't help me get them to talk to me, but at least when they do, I may be able to tell when they're lying."

"Are you going to one of their services at their—what do they call it—Kingdom Hall?"

I looked at her, startled. "I—I wouldn't know what to do. You know I'm not a very religious person."

Hattie shrugged. "You don't have to be religious to just go and see what happens, do you?" She waited, watching me. "It might show you something about this girl and her family. Aren't you looking for suspects?"

I sat still for a moment, thinking. Would everyone there be able to tell that I didn't belong? What would I do? What would I wear?

Sallie leaned in, clearly bored by this line of conversation. "So, this Gerard. Is he handsome? Single? Sexy?"

I stood up. "Yes, I don't know, and no comment." They laughed, and I hid my blushes by reaching to stack dishes. "Time to work for my supper."

————

I FINISHED WASHING THE DISHES AND WIPED DOWN THE counters while Hattie dried each dish and put them away in zippered bags. We could hear Sallie in the dining room polishing the clean silverware before putting it away in the little velvet bags, humming some song as she went. I'm pretty sure it was hip hop.

"Lacey, you know, rapport is really all about making sure that the person you're talking to believes you care about what they say." Hattie lifted the platter from the rack and began to dry it with quick efficient motions.

"Yes, I read that in the stupid book, but I'm not sure how you do that." I lifted the iron grillwork over the gas burner and cleaned around the igniter. "It seems so easy for everyone else."

She snapped the lid on the plastic container where she'd stored the rest of the leftover chicken and handed the container to me. "Next time, watch Sallie when she's talking with you. I swear, she hangs on the words of everyone she meets."

I laughed. She was right. A quick trip to the grocery store always stretched long with Sallie—she'd stop to talk to the butcher, the produce man, the cashier—and they laughed and told her about their lives. Like Gerard, Sallie had the gift of charm, and it never seemed fake or insincere.

"She wasn't always that way. After Haley died, I think she let herself be numb for a while." Hattie spread the wet cloth over the oven door handle to dry, then looked at me. "Coming to Boston to stay with me and George was her answer to despair, and it got her in a small neighborhood where everyone talked to everyone else." From the dining room, we could hear Sallie singing another hip-hop song that was currently famous.

"Was that why you went to California?" After years of playing a society hostess and masking her emotions, it was rare for Hattie to be so open. I watched the play of memories across her face, the deep brown eyes reflecting for a moment a pain long held and deeply felt.

"No. In my case, it was a fear that my naked relief would shock the neighbors." She kissed my cheek and turned off the kitchen light, leaving me in the semi-darkness. "Good night, dear."

CHAPTER TWELVE

When I was seven, my father organized a summer vacation through Texas. Rather than go to Six Flags or another theme park (which I would have preferred) or NASA space camp (which my nine-year-old brother would have preferred), we traveled to battle-grounds and memorials in south and east Texas, which no one but my father preferred. It was July in Texas, which means—depending upon which sub-climate of Texas you're visiting—the weather is hot and humid, hot and windy, or simply unutterably hot. For two weeks, while our Ford station wagon lurched from the Alamo or other free historical monuments to abandoned forts from the now-politically incorrect Indian Wars, my father kept up a running list of who died where or what battle or what massacre the windswept spot was known for. At night, all three of us would share a single room in small-town motels after dinner in the local Tex-Mex joint or Dairy Queen.

It was the summer after my mother walked out on us. I know now that she'd been depressed and unhappy for some time. That year, as the 1990s oil crisis ramped up, my father worked 60-hour weeks as a petroleum engineer and was rarely home even on the weekends, and she finally broke. After she left, he seemed to become our entire world, and perhaps he was. I was old enough to miss our mother, but young enough to be relieved that the tumult of her depression and the fights with my father were gone. My brother took her leaving particularly hard. He blamed our father for driving her away, and all this was complicated by our situation when we all had to move in with our grandmother on her farm. We were left with a grandmother we barely knew when he headed back to the oilfields of west Texas.

That vacation summer, though, the relief of my mother's absence faded, and it became clear that we were broken. My brother's anger bubbled beneath the surface and became a tangible thing in the blue vinyl confines of our white Ford station wagon. Our father was frustrated and unused to the role of disciplinarian, and, as a result, Ryan acted out at every opportunity on the trip. At the historical marker describing the Battle of Gonzales at the Guadalupe River, he pushed over a small monument, and we were escorted out of the Alamo by the Texas Ranger who guards the door when Ryan laughed maniacally in the sacred shrine. When we stopped at a graveyard in some east Texas county to find the grave of a distant great-great uncle to make a rubbing of the headstone for my grandmother, the simmering tension boiled over, and I remember getting out of the car while my father yelled at my sullen and silent brother.

The roads in truly old cemeteries in Texas are really just sandy lanes alongside tall cedar trees that give no shade, and my feet in their plastic jelly sandals sank into the sand on the side of the road. I'd left the car door open, and I could hear my father's frustrated voice as I walked away, at least until the cicadas started their squealing again. I could see an angel a bit taller than me a few graves away, so I headed for her. In between were large squares where several flat, weed-covered graves were marked with weathered and chipped stones, begging God (or someone) to allow people to rest in peace, or, more often, in the arms of Jesus. I walked carefully along a concrete border, my arms out for balance, careful not to step on a grave, humming 'Jesus Loves Me This I Know' to myself. It was the only song about Jesus I knew, but singing it, I felt a connection to him and those people sleeping in his arms. I whirled in circles next to the grave-stones, the angels and stone babies shimmering in the heat, until my father realized I was gone and retrieved me. Later, in a tiny motel room outside Mexia, I woke crying from a nightmare where the bearded white man from my vacation bible school lessons chased me and threatened naps.

Until my mother died when I was 15, that was the last time I was in a cemetery. My mother's family insisted on a full graveside service, where everyone speculated in whispers about her suicide. It was a sunny spring day—in April, I think—and my father, who had never filed for divorce or legal separation, was blamed for her mental illness and was not invited to attend. My brother and I were dressed in stiff new clothes and shuttled to the cemetery and back home by my mother's sister, and neither of us spoke a word in the car or at the service. One of the mourners commented on how much our hair looked like our dead mother's, which was just the catalyst needed for Ryan to begin his hair color experiments. We took off the new clothes when we returned home that night, and—without any discussion between us—Ryan took both outfits out to the trash barrel and burned them.

———

CARRIE'S MEMORIAL SERVICE WAS NOTHING LIKE MY MOM'S HAD been. In defiance of the gray weather outside, Ann Thornton's house was lit with lamps and candles and a fire burned in a tiny fireplace in the living room. The small 1930s Tudor house had been remodeled and the wall between the kitchen and dining room removed, allowing the forty or so people to mingle and move about. The rooms were decorated in whites, creams, and tans, and the furniture was sparse. The art, however, was spectacular. A five-foot tall canvas on one living room wall was vibrant with reds of all shades and hues in a swirling mass that cried out for attention against the neutrals decorating the rest of the room. I wanted to go over and look, but there was a crowd around it, and I didn't want to talk to anyone else just yet. The dining table was crowded with dishes heaped with chips and dips, sliced meats and cheese, and cookies and cupcakes, and I moved some to the side as I added the plate of Café au Lait's finest snickerdoodle cookies that I'd brought. Instead of whispers, people spoke about Carrie with laughter and told stories of her life to people they didn't know.

Both Naomi Jackson and Adam Garrison had invited me, but I still felt awkward when I came in. The woman I assumed was Ann Thornton met me at the door, taking my coat and inviting me in. She was a tall woman—at least 5'10"—and very thin, with straight blond hair chopped bluntly at jaw length, a large Roman nose, and light blue eyes. She didn't wear makeup or jewelry, and even I thought she could use some color. Rather than sad or unhappy, her pale face looked peaceful.

I spotted Naomi sitting on the couch in the living room, her dark auburn hair spiked and feathered around her face. She was surrounded by other young men and women, and, when she laughed at something one of them said, she saw me and waved. I finger-waved back, but headed into the crowd in the dining room. Garrison had promised to introduce me to the other ex-JWs in Carrie's support group, and I wanted to make sure I looked like any other person there to celebrate Carrie Ames's life. If that included loading a plate with deviled eggs, French onion dip, and carrot sticks, so be it.

Adam Garrison was holding court just inside the kitchen. The cabinets had been freshly painted a bright red and the original checkerboard floor was painfully clean, but the counters were crowded with wine bottles, glasses and cups, and iced beer in small plastic tubs.

Garrison paused and lifted a beer bottle in my direction when he saw me, and I waved back with a fork loaded with half a deviled egg.

He exchanged a few more words with his audience before breaking away to come over to me. A few women glanced in my direction as he came toward me, and I saw him through their eyes for a moment: a handsome man in snug jeans and leather jacket, with a strong, intense face and charisma to burn. Was I the only one who saw how calculated it was, how rehearsed? I set down my plate to shake his hand.

"Lacey," he said and reached to give me—oh, wait—a hug. I awkwardly patted his back as he hugged me, and over his shoulder I saw several women giving me the eye. I'm uncomfortable being the center of attention at the best of times, and I'd really wanted to fade into the background at this gathering. As soon as I could, I stepped back out of his embrace.

"Glad you could come. Did you meet Ann?"

"She let me in." An awkward silence fell as we both looked over at the tall, pale woman, and I waited to see if he'd fill it.

He did.

"I'll introduce you to a few people in a bit." He looked around as he talked to me, that odd habit making me feel that he was looking for someone more important to impress. "I'm going to say a few words to get people started, and then a couple of the ex-JWs have said they'd speak with you."

Before I could reply, Garrison left me to go stand by the fireplace. He paused there, and someone tapped a fork against a glass to get everyone's attention. As I watched, a persona settled on Garrison's shoulders as surely as if someone had draped a cape over them. He smiled—a professional speaker's smile—and looked around to make sure he had everyone's attention.

I eased back across the entry hall toward the dining room doorway, where I had a view of almost everyone gathered around in the living room, and I watched as people listened to the man they called The Shepherd.

"Hey, everyone," he began. "For those of you I don't know yet, I'm Adam Garrison. I was a friend of Carrie's, as I'm sure we all were." He gestured with the beer bottle around to everyone, and I realized it was going to act as a prop. "I appreciate you all coming, and I know we all appreciate Ann Thornton for hosting." He led a little golf clap, and Ann dipped her head slightly in acknowledgment before she too faded back out of the limelight. "Thanks to everyone who brought food tonight, and whoever brought this great beer is my new best friend." A few people laughed, and someone shouted "Amen!"

Garrison laughed along with everyone, and then his face stilled and saddened so suddenly it had to be artificial. I looked around, but no one else seemed to have noticed. Most of the people were nodding in agreement. "We're here tonight because we lost Carrie, and this is our way of saying goodbye."

From Garrison's right, a young man with a heavy beard and striking blue eyes muttered audibly: "She was taken from us."

Garrison gave a short, annoyed glance at the man. "Yes, David, she was taken, but that's not something for tonight." He looked back at the group, but I kept my eye on the young man, who glared at Garrison for a minute before looking away and swigging his own, more-empty bottle of beer. "Well, I won't mention the resurrection, but I will say that if anyone deserves paradise, it was Carrie." Several people laughed shortly or nodded, but the rest of us looked as if we'd been left out of a joke.

Garrison continued to talk about Carrie, sounding much as he had the other night, and I looked around at the listening crowd. Several people sitting or standing around Naomi looked uncomfortable or even slightly bored. Ann Thornton watched him with no expression before starting to move around the room to pick up empty glasses or plates. Several young women looked cow-eyed, as my grandmother would have said, following his every move and laughing at every joke, funny or not. An older couple sitting next to each other on the love seat held hands, and I saw the woman wipe a tear away. The young man Garrison had called David didn't look at him at all, but a slightly older man standing behind David watched Garrison avidly. I couldn't tell if he approved of the speech or not.

Garrison wrapped up, and introduced a Dr. Steve Peterson, who had apparently been Carrie's boss at the urgent care center. He looked a bit embarrassed to be called on to speak, but he spoke for a moment to Carrie's kindness to their disabled and poor clients, and how proud he had been of her ability to quickly process new information in her training. Several of the people around Naomi nodded while he spoke, and some teared up as he ended simply: "We'll miss her."

Other people spoke up in turn then, talking about Carrie and her simple gestures of thoughtfulness—cards when they weren't feeling well, cupcakes for the new family in her apartment building, groceries for the older couple when they both caught the flu the same week. They described a life that was small and simple, but full in its breadth.

"It makes me feel warm and ashamed at the same time," Ann Thornton said from my side. I glanced up at her. "You know, like I've not been living right."

I nodded. "It's a nice eulogy, though." I thought of my mother's funeral, where a clergyman who didn't know her recited bare facts about her life and read Bible passages I didn't recognize. "I guess everyone who's here knew her well." *Except me.*

Ann looked over the crowd, and then picked up a glass and plate from a small table near the doorway. "Adam says you'd like to talk to me. I'm not sure how I can help you."

I picked up a couple of paper plates and followed her to the kitchen. "I'm just trying to understand Carrie and her life."

Ann began to load dishes into the dishwasher, and I noted with some concern that she didn't rinse the dishes off first. I didn't have a dishwasher myself, but I was pretty sure you were supposed to wash them before you washed them—at least that's what Sara did. But Ann loaded them in dirty. Rather than make a point of it, I started gathering trash from the counters and mashing it down into the lined trash can.

"That empathy they're describing—it's the best evidence that she'd left the Jehovah's Witnesses behind." Ann didn't look at me as she spoke.

I washed my hands and dried them before responding. "I don't know what you mean." I leaned against the counter and watched her.

"We're not trained to be empathetic—well, not of the world." She finished loading the top rack and began to load small plates. "You're supposed to spread God's message, but you can't feel too much for people who are going to burn in Armageddon." She rolled the rack into the dishwasher and loaded the soap dispenser with a small soap pod, then shut the door and started the machine. I moved aside so she could wash her hands. "It bleeds into how you deal with people. She was kind and gentle. Loving, I guess you'd say." She dried her hands on a towel, then folded it several times, her eyes on her hands. "That's unusual for a JW."

"Could I buy you coffee this week? I can do either during the day or the evening, your choice."

Her eyes met mine and she paused for a few seconds before turning to wring out a cloth and begin to wipe down the counter next to the sink. She spoke without looking at me, her voice tight. "Did Todd kill her?"

I looked steadily at the back of her head, wondering if this habit of talking to someone without looking at them was a JW trait. "He says he didn't."

She didn't speak for several moments as she finished wiping down the counter. Then she turned and looked at me, her face calm and composed. "I can meet Tuesday evening."

———

ANN THORNTON AND I COMPARED CALENDARS AND DECIDED TO meet there at her house on Tuesday evening for dinner. The kitchen was starting to get crowded by that time, so I let other people take over the cleanup duties. Naomi found me in front of the vivid red painting. I think it was a painting of a rose from inside the flower, but I couldn't be sure. I wished I could tilt it to one side and look at it from that angle.

"I was wondering..." Naomi began. I turned to her. She looked distinctly uncomfortable. "I don't know how this is supposed to go, but I have Carrie's things." We moved aside as some people stepped up to look at the painting. "I'm breaking the lease and moving out early. I just can't stand to go back there alone."

"I can understand that."

She started putting on her purple coat. "The furniture is almost all mine—she didn't have anything like that when she moved to Dallas. I called Carrie's dad about her clothes and books and family pictures, but there were only a few things he wanted. I was going to meet him Tuesday during my lunch to give him those, but I have a few pictures of her with Todd and some things he gave her." She dug in her purse for some gum. "Is it weird that I think Todd might want them?" She unwrapped a stick of vividly pink gum and put it in her mouth, chewing hard to soften the gum. "I know her family won't want to see that stuff," she said with the gum tucked in her cheek.

"No, it's not weird." I couldn't watch her mangle the gum, so I turned to watch the people cleaning up the living room. "I thought her family didn't want anything to do with her?"

Naomi looked back at me, her jaw working the pink gum. "No, just her mom. She and her dad met for coffee sometimes at a little bookstore not too far from here. And he stayed in touch." She sniffled a little, and I moved back. I'm not really comfortable with grief, and I was afraid she'd start to cry. She pulled a wadded up tissue from her pocket and wiped her nose, tucking the tissue back into the depths of her coat pocket.

I was mystified more than ever by the Ames family, but I had an idea. "If you want, I could hold on to the stuff for Todd. And I'm happy to meet Carrie's dad and give him her things." I rushed the words, hoping she'd agree. I was intrigued by the thought of meeting the man Garrison had described.

She looked relieved. "That'd be great." One of her friends waved at her, and she nodded to them. "We're going out for a drink. Do you want to come?" I refused as politely as possible, and then we agreed to meet on Monday at their apartment so I could gather Carrie's things. Even better—now I'd get to see the scene of the crime.

———

AFTER NAOMI AND THE OTHER PEOPLE FROM CARRIE'S WORK left, the gathering settled into mostly ex-JWs who'd known Carrie. The exception was the elderly couple, who turned out to be the neighbors Carrie had bought groceries for. They lived in the apartment next to Carrie and Naomi, and were also the ones who had heard Carrie and Todd arguing. Their story placed him in Carrie's apartment after the support group members had left, and they were distressed to hear I was Todd's attorney. It was clear they thought him responsible. I didn't push for a meeting since I assumed the police would have taken their statement.

The room had settled into two groups: one that gathered around Garrison, and another that seemed to avoid him. Garrison introduced me to Carl Grassley, the man who had so closely watched Garrison speak. He told me that he and his wife Susan would meet me on Monday afternoon after he finished his deliveries for the office supply store where he worked. We exchanged numbers and agreed to meet at their home in Garland, which turned out to be a few blocks from where Carl worked.

Most of the non-Garrison crowd had said their goodbyes to Ann Thornton, and I started moving towards the door as well. Nothing like a guest that hangs around after their welcome fades—like fish that stays too long in the fridge, my grandmother used to say, they start to smell bad.

I was putting on my coat when the young man Garrison called

David came up to me. "Adam says you want to talk to us." His brown leather jacket was fashionably distressed, and it complimented his dark blond hair and thick beard. He was a slender, good-looking man in his late 20s, and, in a younger, more different life, he'd have been my type.

I felt old and tired. "You know I represent Todd?" David nodded. "Do you mind visiting with me?"

He looked mulish, but he shook his head before taking another swig from the beer he held. I couldn't tell if this was a new one or if he was still nursing the previous one. "If Adam says it's okay, I guess it is." He seemed slightly drunk, and I hoped he had a ride home. "Do you think Todd killed her?" he asked abruptly.

I hid behind my usual answer. "He says he didn't."

David blinked owlishly at me, and I realized he was far more drunk than I'd thought. "Do you have a ride home?" I asked. He gestured with the bottle toward Adam Garrison, and I waited to make eye contact with Garrison, taking my keys from my pocket and jingling them. He nodded.

"If I can have your number, I'll text you tomorrow and we can arrange a time and place." David rattled off a number and I entered it in my phone under "David JW."

"She was my friend, you know," David blurted out, and I could see tears in the corners of his bloodshot eyes. "Carrie. She was my friend." He turned and walked unsteadily back to Garrison and his acolytes. I let myself out.

———————

MY BLUE MOOD FROM CARRIE'S MEMORIAL SERVICE LASTED most of Sunday evening. I went home and turned my phone off to brood and binge on some old episodes of *Friends*. Life seemed so easy in 1990s New York City. You worked a little, you drank a lot of coffee, and you got to split the restaurant check with five other friends. In between, you lived in an apartment with a living room big enough to dwarf my entire place. It was a depressing reminder of where I was, and where I wasn't.

When I turned the phone back on before bed, there was a voice mail from Gerard, asking me to meet him for breakfast the next day at the Lone Star Club before a seminar he was attending. I sent him a text telling him I'd be there and went to bed.

CHAPTER THIRTEEN

There are several private clubs in the upper floors of uptown and downtown Dallas skyscrapers. They offer sumptuous buffet breakfasts and lunches to their members, and they host seminars, meetings, and dinners in their private rooms. As the elevator door opened onto the 25th floor with a whoosh, I thought idly that only the very wealthy can afford quiet elegance like this. The main room of the Lone Star Club was as long as a football field, with windows facing a cold and intensely blue winter sky. From this height, south Dallas and beyond were crystal clear, the traffic below moving briskly along interstates and highways. In the main dining room, suited men and women spoke in low, confidential tones at scattered tables while a row of black-jacketed servers watched from the side, ready to refill coffee cups or water glasses or clear used plates. Heaven forbid anyone should have to talk business while a used plate sullied the white tablecloth.

I'd pulled a navy blue suit out of the back of the closet for this breakfast with Gerard, and my navy heeled pumps sank into the thick carpet. He'd made the invitation casually, as if being invited here was a daily event. Perhaps for him it was. I followed the maître d' to 'Mr. Gerard's table' over by the window, with a clear view of the rest of the city. Gerard was reading a brief, but he stood when I approached, and I noted his tie wasn't yet tucked away. Or was that just a Courthouse Café affectation?

Once I was seated in a chair adjacent to Gerard's, my napkin spread across my lap by the maître d' and my coffee poured into a tiny china cup, Gerard put his brief away. "Good morning, Benedict. Or should I wait for you to have your coffee?"

I smirked at him. "I'm good, Gerard. I've already had one cup, thank you very much." I smoothed the napkin over my lap, hoping I looked as if I belonged in this rarefied atmosphere.

"Randy, I think we'll have the buffet this morning," Gerard said to the hovering waiter.

"Very good, sir," the redoubtable Randy said, and moved on.

I waited until he was far enough away, and then leaned closer to Gerard to whisper. "I didn't know people actually said stuff like that."

Gerard grinned and leaned forward. "Only in places like this," he whispered back.

He stood and then led the way to the buffet spread along the inner wall of the club, multiple connected white-clothed tables with chafing dishes and bowls of berries, juices, and fruit on ice. A chef in a towering toque manned an omelet and waffle station where people —mostly men—gathered and watched him crafting their breakfast. I recognized several of the men waiting there from trials I'd watched, and I pondered a waffle, but didn't want to risk having to talk to anyone. Instead, I loaded a plate down with scrambled eggs with cheese, several strips of bacon, and a golden brown biscuit at least two inches high. I hesitated towards the end, and then added some chunked pineapple and ripe strawberries. This deep in winter, the expensive fruit wasn't something I bought for myself, and I figured it would offset the bacon somewhere in my food karma.

Back at the table, I realized my plate was quite a bit more full than anyone at the other tables. No one stared, though, and Gerard's plate had much the same things as mine in an even larger pile. I hid a smile as he tucked his tie away and, for a few minutes, we just ate. I'll say this for him: He can be a sarcastic bastard sometimes, but the man does like to eat. And it was good: the scrambled eggs were fluffy and the bacon strips were paradoxically thick and crisp, and I slathered real butter on the biscuit. Even so, I felt virtuous as I ate the fruit at the end.

I finally gave up and sat back, pushing my mostly-empty plate toward the middle of the table. A server was there immediately to clear it, and I was a bit embarrassed when he used a little device to scrape my scattered biscuit crumbs, feeling slightly rebuked for leaving a trail. He refilled my coffee cup, though, and I chose to ignore the feeling as I sipped.

"How'd the funeral go yesterday?" Gerard slipped his tie out and rebuttoned his shirt. I noticed the server didn't have to scrape up any crumbs from Gerard's place as he cleared his plate, and I grimaced. Perhaps the wealthy weren't messy like the rest of us.

"Weird. I haven't been to many funerals, but this wasn't really like any I've seen." I pulled out the notes I'd made this morning and dug in my bag for a pen. Gerard watched me for about ten seconds, then sighed and handed me his Mont Blanc. I happily unscrewed the cap and started a new page for today's notes. "I met a few of her friends, and saw Garrison in action again. He's quite the public speaker. He introduced me to a couple of people, and I've got appointments to talk with those closest to her."

I stopped as Gerard held up a finger, then stood to greet a woman approaching. "Julia, good to see you." They shook hands, and then she turned to me with her hand out.

"Julia Lunsford."

"Benedict, Julia is the ADA on the Carrie Ames case. Julia, this is Lacey Benedict—like I said, she's assisting me with this."

"Nice to meet you, Lacey." She shook my hand and took the seat on the other side of Gerard. "I've got some history with Rob—keep an eye on him." She laughed. I looked over to Gerard, who raised his eyebrows at me.

A server appeared at Julia's side and poured her coffee, and, while she and Gerard exchanged pleasantries about the upcoming criminal bench/bar seminar they were both attending, I looked her over. She had long, lustrous brown hair pulled back in a low ponytail with a red-and-navy patterned scarf, and *her* navy suit had a fashionable long jacket and wide-legged trousers. Women like Julia Lunsford and Dr. Amie fascinated me. They wore scarves and belts, and their earrings, necklaces, and bracelets all matched their outfits. I always wondered how full their closets were, and how often did they shop? How did they fit those hours of matching and shopping into already-full schedules? I tugged on an ear lobe and remembered the earrings I'd set out to wear but forgot to put on.

The server brought a tiny silver pitcher of almond milk at Julia's request, and she stirred some into her coffee. "You've stepped into a bad one this time, Rob." Gerard simply raised an eyebrow and waited. "We've gotten the preliminary autopsy results back." She sat back in her chair and sipped her coffee, clearly enjoying drawing out the suspense. "You might want to talk a deal."

"I wasn't aware we were talking deals yet, Julia." Gerard sat back and regarded her, sounding amazingly calm.

"You should be." She set her china cup on the table and smiled at me serenely. Her next words shattered the pleasant tea-and-crumpets atmosphere. "Carrie Ames didn't die because of the head wound. Your boy smothered her."

I was really starting to dislike Julia Lunsford.

"You said the results were preliminary—how preliminary?" Gerard still seemed calm, but my heart was pounding, and the blood was rushing in my ears.

"We know the preliminary cause of death, but we're still waiting on the toxicology and some fiber testing. You know how much slower real life is than the movies." She and Gerard shared a look, and I wondered how much of a history they'd actually shared. She wore an enormous rock on her left ring finger, so I presumed she was married. "The head wound bled a lot, and it looks like it might have been severe enough to make her unconscious." She folded her hands on the table before her. "So her killer decided not to take a chance on her bleeding out from the head wound."

I fidgeted, wanting to ask questions, but Gerard's slight frown in my direction kept me quiet.

"Right now, Todd Parrish is charged with manslaughter, but you know how Angela feels about domestic violence cases, Rob. She'll push for murder charges once everything comes back." She casually sipped her coffee again, and I realized I was watching an expert negotiator.

Gerard beckoned the hovering server over, and he watched in silence as his cup was refilled. I shook my head at the proffered refill. Not until the server had stepped away did Gerard speak. "We've not discussed pleas with our client."

At his use of 'we' and 'our,' Julia glanced at me, and I could see speculation on her face. "Well, I think the final results will be back by the end of the week, maybe next Monday. If we want to have that conversation and try to get a deal in before Angela gets wind of this, it's going to have to be soon."

She pushed her chair back, and Gerard stood along with her. She folded her napkin in thirds as she looked over at me, clearly speculating. "Benedict...Lacey Benedict..." I could see what was coming, so I stood and stuck out my hand.

"Nice to meet you, Julia. Thanks for stopping by."

Forced to shake my hand, she leaned forward, her voice low. "Are you the Benedict that blew the whistle on Bill Stephenson?" I stopped, the blood rushing to my cheeks, as she continued. "And you represented him, Rob?" She looked from me to Gerard and back. "Well. That's interesting." She stepped around the table and patted Gerard's arm before turning back to me and leaning a little closer.

"Good for you, Lacey. Bill Stephenson is a snake." And with that, she walked away.

I FELT DISTINCTLY WARM AS GERARD AND I RESUMED OUR SEATS across from each other. My mind was racing, jumbled thoughts of Carrie Ames and Todd Parrish, mixed with Bill Stephenson and Julia Lunsford. Clearly, she knew Bill. I didn't know what to think. I put that aside.

Gerard made a signing motion in the air, and the server appeared with the check. I started to speak, but Gerard shook his head, so I stopped. "I'll walk you down and then come back up for the seminar," he said tersely as he signed his name on the bill.

I couldn't tell if he was angry because of Julia Lunsford's comments or something else, so I packed up my pad and Gerard's pen and stood. Gerard stepped to my side and waited for me to head out, stopping me at the front desk so I could search for my parking ticket to be validated.

We stepped into the elevator with several other people, so I kept my silence. On the first floor, Gerard motioned me to the glass doors, and we stepped into a small garden with benches and the ever-present smoker's ashcan. At least there was sunshine today. I sat on a bench in the direct light, and lifted my face to the sun. There's nothing quite so uplifting as a bright winter sun.

Gerard paced. Now that the tenseness at the table had passed, I felt a little numb and tired. I hadn't slept well, breakfast had been filling, and this bench seemed pretty inviting. Maybe I'd have a nap.

Gerard finally spoke. "Sorry about that—but every criminal lawyer, DA, and judge in town are either up there or headed up there for this seminar today." He looked up at the bare branches above us. "The last thing I need is for someone to hear us talking about this case."

I felt a bit embarrassed. I didn't realize there was such a need for secrecy. I thought about apologizing, but Gerard kept talking.

"I've got to have a real conversation with Todd. Julia was being a bit dramatic, but she's right. Angela Broward is looking for publicity before running for re-election next year, and a trial with a pretty victim and a guilty boyfriend is just the type of case to do that."

I sat straight up, suddenly feeling chilled. "That's pretty cynical of you. And Todd said he didn't kill her." I tried to stuff my hands in my pockets, but the skirt didn't have any, so I tucked them under my legs to warm them. "I've asked you this before: why should he plead to something he didn't do?"

Gerard crossed his arms. "Benedict, I can't believe you're as old as you are and still this naïve." He smiled, a cynical, one-sided smirk I didn't like at all. "The prisons are full of innocent men—didn't you ever see *The Shawshank Redemption*?"

My heart pounding, my knees shaking, I stood up and faced him. "And what if he didn't? He's not the strongest guy in the world, with his depression and other issues. What if he's pushed into a plea and didn't do it?" I was so frustrated I wanted to scream. "What's wrong with you? Why would you want that?"

"Benedict, it's not what I want." He rubbed a hand over his hair, clearly frustrated—with me? With Todd? With the situation? "Can't you understand that criminal cases move on whether you want them to or not? If we don't make a deal happen, they'll charge him for the greater offense."

"And so we just convince him to take a deal, even if he's not guilty?" I could hear my voice rising over the buzzing in my head, but I couldn't help it. "How is that justice for Carrie Ames?" For ten beats of my heart, we faced each other. Then he turned away and resumed pacing.

"All right, Benedict. If not Todd, who? You've been talking to all these people. Do we have anyone else to toss in the DA's direction?" He turned to face me again. "Julia is right—Angela Broward needs a good, juicy murder to throw to the press."

I sat down, relief making me feel light-headed. "I think the new autopsy results make Todd even less likely." I'd lost all pleasure in the sun on my face, and now the glare was giving me a headache. "And I don't like Julia Lunsford at all." A question I'd wanted to ask nudged at the burgeoning pain in my head.

Gerard stuck his hands in his pants pockets. "Julia?" Distracted, he looked at me, his eyebrows lifted high. "What's wrong with Julia?"

I sniffed. "She seems really full of herself." I knew—I *knew*—that this was small and petty of me, but I really didn't like the whole negotiating process as I saw it.

He looked baffled, as he should, but he saw it for the distraction it was and came back to the important matter at hand. "Why do you think this makes Todd less likely?"

I leaned back and tried to clear my mind. "When it seemed like an accident, perhaps a fall during an argument, maybe that was Todd losing his temper. But smothering an unconscious Carrie?" I shook my head. "I just can't see it. He doesn't seem the type to be that— angry." I looked at him. "Wouldn't something like that require real, intense anger?" I remembered my question. "How long will it be before the autopsy results become public?"

He ran a hand over his hair again, distracted. "They won't release preliminary results, because they'd have to modify the charges against Todd then—and they won't do that in the Collin county court." He checked his watch and straightened his tie. "So I expect we have that week she mentioned. That means—for a week or so anyway—there are only a handful of people who know how she really died— including her killer. As long as we know that, but the killer doesn't know we know that, we have a bit of an advantage." Hands on his hips, he stood for a moment looking down at me, then held out a hand and helped me up. "Go get 'em, tiger."

That I could do.

CHAPTER FOURTEEN

When I graduated from law school, I had already accepted an offer from Bill Stephenson to work at Stephenson & Associates. I took the bar early in February that year, so I had my license by May and was ready to start work in June. After a quick graduation trip to Paris on funds I'd inherited from my grandmother, I terminated my lease on the tiny apartment I'd lived in through law school, and moved into the biggest, fanciest apartment I could afford on what was left of my student loans. I'd been promised a great signing package and a six-figure salary, and I spent the summer loading up a couple of credit cards with furniture, small appliances, and knick-knacks for the apartment on the 18th floor of the Crystal Walls, a high rise complex overlooking downtown Dallas. I decorated that place like a wife hosting her mother-in-law for the holidays, and I was panicky when I didn't have framed artwork on every wall.

Even though I'm no psychologist like Dr. Amie, I knew what I was compensating for. When we moved in with my grandmother after my mother left, my father sold all the furniture we had in our house. My grandmother—a strong, vibrant woman then in her 60s—had a house full of old family furniture, and it was eminently practical to keep things as they were. 'Eminently practical' was her highest compliment, and I worked hard to earn her approval. For 12 years, I shared a room with an antique sewing machine that had traveled in a wagon with my great-great-grandmother and her six siblings from Tennessee and slept on the bed that had been built by my other great-grandmother's great-grandfather when he moved to Texas shortly after it became a state. My brother shared a room with my father until he moved out to go to college at 18, sleeping on the twin beds my grandparents used back in the late 1950s, just like Rob and Laura Petrie.

To an adult, stories of furniture carried by wagon over the Smokies sounds like a quaint family tale. To a child, it's the creepy ingredient of nightmares about all the dead people sleeping in the bed with you. Every year, I'd ask Santa—or eventually, my father—for a new bed. Every year, he and my grandmother would laugh off the request.

Home felt temporary.

In apartment 1802 of the Crystal Walls, I struggled to make the choices of furniture and colors and patterns feel necessary to my life, but they were so new and awkward that I never sat in any of the chairs, never laid down for a nap on the stiff and prickly-textured couch, never really stopped looking at the art on the walls as if I was visiting a museum. The only thing I really loved was the bed, so I spent much of my time there, reading or working or watching television or sleeping.

Four years later, when I moved into the apartment in the back of the Shelton house, I sold most of the purchases I'd made after law school. The apartment had a small navy blue sofa that just fit the living room and matched a stripe in the brocade upholstery on an old rocking chair from my grandmother's house, and my double bed took up three-quarters of the tiny bedroom. Most of the apartment had been the house's breakfast room and sunroom, and French windows overlooking the back garden comprised the entire back wall of the apartment. Another wall had built-in bookshelves where I could shelve my only prized possessions—my books—and having that many windows took care of the need for artwork on another wall. Five years on, I found the remaining blank walls restful. People who came over sometimes thought I'd just moved in.

I guess I didn't need the new things after all.

————

CARL AND SUSAN GRASSLEY PUT A NEW SPIN ON TEMPORARY.

I coasted to a stop in front of their small three-bedroom home on a busy crosstown street in Garland just before 4 pm. Carl had told me he usually got home about that time from his delivery job, and he pulled into the driveway as I got out of my car, careful to space opening my door in between rushes of traffic. This time of year, the Bermuda grass in their front yard was a yellow-brown, but the yard itself was tidy and close-cut for winter.

Susan greeted me at the door carrying a small child on her hip who regarded me with grave serenity. Susan introduced her as Emma, and I shook her tiny hand with care. I'm no expert on children, but Emma looked sickly to me. Her light brown hair was wildly curly, but her skin was a pasty light cocoa, and her pale blue eyes seemed bloodshot. She had her mother's rosebud mouth.

I followed Susan and Emma into the living room, where a tan couch was joined by a faux-leather recliner in a deeper tan. A nondescript brown coffee table and a TV stand with a small television were the only other furniture in the room. A grouping of a few photos was lost in the blankness of a white wall, and were too far away to be seen from the couch where Susan placed me. She dodged into the kitchen for coffee, but Emma perched near me, her little hand pleating and re-pleating the skirt of the embroidered red dress she wore. I've seen other people charm children, but I never know what to say to them, so we sat in a comfortable silence until her mother bustled into the room carrying three mugs of coffee. She handed Emma chocolate milk in a small cup with a lid and handles on both sides, something that seemed really sensible to me. I could have used something like that a time or two, I thought, and I was about to tell her so when Carl came from a hallway on the bedroom end of the house, pulling a sweater down over his uniform pants. His dark brown skin glistened as if he'd splashed water on his face.

"Adam told us you represent Todd, but he didn't really explain what information you're needing." Carl settled into the recliner, and Susan handed him a mug.

I took mine from Susan with thanks, and then settled back into the couch cushions. Emma followed suit, her tiny feet in red and white sneakers hanging off the edge. "I appreciate you allowing me into your home to speak with you. I'm really just trying to learn as much as I can about Carrie." I took a sip of coffee and tried to control my face—it was loaded with milk and sugar. I swallowed it down and tried not to cough. "I'm not sure anyone thinks Todd killed Carrie, so we're trying to understand her life and see if there are other suspects out there." Emma took a sip of her cup as well, and made a sour face that I was afraid was an imitation of mine. I resolved to control my expressions better in front of children.

Carl nodded, as if he understood the strategy. "We didn't spend too much time with Carrie." He sipped his coffee and seemed to enjoy the taste. He ran the side of his finger over his little brush-like moustache, one side and then the other, a gesture I really dislike, but I tried to remain neutral. "It doesn't do to get too close to someone in a worldly relationship."

My brain hung momentarily on the 'worldly' relationships. I knew Carrie's family hadn't approved of her relationship with Todd, but I hadn't really picked up on a lot of disapproval from the ex-JWs. I wasn't very good with Jehovah's Witness terms, though, so it's possible I misunderstood. "Her relationship with Todd? That's the reason you didn't get close to her?"

Carl nodded again, his expression approving. "'Be in the world,

but not of the world.' John 17." He glanced at his wife, who sat down
next to Emma on the other end of the couch. "We cannot allow Satan
and the evil of this world to take root in us. We are just temporary
travelers here."

I felt like a particularly slow student, something I hadn't felt since
tax law class in law school. "I'm sorry—I had understood that you've
been disfellowshipped and are a part of The Shepherd's—Adam's—
support group." I looked over at Susan, who hadn't spoken since we
sat down. Her arm was around Emma, but she looked down into her
coffee mug. I looked back at Carl, who seemed a little put out at my
statement.

"Right now, we must travel in this world, but that's only for a
short time. We're going to be reinstated very soon." He looked at his
wife again. "Isn't that right, dear?"

Susan didn't answer him, but she finally looked up at me. "Carrie
was a sweet girl—so caring and thoughtful. She brought us flowers the
last time Emma was in the hospital." Her arm tightened around the
little girl. "Remember, Em?" The little girl nodded gravely, her huge
blue eyes on me.

"Emma was born with a type of sickle-cell anemia," Carl said,
nodding at Emma, who sat more still than any child ought, her little
fingers tracing the embroidered flowers on her skirt. "It required some
medical treatments that the Organization has some problems with.
But that's going to come to an end very soon, I'm sure." He sipped his
coffee, his eyes on the far wall of the living room, where family
pictures hung, including a picture of an infant in a blanket looking
much like infants do. "Susan and I pray constantly for holy spirit to
help us through this time as temporary residents in this world."

Susan smoothed a hand over her daughter's ringlets. "We had no
choice," she said in a quiet voice. "We would have lost her, and we'd
waited so long for her." Emma looked up at her mother then back at
me with eyes that seemed far too old.

I remembered with brutal clarity Garrison's words about blood
transfusions and his condemnation of parents who allowed children

to die rather than approving a blood transfusion, and realized he had sent me to Carl and Susan Grassley as a stark example of what he'd called 'blind faith.'

"So you've been disfellowshipped, but you're going to be—I'm sorry, did you say 'reinstated'?"

Carl nodded, his eyes wide. "There's some indication that Watch Tower is re-considering the blood transfusion doctrine." He leaned forward in his chair, eager to convince the unbeliever. "You know, when those interpretations were written, medical science wasn't very far along—it's all a terrible misunderstanding." He took another swallow of coffee and looked at the wall of pictures again. "We weren't very strong when Emma was born—we overruled the liaison committee and allowed the doctors to treat Emma. But we haven't since."

I looked at Susan, who was watching her husband with something like pity and resignation in her eyes. I carefully put my coffee mug on the coffee table, and dug in my bag for a pen and pad. At my motion, Carl looked back at me, and I held up my pen. "Do you mind if I take notes?"

Carl seemed to grasp what I was doing and shook his head. "I'd rather you didn't, if you don't mind." He cleared his throat and smoothed his moustache again as he looked away from me. "As I said, we really didn't know Carrie that well and have nothing much to say. We limit our associations with her and her kind. I Corinthians 15."

I don't know why, but his constant Bible references irritated me. "'Her kind'?" I echoed as I put my pad back in my bag. "Weren't you all in the same disfellowshipped boat together? Didn't you both meet with the group every Sunday afternoon?" Even though I wanted to keep my cool, all the 'let it go' advice Gerard had given me fled from my brain and I pushed further, watching a vein begin to pulse in the side of Carl Grassley's neck. "I mean, you've lived here in Dallas for —two years? Surely you knew her a bit." He stared at the wall, and I gave up needling him. "What did you think when she told the group she was returning to the Jehovah's Witnesses?"

Carl Grassley turned toward me so fast, I jerked back in surprise. His eyes were hot, his expression avid. "If she had truly repented, she would have been given the opportunity of a lifetime." His hands squeezed the recliner's arms. "She would have had the opportunity for Paradise. If she had shown the judicial committee that she was truly repentant."

"Did you tell her this?" I could feel Susan move on the sofa, but I didn't want to interrupt Carl's flow to turn to see.

"I did." He sat back in his chair and took a deep breath. "However, she was still seeing that young man." He shook his head, a tight, judgmental negative. "I cannot believe that she was truly repentant of her sin, if she continued to see him." His face was closed as he looked at the photo wall. "She walked disorderly."

"I don't understand what you mean."

He looked at me and spoke clearly, enunciating every word. "If she was unclean and unrepentant, she would spread her uncleanness to the congregation."

I was chilled by his tone. "And you wouldn't want that." He stared at me and said nothing.

I heard Susan Grassley make a slight noise, and turned to look at her. I was startled to see tears forming in her eyes. She pulled Emma on to her lap and looked over her daughter's head at me. "We got to know Carrie a little. She was very kind to us." She looked at her husband. "You know she was, Carl."

Carl was having none of it, and he seemed really displeased now. "We were careful to limit our interaction with her and her boyfriend." He stood up, and I realized I was being politely moved on. "We don't know anything about her, or why someone would kill her. This world is under the influence of the god of the system of things, and we do not engage with it." He loomed over me, and I realized he truly believed his denial. He clarified his statement. "You know, *Satan*. John 5." He nodded once, as if approving of his own argument.

I looked at him, and then at Susan. "If there's anything you can tell me about Carrie or Todd or anything else, I would appreciate a call." I stood. Susan and Emma stood as well, and Emma took a step towards me, taking my hand in hers. For a moment, I thought of the children who were taught to refuse the blood transfusions that could save their lives, martyrs for their faith, according to the Organization. I knelt and gathered Emma in my arms, squeezing just a little before releasing her to her mother. She smelled confusingly of baby powder and medicine.

As Carl marched to the front door to see me out, I slipped my card into Susan's hand.

———

CARRIE AND NAOMI HAD LIVED IN THE MALIBU, A SMALL BRICK complex near Live Oak Street, one of many left over from the real estate developments of the mid-20th century that were decorated to emulate southern California, with palm trees and *Jetsons*-like architectural details. Most had been renovated extensively, now featuring gated parking, pools, and exercise rooms for the millennials who moved to Dallas for work and looked for housing near downtown. The Malibu had resisted the renovation trend so far, and the futuristic details of 1960s Los Angeles style were the real thing, just painted over a few times.

A central metal gate at the front of the compound barred entry into the courtyard, but Naomi was waiting for me in the twilight, several empty boxes at her feet. I lifted a couple as she let us in, punching a code into a device attached just above the knob. A pair of two-story buildings faced each other across the courtyard where several palm trees struggled against the February cold. Brown-painted iron staircases with geometric details picked out in gold led to the second floors. The white brick of the buildings had long ago been stained by the elements, but several of the brown doors were brightened by wreaths or—in the case of the apartment next to Carrie and Naomi's—Valentine's day decorations. As we passed number 7, the door opened, and the older woman from Carrie's memorial service stuck her head out.

"Oh my dear, do you have to go back in?"

Naomi nodded and allowed herself to be enveloped in a hug, then introduced me to Myrna Lowenstein. Mrs. Lowenstein asked us in for coffee—which we declined—and then she reminded Naomi that she and her husband Benny would be happy to go into the apartment for anything Naomi might need.

As Naomi let us into the door marked with the number 8, she told me a bit more about the Lowensteins.

"They've been great neighbors. I mean, I think they liked Carrie more than me, to be honest." The apartment was cold, with a musty, minerally smell overlaid with bleach and ammonia. "I spend most weekends with my sister up at UNT, but Carrie stayed here all the time. The Lowensteins asked her to dinner a lot, and I think she had dinner with them during Hanukah."

The apartment entry had a folding door immediately into the tiny kitchen to the right, but opened itself into a long living/dining room. There were no windows on the side walls of the room, but the ones at the end were large and looked out onto a grassy area where a little girl waited while a dog did its business under a tree. The décor seemed to be garage sale with a dash of color.

Naomi kept talking from the kitchen, where she was cleaning out the refrigerator into a trash bag. "Myrna and Benny moved here in the 70s, when Benny was still an accountant. I think they were swingers then—can you believe it?"

Actually I could, having lived with my own septuagenarian swingers for four years, but I didn't think Naomi was looking for a response. I set my boxes on the little dining table and wandered over to a small bookcase filled with pictures and knick-knacks while she kept talking from inside the refrigerator.

"I've only been here once since that night, to get my clothes and jewelry. I knew there was milk and stuff in here that would be going bad, but I really didn't care." She closed the refrigerator door and tied up the trash bag. "I'll clean the rest out this weekend when my sister comes into town to help me move."

She came around the corner into the living room and stopped. I noticed her face was so pale in the ceiling fixture light that her freckles looked dark brown. She was looking over towards an old painted cast iron radiator against the left wall, so I looked too. I could see a dark patch on the shag carpet beneath it, and I suddenly realized what we were looking at.

"Myrna came over and cleaned in here when they released the apartment, you know." She blinked rapidly and sniffed. "She didn't have to, but she said she didn't want me to see it." She turned away and faced me. "I can still see it in my mind though. She was lying there, and blood was beneath her head. It looked like she'd fallen into the radiator. They said Todd must have pushed her backwards and she hit her head, but I don't believe it." She seemed to be asking me, but I had no answers for her. "I just can't see him being that angry at Carrie. He never got angry with her, no matter what."

"I don't know him that well. Was he here a lot?"

"Yeah." She made a face. "I tried not to be jealous—I mean, I wasn't really—but you know how it is when you're alone, but your best friend isn't?" I nodded, sympathizing more than I should. It'd been years since I was in a real relationship, and most of my friends were married and having kids by now. "So he was here whenever he could be. They weren't—you know—intimate too much, but he had a key and came over and fixed dinner sometimes when it was raining and his crew was off." She stared at the radiator, and I could tell she was thinking about that night. Time for a distraction.

"Do you need to get more things from your bedroom?" I picked up an empty box and headed to the two doors on the far wall.

Naomi picked up a box and followed me. "I'm good, but I thought Carrie's dad might like her books." The door on the left was open, and showed a messy room vivid with deep pinks and purples, the bed laden with pillows and a dark purple comforter pulled back to show lighter purple sheets, the lavender-colored curtains open to let in the fading light of the evening. It looked like the inside of Jeannie's bottle in the old television show. Naomi opened the door on the right.

Carrie's room had one window that faced the courtyard of the apartments. I could see how that could be a security nightmare, but it was covered in plantation shutters. The double bed was neatly made with a cream-colored spread and a chocolate-brown velvet throw pillow. On one wall was a small, tightly packed bookcase, with books overflowing onto the floor beside it and on the nightstand next to the bed. The two bedrooms shared a common bathroom in jack-and-jill style, and there was a tiny closet with the usual complement of clothes, neatly organized, and a small pile of shoes on the floor. On the one wall without a door or window was a framed photograph of a path, trees arching above it to create a green tunnel, the end shrouded in diffused sunlight. *The light at the end of the tunnel*, I thought. It looked like a photo printed out and framed, rather than something professionally done.

Naomi carried a box over to the bookcase. "The textbooks are my sister's old college textbooks. She'd saved them all, and she let Carrie borrow them. I'll see if Ruth wants them back." She picked up a college algebra textbook and fanned through the pages. "Carrie didn't get to go to college, but she was saving up to go next year. She read these textbooks like they had the answers to everything." Naomi suddenly sat on the bed. "She won't ever get to go now."

I could feel the tears coming, and tried to speak brusquely. "So none of the textbooks. What about the rest?"

She looked around the room. "She tried to find old Jehovah's Witnesses books, and she was always going in used bookstores to look for them." She lifted a small, green clothbound book from the night-stand. "*Millennial Dawn*. She found this one at a flea market we went to sometimes." She gently tucked it into a box, and for a moment, we packed a box with all the non-textbooks we could find.

A small wooden dresser with a scratched top was neatly covered with a yellowed linen cloth detailed with tiny flowers, and Naomi told me about the day she and Carrie had found a box of embroidered linen napkins at a garage sale. She brushed the dust off the cloth spread over the dresser, and lifted a picture frame to hand to me. Todd and Carrie were part of a group of young people, and I was struck by how unusual their posture was. Where the rest of the group had their arms around each other, Todd and Carrie stood next to each other, their arms by their sides, only their shirt sleeves touching.

I mentioned the distance between the couple to Naomi.

"Yeah, we used to talk about that. The JWs are just obsessed with sex—there's no other way to put it. Carrie told me if you hold hands at church, it was like a declaration you were engaged." She rubbed her nose and sniffled a little, then looked around for a tissue. "'Course, she didn't say 'church.' At the Kingdom Hall, she'd say." She blew her nose on the tissue she'd found, tossing it in the trash can by the dresser. "Everything meant something—kissing, cuddling, any kind of PDA. So in public, they just didn't touch."

"Was Todd okay with that?"

Naomi considered. "I don't know, honestly. He seemed to really love her though, and she'd come a long way. Sometimes here at home, she'd cuddle with him on the couch when we were watching a movie, but never in public." She turned to put a picture frame in another, smaller box. "I know her parents won't want the pictures of them together, but I thought Todd might. You know, when this is all cleared up, and he gets out." She looked down into the box, and I could see the next question forming.

She tucked a strand of hair behind one ear and resettled her glasses on her nose. "Do you think he did it?"

I turned to put the picture frame in the small box and gave my usual answer. "He says he didn't." I sat on the edge of the bed and watched her moving items from one side of the dresser to the other. "What do you think happened?"

Naomi gathered several pairs of earrings and put them in a small velvet bag. "I don't know. That night—well, the Lowensteins said they heard them arguing, but they didn't hear him leave." She looked out the window into the courtyard, where antique lights brightened the growing darkness. "And David says he saw Todd leaving when he came home about 8:30."

"David?"

"David Young. You met him the other night at the memorial thing. He lives on the other side in number 9." She opened and closed the drawers of the dresser. "I guess I'll gather her things up and take them to Goodwill. She was always giving things away—I think she'd appreciate that."

"I didn't realize he lived here." I put a few more pictures into the Todd box, and included a Christmas card that seemed to have been from him. I opened the drawer on the small wooden nightstand next to the bed. There was a leather-bound journal in her the drawer, and I hesitated. "Have the police gone through her things?"

"They looked through the apartment that—that night," she said. "They left me a receipt for the things they took." She looked up, dismay on her face. "Should we have waited?"

"I think they'd have told you if they didn't want you to come back in." With a mental shrug, I tucked the book in the small 'Todd' box.

"Oh." She took her glasses off and cleaned the lenses on her purple scrub top. "Could you ask Todd if there's anything else he knows he wants?"

"Sure. I think the other attorney is going to be visiting with him this week." In a little crystal dish in the drawer was a silver bracelet with a heart charm that could have been a boyfriend gift or a parent gift. I put it into the parent box and looked around. "Can you think of anything else that might need to go to her parents?"

Naomi opened the nightstand drawer and pulled out an older, black leather-bound book. "This is her Bible." She smoothed the frayed edges, and a tear fell on the gold-stamped front cover. She wiped the drop away and handed it to me to put in the box.

I locked the box for Carrie's father in my trunk and carried the trash bag to the dumpster, leaving Naomi talking with Myrna Lowenstein. A light rain had begun to fall in the full winter darkness, so I sat in my car for a while, thinking and watching the drops slide down the windshield.

———

CARRIE'S DIARY WASN'T REALLY A JOURNAL; IT WAS A RECORD OF her recovery.

I felt intrusive as I paged through it while I waited for some of Sara's frozen stroganoff sauce to heat. Carrie'd begun it about two years ago, probably a few months after leaving the Jehovah's Witnesses. At first, she'd just put dates in, with a word or two about what she did that day—9/4: *job interview, met with Adam and David* —but as time went on, she included more detail about what was going on in her head—12/16: *don't get the holiday thing, but it seems to bring out the best in people. Is it really so bad then?* and 2/17: *it's hard for me to pray, but I miss talking to God. I'm trying. I need the help* and 3/9: *my birthday, and they got me cupcakes at the office, and I don't know how I should feel, guilty or happy.* There wasn't an entry for every day, but they got more detailed as they continued into last year. 7/16: *Dad said Kyle Barstow was DF'd from Garland. I'll reach out to him. Dad v upset—jud comm didn't listen. Remember to mention to AT and AG* and 9/1: *Dad says the new rules for elders are upsetting, he's praying about them.* And later still: 10/23: *DY off the rails again tonight. AG out of town, needs to know. Remember to mention need for substance abuse groups to AT.*

I flipped over to the last filled-out pages. 1/23: *Talked with Todd, we can make this work. It's important, he understands and it will be OK* was the last entry. I stared at the date. That was four days before she died. If the fight with Todd the night she was killed was about her going back to the Jehovah's Witnesses, it appeared that it wasn't the first time he'd heard the news.

I went over to stir the stroganoff sauce and start water boiling for the noodles. I really didn't want to read her journal, but I could just hear Gerard scoffing at my scruples. I decided that delay was the better part of valor, and put it off until after dinner.

A couple of hours later, I stretched and put the journal back in my bag. There wasn't much to it. I was particularly saddened by a couple of entries about her attempts to reach out to her mother. In one, she reported that she'd called her, but her mother hadn't answered, and she was sure it was because she'd seen Carrie's name on the caller ID. The second time, she'd texted Leah, who'd responded: *Please don't make this more difficult than it is. I cannot speak with you.* Carrie drew a little broken heart in red next to the response she'd written word for word in her journal.

———

I spent the rest of the evening roaming my apartment, starting on the little sofa and ending in the bedroom, considering my home. One of Frank Lloyd Wright's students had designed the Prairie-style home for the Shelton sisters' grandfather, who'd built the home out of expensive red brick in 1917, two years before their father was born. Instead of the foursquare that Wright developed, Dr. Matthew Shelton had built the home much larger than four rooms above and below, anticipating many children and grandchildren. Unfortunately, neither was to be. Matthew Shelton died of the Spanish flu in 1919, leaving only the Shelton sisters' father, Winslow Shelton, to inherit what was a fair amount of wealth back then. He passed away when the girls were children.

When Hattie and Sallie left home in the early sixties, their mother sold the big house and moved to a smaller home in Highland Park. Some of their family wealth was lost in those days, but Hattie and Sallie had apparently married well, and had invested even better. When they both moved back to Dallas about 15 years ago, they found the house in disrepair and on the market. They bought it, and have been slowly redesigning the spaces. I noticed for the first time tonight they'd had Tomas install a new cat door in the connecting door, which explained the cat's recent absences.

The house is on a huge double lot on a corner, with large and mature trees in front and back. The carriage house in the back was renovated into a modern garage—at least on the inside. It still matches the house, and has a full apartment above. The covered entry on the side of the house is my carport, since my 'front' door comes in off that side. An enclosed sunroom is my living room, with one wall bricked in and the other made of French doors and arched windows. In every season but winter, it's a joy: there's plenty of light and views of the enormous back garden where Hattie grows beautiful flowers. In the winter, the glass is cold, but I don't mind (well, as long as I have power and heat). My bedroom has the same kind of wall, and since the back of the house faces the south, I get warming sun through the glass all winter long, and protection from the heat during the summer.

It's a beautiful place to live, but it's not the best office space. The dining table that had come with the place made a perfect desk when pushed against the dining area wall four years ago, but now I'd added a small file cabinet and a little printer table, and I really needed a larger whiteboard. I liked seeing my cases up on a board when I worked, but I had enough work now that my writing was practically unreadable.

I thought again of the Grassleys' house, so neat and orderly, soaked with the sense of temporary, the feeling that they were just biding their time. Carrie's room, while just as tidy, hadn't felt the same. The pictures, the velvet pillow, the jumble of shoes on the closet floor— those were the signs she'd made her place a home, that she was nesting there, getting comfortable in the 'world' where she'd chosen to be.

So why go back?

I checked my emails before going to bed and found one from Gerard.

Benedict:

I'm going to Princeton tomorrow to see grandson. I'll let you know how it goes. I want to hear his response to the news about cause of death and get more details about his argument with girlfriend.

Let's try to get together on Wednesday or Thursday to take a look at all the possibles. We need to be thinking about a plea bargain, if we can't do something else. I don't think he'll do well at trial.

RG

Great, I thought glumly as I brushed my teeth. *We'll have Todd in jail for the rest of his life at this rate.* I hoped Gerard wasn't as persuasive with Todd as I knew he could be with a jury.

CHAPTER FIFTEEN

I can't decide if clients are a burden or a blessing.

After a morning spent chasing money and the clients who owed me money, lunch with Sonja Winston was a gift. A savvy and successful real estate investor with a deceptively cute and fun demeanor, Sonja can bring me out of any funk. She's north of 50 (but no one knows how far north) with a younger boyfriend and an eye for gorgeous bling. Since it was her turn to treat, we were at an Asian fusion place on Royal Lane where she could have Thai and I could get some much safer orange chicken.

I could tell she had news when I sat down. Her highlighted spiky hair practically quivered with anticipation, and her green eyes were dancing. I sat in the booth and gratefully cupped my hot green tea with icy fingers, but she had both hands spread on the table.

"How are things?" I began, but she drummed her fingertips on the table without answering. "New manicure?" I guessed, since her nails were always perfectly polished in some shade of deep pink.

"Lacey! Look!" She waved her hands at me.

"New ring?" I ventured, pretty safely, I thought, since Sonja was known for buying expensive and very large jewelry. Four rings flashed on her fingers.

"You're hopeless," she laughed, rolling her eyes. "Look!" She waved her left hand in front of my face, and I realized what I'd thought was just a gorgeous cocktail ring was an engagement ring. I pulled her hand down and moved it to the circle of light on the table to peer at the huge diamond, surrounded by sapphires.

"Five carats?" I ventured. I thought I did a good job of examination, but she pulled it back and laughed at me.

"You wouldn't know five carats if they hit you between the eyes, Lacey." She gazed down at the ring, holding her hand out to look.

"So Dennis proposed?" I sat back to let the server drop off a plate with hot towels and used one to clean my hands, grateful for the warmth. Another front had come in during the night, bringing clouds and damp, and I was freezing.

"He did, the sweetheart." She used her own towel on her palms, avoiding her rings and bracelets. "Two nights ago at dinner. He said he'd thought about waiting to Valentine's Day, but he was so excited, he couldn't." She admired the ring once more, then picked up her tea cup and took a sip.

"Sonja, I thought you said you never wanted to get married." I gave the menu a quick glance, but we both knew I'd have the orange chicken. I'm nothing if not predictable.

"Oh, I know." She smiled at the server taking away the used cloths, then focused on me. "I still don't."

I raised my eyebrows, realizing as I did so that I was imitating Gerard. *Damn the man.* "Does Dennis know this?"

She smiled at me, the sweet, sparkling smile that so many men had underestimated. "He thinks I'll change my mind." She looked at the ring again. "This ring would almost do it."

"But...." I prompted.

"But no, I don't want to be married." She turned to the server, who'd brought her a vodka martini and a separate glass with olives and juice. "Thank you, Danh! Ooooh, that looks perfect!" She sipped delicately. "Yum! I know what I want today—the Thai Beef Salad. But not as spicy as last time, okay?" She and Danh discussed the merits of more or less cilantro before he looked at me.

"Orange chicken again, Lacey?" He took my menu without waiting for me to answer.

"Good to see you too, Danh." I grinned at him when he rolled his eyes.

"You know, Lacey, we could fix you up something that would taste really good and avoid lemongrass." He frowned at me over his half glasses.

"Once I find something I like, I stick with it, Danh."

He and Sonja exchanged another eye roll before he left.

Sonja settled back into the white banquette and adjusted her silver and navy jacket, chosen—I'm sure—to highlight the new white gold engagement ring. "I know we're meeting to discuss the townhouse sale, but I'm just floating today." Her left hand made a little floating motion, and both our eyes were drawn to the engagement ring. She giggled a little, and I wondered if that was her first martini.

"If no marriage, why take the engagement ring?" I took a sip of tea. "You've made it this long without being married..."

"I didn't want to disappoint him," she said with a head tilt. "He'd planned it all so perfectly, and he picked the perfect ring." She poured a bit of the olive juice into the martini and stirred it with the olive-adorned swizzle stick.

"Are you going to 'not disappoint him' right to the altar?"

"Noooo." She sighed and put her hand in her lap, clearly irritated with my questions. "We'll have a talk soon, and I'll explain, but not right now." She leaned forward. "So why are you so glum? Is it Valentine's Day coming up this week?"

I groaned. "You know I hate that holiday." I thought for a moment about a martini of my own, but decided to abstain, since I had a lot of work to do that afternoon.

"I do know. Is that why you're so cranky?" She took a sip of the icy martini, rings flashing.

I felt instantly ashamed of my mood in the face of her good news. "I'm so sorry, Sonja. I'm happy for you, really I am." I sighed. "Maybe it is Valentine's Day, I don't know. I've tried to avoid all the grocery stores and anywhere that sells chocolates or flowers or cards."

She patted my hand, and then we both sat back to allow Danh to serve our hot and sour soup from a small tureen he then placed between us. While he fussed and ladled and Sonja took a call, I thought about my morning. I'd sat at my desk in my dining room, where all my work was done, and looked around the small space. I loved my little apartment. It had been a haven when my world had fallen apart, and the Shelton sisters didn't mind at all that it had become my office too. All I needed to work was a desk with a computer and printer, and I was good to go.

This morning, though, I looked at the mostly bare walls and wondered if I too was living a temporary life. I'd thought I was being money-savvy by staying in the tiny one-bedroom apartment, but was I afraid to get on with my life? Sonja finished her call with a laugh at the caller, and we ate our soup for a few minutes, discussing the flavor and the bit of heat in the broth.

"See, there's that little line between your eyebrows." Sonja pointed a rose-tipped finger in my direction as I ate my soup. "That frowning will give you the worst wrinkles."

I immediately relaxed my forehead, wondering if there was already a permanent line from the last five years of worrying. "Sonja, do you think I live a temporary life?"

She stirred her ice water with the straw and took a long sip, and I realized she was hesitating.

"You do, don't you?" I was appalled.

She shook her head. "Not completely," she said. She ate a spoonful of soup while I waited. "I've known you—what?—four years now?" She smiled. "You're not the same person I met back then.

You've grown up a lot." I stared at her, stung a bit, and she smiled at my expression. "What? You think adults can't grow?"

I pushed my soup bowl aside, now really cranky. "Of course they can. I just thought I was recovering pretty well." I picked up a crunchy noodle and nibbled.

"Lacey, honey, five years ago you had a very traumatic experience. You lived through it." She smiled up at Danh as he cleared our soup bowls, and then focused on me, serious for once. "But you don't seem to have come out on the other side."

"What do you mean?"

She leaned forward, a fingernail tapping her new engagement ring. "You've never asked me why I don't want to marry. You haven't been curious?"

"Of course I'm curious, but it's not my business to ask. Your reasons are your own."

She pointed that rose-tipped finger at me again. "I bet you think I had a bad love affair in the past." I started to smile, since that's exactly what I'd assumed. "It wasn't me, Lacey—it was my mother." She took a sip of water through a straw and hesitated, and I realized this story wasn't easy for her to tell. "My mother and father were not happy. My mother married him very young to get out of a bad situation, and it was like going from the frying pan into the fire." She paused while Danh placed our entrees in front of us.

"Thank you, Danh, this looks lovely."

It did indeed. The tart orange sauce glistening over the pieces of barely-breaded and fried chicken was almost clear with tiny flecks of orange peel. I inhaled the spicy fragrance with pleasure: I love the smell of citrus. The steamed rice was sticky and perfect, and a little pile of steamed broccoli would give me a green vegetable for the meal —score. Best of all, a pair of miniature spring rolls was Danh's gift to me for his displeasure over my predictable order. I dipped a roll into the orange sauce pooling at the edge of the plate and bit into it, the still-crunchy vegetables warm inside the hot, papery wrapper.

Sonja stirred her salad, tasting and then adding some chili sauce from the bowl on the table. "My father wasn't physically abusive—oh no, that would have been too overt for him. But he was so hard on her. Nothing was right. If dinner was on the table when he got home, he had no time to relax and have a cocktail first. If it wasn't, he considered it late." She dipped a strip of steak in dressing before nibbling on the end. "Either situation was his opportunity to show she'd failed to anticipate his needs."

"Was he like that with you?"

She shook her head. "He didn't really have a chance. They didn't have me until they'd been married for ten years—and believe me, he considered that her fault—and then he died when I was seven." She stirred the swizzle stick in her martini and then ate an olive before continuing. "And she never got over it."

I cut a piece of chicken and rolled it in the rice. I could see she was gearing up to her point.

"She lived the next 20 years trying to measure up to everyone. Me, the church, her parents and sisters, everyone." Sonja looked up at the crystal chandelier in the ceiling for a moment, then dabbed her right eye with the edge of a finger, making sure not to smudge her eyeliner. Then she took another healthy swallow of vodka martini, her dangly silver earrings flashing. "My father was in her head for the rest of her life. She lived it as if he was still there, berating her for everything she ever did."

She looked across the table at me. "Who's in your head, Lacey?"

———

I KNEW THE ANSWER TO SONJA'S QUESTION: ROB GERARD. AND I thought I even knew why. What I didn't know was how to get him out of my head, or at least make him shut up and let me be. Sonja didn't push, however, and we quickly got down to our lunch business, rolling the proceeds from her sale of a townhome in Dallas's cushy Preston Hollow into a new property.

I kept thinking about her question while I drove to meet Carrie's

father in east Dallas. R&D Booksellers is a bookstore in a commercial
neighborhood that's been almost swallowed up by Baylor Hospital, an
enormous and sprawling facility that served much of east and downtown Dallas. Professional buildings had sprung up all around the
main hospital, large anonymous brick buildings with reflective glass
where laboratories and physicians and day surgeries now supported
the patients Baylor served.

This part of town was a haphazard mix of new buildings, old
commercial strips, and homes in all states of repair or renovation. The
small, tan brick building where R&D occupied space had '1921' cut
in stone beneath a green tile roof, and large multi-paned storefront
windows were steamed over in the winter cold. The building had
four separate commercial spaces: on one end, a dress shop I was sure
supplied drag queens with evening wear, then an antique store that
never seemed to be open, and on the other end, two spaces for R&D.
One space rambled in and out of small rooms full of bookshelves,
both open and glass-fronted, where antique and rare books could be
found, if you looked long enough. The proprietors were proud to say
there was no order to the bookshelves. In their minds, the books were
there to be found, and your need wasn't their problem, or the books'
problem, for that matter.

Through a connecting and always open door was a coffeeshop.
The threshold was no-man's land, where books from the store could
not cross. You could bring in your own book or magazine, but you
could not bring books across from the bookstore. There were five
small square wooden tables in the coffeeshop, and the one by the
window in the back was the only one occupied that cold and wet
afternoon.

Samuel Ames was in his late 50s, with thinning dark blond hair
he wore combed back from his face. He was dressed in a dark blue
suit that was old but carefully pressed. His shirt cuffs were a bit
frayed, and the left one had been mended, I could see, with small,
even stitches. His blue and silver tie was wide, and it was a little too
short to lie smoothly over his stomach when he sat. He was reading a

thick hardback book that I was surprised to see was the most recent thriller from a well-known author. He read like I do: a cooling cup of tea at one hand, absorbed completely by what he was reading, losing track of everything around him. The barista nodded to me as I passed. Since I didn't know how this conversation would go, I didn't want to presume we'd be having coffee.

He stood as I approached, taking the time to carefully mark his place with a bedraggled bookmark that looked like it had been made by a child pasting pictures of flowers cut from magazines. It had been laminated to preserve it, but even so, it looked years old.

"Sam Ames," he said, holding out a hand to me.

I shook it seriously, noting his firm grip and calloused fingertips. "Lacey Benedict."

He motioned to a seat. "Coffee or tea?"

I considered. "I'll get a latte, if you have time to wait."

"Of course." He resumed his seat, and started to lift his teacup, grimacing when he realized how cold it was.

"May I get you some more hot water?"

He smiled and nodded, holding the cup out to me. "I lose track of time," he said with a laugh.

I smiled back. "I do the same thing."

A few minutes later, settled in with warm drinks, Sam Ames was telling me about his current book—"one of many I have going at the same time, I fear"—and we were discussing R&D's unique shelving style. "I think it's a brilliant sales technique," he said. "You're looking for one book, but you find three others you didn't know you wanted."

"Yes, but it takes forever to realize they don't have the book you thought they did after all." I took a sip of the excellent latte.

"But then you buy the other three." Sam laughed.

We smiled at each other, two book lovers caught in a moment, and then we both remembered why we were there.

"I'm so sorry for your loss," I began.

He lifted a hand to stop me, his hazel eyes shining a little brighter as he blinked away tears. "I appreciate the sentiment." I nodded, wanting to let him recover. "I understand you represent Todd."

"I do." I watched his face for a moment to see if there was a negative response. "But I'm getting to know Carrie right now—trying to understand her and her life. I have the things Naomi sent, but I was hoping you might speak with me about Carrie."

He looked off at the window, where the gloomy sky threatened more rain. "I'd actually welcome the chance to talk about her." He looked back at me, his face wrinkled in a frown. "You understand—she was no longer in the Truth, and we did not speak of her."

I moved my cup to one side of the small table and leaned forward. "I don't really understand, but I do know she was being shunned."

Sam Ames winced noticeably at my use of the word. "She was outside the Truth, yes."

I tilted my head. "And was being shunned, true?" I didn't know why I felt the need to push the point, but I still felt angry on Carrie's behalf.

He paused, and then nodded. "It's our way."

I felt emboldened to push a little more. "I understand that it's your way, but I just can't understand how you could do it." I waited for a few seconds. "But I know *you* didn't do it, exactly."

He threaded his fingers together loosely in a gesture that made me think of a child praying. "I found it difficult to think of my youngest child out in the world with none of her family." He looked at his hands, and I could see him swallow hard. "It's something I've struggled with, and I pray about it constantly." He looked up at me and then tilted his head to the side. "Are you close to your father?"

I sat back, startled into answering. "I guess I am." I looked down at my own hands, and felt a flush rise to my face. "At least I was. He has Alzheimer's disease, and he doesn't really remember me all that much now." I was appalled to feel hot tears prick at the corner of my eyes.

Sam Ames nodded sympathetically. "But you go to see him anyway, don't you? Even though he doesn't remember you."

I nodded. "Sometimes I think I'm really going for me, to be comforted." I swallowed. "Like I used to be."

Sam looked out the window at the dull gray February day. "Perhaps that's why I saw Carrie when I could. She and I shared a love of books—like you—and a comfort between us." He looked back at me. "We would meet here on her Tuesdays off and talk of history or philosophy. I'd tell her about her mother and sisters, and she'd tell me about Todd or her work or friends." He took a folded white handkerchief from his pocket and wiped his eyes, where the tears had leaked a little.

"Her friends have said she was a smart girl, very kind and loving."

"Oh, she was, she was." His voice broke, and the tears flowed for a bit before he wiped them away with the handkerchief. "She was so intelligent," he said thickly. "She loved to read and learn things and ask questions." He laughed, a hoarse, bittersweet laugh that sounded rusty. "Some I couldn't answer."

I smiled. "Which ones couldn't you answer?"

His smile died. "Too many. Why, why, why—it was always 'why, Dad?' about everything." He looked so sad as he remembered. "It finally drove her away. No one had the right answers for her." He wiped his eyes and nose, and then re-folded the handkerchief carefully before putting it away. "Did Todd kill her?" he asked abruptly, looking at me directly.

I looked back steadily. "He says he didn't."

"Do you believe him?"

It wasn't a question an attorney should answer, but in this case, I felt justified. "Yes, I do."

Sam Ames nodded once. "Then who did?"

"I don't know yet." I adjusted my coffee cup in the saucer to give myself a moment, and he watched me without speaking. I sat back in the cold metal chair. "Did you know she was going back into the Organization?"

He didn't speak for a few seconds, and then he sat back too, straightening the knot of his tie. "She'd told me that the week before she died, yes." I waited for a few seconds, but he didn't continue.

"Were you happy that she was going back?"

I'd thought it was an easy question, but he looked down at the white bit of his shirt showing at the end of his jacket sleeve, adjusting it a little so that the stitches mending the left cuff didn't show. I let the silence stretch, and he finally looked back at me.

"No. No, I was not."

———

I stared at Sam Ames. That was absolutely the last thing I expected to hear him say.

He looked back at his cuff, fiddling with the clear button there, which I could now see was a little loose. He finally looked up at me.

"I know you didn't know her, but being outside the Organization —out in the world—was so good for her." He swallowed hard, and he twisted the button on his sleeve. "We like to believe that when someone leaves the Organization, they're miserable and degraded, like the prodigal son in the parable. They eventually realize—as they're eating from the trough with the pigs—that being in the Truth is where they belong, and they come home."

I didn't know the parable, but I knew what a prodigal son was. "And if they're not miserable?"

He shook his head. "We don't even let that possibility enter into the equation. True happiness comes from service, from being in the sunshine of Jehovah's love and approval." He stared out the window. "But not my Carrie. She was healthy, she was happy and not anxious anymore, she was even thinking about going to college." He looked back down at his sleeve, where he'd worried the button until it hung by a single thread. "I took a few college courses when I got out of the Air Force—before I came to the Truth—and it was the happiest time of my life. The thought that she would go to college, to learn and be challenged—" The slender thread snapped, and he stopped, staring at the pearly button in his hand. "We argued. I told her she needed to consider her decision again, but she was adamant."

His face was taut as he remembered. "I reminded her what reinstatement would require—the hardship that she would have to endure to prove that she had repented of her sin and truly wanted to be back in the Truth." He inhaled deeply. "She said what she was doing was important, and it needed to be done. I implored her to wait, I told her that she would never lose me, that I would always stay in touch." He looked at the button again, and then closed his hand over it and slipped it into his pocket. "She said she had her reasons, and wouldn't discuss it anymore."

He finally looked at me again. "The last words we exchanged were ones of anger." The tears flowed down his face and dripped to his jacket lapels. "I'll never forgive myself for that."

I let the painful silence steep as he wrestled with his thoughts and his guilt. "You didn't speak again?"

He brushed the remaining tears from his face. "No. I waited a couple of days, then texted her over the weekend. She didn't respond."

I had to ask. "Mr. Ames, you said the happiest time of your life was in college." He took out his handkerchief and blew his nose. "Why didn't you go ever go back?"

He shook his head, his eyes soft and sad. "Some things aren't meant to be."

I leaned forward. "Why not?"

He smiled at me, and I could see he was hearing Carrie's questions. "I chose my path, and it leads to a paradise the Bible has promised me. I'll be happy then."

———

THE CLOUDS HAD DARKENED AND THUNDER RUMBLED distantly, and we decided to transfer the books before it began to rain. I opened my trunk and Sam looked through the books in the box

Naomi and I had packed. He opened the Bible, and tucked inside the back cover was a picture of him and Leah and three young girls. He showed it to me and told me about the trip the family had taken to Sweden, where Leah's great-grandparents had been born. It had been the summer before their oldest daughter had gotten married, and Carrie had been a sullen pre-teen who'd found that she loved traveling.

"Leah hated the whole trip. We visited some of her family who are not in the Truth, and it was a bit uncomfortable. But Carrie loved learning about the culture and the people, and I thought perhaps eventually she'd live somewhere else and be happy there." He turned over the picture to the back, showing me where a childish hand had written 'happy times in Stockholm 2006,' and he smiled and put the picture in his jacket pocket with the button.

It began to mist, and we crowded in together under the trunk lid. He frowned a bit when he found some of the Watch Tower-published books, and put them to one side of the box. "I'll send these in," he said mysteriously, and then he picked up a slim volume of Emily Dickinson's poetry, too ragged and water-stained to be a real antique. "I gave her this a few years ago." He flipped through the pages, where a bookmark similar to the one he used marked a page about halfway in. "'Tell all the truth/but tell it slant—/Success in circuit lies,'" he read aloud. "'The truth must dazzle gradually/Or every man be blind'." He stared at the words.

"That's one of my favorites," I said, looking at the marked page.

He took the bookmark out and closed the book. "Take it."

I stepped back. "Oh no, I couldn't."

He shook his head and held the book out to me. "It's hers—I can't take it home, and I cannot donate it like the others." He continued to hold it out. "Please."

I took it and tucked it into my bag. I opened his car door as he lifted the box and put it in the front seat, settling it in as gently as if it had been his young, sweet daughter. "Mr. Ames—" I stopped when he turned to me, drops of mist beginning to coat his hair. He looked so bereft standing there. "I'm so, so sorry for your loss." We looked at one another for a moment, and then he smiled and patted my shoulder.

"And I'm sorry for yours, my dear."

I stood there and watched as he drove away, the mist turning to rain.

CHAPTER SIXTEEN

Carmen, from Gerard's office, had texted me while I met with Sam Ames to let me know that Gerard had spoken with Todd, and to book a meeting with Gerard for the next day. I called her and agreed on a time, entering it into my phone's calendar since I was in the car. I spent a few cold hours at the county courthouse, prepping for some petitions I'd need to file, and then headed out to meet David Young.

After his display at Carrie's memorial, I was prepared to dislike David. I was not prepared for a charming and attractive man in paint-spattered jeans and a light blue, long-sleeved t-shirt that made his blue eyes look even bluer. I was right. He was exactly my type when I was 25 and in law school. I squinted and thought back. Yep, he was pretty much a bearded replica of my law-school boyfriend.

We'd spoken early in the afternoon about time and location, and, when I walked into the fast-food place a few minutes before 5, he was already there. Just looking at the remains of one cheeseburger, two more still wrapped, and the mound of fries in front of him made my stomach growl. But Ann Thornton had promised me dinner tonight, and I didn't want to spoil my appetite. I just hoped she wasn't a vegan.

The first thing David did was apologize for Sunday night. "Sorry if I was rude the other night. I'm not the best when I drink," he said with a self-deprecating grin, "and that's an understatement." He squeezed four ketchup packets onto a corner of the waxed paper and then heavily salted and peppered the large red puddle. I watched as he dragged a couple of fries through it. "Man, I'm starving. We started working this morning at 6 trying to beat the rain and didn't stop until about an hour ago."

"You're in construction, right?" I womanfully stopped staring at the French fries and took out my pad and a pen. "You mind if I take notes?"

He shook his head. "Go ahead." He unwrapped a second burger and lifted the top of the bun to heavily salt and pepper the patty. At this rate, I was hoping he didn't have a heart attack before we finished talking. Although he had a slender and wiry build, he could be a ticking time bomb with high blood pressure. He caught me eyeing his burger and grinned. "Want some?" He nudged the paper with the fries toward me.

I took one, congratulating myself for my self-restraint. I tried not to moan as the crunchy, salty fry hit my mouth and taste buds. David laughed, showing a set of perfect white teeth in a face tanned caramel and bracketed by a light brown beard. "Fries and potato chips—you can't eat just one."

"I'm good." I virtuously wiped my hands on one of his paper napkins and turned to a clean page in my notebook. "So, I know you and Carrie were in Adam Garrison's support group."

David bit off a huge bite and nodded as he chewed and swallowed. "I'm not sure if it's Adam's group or not, but yeah, we both went on Sundays."

I wrote the date at the top of the page, split the page in half, and sat back in the molded plastic chair. "Well, is it, or isn't it?" *Let's get this off on the right, professional footing,* I thought.

He dragged another couple of fries through the ketchup and ate them without answering. I'd thought he was a little unhappy with Garrison on Sunday night, but this seemed to be more than that. The table wobbled slightly as he jiggled one leg. Finally he seemed to come to a decision.

"You know about JWs and being disfellowshipped, right?" I nodded. "Well, Adam left a few years ago, and I got DF'ed about a year later." He took a bite of burger, and then, disconcertingly, talked while he chewed. "Adam was getting the group together a few years ago, and he and I kinda started visiting with people to try to get the best mix for the group." He sucked some of his soft drink down through the straw, and I watched his tanned throat work as he swallowed.

"So you were really involved in getting it set up?"

"Yeah. Adam is kinda a geek, you know?" He grinned at me. "He looks at things in a mostly intellectual way."

"What'd you get disfellowshipped for, if I can ask?" I didn't know the protocol with this, if it was in poor taste to ask. "Or is that something you don't talk about?"

David grinned at me, but his eyes looked a bit annoyed. "I had a girlfriend out in the world. You know, like Carrie and Todd." He picked up his burger. "That's a big no-no in JW-land." He took an enormous bite, halving what was left.

"So you and Adam started this support group…"

"Not just this one. We've been kinda rolling them out in other places too." This was news. I wrote a note to myself, and David watched me.

"I've watched Adam's YouTube videos. He's got quite a following."

David finished off his second burger and started unwrapping his third. *Where did he put it*, I thought. He tipped it toward me. "Last chance. Sure you don't want a bite?"

I smiled and shook my head.

"Yeah, Adam has the social media thing down pat." He doctored the burger with salt and pepper. "That's not really my area."

"What *is* your area?" It might have been my imagination, but he seemed a bit off his feed at this point—or maybe he was just getting full.

"Kids getting out of the JW need help—more than just sitting around in a circle-jerk"—he eyed me with an eyebrow wiggle—"I mean, talking about their feelings." He chewed a bite of burger and swallowed. "They've never rented a place or got a job, or had a girl-friend or boyfriend." He grinned, the charm back. "Hell, most of them are virgins." He put the burger down to swipe a few more fries through ketchup.

I looked down at my pad and took a few notes. I got the distinct feeling that David had not been a virgin when he was disfellow-shipped.

"So these people need more practical help?"

He wiped his hands on a paper napkin and then tapped his nose to show I was right. "*Practical*. Right. That's the word. Adam does the intellectual bit, and I do the practical bit."

"I know you helped Carrie and Naomi find their apartment."

"Carrie was a good kid. I felt bad for how things went for her when she left." He ate another French fry, this time without the addi-tion of ketchup, then crumpled up the remainder of his burger with the partially-decimated pile of fries. "You know, I knew her before."

"No, I didn't. You knew her as a Jehovah's Witness?"

He took a slurp of soft drink. "Yeah. Our families both attended the same Kingdom Hall for a long time, before the Ameses moved to Princeton." He transferred the tray with the crumpled paper wrap-pers and leftovers to the table next to us, and then leaned back.

"Of course, she was a lot younger than me—she and my younger sister were about the same age." He rolled his shoulders and neck, his snug shirt stretching over lean muscles. Out of the corner of my eye, I saw a woman at a nearby table look over. I knew he was well aware how attractive he was—nothing wrong with that, of course, but David gave her a glance and grinned. She looked away. "Her sister Jenny was in my class at school until she quit to go out into service."

I made a few notes. I thought some of this was sour grapes, but there must have been a reason Adam Garrison wanted me to meet with David Young.

He opened the lid of his drink and tipped it up to get a piece of ice, crunching it with enthusiasm. "So anyway, yeah, Carrie came to me when she was out, and I let her know that there was an empty apartment next door. I put in a good word for her with the landlord, and that was all she wrote." He crunched down on another piece of ice.

I checked my list of questions. "You were there on the Sunday she was killed, right?" There was a pause, and I looked up.

He was gazing off, out the window, and I looked out to see what he was staring at. When I looked back, he was looking at me again. He put his cup back on the table before answering.

"Yeah, we all were. The group meets at 5 pm most Sundays." He looked down and picked at a paint spot on his jeans. I waited to see if there was more, but he stayed silent.

"What was the group meeting like on that Sunday?"

He looked at the woman who'd been staring at him before, but she was texting on her phone. He kept watching her as he spoke. "It was pretty intense. We usually just go around the group, and anyone who wants to talk about any issues they're having can talk." He looked back at me with a lopsided grin. "Kinda like AA, you know?" I smiled a little in response, but inside I was thinking, *if this guy is in AA, he's in more trouble than I thought.* "So Carrie told us she had some news that might be upsetting. And then she just dumps it on us." He frowned and shook his head. "She was going back. Back to the Organization." He looked down at his hands spread on his thighs, the right one jiggling. He picked up his cup to get another piece of ice.

"And that upset you."

He exploded at me. "Of course it did!" I leaned back in my chair. The force of his anger was palpable as he leaned forward. "It kills people! If they don't kill themselves, they die inside." He slammed his cup back on the table and looked off to the side. The woman he'd looked at was glancing our way, as were others in the restaurant. I couldn't decide whether to keep the pressure on him or calm him down, but he abruptly pushed his chair back and stood up.

I stood up too, my hands raised. "Hey, David, I'm sorry, I'm sorry." Concerned, I risked a hand to his arm.

He stood there, blinking back tears, swaying slightly. I tried again, making my voice as soothing as I could. "Let's sit down again, okay?" I sat, hoping he would too. The last thing I wanted was him storming off like this.

He sat, rubbing this thighs. "I'm sorry." He blinked away the last moisture in his eyes and looked away. "My sister died because of the Organization, you know."

"No, I didn't know. I'm so sorry." I didn't want to ruin the moment by making a note. "So Carrie deciding to go back was upsetting to the group?"

The question seemed to upset him even further and he blinked rapidly. "Except for that asshole Grassley. He thinks the Organization hung the moon." He took a deep breath, his handsome face twisting into a sneer. "He thinks they're going to reverse their position on blood transfusions and let him back in." He tipped his cup up and got a piece of ice, all cool guy again. "Not likely."

"That's not going to happen?"

"No way. That's one of those things they can't risk undoing." He looked at me with a cold smile and spoke around the ice. "What are they going to say to all the people who've lost family because of that policy? 'Oops, sorry, we were wrong and your husband or wife or son or daughter died for nothing'?" He crunched down. "Not happening.

And Susan knows it. That's all coming to a head soon—Susan isn't going to stand for it much longer. She'll take Emma and leave him."

He shook his head again. "And so he tells Carrie she's doing the right thing for going back. He says he hopes she's truly repentant and ready to heal spiritually." He rubbed his face with hands that shook slightly. "I coulda killed him." He seemed to remember that someone had indeed died that night, and he looked at me with a ghost of that charming smile. "You know, metaphorically speaking."

"What did everyone else think?" I surreptitiously checked the time on my phone. David didn't seem to notice. He rattled the ice left in his cup.

"Oh, everyone was upset. Most everybody was shocked." He sat back. "Garrison just sat there, watching everyone talking. I thought maybe he'd say something, but I think they'd already talked about it, and the asshole didn't have anything to say." He stared out the window at the growing dark.

"What did you say to her?"

He looked back at me for a moment, then looked away. "I told her she was being an idiot. That she'd have to grovel for them to take her back, and then she'd still be shunned while she proved how repentant she was." His mouth tightened. "I reminded her about what happened to Megan, about what it's like in Kingdom Hall—that she'd have to sit away from everyone like she was a leper, that no one would speak to her for six months, maybe longer, to prove herself."

I was appalled. "This is *after* she goes back?"

He nodded. "Yeah. Until she confesses her sins and proves that she's given up all sin. Then she'd have to meet with the elders to show that she's repentant enough. Until then, they'd treat her like shit. That's what they did to my sister Megan, and it broke her heart. As if the disfellowshipping hadn't already done enough." He looked at me and nodded at the look on my face. "They make you miserable first by shutting you out, and then they get to decide if you've crawled enough when you want to come back."

I decided to risk it. "What happened to your sister?"

He sat still, looking off to the side. "She couldn't take it. She was afraid she'd never be judged faithful. She thought she was an awful person for her sins." He tipped the cup up one more time, but the ice there had melted into slushy water. He stared into the cup, his voice mechanical and oddly distant. "She killed herself. She slit her wrists in my parents' bathroom while they were at work."

CHAPTER SEVENTEEN

I left David Young not too long after he told me about his sister, and I found myself thoroughly depressed. The human toll taken in and around this religion seemed to be endless, but I guess that's true of most of them. I had a voicemail from Gerard, telling me that his conversation with Todd had gone well—or at least until he told him the true cause of death. Todd had come back to the apartment about 8:30, Gerard said, but he blamed himself for not going in when she didn't answer. He felt guilty for not being able to help her. Once he knew how she really died, he broke down, and Gerard said he had to end the interview. "I think he's telling the truth, Benedict, but we're going to need him to make a statement soon. I don't want to coach him too much—his truth will come across better if he's just honest about it. And his testimony could help with a timeline to show time of death." He paused. "Be safe, Benedict." So many lives shattered, I thought as I deleted his message.

I drove to Ann Thornton's home, not expecting much. I still couldn't get a handle on her. I'd looked her up on the internet the night before and discovered that she was an artist fairly well-known in Dallas. The vivid red painting on her wall was hers, and was typical of her work. There were magazine photos of gallery showings where she stood with some of the more famous of Dallas's socialites, her pale composure a stark contrast to the glitter of the crowd.

She answered the door dressed in what I thought for a moment was a karate outfit but was, instead, just a pale, unbleached linen pantsuit. As she led the way into the living room, I peered at it, realizing that I was confusing deconstruction with lack of fashion. If anything, her pantsuit was designer. Her ash-blonde hair was straight and blunt-cut to just beneath her chin, and her nose was sharp and pointed. Neither the outfit nor the woman were soft or comforting, and yet her manner was gracious and a bit warmer than polite.

"I'm starving, so if you're okay with it, let's eat as soon as the *tahdig* is done."

I'd had *tahdig* before—I'd been hired by a Persian family to do some real estate work, and I'd had the sticky, crunchy rice dish at their home. When I mentioned it to her, she nodded and seemed pleased.

"We're having a lamb tagine with pomegranate and dates. I saw you'd eaten meat at the service on Sunday so I thought you'd be okay with a hearty meal in this dismal weather."

For a moment, I felt a little disconcerted that someone had noticed my eating, but then I realized it meant I'd get to have comfort food tonight, so I let it go. She'd set the dining table for two with a thick, dark red pottery set. A matching tagine sat in the middle, steaming with a lovely aroma. I decided I was supposed to sit on the side and let Ann sit at the end where the tagine waited.

She came out of the kitchen with a shallow dish of *tahdig*, the long-grain rice flipped over to show a crunchy, golden crust. My mouth watered, and when she took the lid off the steaming tagine, I was glad I'd ignored David's greasy French fries. Well, most of them.

I made all the appropriate noises as she served the lamb, and helped myself to a healthy portion of *tahdig*. A salad with carrots and sweet potatoes had saffron and honey, and as I crunched through the rice, I realized that it had saffron in it as well. Considering how expensive saffron was, this was quite a meal.

I'd learned from my clients that discussion of business should wait until after eating, so I didn't ask Ann any of the questions I'd prepared. Instead, we talked about her travels, where she'd learned to love the food.

"I traveled the first couple of years after Ted—my late husband—died. We'd always dreamed of traveling more, and I felt like I was honoring all the promises we'd made by going ahead to those places. I visited Lebanon, Syria, Israel, Turkey, Jordan, Italy, Spain, France, and Germany—I was able to spend weeks in each place and really discover the art and the cuisine." She speared a date with her fork and considered it. "In Turkey, I learned to tell the difference between the types of dates, something I'd never really thought about before." She ate the date and chewed thoughtfully.

"I just know I love the taste of the spices." I savored the cinnamon and ginger, and made sure each bite of lamb had a little bit of date with it. "Are there pomegranate seeds in this?" I looked through the portion she'd given me (woefully small, I thought) for the ruby-red seeds.

"Pomegranate juice, not seeds." She laid down her knife and fork on her empty plate, and I mourned. She surprised me, though, and helped herself to more of the dish, then turned to me with the spoon raised. I lifted my plate for her to pile on more lamb. We ate for a few minutes in a companionable silence before I gave in to my curiosity.

"How long ago did your husband pass away?"

She made a little frown. "He didn't pass away—he died. There's a difference." Chastened, I chewed a bite of lamb and date and kept silent, hoping I hadn't offended her. Sure enough, she continued. "He died in an accident at the truck repair shop where he worked." She took a bite of *tahdig* but didn't seem pleased with it.

"I'm sorry for your loss," I managed when I finished chewing. Good lord, there was a death around every corner with this crowd.

She made a little flicking motion with her fingers, and I noticed they were stained with paint. "It was eight years ago. I've made my peace."

"Was this before or after you left the Organization?"

She lifted her wineglass and drank the last bit, looking at me over the edge. "Before, actually." She looked at my plate, which I'd emptied completely. If it had been polite to lick it clean, I'd have done that too.

"Let's leave this and have some coffee in the living room," she said, rising and—absolutely—leaving the plates where they sat. A small part of me protested, since I was trained by my grandmother to clean up as soon as you rise from the table. If you don't want to clean yet, you stay at the table with the dishes.

"I could clear these—" I began, but she cut me off.

"Leave them." Her tone was final. I left them.

She went into the kitchen and began to prep a *cafétiere* and tiny cups. It looked like we might be having Turkish coffee, which is black and spicy, and tends to be very strong. I hoped she'd bring some sugar.

I wandered into the living room and found myself in front of the red painting. The paint was laid on the canvas so thickly it looked like cake frosting, and I wanted to touch it. My hand had reached out of its own accord toward the painting when she came in with a small tray, but I snatched it back.

"You can touch it," she said when she saw me. "It's treated so that the paint doesn't degrade when it's touched."

I smoothed a finger over the paint, which I assumed had been laid on with a knife. The thick swirls were all shades and hues of red, ranging from the maroon and burgundies to the fuschias and vermillion, and I felt even more like I was in the center of a deep red rose. I told her so.

"I painted it right after Ted died." She stood with me in front of the painting, her head tilted to the side as if she was remembering her emotions. "I was so devastated and angry." She turned away, so I followed, even though I felt I could stand there and trace the peaks and troughs of the waves of paint a while longer.

She did indeed have a sweetener with the coffee—a small honeypot—but I was hesitant to doctor it while she watched me. She sat down on the couch and dripped a tiny bit of honey into her coffee and then leaned over and dripped a tiny bit into my cup. I wanted to ask her to put more in, but I didn't want to offend her.

I looked around the room. Perhaps it was all this inner thought of temporary lives, but in contrast, Ann's austerely-decorated home didn't look temporary at all. Sure, the furniture was neutral, but I was pretty convinced her use of a neutral palette was artistic and intentional, where the Grassleys' use of tans and browns was Carl Grassley's lack of imagination or desire to nest. Her couch was a low, squared off sofa that made me think of the furniture in the *Dick Van Dyke Show*, one of my favorite black and white oldies. The bookshelves on either side of the fireplace boasted large art books as well as pottery and glassware, and her red rose painting wasn't the only artwork on the walls. I compared it mentally to my own little apartment and felt slightly more depressed. I didn't even have a picture of my brother and his family on my bookshelves.

Ann watched me examining her home, sitting back with her feet tucked underneath her. Finally, she broke the silence. "How is your investigation going?"

I frowned. "I'm not sure it's an investigation."

"Of course it is." She took a sip of coffee. "Aren't you investigating Carrie's life so that you can find the killer?" She looked at me over the cup. "That is, if you're sure Todd isn't the killer."

I felt heat rise into my face, but then I realized she was baiting me. She had a very dry sense of humor, but there was a glint in her eyes that told me she was gently mocking me. I looked around the room as if I was making sure no one was listening, then gazed seriously at her. "Well, I could tell you...but then I'd have to kill you."

A smile started slowly on her face, then became wide and friendly. "You going to drink that coffee or just hold it?"

I looked down into the cup, and inhaled the aroma of the dark brown liquid. I finally sipped. The tiny bit of honey had slid into the flavor of the coffee, and the cardamom and other spices had bloomed in the heat. It smelled somewhat like chai tea, but with a richness that the tea sometimes lacked. It was definitely coffee that you tasted. I made a few happy noises as I took another sip, and she laughed.

"So. You have some questions for me?"

"I do. Do you mind if I take notes?" I set my coffee on the end table.

"Not at all." She watched as I rummaged in my bag for my pad and a pen.

"Adam Garrison told me you let Carrie stay with you when she moved to Dallas."

"I did indeed. She slept on this very couch for about a month." She smoothed her hand over the velvety upholstery. "She was the perfect houseguest. I paint at night sometimes. She made up the bed and was out the door before I even got up in the mornings." She sipped her coffee, her eyes sad.

"And then David Young found her an apartment." I turned to a new page, and split it down the middle as Gerard had suggested.

She rolled her eyes. "Oh, David...yes, he told her about the apartment in his complex. But he really didn't do much to help." She set her cup on the coffee table. "David likes to feel important."

"But he's not?"

She frowned slightly. "I'm being critical, and I shouldn't be." She stretched her arms over her head and twisted her neck, popping it a little. I shivered at the sound. "David felt responsible in a way because he'd known her in the Organization. He felt protective about her."

"Yes, he told me they'd grown up together." I checked my notes. "Once Carrie moved out of here, you and she continued to be friends?"

"Absolutely. I loved her to pieces." She clasped her long-fingered hands loosely in her lap. "She was so different than most of the

Friends I'd known. She was lively and intelligent and empathetic—I think I mentioned that to you the other night. She was kind and thoughtful about all people."

"You didn't know her before?"

"Oh, no. I moved here six years ago from Atlanta, where Ted and I had lived. I wanted a clean break." She gazed at the fire, and I could tell she was thinking about her husband.

"I met Carrie's father. He seemed very intelligent—maybe that's where Carrie got it."

She nodded. "Both Carrie and Adam spoke highly of him." She looked down at her hands, and they tightened slightly. "Did he seem very upset?"

"Oh, yes. I mean, Carrie's mother seemed upset too, but that felt like guilt to me." I thought back to that day in Princeton. "I think he and Carrie had tried to stay close, even though they weren't supposed to see each other." A comfortable silence fell, and we listened to the rain falling down the chimney, hissing as it hit the warm bricks.

"Had you been a Jehovah's Witness long?"

She nodded. "My whole life. I was raised in it. So was Ted. In a way, we were the perfect Pioneers." She looked at me. "You know about pioneering?"

I made the 'so-so' gesture. "Not too much. I've just read a bit."

"Pioneers go out in service to an extreme number of hours per month. When Ted and I got married, it was 90 hours of service per month." She reached over and refilled her cup with the *cafétiere*. "Now, I think it's down to 70." She dripped a bit of honey into the cup and let it sit to bloom. "We did everything right: we pioneered out in service knocking on doors, we went to every meeting and convention we could afford, we hosted study groups, Ted even went through the Theocratic Ministry School to learn to be a better speaker. He could have been an elder, but he truly enjoyed getting out and speaking to people. He would have been so disappointed when the Organization moved to cart witnessing." I'd never heard of that, so I drew a line under the words in my notes. She sat back on the couch and took off her right earring before massaging the ear lobe thoughtfully. "We intended to be perfect, to work our way to paradise. Groups like the JW and others"—she looked at me—"it's hard for me to call it a cult, even now. But fundamentalist religions engage in a sort of magical thinking. The adherents believe it's a transaction with a bottom line: if I do this, and this, and this, then I'll go to heaven. Or I'll be taken up by Jesus in the rapture. Or—with the JW—I'll live in an earthly paradise after Armageddon." She put her earring back on and shook her head again. "It's not even really faith. It's an equation."

She leaned forward to pick up her coffee, and I took the opportunity to ask. "You said Ted was killed. Was it an accident?"

She nodded. "A freak accident, really. He worked at a mechanic's shop that worked on trucks, big trucks. He was doing a routine inspection when something happened with the parking brake on the truck he was inspecting." She took a sip of her coffee. "He was crushed between the truck and a wall. He died minutes later." She sat back and sighed. "I didn't believe the police when they showed up at my door. In my mind, we'd done everything right, and nothing like that could happen." She looked down at the cup cradled in her hands. "The elders in our Kingdom Hall said I should be happy, that he would be resurrected and I could be with him again. But I knew that wasn't going to happen." She swallowed hard, and for the first time I saw tears form in her eyes.

"I'd already begun to have doubts. Ted—oh, he was so sure." She smiled a little. "He was a rock, so confident in the Organization and its interpretation of God's word. I'd been a little more in the world, with my art and the work that I did, and I'd heard the stories, the news about the Organization." She looked at me directly. "Have you heard the stories about the sexual abuse?" I nodded. "By the time Ted died, the whispers had started. Oh, the abuse had been going on for years, but the real stories had begun to circulate with the internet and social media. And then a few months before Ted died, I met one of the victims." She shook her head and took another sip of coffee.

"Talked with her, really listened. And realized I was hearing truth. Which meant everything I'd been told was the 'Truth' was not." She stopped and began to inhale deeply, and I realized she was calming herself.

"Did you tell Ted about your doubts?"

She shook her head. "I'd just about convinced myself that God would take care of everything, and to leave it alone, when he was killed." She refilled my cup without asking. "It's funny. You're told you're going to be spending eternity with all these people in the Organization, and at times, I'd look around and think, 'These aren't people I'd want to spend eternity with.' Sacrilege!" She laughed, and I smiled with her, wondering what that would be like. "And then after his death, I went traveling. Even though I was staying with Friends in some countries where I traveled, there were times I stayed in a hostel or B-and-B or some other accommodation with non-JWs, and—it was the best thing you can imagine."

She sat back and crossed her legs in front of her, a graceful move I —at least 10 years younger—couldn't have done. I sensed a yoga person here. She looked over at her bookcases and the pictures there, her face lighting up and her eyes warming. I wondered how I'd ever thought she was plain.

"Oh, the people I met! The conversations I had...the discussions, the debates, the hours of just sitting and exchanging ideas." She looked back at me. "The thing that keeps a cult going is that they restrict your movements and interactions with outsiders. Whether it's Scientology, or Jehovah's Witnesses, or anything else—one of the keys is shutting you off from the rest of the world. You begin to believe your own bullshit because there's no one to contradict you, no one to really disagree." She shook her head slowly. "While I'd had dealings with 'worldly' people to some extent, in my travels, when I stayed with them, ate with them, laughed and cried with them, I began to realize the things they would say about the JW were true. And there was no going back." The delight faded from her face, and I thought she might cry.

I decided a break was in order, so I borrowed the restroom. When I returned to the living room, the sadness had eased, and she seemed herself again.

"I'm curious—are you still religious?" The question sounded intrusive, and I immediately apologized, but she waved me off.

"I said you could ask me anything you wanted. It's a logical question." She was still sitting on the couch with her legs crossed, and I wondered if her legs went to sleep when she did that. She rested her elbows on her knees and steepled her hands to her chin, staring off into space. "I guess I'm what you'd call 'spiritual.' I still believe there's a God, and I believe that he—or she—loves us. Other than that, I'm not sure." She looked at me and smiled. "Not much of an answer. But I still think and pray and wonder. Perhaps that's what meditation is. On Sundays, I still want to be in sacred space, so in the morning I turn off the electronics and think about life and death and pain and comfort and beliefs. I breathe in and out, in and out. I listen to my breaths, and I look for God in the spaces between those breaths. I find it's easier to do that alone than when I was with all those 'friends' in the Organization."

———

THE DIRTY DISHES WERE WEIGHING ON ME, SO I CARRIED THE coffee cups to the kitchen and convinced Ann to talk to me while I took care of the ones on the table. She humored me and allowed me to do almost all of the washing up while she told me about her travels.

"By the time I got home, the truck company's insurer was almost frantic to settle with me—apparently, me not responding meant I was ignoring them and ratcheting up the potential for settlement. It was enough for me to move here, buy this house and make it what I wanted, and will allow me to paint and do the work I want to do."

"And what's that?" I dried the lovely pottery dishes and carefully stacked them in the cabinets.

She leaned on the counter. "I've started a non-profit foundation that will help young people leaving cults—the Jehovah's Witnesses, mostly."

I stared at her. Why had no one—especially Adam Garrison—mentioned this to me?

She smiled at my expression. "Why are you so shocked?"

"I don't know...I guess it makes so much sense that it blows me away a little." I wiped down the counter and then folded the washcloth. "Is that why you helped Carrie?"

She shook her head. "It was the other way around, really. Helping her and others showed me that something like this was needed."

We walked into the living room. "Was Carrie working with the foundation?" I sat down and prepared to make some notes while Ann paced around the room. I felt—rather than saw—that the discussion was making her anxious. My pen was dying, so I dug in my bag for another, and saw several voicemails from Gerard on my silenced phone. I decided he could wait a bit longer. I finally turned up his Mont Blanc at the bottom of my bag, and I unscrewed the cap with a little bit of devilish glee.

"She and I interviewed Marjory together—that's our therapist—and she was helping to set up the website and resource guide." She stopped at the red rose painting. "We're still a month or so from opening."

"How does her death affect that?"

Ann turned to me. "It doesn't change a thing." She inhaled deeply. "We have a board and some volunteers who are taking over those jobs."

"So she wasn't necessary to the foundation?"

"I didn't say ·that." Her answer was short and cut off my next question. "Our work will continue."

I heard the strain in her voice and wondered if I'd worn out my welcome. I looked through my notes and questions quickly to see what information I needed from her.

"The night she died—you were at the group meeting, right?"

She slid her hands into her sleeves and up her arms as if she was cold, even though she was standing next to the dying fire. "I was."

"Did you know she was going back to the Organization?"

She inhaled sharply and then exhaled slowly, in and out, in and out. "I did. She and I had discussed it the week before." She swallowed, and I saw tears shining in her eyes.

"Did you try to talk her out of it?"

She stared at me, her mouth firming. "No, I didn't." I must have looked surprised. "She knew what she was doing. She'd made up her mind."

"Did everyone seem surprised that Sunday night?"

"Everyone but Adam, yes. No one knew what to say—they were all just stunned." She looked sad. "Carrie was such a support for the rest of them. She'd helped them all to struggle through some really bad days. David slammed out—I think he went drinking again." She shook her head. "They were all upset." She frowned a little. "Except Carl. He thought it was wonderful news. He's in such denial about the Organization that going back would be heaven for him." She sighed again, and I thought she looked tired. "Carl has the worst kind of hero worship for the men in the Organization—to him, they can do no wrong. He's very protective of them and the Organization." She rubbed her forehead as if she was getting a headache.

"David said Susan will leave Carl if he tries to go back."

She looked at me disapprovingly. "I hope you won't repeat that to Carl. She hasn't yet decided."

I was stung. "Of course I wouldn't." I looked down at my pad, trying to decide if I had any other questions, but I couldn't think of any, and I felt hurt by her abruptness. I began to gather up my things when she spoke again.

"Her death *will* change things. I shouldn't have said that." She stared at the fire and shook her head. "The foundation—it was supposed to be for young people like her, to help them move on with their lives. Perhaps fill a little of the space their families leave when they're shunned. Give them some people to talk to. Anxiety—and the inability to deal with it—are two of the worst things we're left with when we leave." She breathed deeply. "There's the anxiety of the impending Armageddon, because now you're outside the Truth, and you're going to burn with the world eventually, and then there's the financial and emotional anxiety you feel, because your life has been spent deliberately *not* preparing for any future."

"Why is that?"

"We've been taught there won't be one." She shrugged. "So many of the ex-JWs I've worked with have trouble with it. We're not used to dealing with problems." She crossed her arms and hugged herself. "Many of the young people have substance abuse or addiction problems."

Like David Young and AA, I thought, but didn't say it aloud. I stood up, sliding the strap of my bag over my shoulder. I felt like I needed to reassure her. "It still can." She turned to look at me. "The foundation—it can still be what you envisioned."

She smiled and nodded, and we walked to the door. Through the little window next to the door, I could see the rain-slicked street. Before I could turn the knob, she stopped me with a hand on my arm.

"I hope you'll come back some time. When you're done with all this." She patted my arm, and I could see that, beyond the fashionable artist persona, she was a bit lonely.

I smiled, touched. "I'd like that," I said, and gave her a little hug. I ran out to the car and looked back when I was inside. She was still standing in the doorway, and she raised a hand as I pulled away.

———

I CHECKED MY VOICEMAIL AT A RED LIGHT. THE FIRST MESSAGE from Gerard was short.

"Benedict. Call me."

I scoffed. Bossy man. The second message, half an hour later, sounded even worse.

"Benedict, I swear to God, you're never around when I need you to be. Call me."

The third message was longer.

"Okay, Benedict. This evening, grandson had a call with his therapist. He told her that he was suicidal, and he's now in solitary. Call me."

I pulled the car over and called him. He answered on the first ring.

"Benedict."

"Gerard, what did you do?"

"Benedict, you ray of sunshine on a rainy night." He chuckled, but he sounded tired. "Apparently, after our visit, grandson felt more and more guilty, and he asked to call his therapist." His voice was sharp and laden with sarcasm.

"Did you have to tell him about the cause of death?"

He paused. "Benedict, I understand that you're new at this, but we have to speak with grandson, and move this along—either a plea, or preparation for a defense. He's our client—we can't protect him from that." He sighed. "And that means honest talk with him."

I tilted my head back to the seat headrest and watched the cars approaching, their lights reflecting the raindrops on my windshield between wiper swipes. In the distance, I could hear thunder rumble. I turned off my wipers and watched the rain running in rivulets down the glass.

Gerard was silent too, and I wondered what he was watching. Was it raining on him too? When he finally spoke, his voice was rough. "Do we have any other suspects?"

"No. Not yet." I thought of all the people I'd met in the last week, and realized that none of them seemed to have a motive to kill Carrie Ames—not even Todd. "Gerard, doesn't this feel like a motiveless crime?" It sounded even worse outside my head. "I mean, there's no reason for her to die. She held no secrets, she had no money, she had friends, not enemies. Why would someone kill her?" I tapped my fingers on the steering wheel.

Gerard rumbled at me. "There's always a motive." I heard a dog barking. "Hold on." There was rustling, and then a door shut. "Good girl." I smiled a little, envisioning him and his dog. "Not you, Benedict." I laughed, enjoying the moment. I imagined him letting the dog out of some palatial mansion in Highland Park, into a park-like backyard. Did he follow along behind the dog, scooping as he went?

"Even nice people do things other people don't like, Benedict. If it wasn't grandson who was unhappy with her, we have to suggest that there could have been many others who were unhappy too."

"Well, if there are, I haven't found them." I closed my eyes and listened to the rain drumming on the roof of the car. "So far, everyone seemed to love her."

"No one is loved by everyone."

"That's cynical and absolutely what I'd expect from you, Gerard."

He barked a laugh. "Hold on." I waited, listening to him crooning nonsense to a dog. A few seconds later, he came back on. "Do we have a meeting sometime soon? Grandson had some information we need to discuss."

"Tomorrow, 3 pm."

"Hopefully, it's at that place with the cinnamon things."

I smiled. "Nope. Your office."

"Damn." I heard a dog's tags jingling. "Maybe I can change it."

"You let me know, Gerard." I turned my wipers back on.

"Be safe, Benedict." He hung up. I signaled, then pulled back into traffic, thinking about Carrie Ames and all the people who loved her.

———

MY FATHER'S MOTHER DIDN'T BELIEVE IN GOD. SHE WASN'T A gentle agnostic unsure about whether there was a God or how he or she might run the universe; she was a card-carrying member of the American Atheists and a supporter of Madalyn Murray-O'Hair, the woman who sued to demand separation of church and state and who was long investigated by the FBI and police forces where she lived and worked. My grandmother didn't force her views on me and Ryan, but we were rarely around religious people, and organized religion didn't affect us much after we began to live with her. She tolerated our desire for Christmas presents or Easter egg hunts, but she always stressed the sectarian or pagan nature of most holidays. In high school, I was invited to visit church with friends, and I came away with a smidgen of comfort from the beauty of the services of the faithful, tempered with a large portion of doubt and—I must admit—suspicion.

People who are members of organized religion don't realize how completely religion pervades American society. Our language is peppered with allusions to religious stories, our laws provide for religious observance to an extreme extent, and people who are not religious are seen as unnatural. I've heard it's not that way in other countries.

My friends who know I'm not religious often envy me for what they see as a lack of added stress in my life. They tell me stories of holidays fraught with family censure and premarital counseling sessions with prying priests or ministers, and I wonder at their tolerance for allowing strangers to pass judgment on their relationships and lifestyles. I find myself wondering about God and the universe, and I realize I'm probably hedging my bets on the subject by staying agnostic. It's difficult to agree with people who believe we are just flesh and electrical impulse, but I also find it hard to create a relationship with a divine being, given the state of our world. I continue to collect data either way.

The work I was doing was steeped in religion, and I felt like I was traveling in a land where I didn't speak the language. I wondered if

I'd understand these people better if I'd been someone who had been raised in a religious family, but, since that was clearly not the case, I figured I'd better make the most of the skills I had and do more research. The ex-JWs didn't seem to notice how often they referenced the Bible or parables or verses in conversation, but I wrote them all down, and—since I'd come home from dinner with Ann Thornton wired from the extremely strong Turkish coffee—I spent a few hours looking up Bible verses.

I started with Naomi and Ruth's story (and felt bad for Naomi's twin sister, who got stuck with what I thought was the less-cool name), and then dug into the Bible verses everyone seemed to know but me. After an hour or so checking references, including the ones Carl Grassley had mentioned (which seemed to be plucked out at random for certain words and with no attention to context), I looked up the parable Sam Ames had mentioned—the one of the prodigal son. Of course, that parable is one that everyone knows to some extent, since it's become part of the American lexicon. Kid decides he's not living his best life at home, so he asks dad for his inheritance early and leaves for the big city. There he parties with all the wrong people, spends all his money, and ends up eating with the pigs. Meanwhile, older brother stays home and does all the dull stuff needed for the family business. Younger son comes home, and Dad throws a party to welcome him back.

I could sympathize with the hardworking older son—the one who stayed with Dad and kept working on—who is quite understandably miffed at the welcome home party, and tells his father so. Dad points out that the younger son 'was dead and is alive again, was lost and is now found.' That seemed nice, but Dad also tries to comfort the older son by telling him that 'you have always been with me, and everything I have is yours.' The Bible doesn't record how older son felt about this, but—given my perspective from the outskirts of religious territory—I can tell you what I think: He never felt like everything the father had was his, or he probably wouldn't have worked as hard as he did. Maybe he'd have taken some time off to go to town and party a little. As Ann Thornton had said, religion often seems like a transaction: $1+1=$heaven, and that means earning your way in.

And the younger son. Poor kid. He thinks he's going off to the big city for opportunity and success, and finds out it's not what he thought it was all along. He comes back and his self-esteem is shot. He tells his father, 'I'm not worthy to be called your son.' For a moment, I wondered if that's what Carrie Ames was feeling when she decided to go back; had she come to regret her decisions? Did she hope her Dad would throw a welcome home party, and was she disappointed he didn't want her to come home? Unlike the father and son in the parable, according to Sam Ames and David Young, the returning JW would have to spend some time proving repentance, perhaps working for months on the 'family farm' and showing how well she'd learned her lesson.

I looked up the parable Adam Garrison had mentioned, about a shepherd trying to find a lost sheep. The final verse of the parable reads: 'I tell you that in the same way there will be more rejoicing in heaven over one sinner who repents than over ninety-nine righteous persons who do not need to repent.' It seemed like a lovely sentiment, but, from all accounts, the Jehovah's Witnesses would have greeted Carrie Ames with more suspicion than joy.

There were numerous explanations of the parable, and several songs that retold the story with dramatic detail, imagining the hardship the shepherd endures to find the one wayward lamb. One hymn, 'The Ninety and Nine,' painted the shepherd much like I think Adam Garrison saw himself: climbing rocky mountains to find the lamb, crossing rivers and suffering injury as he searched. He leaves a trail of his own blood before he rescues the lamb 'sick and helpless and ready to die.'

I went to bed and dreamed of Adam Garrison and Carrie Ames, both with blood on their hands—but whose blood, I couldn't say.

CHAPTER EIGHTEEN

My phone rang at 6:30 am, waking me from a dead sleep and a dream of law school, where I'd lost the combination to my locker.

Ryan and Sara have the only numbers that ring through a nightly 'do not disturb' on my phone, so I knew it was one of them, and I happily dragged myself up from the panic of having no books for criminal law class to answer the phone. It was Ryan, letting me know that a spot had opened up at the assisted living facility he'd wanted to talk about, and Dad had moved up the wait list. If we wanted, he could move in the next week. If we didn't, they'd pass him over to the next person on the list. I told him I'd come to Plano so we could discuss it.

I got out of bed and showered, all the while thinking: *Someone died so my dad would have a room.* The feeling of dread inspired by that thought wasn't banished by the beautiful day outside, sharply cold and with the clear blue sky that only Texas winters bring.

As usual, I left the cat sleeping and bundled up in an old navy peacoat and beanie to do some office supply shopping. During the night, I'd decided that I needed a larger whiteboard to map out all the people Carrie Ames knew. No one—not the police, the DA, or Gerard—believed she was killed by a stranger. If it wasn't Todd, it was someone else I'd spoken with, or someone I needed to find. I had a plan to get a walk in this afternoon and then get all my notes typed and scanned this evening after meeting with Gerard. I could white-board the whole thing tomorrow night when I was avoiding Valen-tine's Day.

After picking up the largest whiteboard the store had, I headed for Plano. I had no court appearances or meetings today until Gerard in mid-afternoon, and I wanted to visit with my dad. I couldn't help but think we were rushing moving him into a facility. As I pulled into Ryan and Sara's driveway, my phone beeped with a text message from Carmen, Gerard's assistant, passing along the name and the number of Todd's therapist, with a request that I call her, since Gerard was in trial. I kept the message, but turned off the ringer on my phone. I'd do that later.

My father was awake, and up talking to Sara. The last time I'd been here, he'd seemed fine—oh, maybe a little fuzzy—but okay. This time was different, the room full of a buzzing tension.

Sara caught sight of me coming in, but I didn't register her slight head shake.

"Hey, Dad, how you doing today?"

He rounded on me. For a moment, I thought he recognized me, but then he began shouting. "Rhonda, Rhonda—come in here! Who are these people?"

Sara laid her hand on his arm, but he shook her off. "I don't know you, young lady." He turned towards the bathroom, calling for my mother. "Rhonda! Come out please! We need to go home!" He stepped towards me, suddenly seeming aggressive.

"Ian, please. Let's sit down." Sara put her hand on his back, but he slipped away and threw out an arm to hold her off.

"I don't know you. I don't *know* you. Why are you holding me here?" He flailed his arms, my once-strong father reduced to fighting off strangers. Sara ducked, and it was a good thing. He would have hit her in the head.

I pulled the beanie off my head. I didn't know what to do, but maybe if he recognized me, he'd calm down.

"Dad—Ian, Ian....please calm down." I put myself in front of him. His eyes streaming tears, he blinked once, then again.

"Rhonda?" His voice quavered, and my heart broke.

"Yes, Ian. It's Rhonda." I warily reached out a hand, but he let me take his arm and lead him back to his bed. "Let's sit here for a minute." I perched next to him, sliding my hand down to his. His skin was so hot and dry, his hand stiff and unyielding. I willed my panic to go away, trying to breathe in and out, in and out, like Ann Thornton had said.

"He's not been feeling well, and his medicine wouldn't stay down. We probably need to try another dose." Sara busied herself in the bathroom while I stroked my dad's hand. He looked down at our joined hands, and his fingers tightened around mine.

Sara returned with a cup of water and two pills. "Mr. Benedict, I know you have a headache. This might help."

He looked up at her without any recognition, or, it seemed, memory of the last few minutes. "I do have a headache. Is this aspirin?"

"It's something like that, yes." She helped him take the medication and a sip of water.

I stood and turned to him. "Ian, why don't you lie down while that takes effect?" He nodded slowly, the air seeming to leave him, and I helped him turn to lie on the bed.

"Rhonda, stay with me. I need to talk to you when I wake up. I haven't seen Lacey and Ryan, and I'm worried." He seemed drowsy and tired, but I rubbed his shoulder and told him I'd be there.

Sara and I stood next to the bed until he slept, not speaking, holding each other's hand tightly.

––––––

We met in the kitchen, and I was shaking in anger and despair. I waited until she pushed the door almost shut, then spoke in a loud whisper. "How long? How long has it been like this?"

She motioned for me to sit, and then checked the water level in the coffeemaker. I recognized that she too was shaking, that the whole ordeal had been traumatic for her, but I couldn't help myself. I didn't want to sit—I wanted to know.

"Sara! How long?"

She inserted a pod in the coffee maker and reached for a cup. It rattled against the machine as she slid it under the pour spout. "A few months."

"A few *months*?" Shocked, I sat down abruptly. "Why didn't you guys tell me?"

She turned to look at me while the coffee brewed, leaning back on the counter, her eyes defensive and a bit angry. "Lacey, we did tell you. We've *been* telling you."

"Not that it's been this bad. You never told me that."

She crossed her arms over her chest, and I realized that Sara was as upset as I'd ever seen her. "Lacey, why do you think I've stayed home this year? Why do think Ryan's been looking for a facility?" She wiped a hand over her face. "This actually wasn't that bad."

I was aghast. "'Not that bad'? He almost hit you!" She looked back at me steadily, and I understood. "Oh, my god. He's hit you before?" She didn't answer. The coffeemaker finished filling the cup, and she turned to repeat the process, putting the filled cup in front of me with a little container of milk and another of sugar packets.

I began to numbly add milk to my coffee, watching as the cream-colored liquid swirled into the dark brown. I waited until we both sat with our coffee, facing one another.

"Have I really not been listening?" My lips felt large and numb, and I couldn't feel my fingers. Part of me knew I was in shock, but the other part of me was sitting to one side, analyzing my response, cataloguing my responsibility and my shame.

Sara slid her hand over to mine, covering it and lightly squeezing. "How could we have really described it to you? We weren't hiding it, but we didn't want to upset you either."

I slid my hand out. "I'm not a child, Sara. I can handle bad news."

She looked at me, kindness and pity on her face, and I felt like crying—something that wouldn't have helped my case about my maturity.

I sighed. I didn't want the coffee. I wanted everything to be the way it had been before I knew all this. "What next?"

"Lace, he needs more help than I can give him. As much as I care for him, I'm not a trained professional. And I'm not as strong as he is physically." She wearily rubbed her face with both hands.

"Were you up all night?"

She shook her head. "Ryan and I took turns. I slept first, and then he went to bed about 2. He had early cafeteria duty." She took a sip of her coffee.

"Do you want to get some rest while I'm here?" Surely I could handle Dad if he woke and was upset. I'd just pretend to be my mother again.

Without answering, she took another sip of coffee and then set it aside, folding her arms on the table and resting her forehead on top. She was asleep before I stepped out of the room.

———

TODD'S THERAPIST WAS A WOMAN NAMED MARIA LONG, AND SHE considered Gerard to be an irresponsible worm for giving the news about Carrie to Todd. I know that because she said those exact words. I let her rail against him for a good five minutes, neither agreeing nor disagreeing, until she trailed off with "Are you still there?"

"I am." I sat at the family desk in the den and put my fingers over my eyes. It was only 10 am, but I felt exhausted.

"Well, what do you have to say for Mr. Gerard?" She said his name with as much vitriol as I used to.

What *did* I have to say for Rob Gerard? "Dr. Long," I began, but she interrupted me with an offended sniff.

"I'm not a doctor. I'm a certified and licensed therapist."

"My apologies. Ms. Long, Gerard had an obligation to tell Todd what the DA told us." *Dammit.* "We also believed that, with him being on his regular medication, he was able to function normally, and could assist us with his defense. Is that not the case?"

There was a slight pause. "I sense that's a legal determination, not a therapeutic one."

"That's true. If he's not able to assist us with his defense, we may have to notify the Court."

"Then I can't really make that determination, can I? I'm not a *lawyer*." From her tone, 'lawyer' was one step up from 'worm.' I pictured her lecturing me, a little old lady with glasses sliding down her nose, her graying hair tucked into an untidy bun, her poking finger inches from my face.

I inhaled, a deep, deep breath laden with the day's frustrations, and then exhaled, watching it go, hopefully leaving me with calm and peace. "Then what can you say about his condition, Ms. Long?"

"While I understand the legal need to inform him of his girl-friend's cause of death and a potential change in the charges against him, it would have been better advised to consider the potential setback that you would have been causing for Todd—if you'd truly had his best interests at heart." She took a deep breath, and I knew more was coming. "Instead, you took it upon yourselves to bring him to the precipice of a nervous breakdown, when we were getting very close to a breakthrough." She ended the sentence loudly, and I could almost see her therapist's finger pointing in my direction.

I rested my forehead in my hand and prayed to whatever deity might be up there for patience. "Ms. Long, I—" She interrupted me.

"I'm not done!" She rapped the statement against the phone. "All of this was based on the faulty assumption that his medication would solve all his difficulties!" She inhaled. "In the five years I've worked with Todd, I've never heard him this upset."

"Ms. Long!" I spoke as sharply as I could. "I'm aware that the assumption we made about his ability to handle the news may not have been correct, but here is where we are." I calmed my voice. "If you have recommendations that we can give to the judge regarding changes to his detention that might help his condition, please email them to Carmen, Rob Gerard's assistant, and we will get those into a motion right away."

There was a long pause. "Well, that's not what I expected you to say." She sniffed again. "I'll get that right out."

"I do have a couple of questions for you. You *did* receive Todd's signed authorization allowing us to ask you questions?" I rubbed my forehead, as if rubbing it would stop the headache building there.

"I did, but I still don't think it's best for—"

My irritation finally bubbled over. "Ms. Long, I'm not going to ask you anything you shouldn't answer, but we are trying to help Todd."

"Oh." She sounded surprised. "Well, then, ask."

"Could someone with his challenges act as he's been accused of and forget that he did?"

She paused, and I could hear her thinking. "The mental health field is not that proficient at predicting violent behavior." She stopped. "In fact, we really suck at that kind of thing." She almost surprised a laugh out of me at that, but I smothered it. "But if something is going to be used as a predictor, we look at past behavior. And before you ask, no, Todd's shown no violent tendencies or had any violent episodes in the past when under high emotional stress—just the opposite, in fact. Even his minor convictions were for non-violent offenses—petty theft, teenage pranks." She paused again. "That being said, anyone under significant emotional distress can act in ways one could never predict."

"Ms. Long, I recently discovered that Carrie actually told Todd that she was returning to the Jehovah's Witnesses earlier in the week before her murder. Assuming he was significantly emotionally distressed like you say, would that have lasted for four days, long enough for him to take action?"

"For someone who has anxiety at Todd's level, if he was that distressed at the news, it could have continued to ramp up to a boiling point." It wasn't what I wanted to hear. She cleared her throat and continued, her voice turning into a sing-song lecture. "You see, when humans are confronted with emotionally stressful situations, our logic mind turns off. Our emotional mind turns on, and we start to think, act, and believe in ways that are self-defensive. We aren't thinking then—we are *acting*."

"And with someone feeling that much anxiety, can they turn it off and on?"

"At that level of anxiety, no."

"Ms. Long, did Todd call you in the four days before January 27?"

There was a pause, and I heard pages rustle. "Yes. We had a scheduled therapy call on Friday, January 25. He was doing exposure exercises to work on his claustrophobia, and then checking in with me weekly."

"And was Todd in that level of emotional distress?"

She paused, and I could sense her natural reserve in talking about her patient. "No, Ms. Benedict, he was not." She sounded very sure. "We reviewed his coping skills and talked about his exposure exercises. In my notes, I recorded that he seemed a bit sad, but he told me he was doing okay." She paused. "And I believe he was."

———

I ARRANGED WITH CARMEN TO MOVE MY MEETING WITH Gerard to 4:00 at Café au Lait so I could stay with Sara until Ryan came home. When my father awoke from his nap, all his obstreperousness had passed, and I sat next to him and helped him eat his lunch while Sara ate hers. He didn't remember our previous interaction or his frustration and confusion. From his expression, he assumed I was a helpful stranger who sat next to him as he watched Raymond Burr play Perry Mason on a streaming service Sara had set up in his room. At one point, he turned to me. "My daughter is a lawyer, just like Perry Mason," he said, with such pride in his voice that I had to blink away tears. Perhaps he didn't remember me now, but he was proud of the Lacey he did recall.

I finally had time for lunch after taking care of Dad's. Sara had pulled some spaghetti sauce out of the freezer for dinner, so she thawed a little for me and served it over a tiny bit of pasta with some garlic toast. It was the highlight of my day. I told her so, and then rewarded her with the story of Carrie Ames and Todd Parrish while I ate. It was no surprise to me that Sara felt sorry for Carrie Ames.

"Poor thing."

"True. She's dead." I got a soup spoon from the silverware drawer and used it to twirl my spaghetti.

"Lacey, you're awful," she said with a reproving look. "I mean, here she's taken this huge step to get away from all that, and then she's killed." She blinked tears from her eyes.

I twirled some pasta, and a drop of sauce was thrown out of the mixture—onto my shirt. I cursed and daubed it with a paper napkin, making it that much worse. I gave up and went back to eating. "I know. But she *was* going back. I just can't figure out why." I managed to get half of the bite of pasta in my mouth before it began to slip off the fork. "And I can't find anyone who hated her enough to kill her."

Sara reached over and tore off a piece of my bread. "How about someone who loved her enough to kill her?"

I twirled some more up and then stopped with my fork halfway to my mouth. "What do you mean?"

"Well, Lace, love and hate are opposite faces of the same coin. I read that somewhere." She nibbled on the bread. "People kill for love all the time. Just watch *Lifetime* movies for a while. You'll see."

I tried to twirl the remaining strands of spaghetti on my fork, but they kept slipping off, so I got up to get a knife. "I don't think that's true. Real love doesn't lead to murder."

Sara shrugged. "How about not-real love?" She sipped her water and then stretched her arms above her head. "Not everybody feels true love—or the real love you're talking about. Maybe it was obsession. Or maybe it was someone who was jealous of her, or someone who didn't feel she was all that."

I cut the little bit of spaghetti left on my plate and scooped up a bite, thinking as I chewed and swallowed. "Several people I talked to didn't like what Carrie was doing. Carl Grassley wasn't sure she was worthy of being reinstated, I could tell that. Her father didn't approve of her choice—Ann Thornton didn't seem to, either." I used the last piece of my bread to sop up spaghetti sauce and ate it slowly. "I don't know if any of them have an alibi." Sadly, I considered my empty plate.

Sara picked up my plate before I could reconsider licking the remaining sauce off. "Then I guess you have a lot of suspects."

I frowned at her. "I came here with too few suspects, and I'm leaving with too many." I could feel my temples pounding at the thought of going back to the starting line with a new theory.

She smiled at me over the sink. "You're welcome." She washed a dish and then casually asked, "Any plans for Valentine's Day?"

I finished putting the rest of the spaghetti sauce away and ignored her.

"You know, Lace, you could come to dinner with me and Ryan. My mom and dad are coming to stay with Ian." She dried her hands on a towel and didn't look at me.

I let out a frustrated breath. "You know how much I hate this holiday. My plans are work and dinner. Maybe Chinese takeout from Cathy's." I held up a hand to stop the argument I knew would follow. "And don't tell me how I'll never meet anyone if I don't get out. It's not where my head's at right now."

I couldn't tell if she was trying to be heard or not, but I clearly heard the murmur as she walked out of the room. "I know *exactly* where your head is at right now."

———

By the time Ryan came home at 3, I had reviewed all the brochures from the facilities he'd visited, and had notes and questions on each. I didn't want us to choose Landover Bridges if it wasn't the best one.

We had a spirited and sometimes heated discussion—just the kind Ryan and I like and Sara avoids—before we all agreed that Landover, with its open spot, would be good for Dad. Once Ryan and I had made the choice, Sara presented us with lists of things to do and the completed documentation for Landover Bridges. I eyed the paperwork, and then Sara, and decided not ask her if she'd filled out only the application for Landover Bridges, assuming Ryan and I would get around to the same decision anyway. She might just as well have filled them all out, but I doubted it.

I took a checklist she'd made for me, which included some transfers and legal document changes that needed to be prepared or filed, and Ryan and I agreed that a decision needed to be made about the sale of my grandmother's farm. For better or worse, we were moving forward.

———

I was looking forward to some cinnamon knots, and maybe a half-priced slice of quiche for dinner if Marie had any left at this time of day, but I walked in to see Gerard and ADA Julia Lunsford in my usual spot. I didn't think it could go any lower, but my mood instantly took a nose dive.

Gerard saw me come in and gave me a little head nod, but I headed to the counter to get a cinnamon latte. Marie shook her head mournfully at me when I asked about cinnamon knots, but she offered a half-priced snickerdoodle cookie in substitution. As reasonable alternatives go, it was a good one. There was no quiche left, the final blow to my morale. I could feel the headache bloom across my forehead.

Once I'd gotten my latte and cookie, I walked as slowly as I could across the room. I greeted Gerard and the lovely Ms. Lunsford, who was dressed today in a navy blue coatdress I could never pull off. She was tall and slim, and the dress mimicked a double-breasted jacket that stretched all the way to her knees. Her sheer navy hose and short navy boots matched perfectly, and she wore a scarf that I'm pretty sure was Hermes. She greeted me with a smile and a firm handshake, and I tried to school my expression, but, given the fact that I started the day with a beanie on my hair and ended it with spaghetti sauce on my shirt, I felt a bit cross and I think it showed on my face. I slid my coat off and stuffed it under the table.

We sat, me and Gerard on one side of the table and Julia on the other, and I noted sourly that Gerard was finishing off what were probably the last cinnamon knots in the bakery.

"Benedict, Julia brought a bit more news."

Julia Lunsford looked at him. "Why do you call her that?"

I turned to face him. "Yeah, Gerard, why *do* you call me that?"

He looked from one of us to the other, his eyebrows coming down sharply. "How did I get to be the subject of interrogation?" He looked to her first. "I have my reasons. Now can we get to the business we're here for? Discussing a possible plea?"

I felt my head pound. "I didn't know that was what we were here for." I took a bite of cookie that sent cinnamon down the front of my shirt. I brushed it off and determined not to eat any more.

Julia looked to me and then him. "Are we not all on the same page here?"

I looked back at her, ignoring Gerard. "I don't know. What page are we on?"

She relaxed against the back of the wooden bench, looking at both of us. "Do you need me to step away?"

Gerard started to shake his head, but I said, "That'd be great, if you don't mind." She hesitated, and then smiled at me and nodded. She rose and walked in the direction of the restrooms.

I rounded on Gerard, but kept my voice to a strong whisper. "What are you doing? We don't have permission to do a plea bargain!"

Gerard looked thunderous. "Benedict, discussing possibilities isn't agreement to a plea bargain." He took a sip of his coffee and then pushed the cup away.

A little voice in my head urged caution, but I could barely hear it over the bass drums pounding inside my head. "Then what are we doing?" I meant it to sound like a valid question, but it ended in a hiss.

He frowned. "I don't know what *you're* doing, but *I'm* trying to engage in a discussion with Julia to see if I can learn what they know about the case. The rules of criminal procedure require that prosecutors have to give us access to information, but the Dallas DA's office policy means we have to know what to ask for." We both looked up as Julia came out of the restroom. "I'm hoping to get an idea of what they have."

The ADA hovered over by the sugar and milk station checking her phone, and I was a little pleased—and ashamed to be pleased—to see a tiny run in her sheer navy hose right over her left knee. "They aren't required to show us everything?"

Gerard looked back at me. "No more than a civil litigant has to open everything up in response to requests for discovery. They give what they're asked to give. We're so early in the process, nothing has really been exchanged formally." He squinted at me. "Are you all right?"

"I'm fine." My head was exploding. "I'm sorry, I didn't know." I finger-waved at Julia, who'd looked up at us. She came over, looking from one to the other.

"We good?"

"We're good," I said. She sat down and saw the run on her knee.

"Damn." She ran a finger over the run. "These were brand new."

"Yeah," I said, feeling sorry and wicked for my pleasure a minute before. "The undersides of the tables aren't that smooth."

"Well, the coffee makes up for it." She smiled at me and settled in. "So, Gerard, I know we're here so you can wiggle information out of me. What do you want to know so I can get home at a reasonable hour?"

I snickered at the look on Gerard's face. He frowned at me again, and then turned to her. "Any final autopsy results in yet?"

She shook her head, her perfect hair shaking and then settling back as it should. "I expect it next week. We have gotten the crime scene reports and the fingerprint determinations." At Gerard's look, she clarified. "No surprises. That place was the home of two young women who didn't dust that often. They had people in and out of there on a regular basis. Most of the ex-Jehovah's Witnesses who'd been there recently weren't in the system, but they'd already been approached to have prints taken for exclusion."

I perked up at that. "'Most' of them?"

She nodded. "All but two. Two of them had been printed before: Adam Garrison and David Young. Both of them had DUIs."

I looked over at Gerard, whose face was a handsome mask. Well, well, well.

———

JULIA LEFT SHORTLY AFTER THAT, AGREEING TO PASS ALONG TO Gerard's office a couple of reports from the Dallas Police Crime Scene Response Section with more information. She'd also confirmed that a man's bloody sweatshirt had been used to cover Carrie's nose and mouth as she was killed, but they didn't know whose sweatshirt it was, and there appeared to be a lot of hairs and other nice DNA-able stuff there. As she'd said at our last meeting, DNA takes a lot longer to come back than it does on television.

My head hurt to keep it upright, but the coffee helped a tiny bit. I moved over across the table and made a few notes about the information she'd given while Gerard checked his voicemails. When he finished, I could feel him looking at me while I wrote.

"What?" I asked crossly, not looking up.

"Are you sure you're okay, Benedict? You don't look okay."

I was even more aware of my wrinkled and stained shirt and flattened hair. "What are you trying to say, Gerard?"

He leaned forward. "I'm saying you don't look okay, Benedict."

"Yeah, well, I've had a long day." I rubbed a hand over my eyes. "Family crap."

"Everything all right?"

I looked at him. What would he do if I just laid it all out for him? Dysfunctional family dynamics, money problems, father issues, everything? Probably run like hell.

"Yeah, it'll be fine." I remembered my call at midday. "Oh, that reminds me. Thanks for siccing the therapist on me. There's now a contract out on us." I smiled evilly. "I gave her your address."

He had the grace to look a little embarrassed. "Yes, well...thanks for taking care of that. I uh, was in trial this morning."

I eyed him suspiciously. "You didn't stay in trial all day. I noticed you were here early enough to get the last of the day's cinnamon knots."

A Cheshire cat smile spread across his face. "They were even better than last time."

I controlled the urge to stick my tongue out at him. "And had time to visit with the beautiful Julia."

He shrugged. "Is she?"

"Oh, come on. Like you don't notice."

He looked at the door she'd exited a few minutes before as if picturing her. "I went to law school with her. I've known her a long time. She's attractive." He turned to look at me. "So are you."

I snorted. "Not like that."

He tilted his head and raised his black eyebrows. "Are you jealous?"

I tossed my head and immediately regretted the motion, as it set the drums pounding harder in my head. "No. Just an observation." I crumbled off a piece of the snickerdoodle cookie and ate it. Another mistake. The movement of my jaw caused the side of my head to hurt more, and I rubbed my forehead.

"You are not okay, Benedict." He touched my hand. "Is it a migraine?"

My skin prickled at his touch. I shook my head carefully. "I don't know. I don't get migraines." Even talking was beginning to hurt. "The therapist had some good information." I started to flip my note pages over, but the sudden motion made my whole body hurt. "I think I'm going to go home."

"I'll drive you."

I shook my head, and moaned as the pain rang a deep bell inside my skull. "I can make it."

"Benedict, you can't even move your head without pain."

"I have a hearing in the morning. I can't leave my car here." I tried Ann Thornton's breathing, in and out, in and out, but the pain didn't let up.

"So I'll drive yours home, and then get a car to bring me back here. It's no big deal." He rose and carried our dishes to the busser station, and then came back for his coat. I watched him, feeling curiously detached from everything. When he held out his hand for the keys, I handed them over without any further argument.

I made it out to the car—barely—and clambered into the passenger seat. Gerard locked up his car and slid in the driver's side, making multiple adjustments to the seat and steering wheel so he could get in. As I sat there, I realized that I'd never been on the passenger's side of my car. Everything looked different and off-center, and it made me feel nauseated. I closed my eyes.

Gerard drove slowly, even sedately, as if he knew the motion was making my head ache. When he spoke, it felt as if he was far, far away. "What time is your hearing tomorrow? Could someone else cover it for you?"

I didn't even open my eyes to answer. The late afternoon sun was so bright. "11. And I don't have a firm of associates to cover hearings for me, Gerard." I could hear the waspishness in my tone, but I really didn't care.

"I know you don't have associates, Benedict. I just meant another lawyer or solo who does what you do."

I felt weary. "I don't know any other lawyers who do what I do. It's me or nothing. I just need to sleep, I think. I'll be fine in the morning." I wasn't so sure, but I couldn't talk anymore.

He pulled into my drive and under the overhang. The shadow over the car was so welcome I almost whimpered. I opened the door, but the movement made my stomach lurch alarmingly. I stopped and hung there, uncommitted, for a moment.

Gerard spoke next to me. "Want me to bring in the whiteboard from the back seat?" I think I murmured yes, but I couldn't tell at that point.

I staggered to the door, which Gerard had already unlocked, and immediately headed for the bedroom. The curtains were open and the afternoon sun poured in, but I laid down on the bed and pulled a pillow over my eyes. Gerard followed me in, and I had no energy to protest as he took off my boots and coat. By that time, I was beginning to shiver in the cold of the unheated room. He pulled the covers up over me.

The next few hours are foggy even now. I remember Gerard talking about my phone, and, at some point, Miss Sallie was there, smoothing my forehead with a cool cloth. I remember pain, and cold, and blessed relief, and that was all.

CHAPTER NINETEEN

I woke when my phone's alarm went off at 9:30, fully dressed in my stained and wrinkled clothes from the day before. I felt slightly hungover, but the movement to turn off my phone didn't make me want to throw up. I didn't remember setting the alarm, silencing the ringer, or closing the curtains over the window, but the room was dark, I'd slept for 16 hours, and I was awake on time, so I counted my blessings.

I showered and dressed in what I thought of as my going-to-court clothes, moving slowly and carefully. The worst of the headache was gone, and I started thinking there was a god after all. Then I began to make the bed and found that the cat had finally emerged, and she'd left the gift of a little hairball on one of my pillows. She was nowhere to be found for a thank you.

I'd already prepped for the Barnstead hearing at 11, so I scooped up my keys and the file and headed out the door, noticing as I did that Gerard had brought in the whiteboard from the car. I felt slightly uncomfortable knowing that I'd owe him for his kindness the day before. He'd also left me a voicemail the night before, telling me to come by the Federal District Court today after my hearing, and we could continue our conversation if he broke for lunch.

I noticed the big white tent set up outside the local grocery store to sell flowers and other Valentine's Day gifts to forgetful husbands and boyfriends on their way home from work. I imagined that most of them would take home a fistful of red carnations or a card and consider it done, and their wives or girlfriends would cry themselves to sleep. Truly, this holiday was my least favorite of all. I was glad not to be out in the mayhem tonight.

I got to Justice Laughlin's court about 10:45, and I watched him dress down an unprepared plaintiff's lawyer I knew before abruptly granting him his default judgment. The lawyer stumbled out of the courtroom, a haggard shadow of his former cocky self. By then it was just me and the judge and his bailiff in the courtroom. He checked his docket and then looked at me, a snowy bald eagle with shaggy gray eyebrows, and then he looked deliberately around the room.

"Miss Benedict, I don't see your opponent in the courtroom." I slowly looked around the courtroom before responding.

"I don't see her either, your honor." I walked forward towards the bar.

He raised an eyebrow, but I swear it looked like he might smile. "Is she still occupying the property?"

I'd gotten an email from my client this morning. "As of this morning, yes, she is, your honor." I leaned on the short wooden barrier between the gallery and the courtroom proper.

"Then let's begin." He looked at his bailiff. "Sergeant Carew, please call the halls."

I stepped forward to the plaintiff's table while the bailiff went out to the hall to call Sophia Barnstead's name. It was 11:01.

The bailiff came back in and shook his head. I breathed a bit easier, then asked for permission to approach. I was halfway through the recitation of the eviction elements and handing the Court a copy of the Barnstead lease and its attached affidavit when Sophia Barnstead rushed into the room, trailed by three women and a man, all in various stages of elderliness.

"Your worship! Your worship! Don't sign those papers!" She was dressed in a vibrant red coat and rain boots, maybe in honor of Valentine's Day, but the coonskin cap still perched on her head.

Justice Laughlin had donned his reading glasses to review evidence, and he peered at her over the half-moons as she burst through the swinging gate and towards the bench. Sergeant Carew moved to intercept her, and—for a wild moment—I thought she might push him aside. Instead she veered off toward the defendant's table where she'd sat before. She pointed a finger at me. "You need to start over."

The glasses came off and the judge's head lowered, and he looked pointedly at the clock on the wall, which read 11:05. "Miss Barnstead. You were present at the coordinator's desk when she told you this hearing was set for 11:00 am today, were you not?"

Sophia Barnstead nodded, sending the coon's tail bobbing. "I was, your worship. But I was unavoidably detained."

At the repeated 'your worship,' I saw Justice Laughlin's quick frown and wondered if it masked a smile. "Miss Barnstead, you may call me 'Justice Laughlin' or 'your honor,' but I am not an English magistrate." He pointed at her with his glasses. "We also begin hearings on time in this courtroom, and only *the court* is allowed to give instructions to counsel."

She sat at the defense table. "I understand, your honor, and my apologies. As I said, I was unavoidably dee-tained." She looked over at me. "Someone—and I'm not saying who—but *someone* made sure my car didn't start this morning."

I felt my mouth drop open. Was she accusing me of tampering with her car so she couldn't show up for an eviction hearing? I looked over at the judge, who was watching Sophia Barnstead with something approaching concern on his face.

"Miss Barnstead, are you—" He stopped, and gave a slight shake of his head. "Let's just get this started." He looked at me and then handed me the documents. "Miss Benedict, please step back and start again."

"Yes, your honor." I moved my folder and documents to the plaintiff's table and waited to begin again. He nodded at me, but before I could speak, Sophia Barnstead spoke again.

"Wait, wait!" I looked at her. She held up a hand in traffic cop fashion to me and spoke to Justice Laughlin. "Aren't we going to have this recorded?"

He'd started to slide on his reading glasses to recite the case, but he stopped. "Recorded, Miss Barnstead?"

"Yeah, you know, with the little woman typing." She waved at the witness box and mimicked typing with long-nailed fingers.

"Do you mean a court reporter?" His tone was icy, but Sophia Barnstead didn't appear to notice.

"That's it! A court reporter." She looked at me. "I want all this on a record." Her eyes narrowed vengefully. "All of it." I kept my eyes on the judge, who appeared to take exception to her tone.

"Miss Barnstead, proceedings in the justice court are not usually on record. All appeals from the justice court are *de novo*—that means that they start over. There is no need for a record." He looked thunderous at this point.

"It's my right to have one, innit?" Her tone was mutinous, and I really didn't know who would win this one. Then Justice Laughlin sat back in his chair and looked—really looked—at Sophia Barnstead.

"You can have a record, Miss Barnstead." His tone was deceptively mild, but she didn't seem to notice. She started to look triumphant, and then he continued. "However, you'll have to pay for it." Her smile started to falter. "In advance." She squinted at him.

"Well, I can't do that." She waved at me. "Go ahead."

I looked at Justice Laughlin, who shrugged and motioned to me. "Yes, go ahead, Miss Benedict."

———

I'D LIKE TO SAY IT WAS MY FINEST HOUR AS AN ATTORNEY, BUT IT wasn't. Oh, I did my job, walking the court through the lease, the notices, the service, but I was interrupted by Sophia Barnstead at every step, and the constant interruptions had me rattled. I'd brought copies of all the documentation for her just in case she showed up, but she insisted on seeing every copy of every document, sure I was handing something to the judge with secret notes not included in her copy.

After a quarter hour of this, I finally finished what should have been a five-minute prove-up procedure and sat down. The judge turned to Sophia Barnstead and asked her if she wanted to speak to the matters I'd raised. She marched up to the witness stand and sat down, clearly intent on having her say. After a surprised hesitation, Justice Laughlin swore her in, and she answered with a ringing "I do" and a look at her audience in the gallery.

She launched into a story about her apartment, its condition, and her feelings of being ignored by my client, the landlord. I listened with growing alarm, watching the judge's face as he listened as well. He seemed to be hanging on her every word.

Because this was an eviction proceeding—where the only issue is who has the right to possession of the apartment—I'd not talked to my client about any complaints or issues with the apartment. When she began to show the judge her phone and some pictures of what she said were roaches as big as rats, I popped up and objected.

Justice Laughlin looked at me. "What's the basis of your objection, counsel?"

I took a leap. "These documents have not been properly authenticated, your honor." He frowned at me and turned to Sophia Barnstead.

"Madam, did you take these pictures yourself?"

She looked at me with satisfaction. "I did, your wor—your honor."

He looked back at me. "Objection overruled." I started to sit again, but his next question stopped me. "Any other objections, counsel?"

My mind cleared. "Relevance, your honor." He seemed to nod a little, so I continued. "These photos, and this line of testimony, are not relevant to possession of the apartment, which is the only issue before the court today."

"Sustained." He turned to Sophia Barnstead. "Madam, do you have any testimony in regards to possession of the apartment?"

She frowned at him. "It's *all* about possession of the apartment."

He turned to me. "Miss Benedict, why don't you ask Ms. Barnstead some questions."

I knew there was a possibility she would be at the hearing, so I'd prepared a list of questions. I pulled them out, and then inhaled deeply. *I could do this.* "Permission to approach, your honor?" He nodded.

I selected several documents, and then moved to stand in front of the witness box. "Miss Barnstead, is this your signature on the lease, which was previously entered as Exhibit A?" I placed the copy of the document with its scrawled signature on the wooden ledge in front of her.

She looked at it briefly. "Yes, it is, but that lease is *not* fair." She drew in breath to continue, but I slid in my next question.

"And do you see here, where this paragraph says you must pay your rent by the first day of every month?"

She squinted to the page where I pointed. "I don't got my glasses on, so I can't see it good."

I looked at Justice Laughlin. "Your honor, we can wait while Miss Barnstead puts on her glasses."

The judge looked at Sophia Barnstead, who scowled at me. "I can see good enough. Yeah, it says that."

"And did you pay the rent listed here in the lease by December 1, or at all in December?"

"Well, no I didn't, but he didn't fix the heat until after that cold snap we had in early December. The heater kept cutting off at 74 degrees." She looked at the judge to explain. "My joints get really cold." She looked like she would continue, so I asked the next question quickly.

"Did you pay the rent listed here in the lease by January 1, or at all in January?"

She crossed her arms over her ample, red-coated bosom. "That was a holiday, January 1, and I hadn't gotten my social security check in the bank early." She looked back at her audience. "None of our money came in before New Year's day, did it, Phyllis?" The judge and I looked at one of the women in the gallery, who shook her head vigorously.

I began to feel sorry for Sophia Barnstead. "But did you pay it late, or let the landlord know you needed extra time?"

She shook her head, and the raccoon skin shook too, little hairs falling out to land on the bright red coat. "That place is in such bad shape, it's not worth that much money."

I ignored the comment. "Miss Barnstead, did you pay the rent listed here in the lease by February 1, or at all so far in February?"

This time, she clamped her lips together and didn't respond. I looked at the judge, who leaned a bit toward Sophia Barnstead and said, "Madam, you must answer the question."

She spat the words out with a glare at me. "No, I didn't."

I shuffled through my papers, and found the notice to vacate. "Miss Barnstead, do you remember this document on your door, the Notice to Vacate, previously entered as Exhibit B?"

She sat up. "That's the one." She looked at the judge. "I never saw no letter on my door."

I flipped over the pages of the notice to the certified mail green card for the notice I'd mailed to her. "Miss Barnstead, I also sent that document to you by certified mail, and it was signed for. Is this your signature?"

She looked at the copy of the card, where her signature was clearly scrawled—the same signature as the one on the lease. Her lips tightened, and she looked at the judge before saying grudgingly,

"Yes." She scratched up under the edge of the coonskin cap, and I swear I thought it was moving on its own.

I found the constable's service return for the lawsuit and showed it to her, but the air was going out of her at this point. "Miss Barnstead, a constable served the petition for this lawsuit on an adult answering the door of the apartment, someone named Julius Barnstead. Do you see the constable's signature here on what's been entered as Exhibit C?" She nodded tightly, and then, at a look from the judge, said aloud, "Yes."

"And do you know who that person is?"

"That's my grandson. He's staying with me." She crossed her arms over her chest, daring me to say something about Julius.

"Is he an adult?"

She snorted. "He's 19, but he ain't no adult."

I returned to the table and put my copies of the exhibits down, my mind clicking through the elements I needed to prove. I turned to face the witness stand again. "Miss Barnstead, are you still living in the apartment?"

She snarled at me—literally snarled at me—before hissing, "Yes." Before I could go on, she ground out, "For all the good it does me. It's falling down around my ears!" She looked past me to her chorus for confirmation, but I didn't look.

"Your honor, I pass the witness."

Justice Laughlin started to speak, but she interrupted him. "Can I say something else?" He paused, and then nodded. She looked at me. "You can win this, but that owner treats me and the rest of us like dogs. *Worse than dogs!* And I will take this to the Supreme Court, see if I won't! before I move out." She drew a breath and then pointed directly at me. "And I'll sue you, too!" She sat back in the chair and looked at the judge assessingly, as if deciding about suing him as well.

I think he was speechless. He looked at her, then me, then at his bailiff. Sergeant Carew—normally impassive—was staring at Sophia Barnstead with a frown on his broad face, unsure if she was threatening the judge or not.

Justice Laughlin finally spoke. "Miss Barnstead, you may return to the defendant's table." As she made her way there, her back stiff, he turned to me. "While I would normally allow you to go last for a final statement, Miss Benedict, I think it best if you make it now. You have two minutes." He took off his glasses and sat back in his big leather chair.

I had absolutely no idea what to say after all that, but I scrambled again. "Your honor, plaintiff has authenticated and admitted the lease with the defendant's signature, which she has testified is the lease she signed, and defendant has herself testified that she has not paid the rent in three months." I paused as Sophia Barnstead seemed about to interrupt, but then I continued when she caught the expression on the judge's face and stopped. "Therefore, the lease has been breached. She's testified that she signed for the eviction notice, and it and the notice of this suit were properly served on an adult in the household of Miss Barnstead." I scanned the documents, trying to decide if I needed something else. "She's still living in the property. Therefore, a writ of possession in the plaintiff's favor should be executed by this court." I looked up at the judge, who seemed to approve. I hoped. I sat down.

He turned to Sophia Barnstead. "Miss Barnstead, you have two minutes for a final statement."

She stood, and took a deep breath. "This is a court of law, but there's no justice being done here. I'm living in a shithole—a shithole! I tell you!—and it's all their fault." She pointed at me. "Her and that landlord!" The coonskin cap quivered with her indignation, and several hairs drifted down like snowflakes. "You may win today, but you'll have to drag me outta there." She slammed her hands down on the table, and then she turned and pushed through the gate toward the gallery, where several attorneys were standing at the door, listening. She bellowed at them, and they scattered in front of her. Sergeant Carew stood abruptly, but she continued out through the back door of the courtroom, her small entourage trailing behind.

———

THERE'S A FIVE-DAY WAITING PERIOD BEFORE A WRIT OF possession can be issued, so that a tenant has time to appeal an eviction proceeding if the judge rules against him or her, which Justice Laughlin did in Miss Barnstead's absence. A landlord has to wait that out before getting a writ of possession served at the property by a constable. I decided I'd need to tell my client the details in person—I wasn't sure he'd believe me even then—because I was pretty sure Sophia Barnstead would be appealing this proceeding to the county court. I texted him that we'd won as I rode the escalator down to the ground floor, where I stepped outside to a sunny day and decided to walk the three blocks to the federal court building.

I was stopped twice on my way, once by a scruffy older man who was selling bedraggled red roses for five dollars each in honor of Valentine's Day, and then again by a tourist couple asking me for 'directions to the place where JFK died.'" I almost sent them over to the site of the old Parkland hospital building where President John F. Kennedy actually expired after being shot in downtown Dallas, but I took pity on them and directed them down two blocks to the spot in the street in front of the Texas Schoolbook Depository where Kennedy was shot, which is what I presumed they meant. They thanked me, and then asked me to take a picture of them with their phone. I'm not sure how exciting the downtown Dallas bus terminal is, but now they have a picture of themselves in front of it.

The air was still pretty cool, but the sun shone down on the street in between the buildings. I was so happy not to have the headache of the day before that I tipped my head back to breathe in the sunshine and almost choked on the exhaust fumes of a passing delivery truck. Ah, well.

All of the court buildings have enhanced security these days, with metal detectors and law enforcement officers scrutinizing the people entering and leaving. After going through security, I checked my voicemail again and headed to the seventh floor, where Gerard was in trial. For a moment, as I stood in the elevator and waited for the '7' to light, I remembered being in this elevator, going to a trial where I was a witness. I expected to feel the same old feelings of fear and dread, but I was pleasantly surprised to find those gone.

Once on the seventh floor, I went through another checkpoint and, unlike the regular civilians going through, I was allowed to keep my cell phone, although I had to show them it was silenced. I slipped into the back of the courtroom, unnoticed by everyone but the bailiff and the judge. The female prosecutor was questioning an expert witness, the jury seemingly hanging on her every word.

Gerard was sitting at the defense table next to his client, an older man in a sharp gray suit. A young woman sat on the other side of the client, assiduously taking notes. Gerard himself sat still, leaning back in his chair, one leg crossed over the other with his hands threaded together resting on the top leg. He always sat like that, I remembered, never taking a note, his expression giving nothing away.

I watched for an hour as the prosecutor walked the expert through her testimony, painstakingly authenticating documents and establishing dates and times. Given my recent experience, I was impressed at how effortless it seemed for her, but the jury was bored to death. From where I sat, I could see one man on the back row who kept falling asleep, his head bobbing forward only to jerk backwards when he woke up. Even though Gerard never seemed to look directly at them, I knew he was watching the jury members, evaluating their interest, gauging their understanding of the complex banking transactions the expert witness was describing.

Eventually, the prosecutor seemed to notice the napping jurors and asked the judge for a recess for lunch. We all rose and silently waited while the jury and judge left the courtroom. Once they were all gone, the mood in the room lightened, and people turned to speak to each other.

Gerard spoke to his client and the young woman at his table, and then he turned to walk to the gallery and caught sight of me. He motioned with his head for me to come up to the front, but I shook mine slightly and smiled. He said something to them and then came over to me.

"Skulking in the courtroom again?"

"I was hoping to see how a pro does it," I responded, hoping to keep it light.

He grinned at me and side-stepped the praise. "Yes, Amy Landry *is* a professional at expert witness direct examinations."

I leaned in and whispered. "The guy in the back row was asleep."

He leaned in and whispered back. "I know. I could hear him snoring." I laughed. "How'd your morning go?"

"Well, I won." I shook my head. "I'm not sure what I won—I'm pretty sure the coonskin cap lady is going to appeal."

"Coonskin cap?" He raised an eyebrow at me. "Is that a new thing with the kids these days?"

I mock-frowned at him. "Are you that old, Gerard?" He lifted his eyebrows at me, and I relented. "It's not a 'thing' with the kids. I think it's a Daniel Boone thing. Didn't he wear a coonskin cap?"

He grinned. "I'm not that old, Benedict." He glanced back at his client and then at me. "Is this coonskin cap lady giving you trouble?"

I groaned. "I'm afraid to think about it." We grinned at each other for a moment, and then I remembered where we were. "I know you've got to get back—when do you want to meet?"

"I've got a moment, but it's going to be a short lunch so I can't break now." He looked into my eyes a little more closely. "How's the head?"

"Still attached," I said lightly, and hoped the leftover pain didn't show. I really did feel better. I swallowed my pride. "I want you to know how much I appreciate you getting me home last night. I don't know how I would have gotten there and inside."

His eyebrows lowered. "Was this your first migraine?"

"Is that what it was?" I considered. "I've never felt anything like that before." I stood up straight. "I'm fine now, though."

His eyes narrowed. "You sure?"

I nodded. "I owe you." He shook his head. "No, I do." I thought.

"Breakfast's on me sometime, okay?" I stuck my hand out for a shake. He just looked at it.

"Benedict, you need a plant."

"What?" I had no idea what he was talking about. I dropped my hand.

"A plant." His eyebrows lifted and fell. "Good grief, Benedict, your place looks like you've just moved in."

I felt my face begin to burn. "Gerard, what my place looks like is none of your business." Okay, maybe he was just saying what I'd been telling myself lately, but how dared he?

He grinned again. "That's true, but it doesn't change the fact that —Benedict, you need a plant or something."

Stung, I blurted out, "I don't do plants—I can't keep them alive." That sounded awful. "I have a cat."

"Well that's something." His client and associate were walking towards us. "How about I bring over a pizza tonight, and we'll break in that whiteboard and figure this out." He glanced over at them and began to walk away. "7? You like pepperoni and sausage?"

"I—I do, but—"

"Good. See you then." He joined them at the back and walked out of the courtroom.

I stared after them, openmouthed. Looks like I'd have plans on Valentine's Day after all.

CHAPTER TWENTY

When I turned my phone back on, I had a voicemail from Ann Thornton. I called her back and found out I'd left Gerard's Mont Blanc at her house. I hadn't even noticed. She offered to meet me to hand it off, and also told me she had a few things to tell me about Carrie. We arranged to meet at Café au Lait at 4:30 that afternoon.

My stomach was still a bit queasy today, so I decided try to eat something at home after I'd changed clothes. When I pulled into the drive, Miss Hattie was out in the front yard, checking her shrouded bushes with Atencio, the head landscape guy for the Sheltons' real estate management company. I waved at her and then went in to get out of my heels. Once back in jeans and a sweater, I joined them in the front yard. Atencio dipped his head and smiled as I approached. Hattie spoke fluent Spanish, and I noticed the two of them switched to English as I got closer.

"Are we going to fix up your patio this year, Lacey?"

I nodded. "I swear, this is the year, Atencio. How are the spring bulbs looking?" Atencio launched into a complicated explanation of weather and soil temperatures. I nodded at what I thought were appropriate moments and looked on attentively when he showed me some delicate green shoots under a canvas blanket. After a few minutes, another worker came up to ask him a question, and they retreated over to a stand of crepe myrtles by the long driveway.

Hattie watched him leave and then turned to me. "Didn't understand any of that, did you?"

I stretched my face up to the sunshine filtering through the still-bare tree branches. Much nicer than downtown. "Not a single word."

She patted my shoulder. "You're a nice child." We walked together around to the side entrance opposite mine, where her new kitchen had been built. "Are you feeling better?"

"I am. I thought I heard Miss Sallie in my dreams—was that real?"

She opened the door and ushered me in. "Very much so. Your young man came and knocked on the front door after he'd gotten you inside. He was very worried about you."

The blood rushed to my face. "He's not my young man." She just looked over at me as she went to the refrigerator and took out a pitcher of lemonade. "He's not."

"All right, he's not." She took two glasses out of the cabinet and filled them with lemonade. "But whoever he is, he was very worried about you."

I sipped the cold drink cautiously. Hattie has been known to spike iced liquids with liqueurs and tonics, but this seemed like simple lemonade. "He said it was a migraine—I don't know. I've never had something like that before." I leaned on the counter. "I'm still fuzzy about last night."

"Sal went with him into your apartment and stayed with you for a bit. You were pretty bad off, she said." She tilted her head to the side. "Are you all right?"

I nodded. "It's mostly gone today." I rubbed my forehead, which still seemed to ache a bit. "It was just a really stressful day that ended in pain."

She leaned back against the granite island, a tall, spare woman in cream colored cotton pants and a white shirt, her gray hair pulled back into a loose bun. Standing there like that, she reminded me of Katherine Hepburn, and I told her so. She smiled gently. "I'll take that as a great compliment," she said. "I always loved her." She watched me for a moment. "Do you want to talk about the stresses?"

I thought about it. "Not most of it—maybe soon, but not just now." I sipped the cold, tart lemonade. It made me think of summer, which was probably why she'd made it today. I set the glass down. "There is something I need to talk about."

I began to pace the small room, while Hattie remained still and watched me. I told her about my recent thoughts about my tiny apartment and comparing it to the homes of the ex-Jehovah's Witnesses. "I'm wondering if I shouldn't try to find a larger place, maybe a two-bedroom so I can have a dedicated office space." I looked out the window at the back garden, where Atencio and two workers were clearing out some dead limbs next to the garage. If I left, I would so miss this place.

Hattie spoke quietly. "Of course, if you feel you need to move, we'll let you out of your lease." She paused. "But Lacey, as long as you're happy with your home, no one else's opinion matters."

I looked back at her, still lounging against the island, braced on her strong, tanned arms, with one leg crossed over the other. I couldn't imagine this confident, self-assured woman ever needing a place to hide or worrying about what other people thought, and I didn't expect I could explain well enough for her to understand.

She seemed to come to a decision, however, and pushed off the island. She opened a drawer and pulled out a set of keys—some small and modern, and others old and skeletal. "I want to show you something, if you'll follow me." We went out the side door of the kitchen and walked around to the back, where a plain panel door, painted white to match the house's trim, was placed next to my bedroom window, and stood in stark contrast to the house's dark red brick. She worked one of the antique keys into the lock and opened the door. "Watch your step," she said as she edged carefully around a dormant rose bush and climbed up into the doorway. Clearly, at some point in the past, a shallow step had been placed before the door, but it was long gone.

Inside was a small room—maybe eight feet wide by twelve feet long, and I realized it shared a wall with my bedroom. On that wall, a doorway had been covered over with drywall and painted on my bedroom's side, but on this side, the studs and drywall that had been added were uncovered. On the opposite wall were shelves, but no furniture sat on the dusty hardwood floor.

"This was the butler's pantry when your bedroom was the breakfast room." She indicated the long shelves that went all the way to the ceiling. "Dishes and glassware were stored here, and on that end"—the wall opposite the outside door—"was a china cabinet and silver chest." The room was cold, and I realized there was no heater vent, only a small cast iron radiator like the one that Carrie Ames had fallen against.

"I've had this idea for a while," Hattie said. "You need an office—surely having your work space on your dining table isn't the best idea." She stepped over to the shelves and blew a bit of dust off. "This room is just sitting here being unused."

I turned around to see the space. There were no windows, but the walls and shelves were painted a creamy white that was a bit yellowed.

"We could put in a door with some glass—maybe a French door—so that some natural light would come in." Hattie put her hands on her hips, a woman used to being in charge and making things happen. "Peter and the maintenance boys could spend a week in here while we're in the slow season on properties, drywall up the closed off opening on this side, get some more lights in, some updated plugs. It's not adding an additional room, so I doubt we'd have to have a permit, but it would need to come up to code."

She kept talking about changes and ducts and construction, but I could hardly hear her over the hopeful pounding of my heart. I saw a small desk, a chair, my books on the shelves, maybe even some of my books currently stored in Ryan's garage, a lamp...a space of my own where I could work.

I interrupted her flow. "Yes." I laughed, and so did she. "How much extra rent?" For a moment, I could tell she was about to say it wouldn't cost me anything extra, but she knew me better than that.

"Whatever you're paying now per square foot—for these extra square feet."

I made quick calculations in my head. I could afford it. I stuck my hands in my pockets and rocked up on my toes. "Deal."

———

I was walking out to spend some early time at Café au Lait before my meeting with Ann Thornton when my phone rang with an unfamiliar number. My finger hovered over the 'decline' button for a few rings—suspecting another robocall—but I thought, *what the hell...maybe it's my secret admirer on Valentine's Day*, and hit 'answer.'

Instead of a computer-generated message, it was Susan Grassley. We exchanged stilted pleasantries, and then she apologized for her husband.

"He's just stuck in his idea of the past," she said, and I could tell she was close to tears. "He grew up in the JW, and he's very—" She hesitated.

"Indoctrinated?" I supplied.

"Fervent," she said, after a pause.

"I understand," I said, and I did. "How's Emma today?"

I heard her sigh, and there was some moving around on her end. Finally she spoke. "She's not doing well. Her hematologist has been warning us for some time that she's going to need something more than the antibiotics she's been getting." She stopped, and her voice got softer, so I upped the volume on my phone so I could hear. "She needs another blood transfusion, and she will eventually need a bone marrow transplant."

"Oh no." I couldn't imagine that tiny body in surgery. She didn't seem strong enough to survive such trauma. "How long can she wait?"

Susan sighed deeply. "Not long. The doctor said we should try to get a transfusion this year."

I had to ask. "Will Carl allow it?"

She was silent, and I had my answer. I was trying to figure out what to say when she spoke.

"I need to speak to a divorce attorney. Do you know one?"

I wasn't as shocked as I should have been. I'd seen the protective look in Susan's eyes as she held her daughter. "I do. Hang on for a moment, and I'll give you her number." I scrolled in my phone to get to the number of the best divorce lawyer I knew. "Do you want me to send you her contact?"

"No. I'll just—I'll write the number down."

I recited the number to her, and promised to speak to the attorney and let her know to expect the call. I expected her to sign off then, but she was silent.

I finally spoke. "Is there something else I can do for you?"

There was more hesitation, and then she answered. "Do you know what time Carrie died?"

"I'm not sure they've determined the time of death yet—but probably sometime between 7:00 and 10:00 that night." I waited. "Why?"

"I—I just didn't know." She sounded anguished, and I thought hard for a few seconds before asking the next question.

"Susan, was Carl home that night?"

She sounded like she was crying, but her answer was firm. "No. No, he wasn't. We had a fight after the group meeting, and he left. He didn't come home until almost midnight. And he'd been drinking."

———

I sat in my car after Susan Grassley hung up and considered her fear. Why was she so concerned that Carl might be involved in Carrie's murder? I checked the time, and, on impulse, dialed Carl Grassley's cell phone number. He picked up on the third ring. I apologized for bothering him at work, and then got right to the point.

"Carl, I didn't ask the other night if you spoke with Carrie the night she was killed—I mean, after the group meeting."

There was a long pause, and I visualized him smoothing his moustache down with his finger while he thought about it. Finally, he spoke, his words precise. "No, I didn't speak with Carrie after the support meeting."

I hated telephone questions, and now I realized how on target Gerard had been about using visual cues to support data gathering. I decided to fish. "Are you sure you didn't speak with her that evening? Perhaps on the phone?"

He seemed annoyed, but he kept his voice low. "Ms. Benedict, are you trying to accuse me of something?"

This was frustrating. I gritted my teeth and thought rapidly, and decided to take a chance with the truth. "No, Carl, I'm not. But I'm trying to find out why you seem so sure that Carrie wasn't repentant enough to be reinstated." I pushed a bit harder. "Why you believed she wasn't worthy to be back in the Truth."

He drew in a breath, and I realized that Ann Thornton was right. Carl would go to great lengths to protect the Jehovah's Witnesses. His low voice sounded strained. "She did not turn from her sin, Ms. Benedict. She continued to walk in the way of Satan. I had no chance to speak with her and help her from her sinfulness." He paused. "She continued in her sinfulness until her death."

"I still don't see, Carl. If you didn't speak with her, how do you know this?"

"Because she was still engaging in whorish behavior with Todd Parrish the night she was killed." He hissed the words, and his anger caught me off-guard. "I saw her kissing him that night. I watched them embrace, before he left."

This was new. "What time was this?"

"Just after 7 pm. I saw them together at her apartment, embracing and engaging in wanton acts." He sounded triumphant.

I couldn't help myself. "That's great, Carl. I appreciate you admitting that, and I hope you'll tell the police."

He clearly didn't expect my words. "Why?"

"You just supported my client's story, and placed yourself at the scene of the crime at the time of Carrie's death."

I wasn't surprised when he hung up on me.

———

I FELT LIKE THINGS WERE MOVING FORWARD NOW, AND I wanted to make sure I had all my notes together before Gerard and I had our meeting that night—and it *would* be a meeting, regardless of what day it was—so I got to Café au Lait early. If I was also early enough to make sure I got some cinnamon knots, well, that was just craftiness on my part.

I usually take notes by hand and then type them up for each person I speak to or document I review. Up until a few days ago, I had been pretty good about staying current on that process. This week, I'd gotten behind, so I spent the time at Café au Lait typing up my notes from the David Young, Carl and Susan Grassley, and Ann Thornton interviews. I'd just finished saving Ann's when she walked in. She waved at me, and went to the counter to order. As usual, she dressed in neutrals, but this time, her fuzzy sweater was a cream that verged on a blush pink, and it gave her face a rosy glow. Looking at her now, all pale hair and skin and eyes, I remembered thinking she looked washed out when I first met her. But she wasn't. Her hair was shiny, her eyes sparkling, and her skin shone with health. If she'd worn makeup or vibrant colors, she wouldn't be herself. I took a sip of coffee and wondered if there was a lesson there.

She brought her hot tea over and I smelled rich mint. "Nice day for tea, isn't it?" She smiled at me.

I smiled back and lifted my cup to her. "Or coffee."

She looked around the bright space. "This must be where you got the cookies you brought the other night." She nodded at my empty plate. "Was that a cookie?"

"Cinnamon knot." I felt it unnecessary to tell her it had been *three* cinnamon knots.

"Ohhh, I've never had those. Good?"

"Everything here is good, but those are my favorites." She sat across from me, arranging her long skirt down over her boots, and I thought, *she's stalling.* Okay, I'd let her set the pace here.

She pulled out Gerard's Mont Blanc. "This is a pretty great pen—perfect for a lawyer." She handed it over.

"Yes, well, it's not mine." I unscrewed the cap and scribbled on my pad. "It *is* a great pen, though." I capped it and slid it into my bag. "Thanks for bringing it. I hadn't even noticed it was gone."

"You're welcome. I guess it had just slid in between the cushions of the chair." She busied herself removing the tea bag from her cup and stirring the tea to cool it. She seemed nervous.

She finally leaned back and looked at me. "I wasn't as open with you about Carrie as I could have been." Her hands were twisted together, and the knuckles were white. "I'm not used to lying—it's something I've tried to avoid most of my life."

Part of me wanted to talk, to comfort her, but I sensed I should stay silent.

"The Organization—the Jehovah's Witnesses—has about eight million members worldwide. Every year, Watch Tower puts out numbers. Its recordkeeping would put the US Census Bureau to shame." She looked down at her hands and untangled them, straightening the fingers with effort. "In the last few years, especially in the US, the numbers of growth are barely enough to keep up with the death rate." She sighed. "At least that's what we tell ourselves. The exes."

She looked out the window at the waning sunlight. "I never thought I'd be one—an ex-JW. But there seemed to be no other way, after I returned from traveling. I saw too much, I knew too much, to go back. And I couldn't just fade away. I was so angry—*so angry*—that I had to tell them why, *why* I was leaving." Her mouth twisted. "As if it would matter. They have a special way to deal with people who leave and speak out against the Organization. They call us 'apostates.' It's a word that means a dissenter, but the Organization has turned it into a word for a traitor, someone who works for the other side, who works for Satan." She looked back at me, and I could see angry tears in her eyes. "That way, they can just dismiss anything we say, anything we try to communicate to the people we love who are still inside. And if those we love speak to us—even *listen* to us—they risk disfellowshipping themselves."

I shook my head. "I still just don't get it. The whole disfellowshipping thing. I saw someone in a video talking about being in front of a judicial committee, and how that felt."

She stared out the window. "All those poor young people. They've either confessed—because that's what we're trained to do— or one of your 'friends'"—she sarcastically emphasized the word —"has informed the elder body that they suspect you've committed fornication." She looked at me. "Maybe they saw you leaving your girlfriend's home early in the morning. Or saw you out with a worldly person. All you might have done is some heavy petting or even less. And for this, your parents will disavow you, your church will excommunicate you."

I stared at her, my mind flipping over all the stupid things I did in my teens and 20s, imagining being forced to leave my home and family, my father and brother never speaking to me again. She read the look on my face and nodded. "Yes, it's just that bad. And we"— she ran a hand through her hair—"all of us, we allowed that to happen, we let them convince us that we were to shun them. Those children." She nodded at the question in my eyes. "Yes, I did it, my sweet, dear husband did it. Everyone does."

"You were brainwashed." My voice was thin and thready, as I imagined what it would be like. "Indoctrinated."

The look in her eyes was cynical. "Yes, we all were." She leaned forward. "But don't ever imagine we didn't know what we were doing. We did. They all do. It's a choice." Her mouth twisted as if she'd tasted something sour and bitter.

She took a deep breath. "Trying to talk to people in a cult doesn't work. They think we're just unhappy out here, that we're saying anything that will hurt the Organization, that we don't speak truth." She leaned forward, putting her arms on the table. "So how do we fight against something like that? A direct assault doesn't work."

My heart was starting to beat faster, harder. I knew what was coming.

"So we send some people back inside." She swallowed, her throat working. "We let some of the strong ones go back, let them go in so that they'll be listened to." Her voice rose. "They live through the reinstatement process and wait. And then when the time comes to ask questions or to support a little dissent, they know what to say. We help them to know what to say." She stopped, breathing hard.

I could barely speak over the roaring in my head. "Carrie was going back undercover?"

She nodded, her eyes on mine.

———

SEVERAL PEOPLE CAME IN, LAUGHING AND TALKING AS THEY looked over the menu board. Ann watched them without speaking, and, even though I was bubbling over with questions, I let the silence steep. Finally, she spoke again.

"Adam Garrison and I have been working on this for years, since we both left the Organization. He and I met when he came to Atlanta years ago. Adam was the one who introduced me to the sexual abuse survivor. He travels for work a lot, and he's got groups established in several major cities." She wrapped her hands around her teacup as if for warmth even though it had to be growing cold. "Social media helps—there are more ex-JWs telling their stories and talking online."

"I've seen some of them. They're pretty intense."

She nodded and leaned back in her seat. "Most people think, because the JW is seen as a mainstream religion and has so many members, that the experience of the members is like someone attending a church. But it's not that, at all." She took a sip of her tea, and grimaced at the temperature, then replaced the cup on the saucer and pushed it away. "It's a life you lead. In infiltrates everything: the people you know, the education you receive, the way you feel about yourself. It truly is a brainwashing. The Friends have horrible self-esteem and anxiety issues—we know that for sure. We don't know numbers on some things, like substance abuse and suicide, because *those* aren't recorded by the Organization." She shook her head. "Or if they are, they don't tell us. Numbers that might actually help someone—those they don't care about. But those situations are rampant."

"Like David Young."

She nodded. "His poor family. When his sister killed herself, the entire family was broken."

"I meant his alcoholism." She looked surprised, and then nodded.

"I suppose it's easy to see from the outside." I winced inwardly at the notion that I was, indeed, an outsider. "There are so many young people inside the JW suffering from addictions as they try to deal with the anxiety." She leaned forward again, intent on her explanation. "You see everyone else in the Organization doing their service, attending meetings, looking so pious and faithful. And you know that you're not always faithful, that you wonder about the world or your sins or your doubts or your resentment of service hour requirements, and you compare yourself to everyone else." Her smile was bitter. "We're great at comparing ourselves. And the anxiety eats away at you, and all the prayer you pray doesn't help." She stopped, and I could see she was remembering her life inside. I let her think as I watched Marie helping someone at the counter, my mind whirling. Finally, I had to ask.

"Who knew about Carrie?"

She looked back at me, pulled from memories. "Me and Adam, and I know she told Todd." She shook her head. "Adam and I haven't told anyone else. The only way this works is to keep it secret. If the Friends inside believe that someone isn't truly repentant or faithful, they'll never listen to them, and it won't work."

"And has it worked?"

Her face closed so quickly it was like a door had slammed. She chose her words with care. "I've told you more than Adam wanted me to. I think I've said enough."

I was instantly angry. "'Enough'? You think you've said *enough*? Have you told the police?" I could see from her expression that the answer was no. "You don't think that the fact that she was going into a cult to expose it is relevant to her murder?" I could see people looking at us, but I didn't care. "How sure are you that no one else knows?" I didn't want to mention Carl Grassley's name.

She shook her head, her face sorrowful. "I don't know if Carrie told anyone else, but Adam and I don't talk about this to anyone. We know how important it is."

I leaned back and willed myself to relax, rubbing my hands over my face and trying to think. Ann looked down at her teacup, her hands settling around the saucer. It was clear she wasn't going to tell me anymore. Marie came by to clear the table, and I realized they'd be closing soon. Although I've begged often enough, Marie doesn't stay open for dinner.

I looked around at the few patrons still in the place. Most were standing up and putting on coats, saying their goodbyes. Ann just sat there, her eyes now on me.

"Why Carrie? Why was she the one who needed to go back?"

Ann bit her lip, and I knew what she was going to say, before she said it. Carrie was the key to her father, Samuel Ames, the rising JW star of the region.

CHAPTER TWENTY-ONE

I left Ann Thornton and decided to take a walk at the lake before going home. There weren't many people walking around. I guess most people were getting ready for their big Valentine's Day dates. I walked for about half an hour, letting everything I'd been hearing roll around in my mind. Now that Ann Thornton had told me why Carrie was really returning to the Organization, I saw every story told to me in a different light.

I finally sat on the end of a small dock and watched the sunset, a gorgeous clear sky painted in reds and pinks and golds fading to a deeper and deeper purple. Dusk fell, and the birds starting nesting in trees, and still I sat, thinking. It wasn't until the chill got to me that I remembered Gerard would be at my house at 7. I checked the clock in my car—6:48—and drove as fast as I could without getting a ticket. I drove up just as Gerard pulled to a stop in front of the big house. He let me drive in under the overhang and then pulled in behind me. He'd changed into jeans and a sweater and looked as put together as

Julia Lunsford always did. I felt a little cross until I saw the Giannel-li's box in his hands.

"Please, come right in," I said and waved him past me. He had a small wrapped package in the other hand. "What's that?"

He tried to hand it to me, but I avoided it. "Consider it a house-warming present."

I rolled my eyes. "I've lived here more than four years now, Gerard."

"Then consider it a birthday present or a late Christmas present, or even a Valentine's Day present, but just take it." I took it and unwrapped it. It was a small, squat blue pot holding a flat blue-green plant with thick leaves spiraling out in a pattern that reminded me of lotus flowers in Indian rugs. I set it on the kitchen counter. He and I both stared at it. "What is it?" I asked.

"It's a plant, Benedict."

I touched a finger to the pointed end of one fat leaf. It didn't exactly cut my finger, but it was a bit prickly. "Is it like a cactus?"

"I think they call it a 'succulent.' Millennials like you are supposed to like them."

"'Millennials like me'? What's that supposed to mean?"

He shrugged off his coat and put it on the back of the couch. "I don't know, Benedict. You're in your 30s, you're a Millennial. I read that Millennials like succulents. Now you have one." He faced me with his hands on his hips, eyebrows beetling in annoyance. "And I hear there's a cat somewhere in here, and this one isn't poisonous to cats. And it's hard to kill."

I was touched, which made me a bit confused and cranky, but my grandmother's training saw me through. "Thank you, Gerard. It's a nice gift."

He looked around the apartment. "Yeah, well. Like I said, you need a plant. Or something. Maybe a picture or two."

I looked around as well. There wasn't much in the room, but at least I was neat and tidy—two qualities my grandmother had praised constantly. "I'm not a big decorator. I used to have more, but now I just have the things I like." I turned and opened the pizza box. "Now *this* I like." I pulled out a slice and bit off the pointed end. The crust was Giannellis' perfect, thinner-than-New York style, but not really Neapolitan, so it was a crunchy, chewy delight. Unlike a lot of places, they make their own sauce, simmering it in big pots on a stove in back, and it goes on the pizza warm—which makes a difference I didn't really understand until I tasted it, since it allows them to cook the pizza for a shorter, hotter time. They also make their own Italian sausage, so it's full of herbs and spices, with just a little heat on the back side. I hummed with pleasure as I walked to the small fridge. "I have beer and soda, and I might have wine. You probably like wine."

He reached over my shoulder for a soda. "This is fine."

I took a bottle of beer myself, then handed him a plate that he heaped with three slices. Because my dining table served as my desk, we stood at the bar and ate, and it was heaven. His first slice disappeared about as fast as mine did. As I slowed down to enjoy my second slice, I tried for small talk.

"How'd you know about Giannelli's?" The pizza place on lower Greenville didn't advertise, so pretty much only the locals knew about it.

He raised his eyebrows. "I've eaten there for years. Have you had their spicy sausage pizza?"

"Yeah, when I don't mind my mouth burning for days." I felt like I had sauce on the edge of my mouth, so I tore off two paper towels and handed him one. I'm nothing if not a good hostess. "Do they deliver to Highland Park?"

Gerard tilted his head, probably because his eyebrows couldn't actually crawl up to his hairline. "I don't know if they do or not. Is it important?" He started in on his third piece.

I shrugged. "Just thought it might be far to do take out." I debated whether I could do another piece and decided to risk it. I did take the smallest piece, which counts when you're deciding.

"Benedict, I don't live in Highland Park." He took a swig of soda. "At least, not anymore."

I was surprised. "Oh yeah? I remember looking you up during the —you know, the Bill thing."

He eyed me over his last bite of crust. "You did, hm?"

"Yep." I looked right back at him. "I figure you knew pretty much everything about me too."

For a minute, we just watched each other, chewing. Then he swallowed and grinned. "I'm over near the lake now."

I felt a spurt of jealousy. Houses near White Rock Lake were expensive. Oh, maybe not as expensive as Highland Park, but they were still pricey. And they tended to be either mansions, or cool modern homes with lots of angles and glass, or architecturally significant vintage homes. "Which part?"

"It's not too far from the old boathouse." He chewed for a minute. "A couple had just built it when they had to move back east, and I picked it up for a song."

I said casually, "I bet *you* have a decorator." I popped the last bite of crust in my mouth.

He looked at me suspiciously as he wiped his mouth with the paper towel, and then he grinned. "Nope. I have a sister." He looked at the pizza box, and I could have sworn he was considering a fourth piece, but he just picked up our plates and put them in the sink. He started running water, and I realized that he was going to wash them —a guest doing the dishes. While I might do that in someone else's home, my grandmother would be spinning in her grave for it to happen in mine.

"I can do that," I blurted out, but no, he was already started, and he told me so.

"Why don't you get the whiteboard set up like you want?"

I thought about it for a few seconds while I watched him squirt dish detergent, and then I mentally shrugged and went to work on the whiteboard.

———

AN HOUR LATER, I'D BROUGHT HIM UP TO SPEED ON THE interviews and my research, and he'd passed along the additional details Todd had supplied. We'd mapped out each of the people Carrie had direct contact with—excluding a couple of her co-workers that the police investigators said had alibis. The important ones who had no alibi were Ann Thornton, David Young, Carl and Susan Grassley, and Adam Garrison—and perhaps Samuel Ames, who had apparently been traveling that night to Waxahachie, a small town south of Dallas, to do a visit on a Kingdom Hall there the next week. But I didn't think he or Ann or Susan could be the killer, and I told Gerard that.

"Maybe they had opportunity, but what would be the motive?" I started re-stacking the reports I'd gathered.

"The same one you want to apply to any of the others."

"I'm still not sure about it." I sat back to look at the notes on the board about David Young, Adam Garrison, and Carl Grassley. "I mean, would why Garrison kill Carrie? That would prevent him from accomplishing what he'd planned."

Gerard shrugged. "So maybe she changed her mind." He stretched, his body taking up my entire sofa—or at least the part the cat wasn't, because she was cuddling up to Gerard. That cat had been living with me for six months, and the only time she had anything to do with me was when the power was off and we were both freezing. She stared back at me, her little gray moustache mocking me as he scratched behind her ears. "Maybe she decided going in and lying to her father about her repentance was more than she could do."

I could see that. "But if she did that, there's no reason for Sam Ames to kill her. He seemed to be sincere when he said he didn't want her to come back. But I can't see him killing her to keep her from doing that." I considered. "I have to admit I'm a bit biased about Carl Grassley. I didn't like him at all." I scratched my nose, which was starting to itch, a sure sign spring was on the way. "Maybe he found out that she wasn't sincere about going back, and he went to see her that night to tell her off."

"Did anyone report seeing him there?"

I'd checked the reports we had several times, but I looked over them one more time. "No."

"Well, that's not helpful. And does David Young have any motive at all? Outside of grandson, they were as close as anyone else. And they grew up together."

"True." I rested my chin on my knees and looked at the board. "No one has said there were any problems between them. In fact, he practically begged her not to go back in. He reminded her of how awful the reinstatement process actually is."

"Well, I think grandson is still holding something back. The old swinger couple heard them arguing at 6:30, and Carl Grassley sees him leaving about 7."

"What did he tell you about that?"

"He said he'd left her about 7:00 and they were okay, but she was upset."

"But then he comes back."

"Yeah. He said he drove around, and then got worried about her. So he goes back and knocks on the door, but she didn't answer. And that was 8:30."

Something teased at my mind. "Wait, wait, wait. Naomi said he had a key to the door. Wouldn't he have opened it up if he was worried about her?"

We looked at each other but I spoke first. "He saw her dead? Or he didn't go in and feels bad about it?"

"He says he didn't go in—he thought that would make her angry. But what if he did? He saw her unconscious and leaves her?" He scratched the cat between the ears distractedly as he thought about it. "Or he sees her unconscious and kills her then—which would make him just as guilty," Gerard said. I made a face and rolled my eyes, which made him smile. "What? I'm just playing devil's advocate. The autopsy results will better pinpoint time of death. Of course, that may be a problem for us at that point, since there is a witness to him leaving."

"I know." I was starting to feel anxious about the lack of real suspects. It seemed so much easier in fiction: suspects appeared out of nowhere. In reality, I didn't know what the next step might be, but I was worried we'd found nothing that would help. I got up to pace.

He stretched, his arms behind his head, as he looked at the whiteboard. "You know, Benedict, you're really good at this. I like the way you organize information." He yawned. "I know Bill said you were amazing with data, but I can't believe you're not working for someone else doing this all the time."

I turned slowly and stared at him. Was he being insulting, or was he just that obtuse? "Excuse me?" My voice dripped ice.

My tone must have alerted him, because he sat up straight. "What?"

"Are you seriously telling me you can't believe I'm not working for a firm? After everything you and Bill Stephenson put me through?"

His look turned wary. "Are you talking about the trial, Benedict, or something else?"

I saw red. "Of course I'm talking about the trial!" My voice rose.

"Benedict, that was five years ago. Why would that keep you from working for a firm now?"

My heart was in my throat, and it was hard to speak past the obstruction of my emotion. "I can't believe you're saying this. No one would hire me, Gerard. Did you think I *wanted* to be broke and on my own?"

His eyebrows went up. "Are you saying you've been blackballed here in Dallas?"

"I believe the term the recruiter used was '*radioactive*'!" I paced the living room. My voice was loud enough that the cat slid off the couch and escaped to the bedroom.

"What recruiter? Which search firm said that?" He seemed confused, and it was the last straw.

"*I don't remember!*" I shouted at him, my voice cracking under the strain. "*It's been almost five years ago!*"

He stared at me from the couch. I stared back, appalled at my shouting.

He stood up slowly, but stayed where he was. His voice was quiet and cautious. "Are you telling me that the last time you looked for a job was immediately after the trial?"

I started to reply, and then realized what he was asking. I blinked. "Well, yes."

He opened his mouth to speak, and then closed it.

The silence yawned.

He sat down again, his hands clasped loosely between his knees. He spoke like someone gentling a wild horse, his eyes on his hands. "Benedict, of course no one would hire you right after the trial. No one knew what had happened. None of us were talking to the press, and most of your deposition testimony was sealed because of the confidential financial details of nondefendants." He raised his eyes to mine. "None of the firms in town knew what had happened. They weren't blackballing you—they were just being cautious."

The blood had drained from my face to my feet, and I couldn't move. Surely he wasn't right. Surely I hadn't scrimped and saved and starved and built a firm from nothing for no reason.

I tried to speak, but the shouting had left my throat dry and sore. I tried again and my words came out in a croak. "She didn't say it was a temporary thing." I swallowed hard. "She didn't say to try again later."

Gerard got up and went to kitchen. He filled a glass with some water and brought it to me, keeping his distance as he did.

The heat abruptly clicked off, and the apartment was so quiet I could hear the metal vents ticking as they cooled. I wish I could say the last four years flashed in front of me, but all I could think was, *I'm an idiot.*

Gerard stood and looked at me. "Benedict, why didn't you take the whistleblower money? Was it all some kind of penance for you? What have you been punishing yourself for?"

I shook my head but didn't answer. I suddenly felt cold and tired, and I just wanted to be alone. I took a sip of water, and it burned its way down my throat.

"You haven't networked or stayed up with the bar here in town, have you?" Gerard kept talking, but I really just wanted him gone. "No wonder the attorneys we meet don't know you. Everyone is so curious about you when I mention you. Julia Lunsford was dying to meet you, and now I get why. Do you not go to bar meetings or continuing education at the Belo?"

I shook my head and took another sip of water.

"Benedict..." He trailed off, and then he stepped close. "Come sit down," he coaxed, and I let him pull me to the couch. "I thought you were choosing your own clients and practice areas because that's what you wanted." He sat down next to me and put a hand on mine. "God, your hand is like ice. You're freezing." He pulled the throw from the back of the couch and tucked it around me.

"Gerard—" My lips felt numb. "Could you please just go?"

"You sure? I think you're in shock."

I nodded. "I am, but I just want to think right now."

He got up and put on his coat. "Want the cat for comfort?" He laughed weakly. "I still can't believe you've had her for six months and haven't named her yet."

I shook my head. "Nah. She's not really a comfort cat." I breathed in and out, in and out. The breaths were coming so fast, it sounded like I was panting.

He headed for the door and then paused. "Benedict, I hate to leave you alone like this." He waited for a few seconds. "Call me tomorrow, okay?"

I watched as he headed to the door. "Gerard?"

He turned back to me. "Yeah?"

"Leave the pizza."

He laughed as he shut the door behind him.

CHAPTER TWENTY-TWO

I sat there for a long time after Gerard left, huddled on the sofa and wrapped in the afghan, my mind flipping through the last four years and replaying events and interactions between me and other people. The longer I sat, the more depressed I got. At one point, I noticed it was no longer Gerard's voice in my head questioning my actions; it was my own. Most of the questions had no answers, but I kept hearing them over and over.

Why did I never look for another job?

Why didn't I get a second recruiter opinion?

Why did I feel like the rest of Dallas's legal community wanted nothing to do with me all that time?

Was Gerard right? Was I punishing myself?

I must have dozed off, finally, because I jolted awake sometime later. The lights were all still on, and the cat watched me from the safety of her bed near the heater vent. It was close to midnight, and, as I started going around turning off lights to go to bed, I realized there was one person who could shed some light on Carrie Ames's actions.

I scooped up my bag and my notepad and headed out the door for Hipster Haven. After a second thought, I nipped back in and grabbed a slice of cold pizza, tucking the box with the last piece into the refrigerator. I threw my bag on the passenger seat and wondered for the ten minutes it took to drive to Deep Ellum if I should text Gerard to let him know what I was doing, but I decided not to. He'd be all concerned and solicitous, and I really wasn't ready for that yet. After everything he'd just said, how could I explain?

I found out that the young, hip crowd went to Deep Ellum for Valentine's Day, even if it was on a Thursday. It took me forever to find a parking space in a pay lot a few blocks away, but the wind wasn't too cold, so the walk wasn't that bad. I passed couples hugging and snuggling as they walked from club to bar to restaurant, and I smiled at a few groups of young people who appeared to have been at an anti-love protest (complete with broken heart stickers). When I came in, Shelley was near the hostess station and recognized me, which made me feel a little better. She smiled at me.

"Hey—Lacey, right?" I smiled and nodded. "Adam's over there," she said, pointing with her chin to a booth by the window where Adam sat, eating a sandwich and scrolling through his phone.

"Thanks. Could I get a cup of coffee?"

She nodded and headed off to the kitchen. The place was pretty busy, with couples and small groups drinking late night coffees or staving off the post-party munchies. The couple next to Adam's booth appeared to be celebrating an anniversary.

I stepped up to his booth and paused. He didn't seem surprised to see me. He moved his half-empty plate and, surprisingly, half-empty beer glass to one side and nodded to me.

"Lacey."

"Hey, Adam. Mind if I sit?"

"Nope. Having a good Valentine's Day?" He smiled up at Shelley as she dropped off my coffee and a little pot of cream.

I slid into the booth and shook my head at the offered menu. "Not really. I'm not a big fan."

He looked directly at me and grinned, that charismatic focus that the ex-JW ladies must love. I felt only the stirrings of anger. "Me either."

Now that I was here, I had no idea how to start this conversation. Adam helped me out. "So I hear you spoke with Ann."

"I did." I started to doctor my coffee with cream and sugar, saying nothing more, wanting to see what he'd say.

"She said you were pretty upset." He took a bite of what appeared to be a Cuban sandwich, and I was glad I'd had that slice of pizza. The smell of smoked ham and turkey was a little distracting even without being hungry. "We didn't lie to you, you know. We just avoided talking about that."

I eyed him over my coffee mug. Having been someone who doesn't tell everything they know, I knew what a wealth of information could be 'avoided.' I didn't respond.

He frowned and wiped some mustard off his fingers with a paper napkin. "You just gonna sit there and not talk?"

I set my cup down and looked at a spot of cream on the table, deciding what I wanted to say. "How could you use Carrie this way? Why use *her*?"

He sat back and shook his head. "You don't get it." He exhaled audibly, exasperated with me. "You know how you get a cult member to change their mind, Lacey? Short answer: you don't. I spent most of my life in the Jehovah's Witnesses, and I know you don't convince a JW by talking to them." He shifted in his seat, his arms crossing over his chest. "I've spent six years outside of it, and the people that listen to me are the people who already know what I'm going to say. When I talk about the Organization and its issues, the people who write me, comment on my posts, respond to my videos are the people who already believe me." His voice was intent, the words uttered with inflection and power, and I thought again how *trained* he seemed to be. A mocking voice in my brain reminded me of Dr. Amie's analogy and how voices from the outside wouldn't convince a victim to leave, but I pushed it away. I didn't feel like being understanding right now.

He looked to the side, at the people at the next table, who were toasting each other with their beer glasses. He kept talking while looking at them, the same habit that annoyed me the first time we spoke. "The people that we need to reach are the ones that are still in. And it's getting worse. People are *dying*, Lacey." He looked at me and leaned forward, intent on convincing me. "Both inside and out. The ones on the inside can't take it anymore: the guilt, shame, the anxiety, the insane rules, the *gaslighting*. The Organization tells you what you think, what you feel, *what you believe* isn't true—that it's Satan affecting and influencing you."

He sat back, his hands lifting in mute appeal. "The ones on the outside—well, we know the problems they have. The issues are the same ones they had on the inside, only now it's magnified by the fact that they have no support system, no family, no friends, nothing. No one to help them. Something has to change." His jaw firmed, and he delivered the power line as his hands dropped again: "*We* have to change it."

I could see why he was so effective with the ex-JW crowd. I also noticed he was avoiding the mention of Carrie. "You didn't answer my question. *Why Carrie?*"

He tilted his head back and narrowed his eyes at me. "You know why. You've met Samuel Ames. He's very well respected in the Organization. Do you know, even though Carrie faded away, he was still kept on as a circuit overseer? You know how rare that is? That should tell you something about what the Organization wants for him." He rubbed a hand over his shaved head, and I wondered at the gesture and his discomfort. "He's trusted. He's listened to in a very large area, with a lot of Friends, in a lot of Kingdom Halls." He breathed in, his nostrils flaring as he looked out the window. "But he doubts. I know he does. And everything that happened with Carrie just seemed to make him doubt more, wonder more. He worried about the young people who left and were failing at life. He'd started to wonder if the shunning was Jehovah's will—or the will of the people in charge." He looked back at me, all intensity and fire. "He began to recognize it as a tool to keep people in line."

I thought about that nice older man and his pain. "Did Carrie tell you that?" He looked down, and I convinced myself it was a reaction to my words. "She did, didn't she? She told you in confidence about her meetings with her dad, and you used that information to set her up."

His face darkened, and he leaned forward, his hands slapping flat on the tabletop. "We did *not* set her up. She talked to me about this a year ago. She knew what she was doing."

I could tell he was getting angry, but I couldn't stop now. I leaned forward too. "A year ago? If she knew about this a year ago, why didn't she go back then?"

He didn't answer, and I knew. "She wasn't sure, was she, Adam?" I thought about her journal entries of a year ago, about praying, about seeing her father and him telling her things about the Organization and people being disfellowshipped. "Why did she wait?" I was so angry, I didn't wait for an answer. "She didn't know if she wanted to do it, did she, Adam? Was it because she would be working on her father, expanding his doubt into full-fledged apostasy? Or was it because she didn't feel like she could go back into that cult and stay strong?"

His hands fisted on the table. "You have no idea what you're talking about. You haven't been in it, and you don't know what it's like to feel that kind of pressure. There's pressure to stay in, and pressure to go back in if you're out. Some people can't do it."

I looked at his flushed face and wondered aloud. "How many people have gone back, Adam? How many of your lost sheep have you sent back?"

He inhaled sharply. "I'm not going to talk about that. We don't publicize what we're doing. If the Organization believes that people being reinstated are working to tear it down, the threshold for reinstatement will get even higher."

I leaned in, angrier than ever. "And do people go back in and lose their nerve? Do people go back in and break under the pressure?"

He looked out the window as a group of the anti-love young people passed by, laughing and hanging on each other. He answered without looking at me, the odd habit fanning my anger. "Yes, sometimes they do. We try to help them, support them with messages and sites, but the Organization is getting smarter about social media. They're pressured to confess about contacts with the outside, and specifically with anyone disfellowshipped. And when that happens, we can't really reach out to them." He ran a hand over his head, then over his face. "The isolation is pretty severe. And the Organization works on you by requiring you to be around people who reinforce Watch Tower's teachings, sisters and brothers looking for weakness or lack of repentance. Sometimes we lose them." He stopped, not looking at me.

"Lose them? How?" He didn't answer. I repeated the word, a bit louder. "Adam—how?"

He looked at me and then away. "Sometimes they stop talking to us on the outside." He paused. "Sometimes worse."

I could hear my heart pounding in the silence. "What do you mean, 'worse'?"

He shook his head but avoided my eyes. "There've been losses. That's all I'll say."

"And you won't tell me how many times this has happened?" A thought struck me. "Was Megan Young one of yours?"

He looked right into my eyes. "I'm not telling you any more about that."

I was stunned and angry, and I couldn't think how to proceed. Shelley brought him a cup of coffee. She seemed a little worried, and I realized our voices had been rising as we spoke.

"Everything okay?" she asked. We both nodded and each of us eased back from the table. She cleared his plate and glass and gave me a cross look, leaving his water and our coffee.

I took a deep breath, exhaling it slowly. I didn't want to be so upset about this that I couldn't ask the right questions. "Why haven't you told the police about this?"

He looked at the couple next to us again, who were now sharing a strawberry shortcake. "If it becomes relevant as to how she died, I will. But I don't believe it is."

I wasn't so sure. "And no one but you and Ann and Todd knew why she was really going back?"

He looked back at me, his attention caught. His eyes narrowed. "Why do you ask that?"

I shrugged. "I was just thinking that if someone knew she was going back—I don't know, what would you call it? 'under cover'?—they might be upset."

He laughed, a short, sharp bark that showed what he really thought. "Who are you thinking? Carl Grassley?"

I sensed him relaxing into his sarcasm, and I thought, I'm off-base—he's relieved. "Yeah. I can see that he would have a problem with this entire scheme."

Garrison made a face as if he was considering it as he took a sip of his coffee. "I don't think Carl would have what it takes to kill Carrie."

I knew I was going down a rabbit track, but I was interested in his opinion about Grassley. "'What it takes'? What do you mean?"

Garrison sneered. "He's not a very strong guy, is he? He thinks he is, but at the end of the day, he's not." He pushed his coffee cup away. "He's a powerless, weak man. He might blow angry, but he has no idea what to do about anything. He won't petition for reinstatement because he knows his wife will leave him, and he won't agree to the treatment his daughter needs, because it would make the Organization think less of him." He looked off to the side, his mouth twisting. "He's pathetic." He pulled his coffee cup back towards him but didn't drink.

Even though I didn't think much of Grassley, I thought Garrison's disgust was a bit overdone. I pushed. "And something like this takes real anger, doesn't it, Adam? You'd have to be angry at her and *stay* angry at her, wouldn't you?"

He looked at me without speaking, so I kept going. "Is it possible that Carrie had changed her mind about going back and doing this to her father? She loved him very much, didn't she? Enough to continue to see him even though she knew it might harm him." I leaned in. "Was she having second thoughts about being the reason he might be disfellowshipped? Is that why it took her a year to announce it to the group, to finally decide? Or did she change her mind at the end? Did she think she might end up like Megan?"

He didn't speak but I noticed that his hands had tightened around his coffee cup until his knuckles were white. Finally, with effort, he released the cup and sat back. "I think I've said all I'm going to say."

———

I LEFT A TEN-DOLLAR BILL FOR SHELLEY AND HEADED BACK TO my car. I was angry. Angry with Garrison and Ann Thornton, angry with Carrie, angry with everyone. I didn't want to see the couples on the sidewalk, secure in their relationships, didn't want to smile at the broken-heart stickers, didn't want to see people, period. I wondered if my anger had pushed Garrison too far. I walked the blocks to my car in the darkness, mentally berating myself for losing my temper, keeping my head down and my hands in my pockets, my mind running over Garrison and his disgust of Carl Grassley. Was he right? Was Carl too weak and ineffectual to kill someone? If not Carl, who had the anger, the will?

I didn't see the guy who pushed me until he was right next to me, and then all I saw was brick wall. The left side of my face exploded— or felt like it—when I hit the wall with enough force to make my head spin. I felt him tug at my bag, and—stupid me—I tugged back. He pushed at me and pulled again, and I felt the strap break and the momentum carried me down. Then I hit the sidewalk. I tried to rise, but my head—my poor, recently abused head—swam, and I thought standing might be a bad idea.

I didn't pass out. I told the people who stopped to help me that I didn't lose consciousness, but I don't really remember much about it. They called the ambulance over my objections, and the paramedics told me the cut on my eyebrow was going to need stitches. I argued, but the blood that kept running into my eyes sort of nullified my protests.

In the emergency room, I laid on a gurney in the hallway, holding a thick pad of gauze to my forehead while I spoke to the police officer they'd called to the scene. I never knew Valentine's Day was such a busy day in an ER, but apparently not everyone spends it sharing strawberries and champagne with their sweetheart. Ambulances brought in the victims of two knifings, a shooting, and several domestic assaults while I laid there, slightly queasy and a little medicated. I practiced breathing in and out, in and out. In between, I thought about Garrison and Ann Thornton and their—I couldn't call it anything else—conspiracy. Perhaps it wasn't a criminal conspiracy, but they were working to bring down a global organization. By dropping people into the mix who would support dissent and question, they were infecting the Organization with a virus intended to bring it down. I understood their reasons, but I couldn't see how it would have caused Carrie's death—unless someone knew what was planned and decided to keep it from happening. It had to be connected, but I couldn't see how.

Officer Garza, who had responded to the scene only to find me being loaded into the ambulance, spoke to several witnesses who'd seen someone in a hoodie, coat, and gloves running away from where I lay bleeding. They'd assumed it was a man, but they didn't know for sure. He was treating it as a purse snatching, and—since I had only some nagging doubts in my mind—I didn't disagree out loud. He left me with an incident number and some information to call to get a police report.

The ER doctor was young and female. She talked me through what she was going to do as she did it, even though I was pretty sure I didn't want to know. With my head elevated and direct pressure on the cut, the bleeding had slowed down a lot by the time she was able to get to me. Head wounds look awful, she told me, because of all the bleeding. Something they'd given me was making me a bit sleepy, and it became harder and harder to stay alert as they ex-rayed me and cleaned the blood away. Her voice was soothing too, so I focused on it while the world wheeled. There were a few needle pricks as I closed my eyes, and then I might have dozed for a bit. When I roused as they moved me, she told me I had seven stitches and a lot of bruises.

It's pretty much impossible these days to get by without identification, credit, or insurance cards, all of which were in my purse. I had a lot of the numbers and other information memorized, and even in my sleepy state, I remembered them. My phone was in my jacket pocket, which was a blessing. I debated about who to call, but decided—since it was almost 3 am—to call Hattie Shelton, who says she sleeps less with each passing year. I told her where to find my extra car key, and she and Sallie were waiting outside the ER when they brought me out.

I climbed into the Sheltons' Mercedes SUV with assistance from the discharge tech, the pain medication they'd given me bringing only intermittent waves of relief from the swelling and bruising in the left side of my face. Sallie was uncharacteristically quiet in the front passenger seat, but Hattie sounded concerned. "Been quite a week for you, hasn't it?" I winced a little when I remembered that it was Sallie who'd comforted me when I had the headache—was it only a night ago? This was a lot to ask from my landlords, and I fretted a bit about the imposition. The pain helped to put all that into perspective.

We drove back to the parking lot, and Sallie got into my little car to drive it home. I stayed in the backseat, dozing as the warmth and medication relaxed me. I think I apologized and expressed my gratitude a few times, but I'm not sure. Both of them came in to help me into pajamas and bed, and Sallie took the cat with her when they left. I'm sure they were all relieved.

CHAPTER TWENTY-THREE

I woke up when the sun made the room too bright to ignore anymore. It was 11:30. I was about to miss lunch with Dr. Amie, and given how fretful she can be when I forget mascara, she wouldn't want to see me like this. I also had an afternoon appointment with Karan Sullivan, the divorce attorney I'd referred Susan Grassley to, who had a matter we needed to discuss. Given that opening my jaw sent shockwaves of pain through my head, that might be a problem.

The doctor the night before didn't think I'd broken my cheekbone, but she'd warned me that I'd be sore. That bit of understatement floated back to me when I got out of bed after texting Dr. Amie to cancel and felt the ground—so firm and stable all my life—roll under my feet. A note from Hattie was stickied to a bag from the pharmacy with my filled pain medication prescription. I was going to owe those ladies big time. I took a pill with a big glass of water and went to brush what felt like hair from my teeth, feeling a tiny bit more alive. Then I looked in the mirror.

I'm not vain. I've been known to forget to brush my hair if I'm in a hurry, and makeup is often a flick of mascara I keep in my car. But even I was appalled at my reflection as I got close to the mirror to inspect. The doctor had put in seven stitches for the cut through my left eyebrow, and there was still some orange antiseptic staining my skin there. Hattie had cleaned my face of any remaining blood before she tucked me into bed the night before, so the red patches on my cheekbone and down the left side of my face were probably scrapes that were already bruising. My left eye was bloodshot, and my jaw ached. I moved it around a bit, and decided not to do that again for a while.

I rescheduled my appointments by text, and moved on to voice-mails. I had one from Sam Ames, and I hesitated before checking it. For some reason, I had the vague worry that all our discussing of him the day before had summoned his call. His voicemail, however, was about the heart bracelet that I'd tucked into his box. No hurry, he'd said, but he knew it was a gift from someone else, and he'd like to meet me to return it. I resolved to call him back after some more rest and medication. I faded off to sleep to dream about men in hoodies running after me.

When I woke, Gerard was calmly sitting in the chair by the window reading one of my paperback novels. I thought it was a dream for a minute or so: his silver hair was lit by the evening sunlight coming in the window, and the novel was one I bought at a garage sale years ago, the cover torn off to prevent resale. I liked the sassy heroine, though, and I kept the book to re-read when I feel blue. It's gotten a bit of rereading in the last few years.

His phone beeped, and the dreaminess left from the pain medica-tion receded. And I realized that *Gerard was calmly sitting in the chair by the window reading one of my paperback novels.*

I would have laid there, waiting for him to finish and leave, but I could tell I was going to have to use the bathroom soon. I opened my mouth to speak, but the motion sent off another wave of pain, and whatever I was going to say turned into a croak of surprise at the intensity of pain in my head.

He looked up, and his eyebrows came down. "For God's sake, Benedict, don't try to talk."

I cleared my throat. "I, ah, need to..." I trailed off and then waved a hand in the direction of the bathroom. Nothing had prepared me for a conversation like this with Gerard.

He frowned, and then that cleared away and he nodded and rose. "Need help?"

"No," I croaked. He left the room, and I stumbled unsteadily to the bathroom.

What I'd seen earlier in the day had only gotten worse. The bruising had a fine head start up the side of my face, and the orange antiseptic had faded, but not by much. My hair stood up from my head like a long, greasy mohawk, and I suspected I was beginning to smell.

I thought about a shower but, since the walk from the bedroom had already made me dizzy, I settled for a wet washcloth and a quick brush through my hair. While I stood at the sink waiting for the world to steady a bit, several questions flicked through my medication-twisted mind: *What was Gerard doing there?* and *Did I manage to click send on my rescheduling texts earlier?* and *Why would I have been the victim of a purse snatching when there were other, more wealthy-looking targets available?* and *What the hell was Gerard doing there?* and, finally, *When did Gerard and the Shelton sisters get so chummy?*

With a final adjustment of my wrinkled pajamas, I exited the bathroom with much more dignity than my entrance and found Gerard gone. There was a bit of a clue in that the front door chain was on, so I assumed he'd gone out the way he came in—from the Shelton sisters' side of the connecting door.

I took another pain pill from the bottle by the bed, wondering how much was too much. My eyes didn't seem to want to focus, so I tucked the bottle into my pocket to see if someone else could read the instructions for me. I used the connecting door to the Shelton kitchen, only to find Gerard at the table with the cat in his lap, a pot of something savory on the stove, and the Shelton sisters being charmed.

"Hey, Benedict. I'd get up, but your cat seems determined to erase the smell of my dog." He rubbed a hand over the traitorous cat's head, who purred and arched a cat eyebrow in my direction.

Hattie's cooking is always perfect for every occasion, and I wondered what the aftermath of a purse snatching would merit. My stomach reminded me that the piece of pizza before running out to meet Garrison last night was the last thing I'd eaten. It seemed like a week ago.

Sallie Shelton got up and ushered me to one of the kitchen chairs, where she sat me down and went off muttering about afghans. Hattie went to the stove to stir in the big pot, and Gerard and I were left alone. After him apparently watching me sleep, sitting together in the kitchen shouldn't have felt awkward, but it was. I resolved not to think about it.

Hattie put a heavy pottery bowl in front of me with something vaguely soupy in it, and I dug in. It was heavenly: an aromatic and flavorful mixture of white beans and carrots and green things and no discernable meat. After a few bites, my stomach and aching cheekbone decided I was done. I pushed the bowl forward as Sallie came back in the room with a soft, knitted throw she tucked around my shoulders and left me with a gentle stroke of my hair that brought tears to my eyes.

The Shelton sisters puttered around the kitchen and refilled Gerard's bowl and coffee cup. Hattie left a minty cup of tea at my elbow. I felt full and drowsy, but I sensed a conversation was coming, and I knew I needed to stay awake for it.

Hattie and Sallie settled on either side of me, and together we faced Gerard and the cat. He ate slowly and calmly, and complimented Hattie on the meal. We all waited until he finished and pushed his empty bowl aside. He sat back with his hands around his coffee cup and looked at me, and I could tell he was looking at the stitches and bruises.

"So what do you think, Benedict? Was this related to the case?"

I took a sip of my tea and wondered what was in it. I could taste some lemon and honey, but the rest was a mystery. At least my voice was back. "I know in the mysteries on TV the banged-up heroine denies any connection between danger and thrilling events, but I can't think of any other reason someone would pick me and my non-designer purse instead of all the Coach and Gucci and Chanel I saw on the street last night."

He nodded. "Did they get anything privileged?"

I shook my head, and inhaled sharply as the motion sent a lightning stroke of pain up my face.

Gerard winced in sympathy. "I'm glad you weren't injured worse."

I waited for him to scold me for being there or being injured, but he just sipped his own coffee and waited, his eyes on my face.

I perked up. "But wouldn't this prove Todd didn't do it? He's in jail and couldn't have been the guy in the hoodie."

Hattie spoke from my right side. "Rob told us that you've been shaking some trees lately, interviewing a lot of people." She folded her hands on the table. "Couldn't it have been one of them?"

I considered the relative testiness of the people I'd been interviewing. "I know the police officer said that no one could tell if it was a man or woman, but whoever it was, they were pretty strong."

Gerard spoke. "It was assigned to Crimes Against Persons, and I spoke with someone there. The witnesses didn't see much. But that area has a fair amount of crime—usually car burglaries, not assault."

"Assault?"

He eyed my bruises. "That was a pretty deliberate shove you received, Benedict."

"I pulled back when he tried to pull my bag off my shoulder." I don't know why I was arguing with him, but my head was beginning to hurt again, and I wished the medication would start working.

His eyebrows lowered alarmingly. "He shoved you into the wall first, the witnesses said."

I remembered the feeling of hitting the wall, and then the tugging. "Oh. That's right."

Sallie shifted beside me, and I remembered one of my questions. I carefully turned my head to look at Sallie. "Did you call Gerard today?"

She tilted her chin up defensively. "Yes. He'd told us to let him know if you weren't okay."

I looked at him, a motion I wished I hadn't made. "What? When?"

"After your headache the other day. Miss Hattie saw me driving your car and then helping you inside." He smiled at her. "And Miss Sallie wanted to come in and check on you. We had a great chat." He turned the charming grin on Sallie, who smiled back.

"I—okay." I swallowed hard. "I appreciate all of you, all of the help." I thought of something else. "My keys were in my bag, and your back door key is on there—"

Hattie patted my hand. "Tomas and the locksmith have changed all the locks. We have new keys, but we're also looking into some electronic security systems. I think it's time, and Rob knew someone we could call." She nodded at Gerard.

I was feeling distinctly surrounded. "I think I'm going to go to sleep for a bit. Gerard, could we pick this up tomorrow? I need to bring you up to speed on some information." I gathered the afghan around me and stood, my head swimming.

He nudged the cat to the floor and rose. "Let me get you into bed," he said, and I suppressed the urge to giggle, a sure sign the medication was kicking in. I'm not known to be a giggler. Behind me, I heard a little laugh from Miss Sallie—who's definitely a giggler.

"I'm good," I said, then promptly fell into the table, almost knocking a bowl to the floor. Hattie took one side of me, and Gerard took the other, and they moved me pretty quickly to the connecting door. Once on the edge of my bed, Hattie and I had a conversation about my medication—I was a little early on the second dose—and Gerard made sure the cat, who'd followed us in, had plenty of water and food. Hattie found me a scrunchie for my hair and helped me put it up, then patted my shoulder and pulled up the covers. Gerard stood over me for a minute, then he leaned in and said quietly:

"Benedict, I think your safety is more important than getting answers on your own in this case. Let's work together from this point on. Don't you agree?"

I looked up at him, all threatening eyebrows and hands on hips, and this time the giggle escaped.

He looked thunderous. "Are you laughing?"

"You look mad. Don' be mad." I could hear my words slurring, but I was soooo tired. "The girl detect've doesn't ever do what she's told...." My eyes closed, and I thought I heard him tell me to be safe, but I might have been mistaken.

CHAPTER TWENTY-FOUR

Saturday dawned bright and unseasonably warm, a sure sign we were about to get a cold front. I woke with the sun and stretched —and felt almost human again. I was right about the smell, though, and I headed for the shower.

I decided I felt good enough to skip the pain medication, and started the hot water running in the shower while I checked my phone. I had multiple text messages from Ryan, another voicemail from Sam Ames, and new ones from Ann Thornton and Gerard. I put a new bandage over the stitches in my eyebrow and climbed in under the water.

After a hot shower, I felt like a new woman. I wrapped my clean hair in a towel and checked my face. The stitches looked a bit puckered and red, but they'd told me to expect that. There might be a scar, the doctor had said, and she gave me a referral to a plastic surgeon. I think I threw the referral paperwork into the trash in the emergency room—there was no way I could afford that and my pitiful insurance wouldn't cover it. My eye wasn't as bloodshot, and only some of the scrapes on my face had bloomed into bruises. All in all, it could be worse.

I made a mental list of the things in my bag as I dressed in a warm robe. One of the blessings of having come close to bankruptcy meant I had only one credit card to cancel, and I'd turned off my debit card on my bank's smartphone app while I was waiting in the hall at the ER. My keys were gone, but with the locks changed, I'd be okay on that. I had one extra car key, and I could get those locks changed at the car dealership on Monday. I called Sam Ames and left him a voicemail to return my call.

I sat on the bed and called the credit card company. They put me on hold while they checked the account. The representative said no one had used the card, so they'd cancel it and send me a new one with a new number. She did helpfully mention my payment was due in a few days, so I guess the thief hadn't paid my bills for me. I'd only lost $20 in cash—which a couple of years ago would have crippled my finances—but I had no ability to get cash without my frozen debit card, so I put a trip to the bank on my to-do list.

I laid across the bed to consider what notes and other paraphernalia was in my bag—and remembered Gerard's Mont Blanc pen that Ann Thornton had returned to me. I felt a bit sorry about that, since I loved that pen, and realized I'd have to tell him about it. My last thought before I drifted off to sleep was wondering what one of those pens cost.

———

I woke up mid-afternoon when Sam Ames called me back. My hair had mostly dried in the damp towel, and I unwound it as I answered.

"Thank you for calling me back, Ms. Benedict," he said.

"Lacey, please, Mr. Ames."

"Then I'm Sam." I could tell he was smiling a bit at our formality.

"I wanted to call you about the bracelet with the heart you'd put into the box."

"It wasn't a gift from you and Mrs. Ames?" I sat up and pulled my robe tighter. The day had clouded over, and it was starting to get cold.

"No, no it wasn't."

"Oh. Well, I can give it back to Naomi, I guess. Maybe she knows who gave it to Carrie."

There was a pause, and then Sam Ames spoke stiffly. "I know who gave it to her, Lacey. It was David Young."

"David?" I didn't expect that at all.

"Yes. You knew she and David were close?" I did not, but I suspected that saying that might stop him from talking. "He gave it to her a few years ago, when she was 18." He paused. "I didn't realize Carrie had kept it."

"Did she not *want* to keep it?"

His response was tart. "She didn't want to *receive* it." He sighed. "David always had more feelings for her than she did for him. We thought that a marriage between them might steady him, but it wasn't to be."

"Were they dating?"

"It's....different among the Friends than it is in the world." He hesitated, as if reluctant to offend me. "A young man wants to know that a young woman will be a good wife, capable and steadfast, as the wife in Proverbs. And she needs to know that he will be the spiritual head of their family, always putting her and their family first."

I didn't want to offend *him*, so I just said, "I see."

He sighed heavily. "Carrie didn't believe they were suited."

The silence stretched a little, so I answered softly. "I didn't realize that."

"Oh, she was kind to him about it, but she finally had to make it clear to him. He took it hard."

I thought back to my conversation with David, who had mentioned none of this. "I know his sister was Carrie's age."

"Yes, poor Megan." He sighed again, and I could imagine him

shaking his head in sadness. "We have all prayed that their family's faith would be strong so they could withstand the forces of Satan and the havoc they cause."

"What happened to her?"

"I don't like to gossip, my dear." He paused, and I could see him considering. "She was never very strong. She left—she left home and the Truth, and then she came back. But she wasn't strong."

"David told me she killed herself."

"She did, poor child."

"Was this before or after David was disfellowshipped?" His silence seemed disapproving. "I know he was disfellowshipped. He told me himself." I waited. "He seems very troubled."

"David left the Truth not too long after we'd moved to the Princeton Kingdom Hall from Breeland. He seemed to go a little wild, as if he'd been holding his feelings inside him. And then everything seemed to rush out after Megan's death, as if it was a festering wound that finally ruptured."

"What do you mean?"

He clicked his tongue, and then seemed to make a decision. "He tried to set fire to the Kingdom Hall in Breeland."

I was appalled. Why had no one mentioned *any* of this? "Was he drinking? Was he arrested?"

"A brother stopped him, and nothing came of it. The elders there did not want to bring ill repute to the Organization by making it public. He was asked to leave and not return." He sounded tired. "He's a good young man, but Satan and his demons have taken control of him. The drinking is a symptom of the hold Satan has over him."

He seemed to realize how much he'd said. "I thought it might comfort him to know that Carrie kept the bracelet after all."

I wasn't sure, but I didn't want to say it aloud. "I'm happy to meet you and get it."

We arranged to meet at R&D Booksellers on Tuesday, when he'd always met with Carrie. I was sure I wouldn't be a good substitute for his daughter, but I wanted to hear more about David Young and Carrie Ames.

———

GERARD HAD CALLED TO CHECK ON ME—NO NEED TO CALL HIM back unless I needed something, he said. He'd talk to me on Sunday.

Ann Thornton had left me a hesitant voicemail about the ex-JW group, which would meet the next day at her house. She said she thought it might be a good idea for the group to remember about Carrie and her strength, and that they might—if given the opportunity—give me more information that might lead to a resolution.

She ended the message: "We all need closure on this." I agreed. I was ready for this to be resolved, but I wasn't sure we were any further along.

I was starting to get hungry. A quick look in my refrigerator yielded the single remaining piece of the Giannelli's pizza Gerard had brought over. It was a little hard by this time, but I shrugged mentally and crunched into it. My head was starting to ache, and I suspected I'd have to take some over-the-counter medication if I wanted to avoid the prescription pills. I wanted to have something else in my stomach before any medication went in there too.

I thought about the support group meeting on Sunday afternoon, and decided I was going to go. A little guiltily, I remembered Gerard asking me to let him know before I went anywhere on the case. I decided a text might suffice.

> *Hey, wanted to let you know I'm going to Ann Thornton's house on Sunday for an ex-JW support group meeting. I want to see if anyone reacts badly to my face—you know, confesses Perry Mason-style when they see the results! I'll let you know.*

My phone rang almost immediately. Gerard.

"Hey, Gerard. Fingers still fat?"

"What time is this meeting?" He sounded irritable, and I wondered if I was interrupting something.

There's just something about cranky people that makes me want to needle them. "And a cheery hello to you too."

He sighed. "Hello, Benedict. How's the face?"

"Still attached." I laughed when he snorted. "I'm good. Feeling better, but still sleeping a lot."

"You suffered trauma, Benedict." He sounded gruff and distracted. "Most women would still be having hysterics."

"What century do you live in, Gerard? Women don't have hysterics anymore—in fact, we never did. We were always just being passionate and misunderstood."

Silence. Okay, maybe I'd pushed too far. "I'm really okay, Gerard."

"Good. What time is this meeting?"

"Um, 5, I think."

"Be sure, Benedict. I'll pick you up a half hour before."

I balked. He'd not been around any of these people. "Gerard, I really don't want to throw these people off. I can do this on my own."

"Benedict, two nights ago, someone pushed you into a wall, stole your purse, and left you bloody. I'm going with you."

He had a point. "Let me check her text." I checked, and also replied to her that Gerard and I would be there. "5 pm."

"I'll see you at 4:30. Try to be safe till I get there, Benedict." He hung up abruptly.

Ha.

I WAS READY TO CURL UP ON THE COUCH AND WATCH OLD reruns when Hattie tapped on the connecting door and poked her head in.

"How are you?"

"I'm doing all right. I felt fine earlier, but then my shower took everything out of me."

She nodded. "Sometimes that happens. Have you eaten today?"

"I had a piece of cold pizza before taking some medicine." I was hoping my eyes didn't look too pitiful, but she smiled at me in that way she has and opened the door a bit wider.

"Chicken pot pie."

I took it for the invitation it was, gathering up the soft afghan Sallie had wrapped me in the night before, and following Hattie to their kitchen.

The chicken pot pie was a real pie, with flaky crust and creamy filling, studded with chunks of chicken and vegetables. I managed to eat half the portion she gave me before giving up. When Sallie switched out the dinner plate with a small bowl of chocolate ice cream, I knew the inquisition was about to begin.

"So... what do we know about Rob Gerard? Who are his people? Does he come from a good family?"

CHAPTER TWENTY-FIVE

S unday dawned with a low, cloudy sky, but I didn't care. I woke up feeling better than I had for two days. I stretched and then showered. Since I was meeting Dr. Amie for brunch, I spent a few minutes drying and taming my hair, and then tried to add some makeup to the colors on my face. The bruises had fully bloomed, and I had dark blues and purples from my (now scar-divided) eyebrow up to my hairline, and back down past my cheekbone. I considered my wardrobe, and decided to avoid some of my wardrobe that had blue and purple tones. A deep red sweater would do—brighter than I usually wore—and might distract everyone from my face. Sallie, bless her, had laundered the blood out of my favorite jeans, so I was able to get a little comfort from those and my usual boots. The hooded jacket I'd worn Thursday night was a complete loss, Sallie said, and—even though she added 'no big loss'—I chose not to doubt her.

I reconfirmed brunch with Dr. Amie and spent an hour adding Garrison's recent information to the notes I had at home. While the thief may have gotten my notebook itself, most of the pages with notes had been torn out and organized when Gerard and I had met earlier in the evening. I felt a little satisfaction at that.

I had an idea about the information I wanted to try out. I created a timeline for Sunday, January 27, the day Carrie died. Something was nagging at my brain, and I knew dealing with facts—not the static of everyone's emotions—would help me think.

- *10 am: Carrie had breakfast with the Lowensteins*
- *3 pm: Todd and Carrie watch a movie in the apartment*
- *5 pm: The support group gathered, and she told everyone her news*
- *6 pm: The support group breaks up, David Young storms out, Todd stays*
- *6:15 pm: Susan Grassley says Carl leaves Susan and Emma at home and stays gone until midnight*
- *6:30 pm: The Lowensteins say they hear Todd and Carrie arguing*
- *7 pm: Todd says he leaves and Carl Grassley sees him kissing Carrie goodbye*
- *8:30 pm: Todd says he comes back to make up with her, door is locked*
- *8:30 pm: David Young says he sees Todd leave*
- *7-9 pm: Carrie is murdered*
- *10 pm: Naomi finds Carrie*

I found it hard to believe that Carrie could tell Todd about her returning to the Organization on Thursday, January 24, and then he could calmly watch a movie with her that afternoon and then kiss her before leaving, all while being so angry that he would need to kill her that night. Todd had refused to tell Gerard what they'd argued about, but I strongly suspected that he was worried about *what would happen* after she went back, given what Garrison had said about losing people he'd sent back. I made a note for our next conversation with Todd, to let him know we knew about Carrie's reasons. He might be more forthcoming if he didn't think he had to keep her secret.

I also realized, with a cold chill, that I had removed her journal—the only evidence that she had told Todd she was going back days before she was killed—from her apartment. Even if the journal was admissible over a hearsay objection, my removal of the document might mean it was excluded as corroborating evidence. I felt embarrassed at my naivete, and made a note to talk to Gerard about it.

A snippet of a fact floated to the surface of my brain, and I looked through my notes from my conversation with Ann Thornton. She'd said that everyone at the support group meeting was stunned and didn't know what to say to Carrie, but David Young had given me a pretty detailed list of the things he'd told Carrie about her going back, and Carl Grassley had said that he'd told her he hoped she was truly repentant. Had both of them said those things in front of other people? I couldn't remember exactly what Ann had told me about when they'd left. I almost texted her, but then I remembered what she'd said about Sunday mornings and sacred times. I'd see her that evening, and I'd ask her then.

———

DR. AMIE WAS ALREADY AT THE M STREET GARDEN CAFÉ when I came in. She loves it there—she says it reminds her of Paris, and I guess I can see her point. There's a saying: 'On Saturday night, Dallas munches; on Sunday morning, Dallas brunches.' We love to brunch on Sundays, and M Street takes reservations only on Sunday because of that. The restaurant is a commercial building dropped right into the middle of a residential neighborhood. Its back is a neighborhood garden where they sell the produce and plants and flowers they grow, and in the spring before it gets too hot and the fall before it gets too cold, they serve high tea under a grapevine-covered patio. The restaurant itself is a long narrow room with a pressed-tin ceiling and black wrought-iron tables with marble tops, the chairs old and wooden and rickety. They proudly serve their meals on chipped, mismatched china, and the old partially-tarnished silverware is sometimes real silver. French music plays softly in the background—just loudly enough to be heard behind conversations that range from the maliciousness of Dallas society gossip to the intricate negotiations of million-dollar businesses.

The place was completely full, and I could hear a shocked silence sweep the room when I walked in. I'd like to think it was the red sweater, but I'm pretty sure it was the bruises. I kept my eyes on Dr. Amie, and fixed a smile on my mouth as I dodged the tables in the tightly-packed space.

Her eyes widened as she looked at me, but the exclamation I expected never came. She did rise to greet me, and I received a hug that made my eyes suspiciously moist.

She had a squat iron pot of tea ready, and she poured me a fragrant cup. As always, she looked beautiful, her red-gold hair pulled back from her face with a paisley scarf that had swirls of pale pink like her turtleneck sweater. Where my (now bloodless) jeans were tough and bootcut, hers were a cream with gold accents that I could never have kept clean. She still had her gold lame jacket over her shoulders, and it caught the light perfectly. I sighed and smiled for real. Just being around her made me feel a bit better.

"That red looks lovely on you." She nodded at my sweater. "You should always wear bright colors—your skin tone can handle it." I looked down at the sweater, pleased I'd picked right for once.

We ordered, a quiche Lorraine for me and eggs Benedict for Amie. We'd once agreed that, given my last name, I should never order that particular breakfast, and I didn't mind. Hollandaise sauce seemed a bit bland to me. Amie eyed me, and then ordered a side of bacon to share.

She waited for me to tell her the story of the purse-snatching, and I brought her up to speed on the non-privileged parts of the investigation. When the server brought our entrees, we paused to eat for a moment. My slice of quiche was at least three inches high, creamy and cheesy, with chunks of bacon and a delicate bottom crust. The custardy flavor of the quiche was familiar and comforting, and the crispy bacon was the perfect counterpoint. I ate about half of my slice before I gave up.

Amie had cut into her poached eggs and eaten a few bites, but had mostly watched me as I ate. I had to admit I was feeling a little tired, and she seemed concerned. I didn't wave it aside, but I did want to focus on something else. I encouraged her to eat while I asked few questions.

"You and I met—what? Four years ago?" She nodded while she cut a small bite of muffin and Canadian bacon, and used her knife to pile a little egg and Mornay sauce on the bite. "Would you say I'm a coward?"

Her bite stopped before it got to her mouth, and she tilted her head and looked at me before eating it delicately. She chewed and swallowed, laid her knife and fork on her plate, and dabbed at her mouth with the white linen napkin before pushing her plate forward. I sensed she was angry, but I don't know why.

"Why in the world would you say that about yourself, cherie?"

I picked up a piece of bacon, but put it back down uneaten. Even though it was perfectly cooked, I'd lost my appetite. I told her briefly about my conversations with my client, Sonja, and with Gerard, and my realization that I might have been mistaken all these years about being blackballed.

Her delicate eyebrows raised. "And this man called you a *coward?*"

"No! No, that's not it." I didn't want her to get the wrong idea. "He was just so....so shocked that I'd never looked for another job, that I wondered if it was my cowardice, my fear." I gently rubbed the left side of my forehead above the stitches, where a permanent ache had seemed to settle in. "And Sonja...when she said that about me not coming out the other side, maybe I haven't wanted to."

The server came to clear our plates, and Dr. Amie arranged for a new pot of Darjeeling and leftovers in boxes. The background music seemed really loud today, or perhaps that was just me. I concentrated on breathing deeply, and Amie watched me closely.

"My dear, have you had anything for the pain today?"

I shook my head. "I'm tired of the fog, and at least with the pain, I don't have that."

"All right," she said soothingly. The server appeared with the new pot of tea and a little jar of honey. I let her doctor my tea and then I sipped at the cup she gave me. The tea warmed as it went down, and the honey made me feel a little bit better right away.

"Cherie, everyone recovers in their own way and in their own time."

"Oh, I'm sure I'll be better in the next few days."

She smiled a bit. "Lacey, I'm talking about your recovery from the Bill Stephenson relationship."

"Oh." I made a face. "I hate the word 'relationship.' He was just my boss."

She laughed softly. "I know. But it was a relationship nevertheless. And you put your trust in someone who failed you. You suffered at his hands, and then you continued to suffer during the trials." She tilted her head. "That was all trauma. And you're still recovering."

"But I've not come through the other side?"

"I don't know exactly what she meant by that. Have you finished recovery? No. Are you better now? I think you know the answer to that."

"I *am* better."

She smiled. "Then what is the question?"

I was frustrated. "If I'm better, why don't I *feel* better? I still feel..." I trailed off, unable to think of the words to describe my frustration with myself.

Dr. Amie was never tongue-tied, but she did use silence well. She waited me out.

"Guilty? Unhappy? Unworthy?"

She tilted her head at my words. "Why would you feel guilty, cherie?"

Her soft tone almost did me in. I couldn't have *not* answered her. "I didn't report Bill right away. For a while—a month or so—I wrestled with it." I looked off at the people eating and laughing next to us, wealthy people eating expensive meals and drinking champagne mimosas. "I thought, *these people know what they're getting into.* Both the clients and the investors. They were all trying to make a buck on the recovery after the recession. Even the riskiest deals were subscribed to so fast we were shocked." I swallowed hard against the memory. "Technology, real estate, pharma—it didn't matter who was going to be on the other side, or what the product was. People wanted to make a fast, easy dollar. Or million dollars." I looked at Amie and felt ashamed. "For a few weeks, I went home and looked at my high-rise apartment with my expensive furniture, and I drove in my convertible with the top down, and I felt like one of them. I didn't sleep at night, and my days were filled with panic attacks while I wondered how long it would take for it to all come crashing down. And finally, my father saw my exhaustion and my guilt, and he pulled it out of me. He reminded me that right is right, and wrong is wrong." I stopped, the burning in my stomach reminding me of the anxiety of those days.

"And the rest is history," she said gently.

I nodded. "And now Gerard's voice reminds me that I should have been there by Bill's side at the defense table." I felt so tired of thinking about all this.

Her brow knitted. "Gerard's voice?"

Risking her thinking I was crazy, I told her about my dreams with Gerard cross-examining me. She tsked. "Cherie, you're not crazy. You've just allowed him to personify your own doubts. The voice in your head is your own. And the one who is demanding the answers is you."

I considered. I'd always wondered why it was Gerard who interrogated me about my career. Maybe she was right. I massaged my forehead tiredly.

"You should go home and rest for a while," she said with concern.

"Maybe I should." I hesitated. "Gerard thinks I was in love with Bill Stephenson."

She looked at me. "And were you?"

I didn't answer right away. I watched the beautiful people at the tables near us, laughing and talking over their brunch, as I thought about the older man, vibrant and larger than life, ambitious and calculating, who belonged in this place more than I did. I shook my head. "Not really. I thought he represented what I wanted to be. But everything he did had an agenda. He was generous because he thought it would benefit him, kind when he wanted other people to see. Take away the money and the power, and there was nothing there to love."

She reached over and put her hand on mine. "Why does what this man thinks matter to you so much?"

"Who? Bill?"

She patted my hand. "No, cherie. Rob Gerard. Why is he, the man who defended Stephenson, the arbiter of your conscience?"

I had no answer for her.

CHAPTER TWENTY-SIX

Gerard was early. I'd come home from M Street and fallen across the bed with my face resting on my good side, sleeping until I heard him knock at the door. I surfaced from a dream of Bill Stephenson and Dr. Amie—my bad angel and my good angel—and stumbled to the door. He looked concerned when I opened it.

"Are you okay?"

I blinked at him. "Yeah, I'm all right." I yawned. "I was asleep. What time is it?" I stepped back to let him in.

"About 4:15. Why is your face so red on the other side?" He reached out toward my face, but didn't touch me.

I rubbed the left side of my face, starting to feel a bit awkward. I didn't even think to look in the mirror before coming to the door. "I slept on it for about four hours." I waved him off and headed to the bedroom. "Have a seat. I need to wake up."

I faced myself in the mirror. What little makeup I'd managed to put on before brunch was gone, and the bruises were vivid against my skin. I splashed myself with cold water and brushed my tangled hair, debating whether putting it up in a ponytail would highlight the bruising or not. I flicked on some mascara and brushed my teeth. As an afterthought, I carried the ponytail holder out to the living room.

"Since we think my guy in the hoodie—can we call him a 'perp' for fun?—is going to be there tonight, do you think pulling my hair back will make the bruises stand out more? What do you think?"

He turned to look at me, and his eyebrows were so far down his face, I was goaded into asking, "What?"

"Benedict, you were assaulted," he ground out. "This isn't funny."

"Hey, Gerard, I *was* there, you know." I felt a bit insulted by his tone. "The other night wasn't funny. But I'm better now." I swung my hair into a smooth ponytail and tightened the holder. "I think we're down to three guys who might have pushed me into a wall, and I really think it's down to two. I want us to look at them when they come in and see what their reactions are to this"—I pointed at my face —"and we might have a better idea."

He stuck his hands in his coat and stared at me.

"What?" I said again.

He shook his head and smiled a little. "You've got a point, but I wish you hadn't had to end up in an ER to make it." He sighed. "It's getting cold and windy outside." He picked up my coat from the chair and held it out like a butler. "Madam?"

———

Gerard was right: there wasn't any afternoon sun, and it was cold and damp. On the way, I told him about Carl Grassley and David Young, describing each in detail so he could help me watch them as they came in. Once he assured with an eye roll that he could handle the assignment, he asked me how I thought this meeting might go.

"It seems like they use it like a support group—you know, talking about the problems they're having integrating into the 'world,' so to speak. And everyone listens, and gives a bit of advice. I don't think there's a therapist there."

"Like AA," he murmured, and I looked at him sharply.

"That's what David Young said when I talked to him." A memory was jogged. "I don't think Garrison drinks alcohol—that DUI arrest Julia mentioned—and he talked about substance abuse issues that people who get out of the JW often have." I turned in the seat to face Gerard. "But there was a beer on the table the other night."

He looked to the side. "Falling off the wagon? Or someone else's beer?"

I shrugged. "I suppose we could ask him, or ask Shelley, the waitress."

"Who do you think it was?"

"Either Carl Grassley or David Young." I looked out the window at the Tudor-style houses in the little subdivision, their stained-glass windows lit against the oncoming evening gloom. "Both of them seem to be boiling kettles of anger to me." I sighed. "I wish it was Adam Garrison. While I think what he's doing is kinda noble, I don't like him at all."

Gerard laughed, a deep chuckle in the gathering darkness that made the hair stand up on my forearms. I rubbed the feeling away and crossed my arms. His voice was chiding. "If everyone we didn't like was a killer, we'd have no one left to prosecute them." *And no one left to defend them,* I thought, but didn't say it aloud.

As he turned into Ann's street, I told him about the losses Garrison mentioned. "He's a cold bastard, there's no doubt," he said. "But is he a killer?"

We pulled up in front of her house, the uncovered windows lit and welcoming. I could see Ann moving around in the living room. "I don't think so. But I think he knows who is."

———

WE WERE THE FIRST ONES THERE. ANN WAS DRESSED IN A PALE

blue linen caftan, and she greeted Gerard with a calm smile. When she went to hug me, I let her, and that seemed to make her happy. Once we came into the light of the entryway, she was noticeably shocked at the state of my face, and I hoped the rest of the group would be as open and easy to read.

I could see lights outside as cars began to pull up, and I wanted to ask her a question before anyone else got there. "Ann, I have a question. The night Carrie told the group she was going back—did Carl Grassley question the depth of her repentance?"

She shook her head. "Carl was excited for her. He kept raving about how lucky she was, and how fortunate she would be when she was reinstated." She thought for a moment. "But they could have spoken before he and Susan left."

"And David Young—did she and David Young argue?" She inhaled deeply, and I sensed something was brewing behind her calm face. "Ann?"

"No, Lacey. He stormed out after she told the group and Carl started congratulating her. He didn't say a word to her."

She and I looked at each other, and I felt Gerard stir beside me. Then the doorbell rang, and with a murmured word, she went to open the door. Gerard and I moved to the dining room doorway where I'd stood the night of the memorial. The dining table wasn't as loaded as that night, but there were soft drinks and coffee, and a couple of platters of sliced cake and cookies.

I thought it might be the right time, so I leaned close to Gerard. "By the way..." He leaned in to catch my low voice. "Your pen was in my bag." He frowned at me and opened his mouth to speak just as the front door opened.

A couple of young women I didn't know entered first, and they looked at us curiously as they moved into the living room. I couldn't tell if the look was because of my bruised face or the fact that we were strangers.

A laughing Emma Grassley came in through the open door behind them, and I tensed. Susan came in next and spoke to Ann, who hugged her as she had me. Carl came in last, and I waited, halfway hidden by Gerard until they were all completely in the entryway. Carl had spoken to Susan, who picked up Emma and kept silent, and then they both saw me. Susan's mouth fell open, and for a brief moment, she looked at Carl.

Carl froze, looking at me, his brow furrowed. I stepped around Gerard and into the entryway, and Emma reached out before Susan could stop her. "Owie?" Emma asked, and touched the side of my face.

"Yep," I replied with a smile for her. "Big owie."

Carl dipped his head to the side. "Are you all right?"

I nodded, Emma's tiny hand feathering over my bruises. "I will be."

"What happened?" Susan whispered.

"Purse snatching." Gerard said from behind me, just as I said, "I fell."

Susan looked from me to Gerard, her face creased with worry. "When?" *She thinks Carl did it*, I thought. *She thinks he killed Carrie, and she thinks he assaulted me.* Neither one of us answered her.

A light knock immediately preceded the door opening, and the two groups split, me and Gerard backing up to the dining room doorway, and Susan and Carl moving into the living room proper just as Adam Garrison took a few steps inside the door.

I was right under the dining room doorway, and I moved back into the light of the dining room. His eyes met mine, and—to my surprise—he looked sad rather than surprised. The cold rushed in behind him, and he stepped to the side as David Young stepped inside the doorway.

He was smiling and laughing, that charming grin stretching his handsome face, when he saw me. It was only for a few seconds, but I saw the look of shock on his face, the widening of his eyes, and then he bowed his head as Gerard stepped in between us. Adam turned to David and put his arm around him, pulling him forward into the light.

THE FOUR OF US CLOSED OURSELVES OFF IN THE DINING ROOM, pulling the sliding barn doors closed as Ann ushered the rest of the group out the front door. She came into the dining room just as David began to talk.

"I feel like I've been in a fog for most of my life. Every once in a while, something—or someone—would break through it. My sister could always bring me out of it. She was so sweet and loving and kind. Carrie was too." He looked up at me and winced, moving his gaze to Gerard next to me instead.

"When Megan died"—he choked on the word—"I couldn't take it. The only reason—the *only reason* she was dead was the Organization. Those people." He stopped, his throat working.

"They said you tried to set fire to the Kingdom Hall in Breeland after she died." I'd forgotten Gerard didn't know about this, and I tried to send him a silent '*sorry*' when he looked at me suddenly.

"I don't know what I was trying to do," David said, a little defensively, I thought. "I was just—so *angry* all of a sudden. I envisioned myself as Samson, bringing down the Philistines' temple." This mystifying comment was met with a small grin from Adam Garrison, sitting to his left. David shook his head as if to clear it, then he looked at me.

"I'm sorry, Lacey. I didn't mean for you to get hurt. I just needed to see what you'd written down after you met with Adam."

"You'd been at the table with Adam before I got to Hipster Haven, hadn't you?"

"Yeah." He sat back in his chair and crossed his arms over his chest. "I came out of the bathroom and the last person I expected to see sitting there with him was you."

"Ah. I thought you'd already left."

Adam spoke. "No, we were done, but he hadn't left."

David looked sulkily at him. "*I* wasn't finished." He looked back at me. "I waited outside for you."

Adam just looked at him. I shifted in my seat, impatient to get to the truth.

"And with Carrie? What happened?"

David looked at me, tears slowly welling in his beautiful blue eyes. "You know, I loved her so much. Even when I was 18 and she was 14, I knew she was the one." He rubbed a hand over his face. "She couldn't see it. Said she couldn't see us together."

"Her father told me you'd given her a bracelet."

His face tightened. "She tried to give it back to me. I don't know, maybe she threw it away."

I saw my chance to shake him up. "No, David. She kept it." His eyes locked on mine. "It was in her bedroom the night she died."

I could see the pulse leaping in his throat. I leaned forward, keeping my eyes on his. "What happened that night, David?"

His eyes slid to the side, looking at Ann Thornton standing just inside the doorway, her arms crossed, her head bowed, tears streaming down her face.

"I couldn't believe she was going back. I thought—I thought maybe someday, if she and Todd didn't get married, she'd see us, in her mind. She'd come to see *us*." He swallowed hard. "I was so angry that she would go back to the Organization, but she hated it when I got mad, so I left. I drove around for a long time and tried to calm down." He stopped and looked at Adam, who nodded encouragingly. "I stopped at a bar and had a drink or two, you know, just trying to relax. Then I came back and he was leaving. Todd."

I was confused. "At 8:30?"

He shook his head, then he drew a deep breath in, his nostrils flaring. "About 7:00. I heard them arguing, but then she hugged him as he was leaving. I waited in my apartment until he left." His leg was jiggling, his agitation apparent. "I knocked on the door and Carrie was crying. I went in, just to talk to her. To tell her. To *remind* her what it would be like, what Megan went through. The extra hours of service to prove that you're worthy. Sitting at the back in the Kingdom Hall. Being ignored. Being *judged*." He blinked back tears.

"I think that's what broke Megan. She was so sweet and kind. She just wanted to talk to people, to feel loved."

I looked over at Garrison, willing him to say something to David —to his *friend*—about Megan and why she'd gone back. He didn't look at me, didn't say anything to ease David's suffering. I raged inside, but I didn't want to stop David's confession.

He breathed in silence, remembering. We all watched him, his body taut with tension. Finally, he licked his dry lips and continued. "Carrie wouldn't listen to me. She told me she had her reasons, that she had a *purpose* to fulfill. I told her I remembered the whole purpose bullshit from the Organization, and I couldn't believe she was buying into it again." His voice rose. "I didn't want the Lowensteins to hear, so I kept my cool, even though she was making me so *angry*." He rubbed his finger and thumb over his eyes, wiping away the moisture there. "She told me I needed to leave. She got up to go to the door and I just...I just—" He broke off as the tears started flowing over his face and down his beard. "I was so angry at her. I just wanted her to listen to me. I shook her—just shook her by her shoulders and— she stumbled backwards and fell and hit her head." Now he looked at me and Gerard, begging us to understand. "There was so much blood everywhere. I just panicked and ran out." He put his hands over his face and wept.

I looked at Adam and Ann, and realized that they weren't surprised. They'd known, just as they'd known about Carrie. How long would they have let Todd stay in jail before saying anything? At that moment, I understood David's cry about being angry. I felt the blood pound in the bruises in my face and realized I was clenching my fists.

"But you didn't just run—" I started, but Gerard put his hand on my arm. I looked at him, and he shook his head slightly. Bewildered, I watched him rise and stood up too.

"We've heard enough." He looked at Adam. "I'll call the assistant DA tonight, and they can arrange for him to give himself up." David's shoulders shook with his sobs, and Adam put his arm around them as he nodded to Gerard.

My mouth was open as Gerard pulled me out of the room. I looked back to see Ann and Adam on either side of David, their arms around him.

CHAPTER TWENTY-SEVEN

Sunday, February 17 (continued)

"What are you *doing?*" I asked Gerard as we walked down the steps. I pulled my arm from his grasp, and my voice rose with each word. "I wasn't finished!" I looked back at Ann Thornton's house.

"Yes, you were." His voice was even and calm, and he strode so fast I could barely keep up with him.

"He's acting like it was an accident! We both know he's lying!" I screeched the last word at him in the twilight. "What's *wrong* with you?"

He took two more steps, and stopped, his head down. Then he came back, looking down at me, his face dark and tight. I realized then that he wasn't calm, not at all, and I barely kept myself from taking a step back. "It doesn't matter what we know or don't know. The moment we knew he was the one who killed the person *our client is in jail for killing*, we were done." He didn't raise his voice, but the control was chilling.

"How can you *say* that?" I was livid, and my voice shook with emotion. I pointed back at Ann Thornton's house. "He's acting like Carrie's death was an accident instead of murder. We both know it wasn't."

He leaned in until his face was inches from mine, his voice tight. "And we know that because of information we obtained in representing our client, Benedict. Don't you think the DA has the right to use that information against David Young?"

I stopped, my mouth open to respond, but I had no argument. He was right. He looked at me for a few seconds more and then turned to walk the rest of the distance to his Range Rover. I stomped after him, the blood pulsing in the bruises on my face.

We got into the car, me slamming my door. He started the engine but didn't put it into gear. He spoke quietly but intensely. "Our job ends when we have enough information to get the DA to agree to a motion to dismiss the charges against grandson." His voice gentled, but he still didn't look at me. "We don't get to tie it up in a neat little bow, Benedict. We just get grandson out of jail."

I growled. "Can't you call him by his name even now?" I crossed my arms against the cold. "What if David doesn't turn himself in tomorrow? What then?"

He continued to look at me. "He will."

I turned to look at him there, so calm and controlled. In that moment, I imagined that I hated him. "How do you know?"

"Garrison and Ann Thornton will go with him." He turned to face the front and put the Range Rover into gear, and pulled away from the curb. "They knew—couldn't you tell?"

I bumped my head against the headrest in frustration. "Yes. I think they told Ann yesterday, or maybe Friday. That's why she invited me tonight. She was trying to make things happen. To get closure." I shook my head. "But Garrison—the so-called Shepherd— he knew about Carrie, and he knew about what happened to me."

He drove in silence for a minute. "Why are you so angry, Benedict?"

I put my hands over my face and gently massaged my forehead

above the stitches, which were beginning to burn. "He's going to confess, saying it was an accident, and they're going to plead him out, aren't they?"

"Probably." He stopped at a red light, and I saw that a fine mist was falling, coating the windshield.

"She's not going to get justice."

He faced forward, not looking at me. "Who?"

I dropped my hands and looked at him. Was he being deliberately obtuse? "You *know* who. Carrie Ames."

He turned to stare at me, and I could see from the red light from the traffic light spilling into the car that he was frowning a little. "What would 'justice' be for? She's still dead."

"Her killer should be punished. We should get that for her."

He turned away, and his voice was quiet in the darkness. "Benedict, she wasn't our client."

"I know that." The windshield wipers automatically swiped the windshield, and I watched them clear the mist from the glass.

"Do you?" The light turned green, and he started the car forward slowly. "You've gotten very involved with her."

My head pounded, and I wanted to cry. "I've spent the last two weeks buried in her life. I can't help but be involved."

"Why does it mean so much to you?"

I rounded on him, angry again. "Why doesn't it mean *anything* to you?"

He pulled into an empty parking lot and put the car in park under a streetlight. Then he turned to me, his nostrils flaring. "What makes you think it doesn't mean anything? Because I'm not screaming at David Young? Because I don't want to throw everything at him to make him confess?"

I leaned in toward him. "Yes, dammit! Because you're acting like it's over! It's not over yet!"

He leaned in too, his voice rising. "It's over for *us*. This isn't a movie where there's going to be a grand confession and a car chase,

Benedict." He shook his head. "Our job isn't to get justice for Carrie Ames. It's to see justice is done for Todd Parrish."

My throat ached from holding tears back. "Why can't it be *both*?"

He was breathing fast. "Because it doesn't work that way." He turned to face the windshield again, where the rain was beating against the glass and the wipers were picking up the pace. For a solid minute, the thrumming of the rain and the intermittent swooshing and squeaking of the wipers were the only sounds in the car until he spoke again.

"This isn't about Carrie Ames. It's about you."

My voice came out in a croak as I whipped around to stare at him. "*What* did you say?"

"This need for justice. It's not about Carrie and David Young. It's about you and Bill Stephenson."

"That's absurd."

He turned and looked at me, and I could see his eyebrows lifting. "Is it?"

I hissed at him. "Yes." I closed my eyes and breathed in a deep breath, praying for control. "Justice was irrelevant where Bill Stephenson was concerned. *You* helped to make that irrelevant."

His voice was quiet. "Did I?"

I lost it and rounded on him. "You *represented* him! You, more than anyone else, know exactly how much harm you did." I could hear my voice cracking, and I cursed my emotions. "If it hadn't been for you—"

He broke in. "What? If it hadn't been for me, he would have had no counsel?" He shook his head. "Come on, Benedict, you're smarter than that. If it hadn't been me, it would have been someone else, maybe someone else without the ability to get him to see reason." He stopped and then exhaled slowly before speaking again. "Someone who might have won at trial instead of encouraging him to settle before the jury returned a verdict."

I stopped short. In all my 'what should have beens,' I never imagined that someone else might have advised Bill Stephenson not to settle.

And then Gerard said the one thing I didn't need to hear. "Benedict, you've got to get past this. You've got to stop reliving this thing."

I could feel the rage burning its way up my throat, over my face, to the ends of my hair. "*I* do? I have to 'stop reliving this thing'? Are you freaking kidding me?" He looked at me warily, as if he could see my hair standing on end. "This 'thing,' as you put it, derailed my life! I was supposed to be quietly practicing law with Bill Stephenson or some other partner, just doing my job and living my life, making a little money, maybe with a husband and some kids!" I tried to breathe past the lump in my throat. "*How dare you!*"

The rain pounded the roof of the Range Rover as we stared at each other. I waited for what he would say.

"Don't be silly, Benedict."

I screamed, a long, one-word expletive of rage.

"*I am not silly!*"

"Benedict." His voice was chiding, and it did nothing to calm me down. He shook his head. "You wouldn't have stayed much longer with Bill Stephenson, even if everything hadn't gone down the way it did." His hand came down on the console between us, and his voice seemed loud in the confines of the car. "Look at what you did on your own. My god! You started your own firm from *nothing*. You taught yourself to practice law, Benedict. You'd never have done all that with Bill Stephenson holding your reins. And this case—look at what you did, without help from anyone." He shook his head again. "You're amazing. You're a justice warrior."

I couldn't speak. I absolutely didn't know what to say. I looked down at my shaking hands and breathed in and out, in and out.

He put the car into gear and pulled out onto the road, driving slowly and carefully, and I couldn't see how he did it. "You can't help yourself." He stopped at the next light and looked over at me. "I know about the Parrish adverse possession fund."

I looked out the passenger window and shook my head, my

stomach churning as he kept talking. "I know you helped the Parrishes get a lawyer who advised them to stay on the property long enough until it could become theirs by law. And I know you helped them start the fund to pay for the lawyer. Even though you couldn't have had much money then." I thought I heard pride in his voice, and I blinked away the moisture in my eyes. I didn't realize I'd needed that from someone. How long had it been since I'd felt proud of what I did for a living?

His voice gentled. "Benedict, that life you described—do you know so little of yourself that you think that would have been the life you'd lead?"

I turned to look at him. My voice came out raspy and hoarse. "It was the one I thought I was going to lead."

He drove the car through the intersection. "You don't think much of yourself."

"And you do?"

He looked over at me. "I do, Benedict." He shook his head and laughed shortly. "I told you, you're Don Quixote, taking on windmills in pursuit of justice. It's who you are."

I could feel my heart pounding hard in my chest. "I thought *you* were Don Quixote, tilting at windmills, and I was your sidekick."

He chuckled, not looking at me. "Benedict, you're nobody's sidekick."

I felt the tears burning in my eyes, and I was glad for the darkness.

We didn't speak as he turned into my neighborhood, and I thought about the evening. "Will David get the deal Julia was talking about? Even though it wasn't really an accident?"

"You don't want to know the answer to that." He pulled into the driveway and stopped behind my car. "If it makes you feel any better, David Young will also have to answer for the assault on you."

I zipped up my jacket and pulled the hood up. "That does make me feel better." I started to open the door, then I turned and faced him. "Why did you say all these things?"

He looked at me, his face half in shadow from the overhang. "Because I like you, Benedict. I admire you, and I like you. You're a good person, and you deserve better than you got."

I breathed in and out, in and out. And I nodded to him as I opened the passenger door and stepped out into the rain.

As I closed the door, I heard him say, "Be safe, Benedict."

EPILOGUE

On Monday, David Young surrendered to Julia Lunsford and two Dallas police detectives. He didn't put up a fight or try to run. He confessed to leaving the scene, but he claimed Carrie's death was an accident. He was represented by counsel by then, and he later pled guilty to manslaughter, a second-degree felony for which he was sentenced to an agreed-upon three years in prison, a portion of which would be served in a court-ordered substance abuse program. He also pled guilty to a class A misdemeanor assault against me, and was sentenced to three months in prison and a $500 fine. The sentences are to be served concurrently, and if he's granted parole, he will get out pretty much right before he goes in.

Also on Monday, Gerard filed an unopposed motion to dismiss the charges against Todd Parrish. It was granted, and he was released on Tuesday. I didn't attend the motion hearing, but Mary Parrish called and left me a voicemail, bubbling over with happiness. Apparently, Gerard had told them there would be no charge.

At noon on Tuesday, I went to R&D Booksellers. At the table by the window, Sam Ames sat alone, sunlight glinting off a silver bracelet on the table. The weather had turned, and it looked like spring might actually happen. He'd heard about David Young, and for a moment, we talked about David and Carrie and Todd. I noticed that the book on the table was a Bible, and I asked him if he'd finished the bestseller he was reading.

"I decided all of this was a sign I needed to become closer to Jehovah, to leave worldly things behind." He looked down at the bracelet on the table. "Even my child had recognized that she needed to come back to the Truth."

For a long moment, I considered telling him about Carrie's true purpose for returning, but I didn't. I didn't do it for Adam Garrison or Ann Thornton or anyone else. If he stays in the Organization or finally gives in to his doubts, it won't be because of me.

I walked him to his car and stood with him for a minute in the sunshine, not wanting to see him drive away. Finally, I offered my hand. "Maybe I'll see you here sometime."

He looked at my hand, and instead, drew me close in a hug. We stood that way for a few moments before he released me with a pat on the back. Then he opened his door, and turned to look at me with eyes that glistened with tears. "I don't think I'll be by this way again."

On Wednesday, Ryan and Sara and Michael and I moved my father into room 14 at Landover Bridges. I was hoping the day would be rainy and gray to match my mood, but instead the sun was shining and the sky was as blue as I've ever seen it. We made sure to have plenty of pictures of the family on the shelves in the room, and Ryan and I stayed as long as they'd let us that evening, me sitting next to my dad on the small sofa in the room, holding his hand while we watched DVDs of old black and white television shows. They said we could come as often as we wanted.

On my way home, I stopped short at a stoplight, and something rolled out from under the seat. Gerard's pen. It must have fallen out of my purse when I threw my bag on the seat on the way to Hipster Haven the week before. It seemed like a lifetime ago. I tucked it into my new bag, but I didn't know if I'd see him again to return it.

On Thursday, a package arrived at my apartment. It was a framed black and white sketch, about the size of a piece of printer paper. In thick lines, a figure with a small shield and a lance sits on a horse, another figure by his side. In the background, windmills spin and the warm Spanish sun blazes: Picasso's *Don Quixote and Sancho Panza*. A card was tucked inside, the message printed in dark, slashing print: *From the short, squat sidekick on the mule.*

AFTERWORD

Although the circumstances and people described here are fictional, the facts contained in this book about the organization known as the Watch Tower Bible & Tract Society and those people known as the Jehovah's Witnesses are accurate, as far as we know. Information on the Internet is, of course, suspect, but there are still quite a few of the original doctrinal books out in the public or in libraries. A few have been imaged and are available online. Others have disappeared from Kingdom Hall libraries or secondhand bookstores. Conspiracy theories abound about the reason why. All factual information contained in this book is readily available online through Watch Tower's own websites and JW-sponsored entries on encyclopedic websites.

I am indebted to those ex-Jehovah's Witnesses who spoke to me about their experiences, and I am also grateful to those who've posted their experiences online, in forums, and on television over the years. Reading and listening to their stories is a sobering experience. Choosing to remain outside a closed society when your entire life's experience tells you to go back takes a great deal of courage. This story is fiction, but whether a plan exists to infiltrate the Jehovah's Witnesses or not is an open question.

For more information on the Jehovah's Witnesses and those that have left the Organization, see jwfacts.org, *Crisis of Conscience* by Ray Franz, and *The Reluctant Apostate* by Lloyd Evans, among others.

A few details have been changed for this story. The Collin county jail facility is in McKinney, not Princeton, and the Dallas justices of the peace do not hold court in the George Allen Courts Building; there is no Kaufman county road 1622, nor does County Road 89 go north to Princeton in Collin county. Other details may have been changed as well, but White Rock Lake, Deep Ellum, and Lakewood are just as wonderful as they sound.

I am grateful to several people who helped with the critical facts in the story. For psychology and therapy advice, Dr. Yvonne Fritz. For emergency medicine, Dr. Ronnie Shalev. Their advice was valuable, and any mistakes are mine.

I am also grateful for my advance readers: Kara Stoner, Sharon Corsentino, Mary Lyons, Megan Flynn, and Neely Franklin, and to my sister Deborah and daughter Tracye, for reading the same chapters over and over again until I got it right. That's family for you.

Finally, I'm deeply grateful to Nathan Pinzon, without whom this story would not have been written, for so many reasons.

NOW AVAILABLE

FROM ELIZABETH BASDEN

BLOOD WILL TELL
Book 2 of the Lacey Benedict Journals

PROLOGUE

"Now watch your step, miss. They've not done any renovation up here."

I followed the appraiser, Jerry Freeman, up the stairs from the second floor to the third-floor attic of the Tarantino house and watched his steps, if not my own, in the murky darkness there. The wooden plank stairs were in pretty bad shape, and they were covered with a thick layer of dust. I hadn't needed to come with him for the interior property inspection, but I was interested to see what he thought of the partially remodeled Tudor in Dallas's sought-after Lakewood neighborhood.

I was also glad I'd worn my old boots for it, even though they'd felt distinctly out of place in the upscale luxury of the renovated first floor. As we passed beneath an overhead light fixture with only one lit bulb remaining, I realized I was unconsciously placing my feet where Jerry had already disturbed the dust. There was no rail on the sides of the narrow stairwell, and the opening itself was only a bit wider than my shoulders. I steadied myself against the plastered side wall, wondering miserably if I was that much larger than someone living in the 1930s.

We crested the stairs on a small unlit landing, and then the stairs doubled back for the second half of the flight. The air seemed thicker up here, musty and warm even though it was only the 26th of February, and I felt sorry for those hardy domestics who might have lived up here when the house was built in 1937. We finally emerged onto a larger landing with doors on either side. Bare bulbs inserted directly into sockets shone brightly in the rooms that led off the landing, but there was no fixture at the top of the stairs. Mr. Freeman had stepped to the room on the left, so I followed.

"See here on this side, you go in and there's this closet here?" He showed me a closet just to the right of the door opening, the door off-centered on the wall. The room itself was longer than it was wide, perhaps 14 feet long and 8 feet wide, the ceiling sloping down pretty dramatically to about three feet above the floor. These two rooms were over the kitchen section that protruded out the back of the main house. The walls were covered in a cabbage-rose printed paper that curled at the top and bottom where it met plain white-painted wood moldings.

This would have been a bedroom for several maids or a house-keeper, twin beds, perhaps, with maybe a dresser or chair. I thought of my own sparsely-furnished apartment, and winced, realizing I had about the same amount of furniture that someone in a *Downton Abbey*-type attic bedroom would. I resolved to get online and buy something frivolous right away.

I dutifully looked in the closet, a small space measuring about two by eight feet and built of bare wood planks, with a sloped ceiling to match the one in the main room. A few empty wire hangers dangled from the wooden pole.

"Now come over here, miss," he invited, as he moved across the hall to the other room, a space that matched the other down to the wallpaper and closet. In this closet, however, Mr. Freeman told me, he'd found something different. "Look in this closet—do you see it?"

Aside from a lack of hangers, this closet looked no different from the other, and I told him so. He tsked under his breath and unhooked a large, square metal measuring tape from his belt. He slid out the metal tape as he stepped inside and measured the length of the closet, and then showed me. Five feet. He looked expectantly at me, and I felt like I'd missed a math lesson.

Then it clicked. This room, like the one across the hall, was about eight feet wide, but this closet was short almost three feet, and the ceiling slope downward ended at least six feet above the floor, not three like the other closet. He nodded approvingly as I looked out in the room, and then back in the closet. There was no light inside, but it looked like any other closet except for the size.

He hooked the measuring tape back on his belt. "I was checking the wiring up here—it's the original Romex wiring from when the house was built in 1937 in these two rooms. It's not a real fire risk, but it needs to be replaced." He continued to chatter on, throwing miscellaneous building terms around like I throw legal ones. I have to admit I wasn't listening.

He picked up a heavy flashlight and a screwdriver, and then he stepped back into the closet, motioning me in with his other hand. I reluctantly crowded into the closet with him. "This made me curious, so I felt around in here for a minute." He pointed the end of the screwdriver to the wooden board that the 'socket' for the dowel rod was screwed into. "Lookee here, miss." He slid the end of the screwdriver up the corner to just below the board, and then dug in. The wall was divided at that line, and as it swung toward us like a door, I could see dark space behind.

Mr. Freeman clicked on his flashlight and shone it inside the space. It was a small, windowless room, and it woke up every latent bit of claustrophobia I didn't know I had. I tried to peer over his shoulder, but he moved back and handed me the flashlight, so I bravely stepped to the entrance and ducked down to see inside. The smell was unpleasant, the air inside stale, and I began to breathe through my mouth. There was a small box on the floor—a blue metal lockbox, it turned out—and nothing else. I don't know what I was expecting, maybe a skeleton or a valuable painting locked away for 80 years, but 'nothing' wasn't it. I shone the light around the floor, but there were no footprints in the thick dust. Like the closets, the walls inside were bare wood, with no wallpaper or plaster.

"I wonder what's in the box?" I asked, as much to myself as to Jerry Freeman, and started to reach down for it. He stopped me with a hand to my shoulder.

"You see that, miss?" He took the flashlight from me and pointed at some discolorations on the wall. They were about three feet from the floor on the back wall, faded brown spots and streaks and smears, and I leaned forward, struggling to see the area clearly.

"What is it, mold or something?" I asked, a bit troubled. Mold is a four-letter word you don't want to hear when you're considering a potential house sale, even I knew that. I started to reach out to touch it, but his next words stopped me.

"That's blood, miss."

Made in the USA
Coppell, TX
12 November 2021